FALLING FOR HIM

CL Mustafic

Doctor Gavin Addison's marriage didn't end on the friendliest of terms, and his estranged wife's continual harassment has the local police visiting his home so often they've started calling him "the doc." One of those cops, Officer Lex Turner, has a crush on the handsome doc, even though he knows there's no chance the doc would ever consider dating a man.

A chance encounter on a crowded dance floor ends with both men in the same bed with the same woman—but with questionable results. When the doc wants to try that again, Lex becomes more involved than he'd dreamed possible as he helps his new friend navigate the kinkier side of sex. Knowing it's just sex for Gavin, Lex finds it hard to keep his feelings hidden. But when Gavin finally figures out he has feelings for Lex that go beyond what a guy should feel for his buddy, will he let Lex convince him to take a chance with him—even if it turns both their lives upside down?

To my family,
who left me alone for enough five-minute increments
to write this book.

ACKNOWLEDGEMENTS

I'd like to thank the people who helped me bring this book to this point.

To Morwen Navarre, who encouraged me to submit my work to a publisher: without you pushing me, I probably wouldn't have taken the chance or survived the numerous rejections.

To Tonna Saunders, for being there for me every step of the way with this story. For reading the darn thing about twenty times and still giving me crap about the dog. Readers like you are the reason I keep writing.

To Christina Quinn and Jamila Lindsey, for listening to me cry and complain about anything and everything and then kicking me in the butt to get me back on track.

To Pippa Brook for her reassuring comments when the nerves really hit.

And finally to BJ Toth, my editor, and also the person who finally took a chance on Gavin and Lex. Thank you for giving me this opportunity, and I promise to make the most of it.

ONE

"I'M REALLY SORRY to drag you guys out here again," Dr. Gavin Addison said to the two police officers who were standing on his front porch. His soon-to-be ex-wife had been at it again. This time both of the back tires on his car were slashed, and the note she'd put on the windshield left no doubt in his mind who'd done the dirty deed. Gavin hated having to call the cops every few days, and they were probably just as sick of responding to file the damn complaints from him.

"It's not a problem; that's what we're here for," Officer Grady said reassuringly. It was definitely a bad sign that Gavin knew most of the officers by name. Grady's partner stood off to the side, silent as usual. Officer Turner was not a talkative man. Gavin couldn't remember the younger officer ever uttering a word in his presence.

"I know, but I still feel bad. You guys want a cup of coffee or anything?" he offered.

"Nah, we have to get this written up and head over to the campus. There's a kegger going on at one of the frat houses, and we've been taking noise complaints all night. Time to shut it down." Grady smiled.

"On a Thursday night? Kids these days." Gavin tsked jokingly. His eyes shifted to Officer Turner who, unlike his partner, had caught the sarcasm in Gavin's statement and smirked as Officer Grady nodded his agreement. It was the first emotion Gavin had seen on Officer Turner's face, and it transformed him. He looked more like one of the frat boys they were going to bust than the stoic cop Gavin had always thought him to be.

Grady handed him the clipboard to get his signature on the statement. With that done, Officer Grady reminded him to make sure all his windows and doors were properly locked and said goodnight. Gavin thanked them again and made sure he locked the front door after going in. He shut the porch light off and checked the time. Christ, he had to be up at six—five hours of sleep if he could manage to settle down again.

Gavin's alarm jarred him out of an uneasy slumber. He sat up on the edge of the bed to stretch and rub his eyes. Feeling like shit and with the thought of a busy day ahead, of rounds to make before a full schedule at the clinic, he got up and stumbled into the kitchen to start the coffeepot. From there, he went on to the bathroom where he showered, shaved, and dressed in record time. He grabbed his biggest travel mug, filled it with coffee, and was halfway out the door when he remembered that his car wasn't going anywhere on only two good tires.

"Fuck, fuck, fuckity fuck," he swore as he went back into the house to call his friend Riley for a lift. Riley swore it wasn't a problem to swing by and pick him up, but Gavin professed his gratitude anyway. He filled a second travel mug from the chilling pot and went to the porch to wait for his ride.

Riley pulled up to the curb a few minutes later, and Gavin climbed into the front seat, handing a grateful-looking Riley the second travel mug. "Thanks again, I know it's out of your way, but the incident happened late last night, or I would have called to give you a heads-up," Gavin said.

"Hey, man, like I said, so not a problem. I can't believe that bitch did it again. How is she not in jail?" Riley asked. He took a sip of the coffee, hummed his approval, and gave Gavin a thumbs-up. One thing he liked about Riley: he never minced words, always saying what was on his mind. Gavin wouldn't usually tolerate someone badmouthing his wife, but Riley got a free pass since he was Gavin's best friend and had known Cassie as long as Gavin had.

"You know that I hate when you talk about her like that. She's just taking the divorce really hard." Gavin repeated what he'd been saying for the past month and a half in defense of Cassandra. "Her cousin's a lawyer, and somehow he's kept her out of jail so far. Not that I want her in jail, but I sure wish she'd leave my damn car alone."

Riley shook his head. "Gav, you are way too nice sometimes. She's the reason you're getting a divorce in the first place, or did you forget that you caught her playing hide the salami with the UPS guy?"

"I know, I know, but we were married for almost ten years, Riley. That's a long time to love someone. It's not that easy to just make these feelings stop. She's the only woman I ever loved, you know?" He probably should hate Cassie, but he couldn't help feeling a little sorry for her. She wasn't an easy person to love. People just didn't get her most of the time. They thought she came across as cold and self-absorbed. Her nickname in college had been the Ice Queen. People thought he was stupid because, yeah, she'd cheated on him, and he was pissed about it, but they could have worked through it if she hadn't said the things she'd said to him. He could forgive her for cheating, but knowing what she thought about him was something he couldn't forget or get over.

"Dude, you need to get back out there and find you a chick that can appreciate what you got to offer. You know all the single nurses and half the married ones would give their left tit to go out with you. All you gotta do is pick one," Riley said. "If I were you, I'd so be hitting up Lacey; that girl is so fine. I'd tap that if Sheila wouldn't kick my ass for it."

"You're a pig, you know that?" Gavin asked. "And Sheila would kick your ass just for talking like that. I should tell her. It's been a while since you've had a good ass kicking."

Riley pulled into the staff lot and parked. "Shit, that woman kicks my ass on a regular basis. Says she needs to keep me in line."

Gavin laughed because both things were probably true. They got out of the car and headed into the hospital. "You here all day, or do you have clinic hours?"

"I'm here all day. You just here for rounds?"

"Yeah, I have a couple of surgical patients I have to see this morning, and then I'm off to the clinic. I was going to buy you lunch as a thank you for the ride, but we'll have to do it another day."

"Sure thing, man, let me know if you need a ride home. I could swing by and pick you up. See ya later." They went their separate ways once inside the hospital.

Gavin made his way up to the fourth floor nurses station and pulled the charts for his patients. He was sitting at one of the desks in a little alcove behind the counter when the giggling began. He looked up and around the corner. The nurses were gathered around the computer tittering like little girls.

"I can't believe that's him."

"Oh my god, look what it says he's into."

"This has got to be a joke."

"No, that's really him."

"I wouldn't mind doing that to him, if that's what he wants."

"That is some sick, perverted stuff right there."

"You'd never guess. He seems so normal and nice."

"How did you find this?"

"There was a sticky note on the computer with the link on it. I had no idea what it was, but this is what came up when I typed it in," one of the younger nurses said to the crowd around her.

"Do you think he put it there hoping maybe one of us would be interested?" asked Janie, another of the younger nurses.

Gavin had to see what was going on. He got out of his chair and walked toward the group. He knew something wasn't right when they noticed him, and Tamara blushed bright red and tried to shut the computer off before he could see what was on the screen.

"Hey, ladies, what's got you all in such a tizzy?" he asked with his most congenial smile. They stood around, gaping at him like they'd never seen him before. He stepped over and then moved around, Tamara and looked at the screen. Gavin couldn't believe what he saw. The blush crept up his neck as he read what was there for everyone to see. It was like a train wreck; he couldn't stop looking at it.

"Dr. Addison, are you okay?"

"Grab him a chair."

"Get some water."

"Doctor, sit down and put your head between your legs." Sandy, the head nurse, pushed him down into the chair and shoved his head between his knees. "Do you need a paper bag? I think you're hyperventilating." Someone shoved a paper bag into Gavin's hands. He put it to his mouth and breathed into it until he felt himself calming down.

The nurses were murmuring around him, but he couldn't make out what they were saying until he heard Sandy's authoritative voice ask, "What the hell is this? Who did this?" Gavin looked up to see Sandy pointing at the computer and eyeing all of her nurses with suspicion. "I want answers, and I want them now!"

"I did it, but it was a mistake," Lisa said. She pointed to the sticky note before adding, "That was on the screen, and I typed it in. I didn't know what it was. I swear."

"That's not the only mistake you made. What made you think it was a good idea to spread this around? You should have reported it to me. This isn't the type of thing that should be viewed at work, and I want to know who's responsible for the sticky note," she lectured. No one took responsibility for the Post-it.

Gavin got up from the chair and took the neon yellow piece of paper off the desk. The gathered nurses stared at him like he was some sort of animal. He turned to leave when Sandy put her hand on his arm. "I'm fine. I have a couple of patients to see, and then I'll be out of your hair. I'm going to take this. The cops might want to see it when I file a report."

"I'm sorry, Dr. Addison, this should never have happened. What you do on your own time is your business, but I really don't think we need to get the police involved. I don't think there's been a crime committed here." Her tone was nonjudgmental, but her posture was rigid.

"I'm not..." Gavin started but took a deep calming breath. "You know that I'm going through a divorce right now?" Sandy nodded, yes, of course everyone knew. "My wife has been making things difficult for me, and I think she may have had a hand in this. I assure you I've never been on this site before in my life, let alone set up a profile looking for someone to peg me," he finished with a grimace.

"Oh, well, okay then. I'll sort this mess out and try to contain the fallout," she said.

"Thanks, Sandy, I appreciate that." Good luck with that; this would be the top gossip for the next week unless a couple of residents got caught fucking in a broom closet again. Gavin fought the urge to hurry through his rounds and get the hell out of there. He considered his options, and no matter how he worked it out, there was no getting out of attending his patients at the hospital unless he wanted to quit his job.

Thankfully, the news hadn't reached the clinic when he got there at ten. His mind was still occupied by what he'd seen and he couldn't wait to get a moment alone in his office to look into it more thoroughly. He'd seen four patients when his pager went off with a 9-1-1 code from Riley. The news had reached the ER. Gavin checked his schedule. Riley would have to wait until he had a small break between the patient he was about to see and the one after.

He did his best to not rush the old man who was in for a consult for cataract surgery. He patiently explained the procedure to the man's wife and daughter and answered all of their questions. When he left them with the nurse to finish up, he breathed a sigh of relief. He made his way to his office and sat down heavily in his chair. He pulled the sticky note out of his wallet and typed the URL into the computer as he dialed Riley. The website was getyourkinkon dot com, and it was like nothing Gavin had ever seen before in his life.

"Hey, man, what the hell? Why am I hearing all kinds of crazy-ass shit about the most vanilla boy I know?" Riley asked upon answering.

Instead of explaining, he asked, "What the hell is pegging?"

Riley's laughter was loud enough that Gavin had to pull the phone away from his ear until it died down. "Holy shit, Gav, it's true, huh?"

"You didn't answer the question, and what's true?"

"Pegging is when a woman fucks you up the ass with a strap-on. There's this crazy rumor going around that a certain doctor is into some kinky-ass sex, and the nurses are all aflutter," he said still laughing, making Gavin want to punch him.

"Fuck you, Ri. I think Cassie might have done this. I don't even know what half this shit is." Gavin was still looking at his made-up profile. Staring back at Gavin was a picture of himself in a pair of cutoff jean shorts and nothing else, giving the camera his best come-hither look. Cassie had taken it one day when he'd been feeling extra amorous and had been trying his best to get her into bed, but it had turned into them giggling over Gavin's sad attempts at seduction.

"I kinda figured you weren't that kinky. You'd have told me if you were. So on a scale of one to ten, how embarrassed are you?" Riley asked.

"Two hundred or so," Gavin replied. He now knew what pegging was but still had no clue what some of the other things were and was quite sure he wouldn't be into them even if he did. "What I want to know is how she could have planted the Post-it note with the website on it at the nurse's station. This is just fucking crazy, even for her."

"You sure it was her?" Riley asked, but his tone told Gavin he was only playing the devil's advocate.

"Who else would do this?" Gavin covered his face, blocking out his own image on the screen. "Oh, god, this is so bad. Everyone thinks I'm some kind of pervert now. How the hell am I going to show my face at the hospital again?"

"Maybe you just gotta own it, bro. Walk in tomorrow and strut your stuff. Who cares what everyone else thinks? To each their own, man. If you wanna be a kinky fucker, you go on and be the best kinky fucker you can be," Riley advised.

"But I'm not a kinky fucker." His words sounded whiny, but damn it, he needed to whine to someone. He looked at the clock. "I have to go. I have a patient in a couple of minutes. Want to give me a ride to the police station after your shift?"

"Yeah, sure, I'll be there. Laters."

Gavin called AAA to schedule them to change his tires that evening, so at least his car would be in working order again. Damn Cassie. He didn't want to hate her, but she was doing her best to make him. He slogged his way through the rest of his workday and gratefully climbed into the car when Riley showed up to drive him to the station.

Riley was smiling when Gavin got in the car. "So, I checked out your profile. Dude, that is some serious kink. Did you see that you got like sixty spanks?" he asked.

Gavin groaned and asked, "Do I even want to know what spanks are?"

"Spanks are what interested people send you. It means that they're into the same stuff and wanna get you tied to a bed, so they can get their kink on, you know, like the name of the web site?" Riley answered through his laughter.

"How the hell do you know that?"

"Hey, I was curious, so I spent a little time checking it out for you. Maybe you should take a couple of those kinky chicks up on their offers. How long's it been since you got laid?" he asked.

"Number one, I am not going out with anyone who would be on that site. Number two, you are a seriously deranged person. Number three, it's none of your damn business how long it's been since I've had sex. Number four, if it was your business, it's been too damn long," Gavin said. All of it was true. He hadn't had sex with anyone other than himself in almost seven months, and before that, sex with Cassie had been sporadic at best for the last couple of years.

Riley shook his head in commiseration. "We should go out sometime, find you someone to release the pressure. You're a good-looking guy, Gav. I'm sure there're plenty of chicks that would go home with you for the night."

"Maybe that's a good idea," Gavin agreed. Casual sex had never really been his thing, but maybe it was time for him to try something different.

"You want me to come in and wait?" Riley asked when they pulled up in front of the police station.

"Nah, go on home. I'll call a cab if I don't feel like walking." He didn't think he could put up with Riley's joking around through the process of filing the complaint, and once he was done, he probably wouldn't want company either. "Thanks again for the rides."

"Always a pleasure to chauffeur your ass around. Talk at you tomorrow," Riley said as Gavin got out of the car and shut the door. He watched Riley drive away before turning to the building behind him. He straightened his spine and headed in to get it over with so he could go home and hide in his bed under the covers.

TWO

OFFICER LEX TURNER had just clocked in at six p.m. for his round-the-clock shift. He'd settled at his desk with some paperwork when Grady plopped himself down on the edge of it. Lex looked up expectantly, waiting to hear whatever gossip his older, chattier partner had to spill. He hoped it wasn't something about him again. Damn cops were like old ladies with their gossip, and his personal life featured more prominently into the rumor mill than he liked.

"So guess who's having a baby?" Grady asked. Lex shrugged. He had a good idea of who it was but didn't really give a damn. "Come on, Turner, not even a guess?"

Lex sighed. Grady wouldn't give up until he guessed. "Leisha from homicide?" The stunned expression on Grady's face was priceless.

"Someone already told you, didn't they?"

"No, it was an educated guess based on the fact that she and her husband have been trying for almost a year, and the fact that you look happy. I know that you want to take the detective's exam and move to homicide." Lex tried not to look smug, but in his opinion, he'd make a better detective than Grady any day. "I take it she's not planning on coming back after the baby's born?"

"Nope, she's actually trying to transfer out to some little hick town up north, from what I heard," Grady supplied as he moved his ass from Lex's desk to his own desk chair.

"Good for her. I hope she gets what she wants." He wouldn't disparage anyone's dreams, even if they were to live a life of a small-town cop in the frozen north. He had his own dreams, but he kept his aspirations to himself. He didn't need to give his coworkers more to talk about.

"How much paperwork we got tonight?" Grady asked. He turned on his computer and started digging through his desk drawer, looking for god knows what.

"Not too much. Gotta finish up that report on the doc's vandalism, and you need to write up that accident report. Then we can get back out there for another fun-filled night," Lex said, making Grady wrinkle his nose.

"That damn woman makes for a lot of fucking paperwork. I've got half a mind to handcuff her to her water heater and forget her," Grady said with a smirk for his own cocky bravado. "Don't know how a nice guy like the doc got mixed up with a crazy bitch like that."

Lex sat back in his chair. That was the question, wasn't it? The doc seemed like a decent enough guy. Why his ex, one Cassandra Addison, would want to make the poor guy's life hell was beyond Lex. It was even more fucked up when you added in the fact that, from what Lex had gathered, she'd cheated on him. He just hoped they wouldn't end up with a *Fatal Attraction*–type ending with this case.

"Yeah, well, sometimes they hide the crazy until they have you in their clutches; then, bam presto chango, psycho chick is in your bed, and you're fucked in more ways than one," Lex said.

"Sounds like you got some experience in that area."

"Don't we all?"

Grady's gaze shifted to something over Lex's shoulder. "Speak of the devil," Grady whispered.

Lex turned around, hoping that Cassandra Addison was not, in fact, standing behind him. Nope, not the bitch, but Gavin was, and he didn't look thrilled to be in Lex's humble workplace. Lex cast an appreciative look over the handsome doctor. He was one fine-looking man, with blond hair that curled wispily around his head and those deep-brown eyes, where you expected to see crystal blue, got Lex every time. Gavin had the greatest smile, and the dimples that peeked out at the slightest grin made Lex want to dip his tongue in them. He shook his head to clear away the thoughts of what he would like to do to the doc, if the doc was so inclined, that was.

"You got him, Grady. You know you're better with this kind of crap." He didn't tell Grady that he got tongue-tied around Gavin and was afraid he'd make a fool of himself.

Grady stood up, smiled, and gestured for Gavin to take a seat by his desk. "Hey there, Doc, what's up today?" he asked as if Gavin's was a social visit.

Color rose on Gavin's cheeks as he flushed a little before answering. Lex was glad he was sitting at his desk because the doc blushing like that did things to his body that weren't acceptable in polite company. "There's been another incident. I can't be one hundred percent sure she did this, but I can't think of anyone else who would want to humiliate me so much."

"So what did she do this time?" Grady asked, "Or allegedly do?"

Gavin handed Grady a little slip of paper. "If you punch that into your web browser, you can see for yourself." Grady took the paper and turned to his computer to type in the web address. He waited a second, and when Grady's brow furrowed at what he saw on the screen, Gavin's blush deepened. Lex itched to see what was on that screen but stayed in his seat.

"Why do you want me to look at your personal ad?" Grady asked.

"Because I didn't post it, and that little sticky note was stuck to a computer at the nurse's station on the fourth floor surgical unit where I happen to do rounds every morning. Everyone at the hospital now thinks I'm some kind of kinky pervert," Gavin explained, visibly upset.

Lex had to see what was on Grady's screen. He got up to look at his partner's computer. He instantly understood why the doc had turned pink when he handed over the little piece of paper. Lex shook his head; that woman was pure evil.

"So you think your wife posted this profile and then planted the sticky note so that your colleagues would see it, and what?" Grady asked.

"How the hell should I know what she was thinking? I just really want all of this to stop." Gavin's voice shook with emotion. Lex feared the doc may be on the verge of tears. That was not something Lex wanted to see. He didn't think he could handle watching the doc cry without giving into his urge to comfort him. He patted Gavin's shoulder in reassurance when he went to sit back in his chair. Gavin looked up at Lex and gave him a thin smile. "I'm sorry. I'm just getting really sick of not knowing what she's going to do next to screw with me. I mean messing with my car or my house is one thing, but my job should be off limits."

"All of it should be off limits." Lex surprised himself by blurting the words out. He couldn't help it; something about the doc brought out the protective side of him. If he had his way, no one would mess with Gavin.

"That's true," Grady agreed. "But as long as she has that lawyer of hers, we're never going to be able to keep her in jail on petty vandalism charges."

"Isn't this like stalking or something? Couldn't you find something else to charge her with?" The pleading tone in Gavin's voice went straight to Lex's gut. He could tell the doc was at his wit's end.

"Well, sounds like you've had a change of heart. I remember when you begged us to just file a report but didn't want us to arrest her," Grady said.

"Yeah, well, it's hard to do that to someone you love, but I think she finally crossed the line with this one." He looked from Grady to Lex. Lex nodded his agreement; yes, she'd definitely crossed the line.

"Okay well, I'm not sure what we can do with this. I'll have to take it down to our computer-crimes division to see if there's been an actual crime committed. If so, we'll see if we can prove that your wife is responsible for it. It's probably going to take a few days before we have any answers for you. Sorry, but that's the best I can do," Grady said.

"I understand." Gavin stood up. "Thanks for your time. Sorry to be such a bother, really sorry. Let me know if you need anything more from me, and if you could keep me updated on this, I'd appreciate it." He shook hands with Grady and then turned to Lex. Lex was surprised but stood quickly and grasped the doc's hand. Gavin smiled as they shook. "Thanks for taking this seriously."

A pleasant tingle ran up Lex's arm at the thrill of touching the man he desired. He reminded himself to let go of Gavin's hand before it got awkward. "Sure, it's our job." Dumb, he sounded like an idiot, but at least he hadn't stammered. Gavin's smile brightened a little before he turned to leave.

Lex watched as Gavin made his way through the desks and out the lobby door. Why were the straight ones always the ones who got to him the most? Lex turned back to find Grady eyeballing him. "What?" he asked.

"What's with that look you were giving the doc?"

"What are you talking about? What look?" Lex asked.

"Like you wanted to give him a hug. Kiss his boo-boos and make 'em all better." He accompanied his statement with kissy sounds.

"Shut up, Grady. I just feel bad for the guy. I wish we could do something more to stop his wife from harassing him. It's gotta be rough on him." Lex sat down at his desk and stared at Grady.

"We're doing what we can. You write up the report; I'm going to run this down to Don and see what he makes of it. Maybe they can get her on something more serious because of the computer stuff." Grady got up and took the little slip of paper off his desk. He headed off to see the geek squad and left Lex to do the grunt work.

Lex had finished his reports, and Grady still hadn't returned. He turned Grady's monitor so that he could punch the URL into his own machine and bring up the profile with Gavin's picture on it. Shit, the look on the doc's face had him hard in a second. He suddenly wished he was at home. He'd definitely spend some time alone with his hand and that picture when he was off shift in the morning. He wrote the web address on a slip of paper and stuck it in his pocket. He closed his browser and went to the break room to grab a pop before they headed out. Grady met him on his way out of the break room, and he didn't look happy.

"Don told me there's probably not going to be anything we can charge Addison with. He said he'd look into it, and if he can prove she's responsible, the doc could maybe take her to civil court and sue for defamation. That's about all though," Grady said as they walked to their cruiser together.

Lex wasn't happy about that either. He dreaded having to tell the doc or being there when Grady told him since he probably wouldn't be able to string that many words together in the doc's presence.

Lex got in the driver's side because Grady was a menace when he was behind the wheel, and Lex didn't feel like writing up an accident report for their car again. The first half of their shift passed pretty uneventfully, a few traffic stops, a couple of noise complaints, and an accident—quiet for a Friday night. They were sitting at the truck stop café, taking their lunch break, when Lex's cell phone rang.

"Who the hell's calling you at one in the morning?" Grady asked.

Good question, Lex thought before he pulled his phone out and checked the caller ID. Great, it was his mom. "Hey, Mom, what's wrong?" he asked because there had to be something wrong for her to call him at that time of night.

"What kind of greeting is that?" she asked.

"Sorry, but really, what's wrong?"

"Agent is sick. He's been throwing up since I fed him his supper."

"Okay, what do you want me to do about it?" he asked.

"Well, nothing I suppose, but I thought that you'd want to know."

"Mom, it's one in the morning, and I'm working. If the dog is still sick in the morning when I get home, I'll deal with it. You should try to get some sleep; just lock Agent in the laundry room so he doesn't make a mess on the carpets." He flipped off Grady who was snickering at him from across the table.

He could hear his mom huff through the phone before she said, "Fine, so sorry to bother you. He's your dog; I thought you'd care that he was sick; my mistake."

"Mom—"

"No, no, I'll deal with it; don't worry about a thing, good-bye," she said before she hung up. He'd probably be in for a huge guilt trip when he got home. Putting his phone back in his pocket, he shook his head at Grady.

"That's what you get for still living with your mommy."

"Yeah, yeah, shut it, why don't ya." He spared an annoyed look for his partner. He hadn't told anyone the reason he lived with his mother. He didn't need people looking at him funny because his mom was a bit of a nut job. She couldn't help it really. After his dad had passed away a year and a half ago, she'd just lost it. Lots of odd behavior and one suicide attempt later, he'd packed up her house and moved her into his rented condo where he could keep a better eye on her. She still had her moments, but having Lex to dote on, and a dog to keep her company when he couldn't, had helped a lot. She was doing much better.

Grady smirked as they paid their bill and went back out on patrol. The rest of their shift dragged, and Lex found his mind wandering back to Gavin. He hadn't been with a man for quite some time, probably going on six months. Not that many men caught his eye and made it worth him risking his secret getting out, but the doc, if he was willing, would be worth it. He ran through a few fantasies as they sat in the parking lot just off the college campus, waiting to see if they could catch any late partiers driving home after drinking a bit too much. Really they were just trying to kill the last hour before they could head back to the station to do some of their paperwork and go home.

"SEE YOU MONDAY morning, Turner. Try not to get into any trouble," Grady called to Lex as he left the locker room.

"Yeah, see ya," Lex hollered back as the door swung shut behind his partner. Thank god he had the next couple of days off, and then it was back to the day shift for two weeks. He grabbed his bag and headed for the door.

"Hey, Lex, got any plans for your days off?" the front desk officer asked him before he could get out the door.

He turned to the woman behind the desk. Officer Landry was a good-looking woman. It was no secret that she was interested in more than friendship where Lex was concerned, but he'd never dip his wick at work, so in his mind, she was off limits. He smiled. "Not really. Gonna get some sleep and then veg out in front of the TV, most likely." And probably take his dog to the vet to appease his mom, but she didn't need to hear about that little saga.

"That doesn't sound like any fun. A bunch of us are going out to Stucky's tonight. You should come," she offered.

"Yeah, if nothing comes up, maybe I will. Gotta get going. Need to hit the sack soon, or I'm gonna pass out right here."

"Okay, see you later, Lex."

Lex parked his pickup in the driveway and went into his condo. He stopped in the kitchen to give his mom a kiss. He was surprised to see her up, making him breakfast. "Hey there, Mamacita, what's cooking?" he asked.

"I made you an omelette, and there's coffee too," she said as he kissed her cheek.

"How's Agent?"

"Oh that stupid mutt decided that he was just fine after I called you. Of course, he puked up a sock, so I'm thinking that he didn't just magically get better to spite me. He's sleeping in my room right now. Sit down. This is done."

Thank god, the dog was fine, and it looked like his mom was going to forget that she was upset with him. Lex sat at the breakfast bar and let her serve him. She bustled around the kitchen while he ate. "Hey, Ma, are you going over to Sally's tonight?"

She turned and looked at him for a minute before answering. "I planned on it. Why, do you have a girl coming over?"

"No, some people from work are going out, and I thought I might meet them for a beer at Stucky's."

"Then why do you care if I'm going out?"

"I don't want to leave you sitting here alone after I've been on nights for the last two weeks. I know that you get lonely, and I feel bad," he explained.

"Honey, I don't need a babysitter. I'm a grown woman, and I'm used to being alone sometimes. Besides, I go out during the day. I have my quilting club and the church group. I'm not lonely. You go and have some fun; you deserve a night out," she said firmly.

He smirked around his last bite of omelette. "Okay, Ma, you win. I'll go out and get hammered because you told me to."

She swatted the back of his head. "I didn't say to get drunk, you nincompoop. I said to have some fun. Just make sure to call if you're going to get in late so I know not to worry." She cleared his breakfast dishes and gave him a peck on the cheek when he made his way past her to his bedroom.

He put his gun in the safe and sat down at his computer to take a look at the object of his recent obsession before hitting the sack. He studied the way the jean shorts clung to Gavin's slim but muscular thighs. He memorized how the shorts hung low on the man's hips and followed the trail of blond hair, slightly darker than that on his head, which lead from his navel to the waistband of his shorts. But it was those eyes that he couldn't stop looking at. They were brown, and at first glance nothing special, but the camera had caught the amber flecks that made them completely hypnotizing.

He saved the image on his computer just in case the doc decided to remove the profile. He shut the machine down and stripped naked to crawl into bed. The blackout shades on his windows left the room pitch-black when he turned off his bedside lamp. Lex didn't even have to close his eyes to shut out the world while he imagined what it would be like to take the doc to bed. He brought himself off quickly, fumbled for the tissues on his nightstand, and fell asleep after making a few halfhearted swipes to clean his belly.

THREE

"I WON'T GIVE her the house. It's mine. My uncle left it to me before we got married. I won't budge on this. I don't care what she does, the house is mine." Raising his voice at his lawyer probably wasn't endearing Gavin to the poor man. He couldn't help it. Cassie was demanding that he either give her the house or sell it and split the proceeds with her. What should have been a fairly quick and painless divorce was turning into a nightmare because, in Gavin's view, Cassie was being unreasonable.

"I'm sorry, Dr. Addison, but she contends that since she worked during your years in medical school and basically supported the both of you, she's entitled to a share of the house. I really don't want to take this before a judge because I can't guarantee you'd come away with the property," Mr. Goldfarb, his attorney, advised.

"But she cheated on me. That should count for something. Plus, shouldn't the fact that she's been harassing me for the past three months put some weight on my side too?" Gavin asked.

"If we can't come up with some sort of an agreement, this will drag on forever. It's in your best interest to get this settled so we can draw up the agreement to send to the judge; then it's just a matter of a couple of weeks, and you'll be a free man," Goldfarb explained. "I guess you need to decide what you want more: your house or to get that woman out of your life as quickly as possible."

Gavin sat back in the plush chair and rubbed his slightly stubbled cheeks with the palms of his hands. He didn't know what Cassie was playing at, but she was hell-bent on winning. She knew he loved the house. He'd spent weekends and weeks in the summer there with his uncle; it held countless memories for him. There was no way he'd give her the house, but the thought of selling it killed him. Then it was like a light bulb went off in his head.

"What if I got a loan for half the house's value and paid her off? Would she agree to that?" he asked. The idea excited him—maybe he could get out of his marriage and keep his beloved house. It would mean putting his plan to fast-track paying off his student loans on hold. Adding a mortgage payment to his monthly budget would mean less for those payments, but if it meant not losing the house, he'd do it in a heartbeat.

Goldfarb didn't look as excited as Gavin felt. "I can talk to her attorney, but I believe this demand is more out of spite than it is about the money. I'll call her attorney and let you know, but you need to think about what you want to do if she doesn't accept the offer. It would be best if you made up your mind by the next time we speak." Goldfarb stood up.

Gavin took the gesture as a cue and stood too. "I'll decide and have an answer for you, but I really hope she accepts." He shook Goldfarb's offered hand and let the man walk him to the door.

"I'm sorry about this, Gavin. If the law was fair, you wouldn't have to go through this. My advice is next time you get married, make sure you have her sign a prenuptial agreement," Goldfarb said. Gavin always found it funny how his lawyer became strangely casual at the door to his office.

"Thanks, Marvin, I'll keep that in mind. Let me know what you find out."

"Will do. Take care now." Goldfarb opened the door to let Gavin out into the hallway.

"You too." Gavin walked to the elevators and slumped against the wall as he descended to the lobby.

GAVIN WAITED A week and a half to get an answer from Goldfarb, but when it came, he felt the world lift from his shoulders. Cassie had accepted the offer. Gavin was glad he'd been proactive. He'd had his little house appraised and had been preapproved for the mortgage he needed to pay her off. Goldfarb had already drawn up the agreement with Cassie's attorney, and all they needed was to sign it so it could be sent to the judge.

He called Riley with the good news. "It's finally going to be over. She accepted the offer! I have to run downtown to sign the papers, and then it's as good as done!" Gavin couldn't keep the excitement out of his voice.

"Cool beans, man. Congrats! We should go celebrate. Let's go out on Friday."

"Yeah, we should do that. We can celebrate the divorce and the fact that it's been almost two weeks since she's fucked with me. I feel like a free man at last."

"Oh man, we're going to go out and get shit-faced and find you a fine young thing to get you laid, finally." Riley's smile was evident through the phone. "I'll pick you up at seven, so we can go eat and then hit Stucky's. You mind if I bring Sheila?"

"That sounds like a plan, and of course I don't mind. She's a way better wingman than you are anyway. She's got much better taste in women," Gavin said with a chuckle.

"That's because she'll try to find you a nice girl to settle down with, while I on the other hand, am going to try to find you a naughty girl that will suck your nuts and let you fuck her in the ass," Riley stated proudly.

Gavin laughed because it was true—that was exactly the type of girl Riley would look for. "Man you are so gross. I'd love to hear what other colorful characteristics you'd look for in a girl for me, but I have to get going if I'm going to be on time for my appointment. See you at work tomorrow."

"Not if I see you first. Later."

Gavin was on cloud nine. He called the bank and had them start processing his loan and then signed his divorce agreement with a flourish. It seemed everything was going his way.

ON FRIDAY NIGHT, Gavin was feeling all right. First, he, Riley, and Sheila had a nice dinner at his favorite steak house, and then at Stucky's, they'd grabbed a great table near the dance floor. Riley went to the bar to get drinks since getting a waitress's attention on a busy Friday night would mean waiting half an hour for a beer.

"Oh my god, Gavin, I'm so glad that all that business with Cassie is finally over. The way she's been treating you is a mark on the face of all womankind. How anyone could be so mean to such a sweet guy is beyond me," Sheila said. She was shaking her head, and her frizzy brown hair was flying around her like it had a life of its own.

Gavin put his arm around her shoulders and gave her a squeeze. "Thanks, hon. That means a lot coming from you." Gavin liked Sheila, and he was still trying to figure out how a dork like Riley had landed such a great woman.

"Hey, man, get your mitts off my woman," Riley said as he put the beers down on the table in front of them. "There are plenty of hot chicks here; you don't need to be gettin' all up on mine."

Gavin and Sheila laughed as they separated. "I thought you were going to get us some shots to start us off right." Gavin eyed the three beers.

Riley lifted the corner of his mouth in a smirk he thought made him look devilish, but Gavin had tried over and over to tell him it only made him look constipated. "I couldn't carry the whole order, so one of the waitresses is going to bring it over." He tipped his beer back and drained most of it in one pull.

Oh boy, Gavin didn't even want to wager a guess at how much booze Riley had ordered. He looked out over the crowd while taking a drink of his beer. Riley was right; there were plenty of good-looking women around. Gavin was hoping that maybe he could find one who wouldn't mind spending some time with him, like maybe some sexy, naked time. The waitress showed up with a tray. There were twelve shots and six more beers on the tray.

Gavin raised an eyebrow at Riley. "You weren't shitting when you said you were going to get me drunk." He downed one of the shots set in front of him and cringed at the taste. He drank some of his beer to wash away the burn.

"We need to get you good and liquored up. Then we're going to get you laid." Riley held up his shot for Gavin to clink against his own. After drinking the shot, it was evident Gavin was buzzed when he clumsily set his glass down, almost knocking over his beer. "Lightweight."

"Costs less for me to have a good time that way," Gavin joked.

"Let's dance." Sheila grabbed Gavin and pulled him out of his seat. Gavin sent a pleading look toward Riley and got a shrug and a grin in return instead of assistance. Finding no help in that direction, Gavin looked for anyone else who might come to his aid but came up empty. Defeated, he let Sheila lead him out into the middle of the already crowded dance floor.

Stucky's was not a dance club; it was a bar with a tiny square where there were no tables. It was always so packed that chances were if you needed to scratch your ass while on the dance floor, you'd be goosing the guy behind you, so one needed to be careful while dancing at Stucky's.

Sheila had some moves, which made up for the fact that Gavin didn't. He watched and swayed and tried out some jerky motions he knew made him look like a big dork, while she shimmied around him. She was finally ready to go back to the table after five songs. As they were leaving the floor, Gavin caught sight of a petite redhead who he swore was checking him out. Gavin smiled at her, and she winked back.

"Nice. She was totally checking you out the whole time you were doing whatever it was you were doing out there while Sheila was dancing. Seriously dude, at one point I thought I'd have to come out there because it looked like you were having a seizure," Riley said when they got back to their table. Riley grabbed Sheila and gave her a sloppy kiss. She slapped him on the arm when he released her. "Had to make sure the little ginger over there knows that Gav's not with you. Can't have a fine woman like you cock blocking my man here."

Gavin chuckled and downed a shot and half a beer. "She is pretty cute." Gavin looked in her direction again. She was talking to another girl but gazing at Gavin. When their eyes met, she smiled and licked her lower lip before pulling it in between her teeth for a nibble. Gavin's pants got a bit tighter, and he reached down to adjust himself.

"Holy shit, you really do need to get laid if just a little lip licking has you popping a chubby," Riley said, having noticed Gavin's adjustment.

"Quit looking at his crotch, you big freak." Sheila elbowed Riley in the ribs. "And stop checking out that girl before I start thinking that you're not just here to get him laid." She scowled at Riley, and he gave her a wide-eyed innocent look before he leaned in to kiss her.

Gavin watched the two of them and thought about how much he missed having someone to be with like that. He quickly downed two more shots and the other half of his beer. When he stood up, it took him a couple of seconds to get steady on his feet. Good, he thought, the booze was doing the trick.

"Gotta hit the head," he said to the canoodling couple. He made his way through the crowd and to the bathroom without knocking into anyone. He did his business and checked himself in the mirror as he washed his hands. His face was a bit flushed from the alcohol, but his hair gel was still holding. He nodded at his reflection and decided that after one more drink or maybe five, he'd be ready to talk to the hot chick who was checking him out.

His plan didn't work out because the redhead was sitting at their table when he got back. Riley had his arm casually draped around Sheila's shoulders, and he was talking animatedly to the girl across from them. She smiled up at Gavin as he took the seat next to her.

"Hey, man, 'bout time you got back. Everything come out all right?" Riley asked and winked. Sheila groaned at the middle-school joke and elbowed Riley again.

"Gavin, this is Rachel," Sheila said as if she was introducing him to an old friend.

"Hi, Rachel, nice to meet you." Cripes, could he be more of a geek? He sounded so stiff and formal. Riley would have had a way better opening line than that. Gavin's nerves kicked in; he'd been out of the dating game for a long time. What if he didn't know how to do it anymore? Riley pushed a shot toward him. He didn't hesitate to tip it back. Yep, that was what he needed—some more liquid courage.

"It's nice to meet you too, Gavin. Your friends have had nothing but good things to say about you," Rachel said with a wide, friendly smile.

"That's only because we haven't gotten to the good stuff yet," Riley joked. "Like that time in med school when Gav—"

"Ri, I'll kill you if you finish that sentence. Remember which one of us knows more embarrassing things about the other." Gavin tried to sound menacing, but the giggles made that pretty much impossible.

"Then you both better watch it because I have the power to bring all ya'll down." Sheila upped the ante.

Rachel watched the back and forth with a grin. "I take it you guys have known each other a long time," she said.

"Oh yeah, we go way back. If there's anything you want to know about boy wonder here, you just go ahead and ask," Riley said.

"Does he have a girlfriend?" Rachel took a drink to hide her smile.

Riley and Gavin, who were both drinking their beers when she asked her question, sputtered and choked. Sheila stepped up to answer. "Nope, no girlfriend. He's single and ready to mingle."

"Hey, stop trying to pimp my boy out; that's my job!" Riley exclaimed in faux outrage.

Gavin laughed at his friends. "You'll have to excuse them. They don't allow weekend passes from the psychiatric hospital very often, so they have no social skills. You also have to figure in the fact that alcohol and antipsychotics don't mix very well," Gavin stage whispered to Rachel.

She laughed! Gavin mentally patted himself on the back for being so witty. Then he mentally smacked his forehead for being a big enough loser to have to pat his own back, mentally or not.

"Gav, you promised not to tell!" Sheila said through her laughter.

"What happened to doctor-patient confidentiality? That's so not cool, bro." Riley winked at Rachel. Gavin downed another shot. He was really enjoying himself. Rachel shifted a little closer, causing their knees to touch.

"So, do you want to dance?" She leaned in to ask Gavin.

"I'm not much of a dancer," Gavin said. "Ow, what the hell, Ri?" He glared at his friend who had kicked him in the shin under the table. Riley made a face at him and tipped his head toward Rachel.

Sheila was just as subtle when she blurted out, "She's asking you to go out and grind your bodies together, and you tell her you can't dance? Gav, are you being dense on purpose?"

Gavin looked from his friends to Rachel, who was sitting there with an amused look. "I guess I want to dance?"

Rachel stood up and reached for his hand. "Come on, I'll teach you some moves." He gulped one more shot for good luck and allowed her to lead him to the middle of the dance floor.

Rachel was probably six inches shorter than Gavin's six-foot-three height, the top of her head coming up to his nose. The first thing she did was grab his hips and got them moving to the beat. She then straddled one of his legs and started grinding on him. Gavin had never thought dancing was much fun, but Rachel was quickly changing his mind.

At some point in their bump and grind, Sheila and Riley joined them on the floor. Gavin's friends gave him exaggerated grins and a thumbs-up behind Rachel's back. He shook his head at the two goofballs as they did some nasty-looking grinding of their own. After a few songs, Gavin was sweaty and thirsty. "I'm parched; let's go grab a drink," he said. They left the dance floor and went to the bar where he bought them both a beer.

"You're not as bad of a dancer as you think," Rachel said.

"Well, I'm not exactly sure what we were doing out there qualifies as dancing."

Rachel smirked and leaned in close. She stood on her toes to try to get closer to Gavin's ear. He ducked his head to help her in her endeavor. "What would you call it then?" Her breath was warm on the shell of his ear, and it raised goose bumps on his arms.

"It felt more like foreplay," Gavin admitted before he could stop the words.

Rachel let loose a throaty laugh. "Maybe it was. Wanna go back out there and see if it leads to what usually comes after?"

Oh shit! Gavin thought, did she just say what he thought she said? He nodded because he didn't think he could talk, having almost swallowed his tongue at her obvious come-on. He drained his beer and followed her back into the fray.

Riley grabbed Gavin before he could attach himself to Rachel again. "Man, looks like you got a live one. Would you mind if Sheila and I bug off?"

Gavin thought about it for about a second. "Sure, I'll just get a cab. Thanks for coming out with me."

"Not a prob, bro. You have some protection on you, right?" Riley asked with a cheesy grin. He busted a gut laughing at the expression on Gavin's face. "You didn't bring any rubbers? I told you we were getting you laid tonight." Gavin flushed in embarrassment over his lack of planning. He squeaked when Riley shoved a hand in his back pocket. "I came prepared, and now you are too. Give your best buddy in the world a squeeze, and go get your kink on."

Gavin punched Riley in the shoulder and gave him a one-armed man clutch. "Thanks, Ri, but you touch my ass like that again, I'll tell Sheila on you," Gavin said when they separated. Sheila appeared out of the crowd as if summoned. She gave Gavin a hug and a whispered good luck, and then they were gone.

Rachel wrapped herself around Gavin once again. He got lost in the music and the feel of a warm, soft body pressed against his, so when his eyes met a pair of familiar blue eyes at the edge of the dance floor, he just stared into them. Gavin hadn't figured Officer Turner for the dancing type, but the man had some serious moves.

FOUR

LEX HAD WATCHED the doc and his friends from across the bar for most of the night. He tried a couple of times to get up the nerve to go say hi, but he wasn't sure if he'd be welcome. It's not like writing up a few reports for the guy made them friends or something. When Rachel joined them, Lex almost went over. He knew Rachel quite well and could use that as an excuse to insert himself into their group. When Lex saw how she was flirting with the doc, he decided to keep his distance. Gavin deserved to have a good time after all he'd been through with his ex-wife, and Rachel was definitely a good time.

Lex sat on his stool in the corner and watched Rachel grind on the doc until he couldn't take it any longer. He grabbed a random but willing woman and went to do what he'd come to Stucky's for in the first place—he danced. Lex reveled in the feel of the sweaty mass around him. The press of fabric and occasionally damp flesh against his own never failed to lift his mood. He also liked the fact that the crowded dance floor meant the bodies pressed against him weren't always just female. The smell of flowery perfume mixed with musky male scents nearly drove him insane with desire.

After a few songs, Lex was in his favorite headspace. His heart was pounding from the dancing, and his groin was throbbing from the sights, smells, and press of the crowd. He turned just in time to catch the doc staring at him. A slow, sensual smile lifted the corners of his lips as he made his movements a little more seductive. I'm a maniac on the floor, Lex thought as he moved to the music.

When Rachel noticed her partner's inattention, she followed Gavin's gaze. Rachel smiled and waved Lex over. She turned in the doc's arms as Lex moved through the crowd toward them. The thoughts he was having about where the night could go were making his heart pound.

"Hey, Lex, nice moves," Rachel said as she reached out to pull him in. He moved with her in a sensual rhythm, his half-erect cock enjoying the contact.

"Thanks, Rach, not doing too bad yourself." Lex smiled down at her before he raised his eyes to Gavin. "Hey there, Doc. Having a good time?" he asked a stunned-looking Gavin.

"Yeah, thanks," Gavin said.

"Oh, you guys know each other?" Rachel asked. Lex knew exactly what she was thinking from the small, sexy smile she aimed his way.

"We've met," Lex said.

Rachel was still moving between them when Gavin stepped back as if to leave. Rachel pivoted to face him and grabbed his hips and pulled Gavin in close. Lex stayed where he was and continued to move to the music. When Rachel had Gavin secured, Lex plastered his body against her back. Lex wasn't going to give an inch when he was only a couple of inches from the man he'd been fantasizing about for the past couple of months. So close he could smell the intoxicating combination of the doc's cologne and his sweat.

Gavin looked from Rachel to Lex. "I can go—"

"No!" Both Lex and Rachel said in chorus, making them laugh.

The doc raised one eyebrow. "Okay." The one word was a long, drawn-out affair.

Rachel wrapped her arms around Gavin's waist while Lex put his hands on her hips. Gavin's arms rested at his side, and he looked uncertain about where to place them. The doc was tall, having at least three inches on Lex, so it almost felt as if they were dancing alone when Lex looked up into his spectacularly beautiful brown eyes over Rachel's head. Grabbing Gavin's hands, Lex brought them to Rachel's hips, where his own had been only moments before. He risked leaving his own on top of the doc's for a couple of seconds and inwardly rejoiced when Gavin didn't flinch away from his touch.

Biting his bottom lip, Gavin lowered his eyes. Lex's breath caught, and he moved his hands up Rachel's sides, feeling the doc's firm abs on the backs of his fingers. They swayed to the music, and Gavin seemed to relax little by little. Lex got caught up in the rhythm and the feeling of the body pressed against him, but Gavin's eyes flew open wide when Lex grabbed his hips and pulled both his dance partners closer.

"Relax, baby," Rachel murmured to Gavin from her spot between them. Rising to her toes, she pulled his head down and kissed him, Lex getting a nose full of the doc's hair when he refused to move out of the way. Fighting back the urge to lick the sweat from Gavin's temple, Lex couldn't resist turning his head enough to make it seem accidental when his lips brushed the moist, heated skin there. Rachel released Gavin, who then looked at Lex as Lex swept his tongue across his lips to get his first taste of heaven.

In hindsight, it probably wasn't the smartest move. Lex was trying not to freak Gavin out. A straight guy wasn't likely to want another guy macking on him, especially not in public. As Lex shrugged away his little gaff, Gavin shook his head and returned a shy smile. Phew, Lex thought, disaster averted, at least for the moment.

Lex bent to Rachel's ear and asked, "You want to get out of here?"

She looked up at him, and he put his ear to her mouth. "With both of you?" she asked. Lex nodded. "Oh, yeah."

"I'll be in the parking lot. I'm parked toward the back." Lex released Gavin's hips, gave the man a nod and walked away, trusting Rachel to get the doc out to his pickup.

Lex made his way out of the bar and through the parking lot where he leaned on his truck, waiting for Rachel and, hopefully, Gavin. It didn't take long because Rachel was good at getting what she wanted, and it wasn't the first time he and Rachel had played together. Threesomes were her kink, and he didn't mind one bit helping her get her fix. He did have a couple of fleeting reservations about what he was about to drag the unwitting doc into. Usually their third was well aware of what was going to happen and was fully on board. He prayed that the doc didn't bolt when he realized what they had planned.

Gavin was the king of wide-eyed startled looks. Lex thought it was as cute as hell how innocent Gavin always looked. It made Lex chuckle to himself. Gavin's steps slowed when he realized they were heading for Lex's truck. Rachel kept her hold on Gavin's arm and pulled him along with her when his steps faltered.

"Come on, Gavin. I promise you this will be a night you'll never forget," she assured him.

"But...I'm not really sure this is a good idea. I've probably had more to drink than I should have and I'm not thinking clearly," he said as he eyed Lex. "You know he's a cop, right?"

"Last time I checked, going home with two guys wasn't against the law," Rachel said and then added, "Or in your case, a girl and a guy."

Gavin hesitated when Lex opened the passenger side door for them. "You guys aren't going to kidnap me and chain me to the radiator, are you?"

"Like we'd tell you if we were," Lex said while maintaining a straight face. The wide-eyed look was back as the doc looked around the parking lot for help. "Oh shit, calm down. I'm kidding. I'm a cop, remember?"

Rachel was giggling as she climbed up into the cab. "Come on, baby. Let's go have some fun." Rachel extended her hand to Gavin, who took a moment to decide but eventually climbed in beside her.

"By the way," Lex said as he leaned into the cab, "I'd use handcuffs, not chains, if I wanted you restrained, and it wouldn't be to the radiator."

The look on Gavin's face kept Lex amused as he closed the door and went around to the driver's side. He started the truck while Rachel kept Gavin too busy to think about what might be in store for him when they reached their destination. Lex had a hard time keeping his eyes on the road because of the sexy little moans coming from the doc. He got them to Rachel's apartment building in one piece. As soon as he turned the engine off, Rachel was in his arms. He moaned because he was sure he could taste the doc on her lips as she kissed him.

Lex pulled free of her embrace. "We need to get inside, or something we could get arrested for might happen." Rachel nodded in agreement, and they exited the vehicle. Gavin fidgeted as they stood outside Rachel's apartment door waiting for her to unlock it. He shifted his eyes from Rachel to Lex and back a few times. He ran his fingers through his hair and touched his kiss-swollen lips.

"Hey," Lex said to get Gavin's attention. Lust surged through Lex when Gavin looked at him. God, the man was pretty, and those puffy lips of his were begging to be kissed. "Don't be so nervous." The doc nodded but continued to look nervous as hell.

Rachel finally got the damn door open and led them into the apartment. She took her shoes off and went straight down the hallway toward the bedroom. Lex slipped his boots off and waited for Gavin to do the same before letting Gavin go ahead of him. He watched the sway of Gavin's hips as he walked and wished he would be lucky enough to be buried in that ass tonight. He scoffed at himself as he thought, *Dream on, buddy boy. That there is grade A, All-American straight boy, so hands off.*

Rachel had already pulled everything except the fitted sheet and pillows off the bed. She was standing there in a black thong and a pushup bra. Gavin stopped to give her an appreciative head-to-toe sweep. Lex could hear the doc's breathing speed up. Maybe it had been awhile for the doc. Rachel twirled to show off her backside before she took a couple of steps to Gavin. She pulled him down into a kiss as her hands went to the button of his jeans.

Lex stripped out of his shirt and shucked his pants, leaving his tight boxer briefs on. He didn't want to shock the doc too early and risk him running away. Lex approached Rachel from behind and unhooked her bra while she continued to undress Gavin. Gavin was naked from the waist down, but when their lips parted and Rachel tried to take his shirt off, he stopped her.

Gavin looked at Lex who had his hands on Rachel's breasts. "Um...I don't know how this works exactly," he admitted, eyeing Lex warily.

Lex kept his eyes above the doc's waist. Though he was dying to see what the doc was packing, he figured if Gavin caught him checking out his junk, he may freak out. He was already a bit skittish. Lex realized as much as he wanted this to happen that it might not be worth the hassle. Threesomes went much smoother when each of the participants weren't afraid to be touched by the others. Lex liked the doc, but if things went badly, Gavin would probably never be able to look at him again.

"Don't worry. Lex won't do anything that you don't want him to. Are you gonna be okay if he touches you?" Rachel asked, giving voice to Lex's thoughts. She turned to shoot Lex a look. She wasn't thrilled by the inexperience of their third, and he'd probably hear about it later.

Gavin took a second to answer and Lex imagined he could see the thoughts running through Gavin's head as his emotions played out on his face. Lex wondered if what he was seeing was revulsion at the idea of being intimate with another man, but then Gavin surprised him.

"Depends on where he touches me and with which appendage." Gavin cocked his head and smirked at Lex as he yanked his shirt off. Well, well, maybe the doc would surprise them.

Lex took that as an invitation to see which appendage Gavin was most worried about, though he could hazard a pretty good guess. He reached out over Rachel's shoulder and ran his hand down Gavin's arm. "This okay?" he asked. Gavin nodded without hesitation. Lex rubbed his hand down the center of Gavin's chest. "This okay?" Gavin paused before nodding once again. Lex rubbed his thumb over one of Gavin's nipples and then gave it a little tweak. Gavin gasped. "How 'bout that?" Gavin put up his hand and made the so-so gesture with it. Lex smiled He was having fun.

Rachel, who he'd almost forgotten was there, dropped to her knees between them. The look of surprise on Gavin's face told Lex what she was doing without him having to look. Gavin licked his lips and moaned softly. Lex put his hand on the side of Gavin's jaw and ran a finger over the man's lips. "Still okay?" Lex asked. His voice had gone all husky, and he wasn't doing a good job of keeping the lust out of his gaze, but Gavin slowly nodded again. He leaned in and brushed his lips lightly over Gavin's. Gavin jerked back. He shook his head; alrighty then, so kissing wasn't okay.

Gavin looked down at Rachel, who was on her knees at their feet. Lex watched as Gavin's cock was revealed when Rachel moved off him. His knees went weak with want, but there was no way a man who wouldn't even accept a kiss from another man would let said man suck his cock, no matter how much he wanted to. Rachel pulled at the front of Lex's underwear to free his erection. Gavin averted his gaze after only a glimpse of Lex's cock. When their eyes met, Gavin quickly closed his.

Rachel was in her element and played her part like a seasoned porn star. She jerked them off in tandem while alternating licks and soft sucking kisses to the heads of their cocks. Lex couldn't keep his eyes off Gavin, no matter what was going on below his waist. He didn't want to miss anything; his gaze bounced from the doc's face, over his flushed chest and down to his cock. When the urge to grope Gavin became overwhelming, Lex reached down and pulled Rachel off the floor. He turned her to him and kissed her while running his hands over her body.

Gavin stood there looking a bit lost. Suspecting that Gavin wouldn't take any initiative, Lex stepped Rachel back into the doc and grabbed the man's hands to place them on her tits. "You know what to do with those, right?" he asked the befuddled-looking man. Lex felt bad for Rachel and turned his attention to her. "You okay? What do you want, sweetie?" he asked between kisses.

"Double stuff," she moaned.

Gavin snapped out of his stupor and started nuzzling Rachel's neck as he worked her nipples with his deft fingers. Lex wanted to tell her there was no way that Gavin would be okay with what she was asking for, but just the thought of feeling the doc's cock so close to his had Lex groaning. Besides he owed Rachel, and he'd do his best to give her what she wanted.

"On the bed, Rach on top," Lex instructed. He went to the drawer in the nightstand and grabbed condoms and lube. Rachel had Gavin on his back on the bed. She grabbed one of the condoms out of Lex's hand. She rolled it down Gavin's considerable length, threw a leg over him and unceremoniously impaled herself on his cock.

"Oh holy fuck," Gavin gasped out.

Lex got on the bed behind Rachel and lubed his fingers. She lay forward on Gavin's chest. Lex entered her with one finger, causing both of his lovers to moan at the extra stimulation. It didn't take long for him to add a second finger and start a scissor motion inside Rachel. She liked having her ass fingered, but Lex made quick work of the stretching because the doc was making noises, and his hips were jerking as he tried to fuck up into Rachel. He probably wouldn't last too long, and Lex didn't want Gavin to finish before he'd even had the chance to start.

"You ready, Rach?" he asked as he put on a condom and lubed the hell out of it.

"Yeah, now baby, fill me up," she pleaded.

Lex straddled Gavin's thighs. A shiver ran up his spine when his balls rubbed the doc's naked skin. He lined up and slowly pushed past the initial resistance. All three participants moaned. Lex waited until Rachel started moving, letting her set the pace. Gavin made little whimpery noises under them as she moved slowly.

Lex felt Gavin's cock moving in and out of Rachel's body, and the added sensation drove him crazy. He set a rhythm that had him and the doc moving against each other inside the woman between them. Lex closed his eyes and imagined that it was just him and the doc, and the image had him clenching his teeth to fight off his orgasm. He reached around, found Rachel's clit, and worked it like he owned it. She leaned back with her head on Lex's chest. Gavin fondled her tits, making Rachel moan for more.

"Harder, please more and harder," Rachel asked for and got it. When she came, both her orifices clenched down on the cocks they were stuffed with. Lex fucked her ass faster, chasing his own release but holding back his strength because he didn't want to hurt her.

"Fuck, that...oh shit...it feels...ah f...feels so, oh GOD!" Gavin shouted the last word as he came. Lex finally let himself go. He filled the condom and fell forward, catching himself with his hands on Gavin's chest before he crushed Rachel between them. The three stayed in that position as they waited for their breathing to go back to normal.

Lex came down from his orgasm when he felt Gavin trying to shift underneath them. Their balls were pressed together under Lex's weight and Lex wiggled a little just so that he could feel Gavin a little better. Rachel groaned at his movement. He kissed the back of her neck and reached down to hold the condom in place as he pulled out. He made sure that he got a good grope of Gavin's balls and the base of his cock as he did it. Yeah fine, he was a sneaky fucker, but when would he ever get the chance to feel the doc up again? Gavin shuddered at his touch, and Lex wondered if it was because he was creeped out by it or if just maybe, he liked it. Lex pulled the condom off and tied it. He got off the bed and watched as Gavin and Rachel separated. He held out his hand for Gavin's condom. Gavin raised an eyebrow at him.

"Christ, we just got done fucking the same woman. You expect me to get squicked out by touching your used condom?" he asked. Gavin handed it over with a grimace. Lex took the used rubbers to the bathroom to dispose of them. He shook his head at his reflection as he washed himself in the sink. That was definitely not the best sex he'd ever had. He'd never been so lucid and in control of himself during the act; babysitting the doc had really sucked the fun out of the entire thing.

When Lex opened the bathroom door, the doc was standing there with his shirt on and holding the rest of his clothes. Lex didn't much care for the look on his face. It looked suspiciously like regret.

"I, ah, have to be at the hospital for rounds early tomorrow," Gavin said. Lex nodded and stepped out of his way.

He went back to the bedroom. Rachel was lying on the bed with a sheet thrown over her. She didn't look pleased. "Well that was probably the most awkward fucking threesome I've ever had, and I had one with a couple of brothers once. They were less weird about a stray body part touching them than that guy was. What the hell is with him?" she asked.

Hadn't Lex just been thinking the same thing? "I think he may have been overwhelmed." Lex made an excuse for the doc because he felt responsible for the whole thing. He would take the blame for the mess he'd created. He'd known the doc was straight, and from his reaction to the website incident, he was probably pretty straight-laced too. Lex shouldn't have pushed it, but he'd just wanted to get close to Gavin.

Awkward or not, he'd fucking lock this night away in the spank bank and bring it out often for a long time to come.

"Lex, I have no idea what's with you, but I may never trust you to pick a third again," Rachel said. Then a slow smile crept across her lips. "I think you got a big old man crush on that guy."

"Rach, shut it, or he'll hear you."

"Oh my god, you do, don't you?" she asked, her eyes widening before the giggling began. Lex shook his head and put his boxers back on. He'd just sat down on the bed and was trying to think of what to tell Rachel when Gavin came back into the bedroom.

"Hey, um, I hate to...you know...and run, but I have to work early. So I'm going to just, like, go," he stammered. He looked so embarrassed it was hard for Lex to watch.

"I can give you a lift home," Lex offered.

"Um no, really, I'll just call a cab and wait outside. Sorry, I mean—"

"Really?" Rachel asked. Her tone irritated and bitchy. "What the heck, man? You need to chill. We're all good. No need to strain your brain. You need to go, then go. No worries."

Gavin blushed bright pink, turned, and hurried out. Lex listened to the door shut before he said, "Real nice, Rach. God, could you give the man a break? You didn't need to be such a bitch."

She pushed him with her foot. "Fuck off, Lex. Go crush on that weirdo somewhere else. I need a shower and sleep."

Lex got dressed and left. He wasn't going to stay around and listen to anything else Rachel had to say to disparage his doc.

FIVE

GAVIN WALKED FIFTEEN blocks in the opposite direction from his house before his head cleared enough to call a cab. He had to look for a street sign to give the cab an address. Thankfully, in a smaller city like the one he lived in, it only took the taxi a few minutes to show up. He slumped down in the seat and rubbed his temples the whole ride home. He couldn't wait to put the night behind him. What had he been thinking getting himself into a situation like that? Could it have been more awkward? He paid the cabbie and went into his house. He'd never been so glad to be home, but that feeling only lasted for exactly ten seconds.

The smell hit him first, and Gavin crinkled his nose, his mouth dropping open as he entered the kitchen through the side door. He took in the scene in his kitchen before he walked through to the living room where he fell to his knees. Why? Why would any sane person do this to another? There was no doubt in his mind that Cassie had been in his house. Then he thought, what if he was wrong and someone broke in, and they were still there? He sounded like a bad movie, even to himself. Who would break in, trash the place, and then write those things on his walls? No, this had his ex-wife's name all over it.

He pulled out his cell and dialed 9-1-1. When asked what his emergency was he hesitated, this wasn't technically an emergency, was it? Oh fuck it. "Um, someone broke into my house and I...uh need some police, probably?"

"Sir, are you inside the residence?"

"Yeah, I'm inside," Gavin answered.

"Are you safe? Has the intruder left?"

"I think so. I don't think there's anyone here but me," Gavin said. The woman's voice helped to calm him, and his brain was slowly starting to come back online.

"I'm sending officers to you right now. Can you give me your name and address please?"

Gavin gave her his details, and she insisted on keeping him on the line until the officers knocked on his door. He thanked the operator and stood up to open the door for the cops. It was Officers Santiago and Larson, the smiles on their faces falling as soon as the stench reached them.

Santiago grabbed Gavin's arm to pull him outside onto the porch. She put her hands on his shoulders to make him look her in the eyes. "Hey there, Dr. Addison, are you okay?" Her eyes scanned his face. He heard Officer Larson cursing inside the house. Santiago pulled what Gavin hoped was a clean cotton hanky from her pants pocket and started swiping at his wet face. Gavin grabbed her arm to make her stop.

"Is that human shit?" Larson asked when he came back out on the porch after taking a look around. Gavin gaped at him.

"I think he may be in shock," Santiago said.

Larson gave Gavin a once-over and shook his head. "I'm calling this in. I think we're gonna need some help," Larson said as he walked down the steps.

"Can you tell me what happened?" Santiago asked.

"Ah, I went out, no shit; I came back, shit storm," Gavin said, giving her the short version. She didn't need to know what he'd been doing while he was out, right?

She covered her mouth and coughed. It was plain to see she was trying not to laugh. "You think your ex may have had something to do with this?"

"No shit, you think?"

This time she did laugh, and Gavin glared at her. "I'm so sorry," she said when she calmed down. "Do you know if anything was taken?"

"Yeah, it looks like a couple of hundred dumps were taken all over my living room and kitchen. How the hell would I know? It's not like I spent time digging through that shit to inventory my shit to see if it was all there!" Gavin's voice had steadily increased in pitch, but goddamn it, this was just the shit frosting on his crappy night. All he'd wanted to do was climb into his bed, crawl under the covers, and forget about his botched foray into the kinkosphere, and now he had to deal with this...this...CRAP!

"Doc... Doc... Doc... Hey, Do—"

"WHAT?" he shouted when Larson chanting his nickname finally penetrated his thoughts.

Larson put his hands up in front of his chest in a placating gesture. "Whoa, calm down there, Doc. I think you need to have a seat and get ahold of yourself. Is there anyone you could call to come sit with you?"

Gavin's mind pulled up a picture of startling blue eyes giving him a heated look he couldn't reconcile with the very male face they were set in. He shook his head to clear it. Why would Officer Turner pop into his head like that? Santiago was right; he must be in shock. "Maybe my friend Riley. I'll call him." Larson nodded as Gavin pulled out his phone and checked the time. Ugh, almost four in the morning. Riley would not be pleased.

"Hey, Ri," he said after the grunt from the other end let him know that his friend had answered.

"Ugggghhh, god, Gav, you coulda waited till morning to give me the deets," Riley grumbled.

"Sorry, Ri, but could you come to my house? I kind of need someone here," Gavin said, and for the first time, his emotions bubbled to the surface. His breath hitched, and he held back what would have been a very unmanly, embarrassing sob.

"Gav, what's wrong? Are you okay? Are you hurt?" Riley asked. He was awake now for sure, and Gavin could hear Sheila's worried voice in the background.

Gavin took a deep breath, their concern making him want to cry even more. "I'm okay, my house..." This time he did let out a little sob. "She shit on my house."

"We're on our way. Just hang in there, buddy." Gavin could hear rustling and Sheila saying she had the keys.

"Thanks. See you in a few then," Gavin said.

"Yeah, 'kay, bye." Riley hung up.

Gavin sat on the porch steps as more cars pulled up in front of his house. Some of the people weren't wearing uniforms, so he had no idea what type of personnel they'd called in for this. He really couldn't be bothered to ask any questions, and other than some concerned looks, they pretty much left him alone. He was tired and emotionally drained. He stood up when Riley's car pulled into his driveway. Both of his friends rushed to him and wrapped him in their arms.

Riley pulled back and let Sheila to do the physical comforting. "Dude, what happened? Are you really okay?" Gavin was well-versed in Riley speak, and that question meant Riley was really concerned because there wasn't one curse word to be found.

Gavin clung to Sheila. "Yeah, I'm fine. I'm pretty sure Cassie was in my house though. There's shit everywhere."

"Don't worry, honey; we'll help you clean it up," Sheila assured him.

Gavin shook his head. "I'm not sure you get what I'm saying. There's, like, literal shit everywhere. You might change your mind after you see it. Or, I guess, smell it," he clarified. He watched Riley's face go from concern, to disgust, and finally settle on rage.

"That bitch! I'm going to find her and when I do—"

"Oh hush up, Riley. We're going to let the cops handle this." Sheila broke out the mom tone.

"Yeah, like they've been doing such a great job so far," Riley said loud enough for the cops to hear. They received a few dirty looks, but Riley just gave them back as good as he got. "This is breaking and entering, and that's got to be more than a misdemeanor. If they can't hold her on this, then they're incompetent."

"Calm down, Ri. Pissing off the cops isn't going to do me any good. They've been pretty nice to me through all of this," Gavin said. He hoped the officers heard him as well as they did his friend. Last thing he needed was for the cops to hate him when he needed them.

"Do you want to come to our place?" Sheila asked.

"I don't think I can stay here tonight, so that would be great. Let me go talk to the cops and see what they need and how much longer this is going to take," Gavin said. He walked over to where Larson was standing with a guy in a cheap, ill-fitting suit. He waited until Larson finished and stepped up to them.

"Hey, Dr. Addison, this is Detective McDaniels. He's going to be handling your case now that we've crossed into his territory. Detective, this is the homeowner, Gavin Addison."

The detective shook Gavin's hand. "I know they asked you this before, but did you notice anything missing from your home?"

Gavin shook his head. "I don't know for sure, but it didn't look like she took anything. My electronics are all there, and they're the only things worth stealing. Is that really important?"

"It is because the degree of the crime changes. If there's just vandalism, it's fourth degree, but if there's something stolen, it bumps up, and depending on what was taken and other factors, it would fall anywhere between first and third degree," he explained.

"And that affects me how?" Gavin asked. He didn't want to be an ass, but really, why should he care as long as they put her in jail this time? Oh, fuck. "Are you seriously telling me that if she didn't steal anything she's going to get off with a slap on the wrist again?"

"So, you're pretty sure that it was," the detective looked at his little notebook, "your ex-wife who did this?"

"Who else would do this?" Gavin asked. He was getting shrill again.

The detective looked at him with a dispassionate stare. He took a deep breath. "We'll do our best to find out who is responsible for this and then make sure they're charged to the full extent under the law."

"I know and I'm sorry. I'm just really tired, and this is not how I wanted to spend the rest of my night," Gavin said in defeat. He was getting sick of apologizing to the cops.

The detective turned and had a quiet conversation with a man who had come up behind him while they were talking. After some nodding and gesturing at Gavin and the house, the man turned and left. McDaniels expression softened a little when he looked at Gavin. "That was our forensics guy. He's pretty sure the excrement isn't human waste, some sort of animal feces more likely than not. They should be done in there by the time I'm done taking your statement."

Gavin sighed and patiently answered all the questions the detective asked, including who he'd been with that evening, at least he didn't have to tell them what he'd been doing with those two people.

"That should do it," McDaniels said, closing the pad he'd been writing notes on. "We'll be in touch once we have any information for you or if we need anything further."

"Thanks." Gavin shook the detective's offered hand again. He got the feeling the detective wasn't overly thrilled with him, but right then he couldn't care less. He waited until the cops all cleared out of his house before locking it up and going back to where Riley and Sheila were standing. They took him to their condo where they put him in the spare bedroom with borrowed clothes and a promise from him to fill them in on his night after he got some sleep. He showered in the attached bathroom and fell into bed. Finally, he could be alone to nurse his wounded ego.

"THE HELL YOU did!" Riley exclaimed. His eyes danced with mirth above the face mask he wore to help with the stench. "So who was the guy?"

"I didn't know him," Gavin lied. He wasn't sure why, after all he'd told Riley, he didn't want to tell him that he knew the guy he'd shared a woman with the previous night. He watched as one of the cleaning crew picked up another bag of trash to move it to the porch with all the others. Riley had been attached at the hip to him the whole day, driving Gavin around to run a few errands before going back to his house where the people from the cleaning service Sheila had helped Gavin find were into their third hour of work removing everything that was broken or soiled beyond repair.

Gavin sighed at the thought of his poor house. They'd gotten most of the trash picked up. Cassie had emptied the contents of his refrigerator and all of his cupboards. There had been broken dishes and food mixed in with a healthy dose of what the cops told him turned out to be dog droppings. The living room was much the same with the added bonus of words written on the walls in canine crap. She had, thankfully, stopped there, leaving the two bedrooms and bathroom untouched. Maybe she'd run out of puppy poop.

Riley had stood on a ladder and reprogrammed the garage door opener to assure that Cassie wouldn't have access to it again. How Gavin had missed the fact that she still had one of the remotes was beyond him, but now that the problem was remedied he felt much more secure.

Gavin had been working up the nerve to tell Riley about his walk on the wild side all day. He'd finally just blurted it out, even the mortifying details, like having a guy kiss him. Now he had to deal with Riley and his obsessive need to have every single detail about it. Sometimes Gavin wished he could just keep his mouth shut.

"So was he hot?" Riley asked.

"What do you mean?"

"I mean, was he better-looking than you? Were you weirded out because he was like a male model and had a huge schlong? Were you all like 'he's so hot and I'm so not' and that's maybe why you were weird about it?" he asked. "You know, thinking the cute little redhead was comparing you gave you performance anxiety?"

Gavin thought about it. He supposed that Lex was attractive. He had kind of the boy-next-door, "ah shucks, ain't nothing, ma'am," corn-fed, farm-boy-type of look to him. Not anything to write home about, though: plain brown hair, worn probably just short enough to pass regulation, blue eyes, pretty striking—not that Gavin would tell Riley that—a chiseled jaw, strong nose, and a body that most guys would...oh shit. He wasn't going to tell Riley that he had actually checked the guy out.

"No, I mean, I don't know. I didn't really check out his equipment, you know? I don't think he was that good-looking; not that I make a habit out of looking at guys like that," Gavin said. "I'm not a fag you know."

Riley looked at Gavin in astonishment. "Dude, I didn't know you were homophobic. Holy shit on a shingle, Mr. Perfect has a little smudge on his shiny reputation now. I'll never be able to see you in the same light again. Your halo is tarnished," Riley said in a mockingly disappointed tone as he clutched his chest.

Gavin was taken aback. Even if Riley had been sort of joking, Gavin didn't think he was even remotely bigoted. In fact, there had been a time, a very brief time, when Gavin had thought he might be in love with Riley. He wouldn't tell his friend that though; he'd never hear the end of it if he did. Gavin had never acted on his feelings. He knew from his psychology courses that sometimes people confused deep feelings of friendship with romantic feelings. The fact that Gavin had yet to have his first romantic relationship meant he'd been transferring those feelings onto his best friend. He'd convinced himself that it was nothing, but now, with Riley thinking he was homophobic, he considered telling him just to make himself feel better.

"I'm not homophobic, and you know it. I know gay people, and I don't have any problem with them," Gavin said in his defense. What he'd said was just a word they'd tossed at each other all through college, so when did Riley start to take offense at that word?

"I'm just giving you shit, buddy. But wow, did you just get all defensive. Maybe you need to look into that." Riley shrugged as he turned to the wall. "Why did she write this on your walls?"

Gavin looked over at what had been written: PERVERT, SICKO, WEIRDO, and DEVIANT had been scrawled on his walls. "I have no idea. Maybe she's still trying to hurt my reputation, like with the website thing." Who knew what Cassie had been thinking? He wondered if maybe she did need some mental help.

Even dealing with his current ex-wife crisis couldn't keep his mind from returning to what Riley had said about him being homophobic. Going back to his earlier thoughts, he *had* wondered about what it would be like to be with a man sexually, but that curiosity had died when he realized his feelings for Riley were displaced. He'd met Cassie and never looked back.

Gavin's thoughts naturally led him back to the previous night, which bugged him more than he'd admit to Riley. He'd made a damn fool of himself in front of both Rachel and Officer Turner, aka Lex, the god of awesome, kinky, threesome sex. Lex hadn't had a problem at all with what had happened. Why had Lex kissed him? Was it just that the guy was so secure in his masculinity he could get away with kissing another guy and not question it? Not that Gavin wasn't secure, he'd just found it awkward. Or maybe Lex had seen that Gavin was nervous, and he'd had to push it and make Gavin feel stupid. Yeah that was probably it—Lex obviously was okay with kissing a dude, and he wanted to point out Gavin wasn't for some reason that Gavin couldn't fathom.

Gavin started to get angry at that stupid cop for making him feel the way he did over something that was new and strange and for making him feel inadequate in front of a woman he found attractive. He knew if he had another chance he'd do it better. That's when Gavin realized that he wanted a do over. No, that wasn't right—Gavin *needed* a do over.

"I need a do over," he blurted out.

"What?" Riley asked.

"Nothing, just thinking and talking to myself. I think the fumes are getting to me. Maybe we should call it a day," he said. He couldn't tell Riley what he was thinking. Gavin wasn't even sure *he* knew what the hell he was thinking. "Is it okay if I stay at your place again tonight?"

"Hells yeah, we'll have a slumber party. Just don't go getting any ideas about a repeat performance. I don't share Sheila. She's mine," Riley joked.

"Why don't you just get your name tattooed on her ass so everyone knows? You're such a Neanderthal." Repeat performance, the phrase danced through his head. He needed a plan, one that would help him get his pride back.

"Yeah, I'm trying to talk her into that already," Riley said.

Gavin talked to the man in charge of the cleaning crew. He was assured that the house would be locked securely when they finished up. They would be back in the morning to clean the living room rug and the furniture.

He followed Riley home in his own car and spent the whole drive trying to think of a way he could get himself into the same situation he'd been in the night before. Would hanging out at Stucky's, waiting to catch Lex and Rachel there at the same time, seem creepy? Probably. Maybe he could tell the cop he wanted to try again. Yeah and say what? "Hey, I know last time we were naked together it wasn't so great, so I'd like to prove to you that I can do better"? There just wasn't a way to tell Lex that he wanted to try it again without making himself sound like a complete lunatic. He didn't have Rachel's phone number, and she probably wouldn't appreciate him showing up at her apartment uninvited; add that to the fact that she hadn't been exactly pleased with the way he'd left, and she was even less of an option. So the only avenue left to him was Lex, at work, in the cop shop.

Gavin cursed himself as he and Riley walked into the condo. Why did he feel the need to prove himself to someone he didn't even know? He was being crazy, driving himself crazy for a completely stupid reason, and he was going to stop. He'd been humiliated, but he was going to put on his big-boy pants and suck it up. Screw it. He didn't need to prove himself to some meathead cop. He had more important things to worry about, like if the cops would actually put his psycho ex-wife in jail this time. Yeah that's right, time to think about the important things. So why couldn't he get Lex's face out of his head?

SIX

LEX HAD SPENT two days beating himself up over how his Friday night had ended. He'd screwed up big time and not just with the doc. Rachel had been pissed enough to text him to let him know how very not pleased she was. She'd had time to think and knew what had been going on. She had blamed Lex for using her as a tool to get the "weirdo" into bed. Rachel felt used and rightly so. He'd known that he'd been ignoring her needs, while being preoccupied with keeping Gavin from freaking out, and that just wasn't right. He'd apologized and even sent her a little bouquet of flowers. He'd never been such a selfish prick in bed before, and it nagged at him.

Lex had resolved to put his feelings for Gavin out of his mind. The doc was straight and obviously not bicurious at all. He felt almost as badly about what he'd done to the doc as he did about Rachel. He'd never pushed anyone like that sexually, and he felt pretty dirty about the whole business. He wanted to apologize or do something to make amends. He didn't send Gavin any flowers—he wasn't a complete idiot—he just couldn't think of anything he could do for the guy.

When he reported for his shift on Sunday night—his two-week night rotation going from midnight to noon—Grady was standing in a group of other officers. They were listening to Santiago tell what was apparently a very engaging story. Lex walked up to see what he'd missed.

"And Larson was gagging and swearing. The poor doc looked like he was in shock, with tears and snot all over his face; you'd have thought he just found his mom dead in there. The worst part was he kept saying the word shit, and I couldn't stop myself from laughing even though I knew it wasn't funny. God, the smell was just horrible," she stopped and looked around at the assembled group. "Thankfully, his friends came and took him home with them after McDaniels took his statement. When Larson questioned the neighbors, he was able to get one of them to pin the ex. The old guy across the street said he saw her pull into the garage at 9:30 p.m., and then she left somewhere around midnight." Larson's chest puffed up at his partner's shout-out.

"Why didn't he call it in?" Grady asked.

"He said he didn't think anything of it; she'd lived there for years. He figured that maybe they were meeting for something," Larson said.

"Yeah, but everyone in that neighborhood has to know what she's been doing. You'd think they'd find something fishy about her being there, especially when the doc was out," Lex said. He only realized what he'd said when all eyes turned to him.

"How did you know the doc wasn't home when she showed up?" Grady asked with narrowed eyes.

"I guess I figured he wouldn't just let her in if he was home," Lex said drolly, thinking fast on his feet and schooling his expression. The group chuckled and nodded in agreement.

"So who got the honors of bringing that bitch in?" Merriweather asked.

"No one yet. She wasn't at home, and she hasn't been answering her phone. McDaniels even called her lawyer and her parents. So far, she's MIA, and no one's heard from her," Larson said.

"He did manage to get an arrest warrant for her though, so we can bring her in if we see her," Santiago said. Everyone seemed pretty happy to hear that. They were all sick of dealing with the domestic drama Cassandra Addison kept creating.

Lex looked around the group. Everyone there had responded to a call or two to the doc's house in the past couple of months. They would be happy to see that woman get her due, because every one of them liked the doc, but Lex secretly hoped he'd be the one to arrest her. To be able to do that for the doc; shit, he'd be like Gavin's hero or something. Lex was going to memorize Cassandra Addison's license plate number and make sure her neighborhood was well patrolled. He'd found something he could do to make it up to Gavin.

WELL YOU KNOW what they say about the best laid plans, Lex thought as he sat at his desk. It'd been a week and a half since "The Shit Happened," as they were jokingly calling the vandalism of the doc's house, and Cassandra Addison was nowhere to be found. He and Grady had just come in off patrol when the extension on Lex's desk started to ring. Both he and Grady looked at it like they'd never seen the thing before because it was rare for any of the patrol officers to get calls on desk phones.

"Officer Turner," Lex answered the line.

"Hey, Lex, there's a message here for you concerning one of your cases," the front desk officer stopped to snigger before continuing. "The caller was Gavin Addison. He said he had something he thought might be of help concerning his case."

"That's McDaniels's case. Why didn't he call him?" Lex asked, perplexed as to why the doc would be calling him. Patrol officers didn't have cases; the detectives handled them. Gavin should have McDaniels's phone number with the instruction to call him if he needed anything or had any information pertaining to the case.

"I told him that, but he insisted that he wanted to talk to you. I told him you were out on patrol, and he left a message."

"Okay, give it to me then," Lex said. He wrote down the phone number Gavin had left and sat back in his chair. Grady eyeballed him across their desks.

"So, what, you're stealing the dick's cases now? Since when are you and the doc so buddy-buddy?" Grady asked.

"How do you know it was about the doc's case?" Lex asked. He had no idea why Gavin would call him. Of course, he was itching to find out just that but not in front of Grady. If it had something to do with the thing that had nothing to do with the case, he didn't want Grady overhearing any of it. Why would Gavin call about that though, unless he wanted to lay into Lex because he figured out Lex was perving on him, and he wanted to give him a piece of his mind?

"Because every time someone mentions that guy, you get all weird. What the hell's going on with that?" Lex's silence to Grady's question must have triggered his partner's faulty detective reasoning. "You're not sticking it to his ex, are you? Holy crap, Turner, you are; aren't you? That's why you avoid talking to the guy and get all weird about this case. I wondered why our patrol route all of sudden included his house and her apartment three times a shift." Grady was really warming up to his theory.

"You got it all wrong." Lex tried to get Grady to listen, but it was futile.

"Don't give me that shit; there's no other reason for you acting so cagey. She's psycho. She really must be something in the sack for you to put up with her kind of crazy." Grady was leaning over his desk, and his eyes were bright when he asked, "So is she really a hellcat in bed?"

"God, Grady, get a grip. I'm not fucking her, and shut up before people hear you. That kind of talk could ruin my reputation." Lex was peeved at his partner. All he needed was some baseless rumor derailing his career.

"Then what is it?" asked Grady, daring Lex to give him a reason to believe what he thought wasn't true.

"I can't explain it to you. It doesn't have anything to do with me and his wife though. I don't even know her." He was being evasive, but he couldn't very well tell the truth and not explain himself to Grady. "When you find her, you can ask her yourself."

Grady stared at Lex for a while longer. "Fine, but if I find out that you're hiding something about this case from the detective, I'll make sure that everyone knows, and then where will your precious reputation be?" Grady's tone lacked the conviction of his earlier statements, but still, it pissed Lex off.

"Fine, but there's nothing, so don't go spreading rumors, or I'll make sure you'll be the one to pay," Lex threatened back. The two men glared at each other until finally Grady grunted and got up to leave.

Lex slumped back in his chair, letting his head flop back. He looked up at the flickering florescent light and wondered how the hell his life had turned into such a fucking mess. He waited until Grady walked back through on his way out before Lex headed to the locker room. He'd wait until he was home to call Gavin back.

During Lex's drive home, his thoughts bounced from one thing to another. His conversation with Grady, what the doc could want, and what he would say if it wasn't the case Gavin wanted to talk about. He was greeted at the door by Agent. The old mutt jumped up and put his paws on Lex's stomach. He'd never been able to train the stupid pooch not to do that. He rubbed his dog's ears and scolded him at the same time, probably one of the reasons he'd never been trained right.

"Hey, Ma, you home?" Lex called after he'd pushed the dog off. He went to the kitchen, but his mom wasn't there cooking him lunch like she normally would have been. He walked down the hall to her bedroom door. He listened before he pushed the slightly ajar door open. "Ma, you in here?"

She was there. Lex found his mom sitting in the middle of her bed surrounded by photo albums and crumpled tissues. Lex sighed and walked across the room to the bed. It looked like one of her bad days again. He saw the books, and his heart sank because it wasn't the wedding album like usual. No, today of all days, it had to be the one with the pictures of his older sister. Lex chastised himself for forgetting that in a couple of days it would be the anniversary of his sister's death. His mom looked up at him when he sat down on the edge of the bed.

"Hey, honey, sorry I didn't make lunch, but I had a dream about Liz. I thought that maybe..." She trailed off and the tears started again.

Lex looked her over and noticed she was still in her nightclothes, which meant she'd probably started this latest episode the minute she'd woken up. He gathered her in his arms. "It's no problem, Mom. I'll make you lunch today. Did you take your pills this morning?" he asked. She shook her head. "Okay then, you need to get up, wash your face, and get dressed. I'll go see what I can scrounge up for lunch. After you eat, you're going to take your pills and then maybe a nap."

Lex stood up and waited for his mom to crawl off the bed. If he didn't stay there to make sure she grabbed her clothes and went into the bathroom, she'd go back to bawling in the middle of her bed. It took him back to his childhood and how much he hated to get up for school. The roles had been reversed then, and he thanked god that his mother had been a patient woman because this was just annoying.

She gathered her things, and Lex stepped back to let her pass by into the hallway. He snatched up the albums and the used tissues, which he then threw in the trash as he gave some serious thought about throwing the albums in too. He couldn't do it. He settled for putting them in her closet on the highest shelf. That wouldn't stop her from taking them out again, but out of sight, out of mind was something that worked most of the time with his mom, at least for a little while.

In the kitchen, Lex poked through the fridge and found a container that held enough leftover casserole to feed them both. His mom joined him just as the microwave pinged, signaling that their lunch was ready. He spooned it onto two plates and set one in front of her.

She took a watery breath. "I'm sorry for the meltdown. It's just hard this time of year, you know?"

Lex knew. How could he forget? The middle of May was always hard on his mom, since his sister had died sixteen years ago. It seemed time had done nothing to lessen the loss for her. Liz had been about to graduate from college. His parents had already rented one of the convention rooms at one of the nicer hotels for the party. The cake had been ordered, the caterer and DJ had been hired, and the invitations sent out. They'd pulled out all the stops because Liz was going to be the first in their family to graduate from college. The call that came five days before the party was set to take place was the only thing that hadn't been planned.

His sister and three of her friends had been in a car accident on I-94 on their way back from a shopping trip in the Twin Cities. Three died and the other was paralyzed from the waist down. His parents had been inconsolable. Lex'd had his breakdown in private and had then gone on with his life. He'd been just about to finish his junior year of high school and was old enough to know that some people viewed him as a bit callous for his lack of public emotion shown over the tragedy. Even though he'd loved his sister more than anyone else on earth, he knew no amount of raging or crying could bring her back. Lex had always been a practical person, not one to dwell on things he couldn't change, but Liz's death gave birth to his aspiration to become a law enforcement officer.

"I understand, but you still need to take care of yourself. Not taking your blood pressure pills isn't going to help anyone," he said. He covered her hand with his own. "You're all I have. I need you to promise me you won't forget that."

Her sad eyes met his and held for a long moment, one tear tracking down her cheek. "I know and I won't forget my promises to you. I just need to get through this, and everything will be back to normal," she assured him. Lex watched as she ate a few bites of food. She looked thoughtful as she ate. "You need to find you a nice girl and settle down."

Whoa, that came out of nowhere. "It's not that easy, Ma. It's not like it was in your day; women aren't just about getting married and having kids these days. They want to have careers first, and most people aren't getting married that young anymore," he said.

"You're not that young anymore," she said with a snort.

Lex wanted to point out that he wasn't the one drawing social security but thought better of it. "Thirty isn't that old, Mom. I still got time," he said. She shook her head but didn't argue, and they finished the meal in silence.

Lex watched her take her pills and then got a kiss on the cheek as they each headed for their bedrooms. It was almost two o'clock, and he'd planned on a short nap since he was off for the night, but it wasn't worth it if he'd just have to drag himself out of bed more tired than when he'd lay down or run the risk of sleeping the rest of the day. Better to stay up and turn in early.

Lex thought about his mom and how hard the next week or so was going to be on the both of them. He'd have to be there for her because when she got depressed she tended to do stupid things. He needed a distraction from the hopeless feeling he always got when he thought about his mother's bottomless well of grief over her lost daughter and husband.

Lex turned on the TV in his room and sat on the bed to flip through the channels. His mind wandered, and he started to drift off. He shook himself awake. He needed to do something other than watch mind-numbingly boring daytime television. It was then he remembered he had a phone call to make. He got up to grab his cell phone and the slip of paper with the doc's number on it from his dresser. Sitting on the edge of his bed, he tried to figure out what he was going to say. Gavin had said he had information on the case, so Lex would keep the call professional.

Lex dialed the number, listening to it ring until the voicemail picked up and he heard Gavin's smooth voice telling him to leave a message. He hung up. No way was he going to leave a message. The doc was probably at work, so he'd try again in the evening, but when he went to put his phone down, it rang. He answered with a tentative, "Hello?"

"Um, I just missed a call from this number and uh..."

The frickin' doc was one of those people who called back even when they didn't know who was calling them. "Is this Dr. Addison?" Lex asked, though he'd recognized the voice immediately.

"Yes, this is he. Who's this?"

"This is Officer Turner. You left a message for me to call."

"Oh yeah, I mean yes, I did. I um thought you would...I mean the cops, the police would want to know that Cassie's parents called me this morning," Gavin said, stumbling over the words. Lex wondered what had made him stutter like that. Maybe the parents had threatened him? He bristled at the thought.

"That may be helpful, but really you should call Detective McDaniels with any information since he's handling your case," Lex said, repeating what the front desk officer had told him.

"Yeah, I...um... Woo...uh...could we...um... I mean... Wouldyouwanttogetadrinksometime?"

"Huh?" Lex couldn't believe his ears; they must be playing tricks on him. The doc surely hadn't just asked him out?

There was a nervous chuckle on the other end of the line and then a few deep breaths. "Would you want to go out and get a beer with me sometime?" Gavin asked slower this time.

"Um...I guess..." Stuttering was contagious, and it didn't help that Lex's mind was running wild. He had to get a grip and play it cool. Gavin wanted to go out for a beer. That was all. He took a deep, cleansing breath. "Sure, we could do that. When's good for you?" Lex was proud of how normal he sounded.

There was an audible sigh from the doc's end. "Um, any night, really. I'd, ah, prefer sooner, rather than later though."

"Tonight?" Lex asked and then quickly added, "I'm off tonight, and then I have three midnight to noon shifts, so I wouldn't have another free night until Sunday." There was what seemed to Lex an extremely long pause, and the dead air made him nervous. Maybe he'd been too eager? "Doc, you still there?"

"Yeah, I'm still here," Gavin said. He didn't say any more than that though, which left Lex pondering what the doc was thinking.

"It's fine if tonight doesn't work. I didn't mean—"

"No, no, tonight's fine, I was just...um...Stucky's? I mean do you want to meet at Stucky's?" Gavin interrupted to ask.

"Depends on what you have in mind," Lex said.

"Wh-what do you mean?"

"I mean, if you want to talk, somewhere without the loud music would be better," Lex said. "There's a little pub on Washington. I've been there before. It's quieter and not quite as busy."

"Yeah, okay, that sounds fine. Do you have an address? I don't think I know which bar you're talking about," Gavin asked. He didn't sound excited by Lex's choice of venue. Lex wondered if he'd made the wrong choice by suggesting it.

"I could pick you up," Lex offered.

"I don't think so. I'd rather drive myself if that's okay."

"Yeah, no problem. So it's Carlson's Pub, next to the appliance store. You can't miss it. Is seven okay? I'm not sure how late I'll be able to stay awake. I haven't been to bed yet," Lex said.

"Oh crap, really? I'm sorry if tonight's not going to be good. We could wait."

"No, it's fine. So, seven?" Lex asked again.

"Yeah, seven. I have to go. Patients to see, you know?"

"Yeah okay, see ya tonight then," Lex said. He couldn't keep the smile out of his voice because he had a date with the doc.

"Okay, bye."

Lex fell back on his bed. Who'd have thought after what had happened that night with Rachel that the doc would be the one to call him and ask him out? He tried to contain his excitement by reminding himself Gavin was still the same straight man who had refused his kiss. God, he was stupid; Gavin probably just wanted to be friends, or maybe Lex had gotten it completely wrong, and the doc actually wanted to talk about his case. But why out of all the cops, would he pick Lex for that?

Lex let his thoughts drift with fantasies about Gavin. He couldn't wait to see the doc again and was glad that it was only a few hours wait.

SEVEN

GAVIN STARED AT the blank screen of his phone as he sagged against the wall. That was possibly the worst telephone conversation he'd ever had. What had made him think that it was a good idea to call Lex and pretend he needed to talk to him about his case? He was such a chickenshit, but that was going to change tonight at the bar. Gavin was going to lay it all out there, and if the officer decided he was crazy, so be it. Not like he could be more humiliated anyway. Ugh, why did he care so much what Lex thought of him?

Gavin finished with his patients and drove home. He needed to hurry if he was going to get a shower in, find something to wear, and get there on time. He calmed down a bit while he showered. He'd been wound tight since he'd called the station, and the tension had mounted the longer he'd waited for Lex's return call. The ensuing conversation was nerve-wracking to say the least, but with the warm water now sluicing over his body, he felt better about his decision to contact Lex.

Gavin styled his hair, making sure his curls weren't sticking out every which way, and then spritzed himself with his favorite scent. He put on a pair of faded, well-worn jeans, which hugged his butt just right, and a tight, long-sleeved, V-necked T-shirt he'd been told made his eyes really pop. He stopped and wondered why he was dressing like he was going on a date instead of like he was meeting a friend for beers. He excused his strange behavior by telling himself if he expected a man like Lex to consider what he was going to propose, he needed to show he was worthy.

He had a nice body. He'd seen the look in Lex's eyes, and though it had confused him at first, he now realized Lex had liked what he'd seen. It had taken Gavin some time to come to grips with the fact that for the first time in his life another man may have been attracted to him. If playing up his assets was what it took to get him a do over, then dammit, he was willing to pull out all the stops.

As he walked through the door of Carlson's Pub, he glanced around, approving of the dim, cozy interior, and the low and mellow music. A quick look at his watch told him he was ten minutes late, but when he looked up, he spotted Lex sitting in a corner booth near the back of the bar. Lex was picking at the label of a beer bottle with studied concentration.

Gavin walked over and coughed to get Lex's attention. Startled, Lex looked up, and Gavin had to admit the slow lazy smile that came over Lex's face only made him more handsome. Gavin hadn't ever seen the relaxed, at-ease side of Officer Turner he was getting a glimpse of at that moment, and that was saying a lot since he'd seen pretty much all of the man. Lex stood up, extending his hand to the one Gavin offered, enveloping it in his warm grasp.

"Hey, sorry I'm late. I feel bad knowing that you'd probably rather be in bed right now," Gavin said as he slid into the opposite side of the booth.

The smile didn't leave Lex's face. "It's okay, Doc. My sleep schedule is so screwed up that I'm used to doing without. Besides, I got plenty of time to catch up; don't have to report in until midnight tomorrow."

"Wow, you have a crazy schedule. Sounds like my days back in my residency. You couldn't pay me enough to do shift work again." Lex kept smiling as he raised his hand to get the server's attention.

"Yeah, it's rough, but someone's got to do it. You want a beer?"

"I have to order something to eat. I didn't have time to grab anything. I hope you don't mind. I'll have a beer too, though." He ordered an appetizer basket that could feed four and two more beers, planning to offer to share the food with Lex since he hadn't ordered anything. The server brought the beers over right away, and Gavin was glad he had something to focus on besides Lex's smile.

Lex took a swallow of his beer. "So did your ex's parents really call you this morning?"

Gavin's face heated before replying, "Uh, they did. They wanted to know if we could just work this out between us. They want me to drop the charges, said Cassie's having some problems and needs medical help, not jail time."

"So what did you tell them?"

"I told them I couldn't wait for her to kill me before she got help."

"You think she'd actually do something to you?" Lex asked. Gavin took note of how Lex's jaw clenched and his body tensed.

"No, I really don't think she'd do anything to me, and I truly can't figure out why she's been doing the things she has. Our marriage wasn't exactly perfect the last couple of years, but I thought we could work through the rough patch because we loved each other enough. Then she cheated on me." Gavin had no idea why he was spilling his guts to a stranger, but his words had Lex relaxing back against the booth, one arm slung casually across the back.

"I'd heard something about the cheating bit; makes it strange that she's the one who has it in for you. You should make sure you call McDaniels and let him know that the parents called you. Most likely they know where she is, and he can lean on them a bit until they tell him."

Gavin looked down at the table and fessed up. "I called him too. He said the same thing you just said." When he looked up at Lex, the man had a huge grin on his face.

"That's good. So did you get your house cleaned up?" Lex asked, changing the subject abruptly.

The server brought Gavin's food, and Lex ordered them each another beer. Gavin's stomach rumbled. "I did. I hired a service, but now I have to somehow convince my friends to help me paint the walls. Cleaning that shit up scratched the paint up something awful." Gavin answered before he started shoving food in his mouth. Lex watched him while he gobbled down wings, French fries, onion rings, and a cheese stick before he remembered his manners. "Eat some before I suck it all down," he offered while reaching for another wing.

He couldn't place the look on Lex's face, it was somewhere between amusement and the look his grandmother got when she fed him cookies. He picked up a fry and dipped it in Gavin's ranch dressing before eating it slowly. He never took his eyes off Gavin, which made him squirm under the attention.

Lex noticed and a mischievous smile pulled at his lips. "So you gonna tell me what we're really doing here?"

Gavin choked on the wing he'd been gnawing on. He put the bone down, took a drink of his beer, and wiped his hands. He was stalling. "Um, it's about the other night actually," he said without stuttering; thank god. The look on Lex's face became guarded. "It's nothing bad. I, uh, was just wondering if maybe... I mean, if you wouldn't mind if we could have ah, um, a do over?"

Beer came out of Lex's nose and splattered the table before he could put his hand up to catch it. He coughed and reached for a napkin. When Lex got himself cleaned up and back under control, he gave Gavin a long look. "So you want to call a mulligan?" he asked. The amused look was back on his face.

Gavin was blushing, but he couldn't stop. "Yeah, is that possible?" He had to chuckle at himself because he realized how ludicrous the idea sounded now that he'd put voice to it. "A sexual mulligan—it would probably be a first."

"Why?"

"Why what?" Gavin asked.

"Why do you want a do over?"

"Because...I don't know. I just don't like how I feel about myself after that whole mess," Gavin said with a shake of his head. "Never mind. It was a stupid idea, and it was just because my ego was bruised. I shouldn't drag you into my own neuroses."

"What? Why was your ego bruised?" Lex asked, his amusement finally fading to be replaced by a genuinely confused look.

"Oh, come on, that was probably the lamest threesome the two of you ever had. It was all because of me. I was pathetic, like some scared virgin. Don't tell me you didn't notice," Gavin said. Then he had a mortifying thought. "Is Rachel your girlfriend?" Did they sit around and talk about what a loser he was?

"No, she's just a friend. We have some of the same tastes, you know, in the bedroom. So if you were to get this do over, would you want it to be with her then?" Lex asked.

Gavin fidgeted. What did Lex mean? Did he know other people who did this sort of thing on a regular basis? Oh...oh...oh...oh was there a club? He wanted to ask but didn't want his ignorance to show once again. Then he thought about Lex's question. Maybe it would be better if it was with someone new, someone who hadn't witnessed his complete and utter failure already. But wasn't the reason he wanted a do over because he wanted to prove himself to them, both of them, not just the man sitting across from him? If Gavin was truthful, Rachel hadn't been the one he'd been thinking of lately, but he didn't know what that meant.

"Don't overthink it. It was just a question," Lex said, amused once again.

"I guess the whole point of the do over is to show you and Rachel that I'm not usually that bad in bed. God, that sounds really bad doesn't it? I don't know how to explain it." Gavin put his head on the table and then knocked it against the tabletop a couple of times. He only stopped when he felt a hand on the back of his neck.

"Hey, stop beating yourself up. I bet you're the kind of guy who always does everything he tries perfectly, huh?" He'd gotten up and rounded the table to sit next to Gavin as Gavin was beating his head. As he rubbed Gavin's neck, Gavin gave in to the pressure, letting Lex's massaging hand ease some of the tension from him. He nodded a yes to answer Lex's question. "So the thing the other night; it didn't go so well for you, right?" Gavin nodded again. Lex's fingers moved into his hair and started massaging the back of his scalp. "So it's only reasonable you'd want to try to get it right. If only to prove to yourself that you could, right? Because that's just a part of who you are? Just a big old overachiever?"

Gavin took a deep breath. He had to hand it to Lex; the man had his number. "Yeah," he sighed out. He didn't move because the fingers in his hair felt damn good. It'd been a long time since someone had touched him with such tenderness and care.

Lex's warm breath ghosted across his ear as he said, "Then you can have your mulligan."

Gavin turned his head so he could look at the man next to him. There was no malice in Lex's eyes, only understanding. Gavin knew then that Lex Turner was one of the good guys. He was the kind of guy Gavin would like to have as a friend, and maybe they could actually be friends.

"If it's too weird... I don't want you to do anything that would be weird for you," Gavin said.

Lex pulled his hand from Gavin's hair and sat up. "It wouldn't be weird. I've had plenty of practice. I don't think Rach is an option though. She was a bit pissy last time we talked."

"Oh, I suppose that's my fault, huh?" Gavin hated that he'd probably ruined a good thing for Lex.

"Nah, that's all on me."

"How so?" Gavin asked.

Lex blew out a breath. "Well, Doc, I guess it was because I made a mistake, but you're not ready to hear about that yet. Maybe someday I'll tell you," he said with a sad little smile.

"Okay. So then how does one go about finding a girl who will...you know?" He sat up to face Lex.

"Leave it to me. I know a few who might be interested. It may take me a while to set something up, but I think I can manage." Lex's smile brightened a little while he was thinking.

Gavin chewed over his own thoughts before asking his next question. He didn't want to offend Lex, but he wanted to know. "So are you bisexual then?"

Lex cocked his head and looked like he was considering his answer. "I am. Is that a problem?"

Gavin shook his head. He didn't think it would be. "Is that why you kissed me?" he asked because curiosity had won out over embarrassment.

Lex smiled and leaned in close. "No, I kissed you because I have poor impulse control," he whispered at Gavin as though it was a secret between the two of them.

Gavin laughed, a big loud belly laugh, and it felt really good. Lex was a character. He liked Lex now that he'd gotten to see something other than the standoffish cop and the awesome threesome-sex-god persona. Gavin decided they were going to be friends when Lex joined in his laughter, and Gavin felt better than he had in days.

"So, then we're going to do this?" Gavin asked.

"Yeah, I guess we are. Are your evenings usually free?"

"For the most part, yes. If I have something scheduled, it's usually enough in advance that I can plan around it. I suppose your schedule is totally fucked up."

"That it is, but the nice thing is we get it a year in advance, so I know what shift I'm working and what days I have off for the rest of the year," he said, his last few words almost unintelligible as he yawned.

"Oh crap, I should let you go home so you can get some sleep." Gavin had forgotten Lex had been up all night and all day too. The time had flown by, and if he was even a little tired on a full night's sleep, Lex must be ready to fall over.

"I should probably head home. It's been kind of a rough day." Lex pulled his wallet out of his back pocket. His thigh brushed Gavin's as he shifted and signaled to the server for the check.

"Hey, I'm going to pay. I asked you out," Gavin protested. He didn't have time to blush at the way his words made it sound like they'd been on a date because Lex was also a quick-witted comeback king on top of everything else.

"Don't worry. I don't expect you to put out tonight just because I'm picking up the tab. Maybe next time though." Lex winked and nudged Gavin where their legs were touching as he handed over his money. Gavin flushed at the innuendo, making Lex chuckle.

"Thanks for dinner then," Gavin said as they stood up. "And for not expecting me to jump into bed with you as a thank-you." He was trying to be as cool as Lex about the situation but thought maybe he came off as nervous.

Lex laughed at Gavin's joke. "If I remember correctly, that was exactly what you were asking for just a bit ago." Gavin's mouth hung open as Lex threw an arm around his shoulders and led him to the door. "Don't worry. You're not the first guy who's asked for seconds. Your reasons may be different and a bit odd, but I won't hold that against you, Doc. You're good people, so you get a pass."

They were standing in front of the bar, but Lex made no move to release Gavin. "I'm parked down the street that way," Gavin said, hoping Lex would get the hint and stop touching him, but of course, the man just turned them and started walking toward Gavin's car.

"So I'll see what I can come up with and give you a call. I'll be on days for my next rotation, but I've got some stuff going on at home. I'm not sure when I'll be free," Lex said.

Gavin wondered who Lex had at home. He hoped it wasn't a wife and a kid or something. But he really didn't think that was the case since Lex didn't exactly take measures to ensure he wasn't seen with another woman when they were at Stucky's. Gavin didn't ask, though, because he didn't want to pry.

"It's fine, whenever you have time. It's not like I'm in a hurry to embarrass myself again," Gavin said.

Lex dropped his arm. He gave Gavin a long, studying look. "I thought the whole idea of a mulligan was to do better on the second try. What's the point if you think you're going to walk away from the next experience feeling the same as you do now? Won't that be even worse? To know you failed twice?"

Gavin thought the look on Lex's face, his scrunched-up nose and furrowed brow, was kind of cute. Gavin started to panic, and his mind tried to formulate a response. He didn't want to tell Lex that he was the reason Gavin was nervous about the next time. What if the same thing happened? What if Gavin froze up and looked like a fool again? Why hadn't he thought this through better? What in the world made him think that trying this again would prove anything except that he was the inexperienced, uptight prude he'd shown himself to be the first time? Why did he think another man's confused expression was cute?

Lex's hands were on his shoulders, and those crystal-clear blue eyes were staring straight into his. Lex was so close Gavin could smell the beer on his breath. Thinking Lex was going to kiss him, Gavin's stomach gave a nervous flip.

"Calm down, Doc. I'm not trying to freak you out. You have your reasons for wanting to try this again, and I respect the fact that you're man enough to ask me to help you out." His voice was soft as his eyes searched Gavin's face.

Gavin made an effort to slow his breathing. He'd been working himself up into a pretty good fit as his mind went into overdrive, imagining how badly the next time could go. Lex was so solid and sure. Gavin was tempted to tell Lex he was afraid that he'd shy away from his touch again. That he'd make things awkward because the thought of letting another man really touch him scared the crap out of him for reasons he didn't even fully understand.

"You know you could always call it off. You don't need to prove anything to me or Rachel, for that matter. She couldn't care less. Me and you though, we're good no matter what you decide." Lex released Gavin's shoulders and stepped back.

"You're a really nice guy. You know that?" Gavin couldn't stop himself from saying what he was thinking.

Lex smirked and shook his head. "You got it all wrong, Doc. I'm not the nice one in this situation. I got my own reasons for helping you out," he said. He looked Gavin up and down and wiggled his eyebrows.

"Oh...ohhh...um...I'm...er..." Gavin didn't really know what to say to that, and it didn't help that Lex was laughing at him again.

Lex clapped him on the back. "Oh, Doc, you are something else. I don't think I've ever met someone quite like you before. This is gonna be so much fun," he said through his laughter. "But right now, I really gotta get going. If you weren't so amusing, I'd be sleeping on my feet."

"Okay, well, I'm glad I'm entertaining at least. You going to be okay to drive home?" Gavin would hate to be the reason something happened to Lex if he fell asleep at the wheel.

Lex stopped laughing at him. "Yeah, Doc, I'm good. I'll give you a call when I have something to tell you." He waited until Gavin walked to the driver's side of his car and opened the door. "You drive safely, Doc, and have a good night."

"You too, Lex, and thanks again." Gavin got in his car and watched Lex walk back toward the bar, before starting it up and pulling out. When he passed Lex, he waved and got one in return. And then he realized Lex's truck was parked on the street in the opposite direction from where his own car had been parked. The realization that he'd just been walked to his car, after letting a man pay for his meal, made him roll his eyes.

EIGHT

LEX HAD A completely shitty week. He'd floated through his shift the night after he'd been out with Gavin, but after that life had not been easy. Grady was riding his case about his "theory" when he was at work, while at home, his mother had taken to staying in bed for most of the day.

His mom looked pale and gaunt because she refused to eat more than a couple of bites of whatever Lex put in front of her. The day that marked sixteen years since his sister's passing had been the hardest of all. He dealt with his own grief in his way. He sat on his bed and remembered how much he'd loved his sister. He acknowledged how much he missed her and remembered some of the best times they'd had together. He shed a few tears and then went on with the task of helping his mother through her period of mourning.

Lex and his mom went to the cemetery to pull weeds and place flowers. He left her to have her talk with the headstone as that was the usual course of things. He wandered around looking at other gravestones until he heard the loud sobbing that signaled it was time to go. Returning to her side, he led her to the car so he could take her home where she spent the rest of the day in bed crying. Lex checked her periodically, usually when she was quiet for too long, just to make sure she was okay.

She had finally started to come around after a week of depression so deep Lex feared he'd need to take her to the hospital. He was happy to see she'd cooked him breakfast before he'd left for his shift that morning, and they'd even had a bit of conversation not revolving around the dead. It wasn't a great deal of progress, but Lex would take what he could get.

Lex had just come in off patrol and was enjoying that magical time of day while getting his paperwork done when a commotion in the lobby caught his attention. A few of his fellow officers rushed past to see what was going on, and Lex followed, stepping through the door in time to watch Cassandra Addison stomp one of her high-heeled shoes onto Merriweather's instep.

Merriweather pushed her away, while hopping around on one foot, so Grady, who'd beat Lex into the lobby, stepped forward and grabbed the woman's arm to steady her when she stumbled away after Merriweather's shove. She glowered at him, and Grady jerked his hand back.

"I want my lawyer. I'm suing for police brutality!" Cassandra screamed at the assembled crowd.

"Calm down, Mrs. Addison. There's no need to shout. You can call your lawyer as soon as you're done being processed. I'm sure you know the drill by now," Grady said, asserting himself once more.

"Don't you call me by that pervert's name. I'll sue for defamation too!" She glared at Grady.

"What the hell's she talking about?" Merriweather asked. He'd hobbled over to stand next to Lex by the wall so he could baby his foot.

"No idea. I think she's insane," Lex answered, his attention still riveted on the scene in front of him.

"What would you like us to call you then, ma'am?" Grady asked in that voice every police officer used when confronted with someone they thought was unbalanced.

"Ms. Stevens would be fine. I took my maiden name back when the divorce was finalized." Her tone and posture completely changed as she smoothed her jacket and stood ramrod straight.

"Multiple personality disorder," Merriweather whispered to Lex. Lex nodded, thinking it was as good an explanation as any.

"Okay, Ms. Stevens, let's get you all booked in, and then you can have your phone call. If you cooperate, things will go quickly, and you can make that call sooner." Grady was really pouring it on thick. She glared at him again but then nodded and let him lead her into the back. "Did anyone let McDaniels know that she's been brought in?" Grady asked as he passed the front desk.

"Yeah, I called it in on the way," Merriweather said.

"You just going to let him take over your collar?" Lex asked.

"Fuck, yes. I don't want to spend another minute with that crazy bitch," Merriweather grumbled as his partner came to help him hobble through the door to their desks. Lex followed them. "Gotta fill out all the damn paperwork anyway."

Lex sat at his own desk. He argued with himself over calling the doc and letting him know they'd finally brought his ex-wife in. Someone would eventually call him, but Lex wanted to be the one to give Gavin the good news. He'd been itching to call him anyway just to hear his voice. Lex went into the locker room, checking to make sure he was alone before pulling out his cell. He found the doc's number and pressed send, assuming he'd get voicemail since it was still before six.

"Hello?" Gavin answered after only two rings.

"Hey, Doc, it's Lex."

"Um yeah, I know. Caller ID. What's up?"

"This isn't an official call or anything, but I wanted to tell you that your ex-wife was brought in just now." Lex heard the deep breath the doc took through the phone and the shaky exhale that followed. "Doc, you okay?"

"Yeah, yeah, I'm fine. That's...that's good news, I guess, right?"

"That's great news, Doc," Lex assured him. "I'm sure McDaniels will call you as soon as they're done processing her. I just wanted to give you a heads-up."

"Thanks, Lex. I really appreciate it." Lex could hear a trace of a smile in the doc's voice, which made his own lips turn up in response.

"It's no problem. I've gotta go. It's the end of my shift, and I have paperwork to finish. I just wanted to be the one to tell you." Lex bit his tongue. He hadn't meant to say that.

"Oh, yeah, okay. Um...thanks again."

"I'll give you a call soon about the other thing, okay?"

"Yeah sure, whenever you have time. Talk to you soon. Bye," Gavin said and hung up before Lex could get his own good-bye in.

Lex got a high just from talking to the doc on the phone and decided to make a few phone calls after his shift to get something set up so he'd have a reason to do more than just talk to Gavin on the phone. He went back to his desk with a renewed sense of purpose. He was going to finish his paperwork so he could get the hell out of the station. He had things to do. Grady came back a few minutes before their shift ended.

"So how did that go?" Lex asked.

"Wow, that woman is totally delusional. I think they may be able to get her off on an insanity plea," Grady said.

"Really? What did she say?" Lex wanted to know if she'd said anything about Gavin.

"She said she had to let the community know what kind of pervert was living among them. Nobody would believe her when she told them, so she had to take more drastic measures," he said with a shake of his head.

The doc, a pervert? "What kind of pervert did she say he was?" Lex asked.

"She wouldn't say anything more because apparently her lawyer advised her against expounding on her views of her ex-husband in the company of law enforcement," Grady said with a snort. "You'd think he'd want her to make us think she's bat-shit crazy, makes her case that much easier."

"Yeah well, the doc doesn't strike me as the kind of guy who would do anything that would brand him a pervert," Lex stated his opinion and then asked, "So did you ask her if I was fucking her?"

Grady rolled his eyes. "Nah, I decided that even you're not hard up enough to put up with that kind of crazy."

"Gee, thanks, I think." Lex shuffled the papers on his desk. "I'm done with all our paperwork. Thanks for the help with that by the way."

"Sorry, couldn't pass up the opportunity to help my fellow officers," Grady said with a pointed look at Merriweather, who in turn, flipped him the bird.

"You're such an ass, Grady. Let's get out of here before you get into any more trouble," Lex said. He lingered in the locker room to avoid having to make off-time small talk with Grady. He got enough of the man while they were on the clock.

On his drive home, he started making plans for setting up the doc's mulligan. He could use something to help him relax after the last few weeks. It had been too long since he'd had a release that didn't involve his hand. The last time he'd been with anyone was the botched threesome with Rach and the doc. He may as well go join the monastery at this point. If he was going to be celibate, it should at least be for a reason.

Lex got an unexpected surprise when he entered his house to find his mom not only cooking supper but also singing along with the radio. "Hey, Ma, looking good," he said when he saw she was dressed up a little.

"Hi, Lex, how was work?" she asked with an actual smile.

"It was good; they finally caught that woman I was telling you about." Lex always shared some of the more interesting aspects of his job with his mom, and the doc's case was something he'd been regaling her with for a couple of months. It amused him when she tutted over the things she found outrageous.

"Oh, that's good. I prayed for that poor man. I hope he gets some closure now."

"Yeah, I hope so too. I'm gonna take a quick shower before we eat." Lex kissed her on the forehead as he passed, heading for his bedroom.

Lex stripped down and showered, but before he went back to eat, he pulled out his phone. He'd been trying to think of the right person to ask about the doc's do over. It had to be someone who wasn't as demanding as Rach yet still someone who knew what she wanted. He knew six women who were in the scene, including Rach. He went through his mental list and decided he'd try Becca first since she was pretty easygoing. He dialed her number.

"Hey there, sexy Lexy, been a while," she said as a greeting.

Lex smiled. He liked Becca. She was one of those free-spirited people. "Hey, Becs. Yeah, I know it's been a while. I've been really busy with work lately."

"Oh yeah, I forget what a hotbed of crime this little town is."

"Hey now, there's plenty of trouble you can get into in this little town, if you know where to look for it," Lex joked.

"And you know right where to look, dontcha, big boy?"

"Sure do, baby."

"So, not that I don't like to shoot the shit with you and all, but I'm sure there's a reason you called me out of the blue." She knew damn well why he was calling.

"Well, you see, I have sort of a little problem."

"Oh, honey, from what I remember there's nothing little about you at all," she purred.

Lex had to shift. He really needed to get laid if just talking to a potential sex partner was getting him hard. "It's good to know you're not disappointed in that department. But listen, I have this friend, and we had a playdate a few weeks ago, and it didn't go so well. He'd like to try again, and I know that you're pretty flexible, so I was wondering if maybe you'd wanna help a guy out?"

He heard her hum as if she was thinking about it. "So what's wrong with the guy? He a troll?" she finally asked.

"God, no. Have I ever picked up a bad-looking guy for us? He's one of the prettiest men I've ever seen, and he's got a great body; hung too," Lex said without even having to think about it.

She chuckled. "So then, what was the problem, babe?"

"Well, he's kinda green is all."

"How green?" she asked.

"It was his first time, so this will be the second try."

"Oh god, Lex, seriously? Okay, well before I agree, I want to hear the whole story."

So Lex told her the whole story. He even told her about it being his fault because he was crushing on Gavin. He wanted to be totally up front with her so there would be no misunderstanding this time. "So, what do you think, Becs? Would you want to do it?"

"Listen, Lex, I've always had a really good time on our playdates. Hell, you're one of my favorite playmates—"

"But?"

"I really don't want to lose that. If this goes wrong with your friend, it could change what we have, and that would suck," she said.

Lex couldn't fault her logic. He'd seen what it had done to him and Rach, but he really wanted this. "Please, Becs. I promise I'll go over everything with him, and it will be fine. No matter what happens, nothing will change between us." He begged. He wasn't proud of the fact that he did, but she was his best chance.

"Okay, but only because it's for you, Lex. When do you want to do this?"

Lex had to stifle the urge to tell her that he loved her and that he'd forever be in her debt; instead, he asked, "When's the soonest you could do it?"

"A little anxious, are we? I'm free tomorrow and after that Monday and Friday or maybe Saturday next week," she said, probably checking her calendar.

Lex did have to look at his calendar and what he saw didn't make him very happy. He hoped the doc would be free on Monday because he was on duty the next weekend. "Pencil us in on Monday. I gotta call Gavin to see if that will work for him. I'll let you know."

"Okay, I'll do that. It was good hearing from you again, Lex. Let's not wait so long next time, huh?"

"Sure, Becs. Talk to you later." There was a smile on his face as he hung up.

He needed to eat supper before he called Gavin, or his mom would start to wonder what was keeping him. They had a nice meal, and then his mother went out to visit a friend. Lex was happy that his mom was on the mend, so he wouldn't have to feel guilty about turning his attention elsewhere.

Checking the time before he called Gavin, he saw it was two hours after his workday ended, which should have given the doc enough time to have driven home and maybe to eat dinner too, so Lex wouldn't be interrupting if he called. He admitted he was anxious to tell Gavin he had something set up. The potentially awkward conversation that would come afterward, where Lex intended to clue the doc in on a few of the unspoken rules and some of Becca's preferences, was something he wasn't looking forward to.

LEX COULDN'T BELIEVE he was really going to do what he was about to do. He walked up the porch steps like a man going to his execution. His gut was telling him this was a super bad idea, but the doc had insisted that talking about their upcoming sexual tryst would be better done face-to-face. Lex had agreed to hop in his truck and drive to the doc's house to have a couple of beers and a little chat.

It was unseasonably warm for the end of May, and Gavin answered the door wearing the infamous cut-off jean shorts that had starred in so many of Lex's fantasies and a T-shirt tight enough to show off every line of his toned torso. Lex's mouth went dry, and his pants got a little too tight for his comfort. Standing on the doc's porch with his mouth agape and his erection tenting his pants was probably not the best segue into the evening.

"Hey, Lex, come on in." Greeting Lex with a dimpled smile that did nothing to dampen Lex's libido, Gavin stepped back to let him in. It was warm in the house, and Lex noticed that all the windows were open, but there wasn't much of a breeze blowing through. "Sorry, it's a little stuffy in here, but I refuse to turn on the AC. I miss the fresh air through the winter, so I take every opportunity I can to have the windows open in the spring," Gavin explained as he led Lex into his living room.

"I'm the same way, but my mom can't stand the heat, so our air has been on for a week already," Lex said. Lex mentally smacked himself for mentioning his mom lived with him when the doc smirked at him knowingly.

"Have a seat. I'll grab us a couple of beers." Gavin pointed to the TV and asked, "You mind if I leave the game on?"

Lex managed to tear his eyes off the doc and spare a glance at the TV. The Twins game was on, and they were ahead three runs to one. "Nah, it's fine as long as it doesn't distract you too much."

"Don't worry, baseball's not my favorite, but I keep up with it so I'll know what the hell Riley's bitching about in the morning," Gavin said when he returned with the beers. He handed one to Lex and sat on the couch, pulling one of his long, golden legs up and folding it under his butt before he looked at Lex expectantly.

"Riley?" Lex asked.

"Yeah, he's probably what you'd call my best friend. We went to med school together."

"Probably your best friend?"

Gavin looked at his beer as he answered. "Cassie thought terms like that were so junior high, so she hated it when I called him my best friend. She'd ask if I wanted her to buy us those necklaces, you know the ones with the heart in two pieces that say 'best friends forever.'" He looked embarrassed. Lex wondered if it was because of what his ex had said, or if it was because he'd been married to that woman.

"Ah, I see," Lex said. "She sounds so...delightful?"

Gavin chuckled, "She had her moments. So...you said there were a couple of things we should go over...to make this goes better this time."

Okay then, they were going to get right down to business. "Doc, can I ask you something first?"

"Sure, I guess," Gavin said.

Lex didn't know how the doc was going to respond to his question, but he had a suspicion that this one question was going to get to the heart of the reason the first threesome went the way it did. "Are you uncomfortable being touched by another guy?"

Gavin blushed a furious red in less than a second.

"Hey, Doc, it's not that big of a deal. A lot of guys aren't comfortable with it. We're told that it's wrong or that it's gay, and that gay is bad. It starts when we're just kids, and by the time we're old enough to know better, it's so ingrained that we can't change it. It's a lifetime of conditioning you're fighting, but if you really want to do this thing, you're going to have to get over some of that," Lex explained.

Gavin shifted on the couch so he was facing Lex. His eyes were big and the look on his face completely earnest when he said, "I want to, but I'm not sure if I can."

"Then why go through with this? I'm sure there're plenty of women out there who would love to go out with a guy like you. You could get a piece of ass anywhere. Why not just let it go?" Lex asked. He wanted to know what was going on in Gavin's head. Why was this so damn important to him?

Gavin looked agitated. He stood up and started pacing. He stopped right in front of Lex, and oh god, his ass and then his crotch, when he turned around to face Lex, were at eye level. Right there in Lex's face. Lex couldn't, he just really couldn't stop looking at it. It was right there, so close. If he leaned just a foot or so he could bury his face in those lovely shorts, and maybe he'd be able to...

"Lex?" Gavin's sharp tone startled him from his trance.

Lex stood up, putting him just inches from the doc, who hadn't moved from his position over Lex. He grabbed the doc's hips and pulled him in those last couple of inches. He ignored the wide-eyed, shocked look on Gavin's face as he went in for a kiss. At first, Lex thought he was going to wind up on his ass when the doc overcame his shock. He wasn't at all prepared for the soft lips beneath his to open or the needy little whimper that escaped from the man in his arms.

NINE

GAVIN'S MIND SHORT-circuited when Lex's hips came into contact with his. He could feel the other man's arousal pressing into him. By the time their lips met, he was sure there was already brain matter leaking from his ears. There was no explaining why he'd opened his mouth and let Lex explore it with his tongue. The soft lips and taste of beer on Lex's tongue made the kiss familiar, but the scratch of the stubble against his own reminded him that this was no ordinary kiss. The moan coming from his body was what broke him out of his stupor.

He pushed out of Lex's grasp. Gavin turned and ran to his bedroom before either of them could say or do anything else. He slammed the door and stood with his back pressed against it. His heart pounded, and his mind reeled. What the hell had just happened? He looked down at the front of his shorts, and hell, if he wasn't harder than he'd been in a long time. He slid down the door until he was sitting on the floor with his head in his hands.

"Doc," Lex said through the door as he knocked. Gavin didn't answer. "Doc, come on, let me in. I'm sorry. Please just open the door."

There was no way Gavin was opening the door. He could not face Lex, not after he'd acted like a sex-starved teenager getting a boner from just a kiss. Oh holy shit, Lex had kissed him again! Gavin was confused because he'd maybe, kind of, somewhat, enjoyed it. What the hell was going on?

"Doc, please, just talk to me," Lex pleaded, but to Gavin, he sounded put out. Maybe he was sick of Gavin's shit already. He'd freaked during sex; he'd almost had a panic attack at the thought of more sex, and now he was wigging out over a kiss. Lex would write him off as a lost cause soon, if he hadn't already.

"Could...would you..." Gavin just wanted to ask him to leave, but he didn't want to be mean about it.

"Would I what?"

"Leave? Please I...I just need..."

A heavy sigh came through the door. "Yeah, okay, I can go, whatever, no problem."

Now Gavin knew Lex was pissed. His tone was neutral, but the words spoke for themselves. It took a few seconds, but Gavin heard footsteps and then the front door opening and closing. He knocked his head back against the door. He needed to think, and maybe he needed some help.

He got off the floor and went to the phone in the kitchen. He dialed Riley. As he waited for his friend to answer, he stared at the two bottles of beer sitting on the coffee table. What the fuck was he going to do about Lex?

"Yo, bro, what's up?" Riley answered. "You watching the game? The freakin' twinkies just blew a two-run lead."

"Yeah, I have the game on," Gavin answered. He took a deep breath, steeling himself to ask Riley what he should do.

"Dude, I know that sigh. What the fuck happened now? I really hope it doesn't involve cleaning up more shit 'cause, dude, you already used up like half of your solids for the last time."

"No, no shit this time, at least not literally. Can I come over? I need some advice, and like it or not, you're the only person I trust to not freak out about it." At least, he hoped his best friend wouldn't freak about it.

"Sure, I need some more beer anyway; so stop and grab a twelve-pack, would ya?" Riley asked.

"Yeah, okay. I'll be there in a few."

"See ya." Riley hung up.

Gavin grabbed his keys, wallet, and cell. He didn't think to change clothes, and when the liquor store clerk gave him a funny look, he ignored the old man. Of course he couldn't ignore Riley's whistle when he met him at the door.

"Wow, Gav, looking mighty sexy tonight. You didn't have to get all dressed up for little old me." Riley playfully pinched Gavin's ass.

"Not really in the mood, Ri," Gavin grumbled as he pushed past. He put the beer in the fridge after pulling out two. He handed one to Riley and followed him into the living room.

"Oh, touchy tonight, huh? What's got your panties in a bunch?" Riley plopped down on the couch and waited for Gavin to settle next to him.

Gavin took a drink of his beer, trying to think of how to broach the subject. He decided his best course of action was to come completely clean. "You remember when I told you about that threesome I had a few weeks back?" Riley nodded. "Well, I lied."

"What do you mean you lied? You didn't have a threesome?"

"No, I did. I lied about not knowing the guy." Riley raised an eyebrow, prompting him to add, "Well, I sort of know him. He's a cop."

"Okay, so what's the big deal? It's not like he can arrest you for having bad sex, right?"

"No, it's nothing like that. I um...asked him if we could do it again." Gavin couldn't look at his friend. If it was embarrassing admitting to that, then how was he going to tell him what had happened earlier?

"What? No way. Why?"

Gavin couldn't explain his reasons and still sound rational, but he needed someone to talk to about it. He had to try. "I wanted to try again to see if I could get it right this time, but I think I've screwed up again. Lex is a really nice guy, but he kissed me again, and I freaked out about it, and he probably doesn't want anything to do with me anymore, and that means I won't be getting my do over because..." Riley's stunned face cut Gavin off. "What?"

"Did you say he kissed you *again*?" Riley asked. The look of total disbelief on his face made Gavin wonder if he was really so undesirable that Riley couldn't imagine a man wanting to kiss him more than once.

"Yeah, is that so far-fetched? I'm not that ugly." Riley laughed and Gavin's glare only made him laugh harder.

"Oh...oh Gav...oh my...god...oh oh...shit...oh, you're so fucking funny," Riley gasped through his laughter. Gavin punched him in the arm, and when that didn't stop the giggles, he decided to wait them out.

"So, you done now?" he asked as Riley calmed.

"Gav, Christ, sometimes I really wonder how you've made it this far in life. I wasn't surprised someone kissed you, you big dork. I'm wondering how exactly it happened: when, where, why?" Riley asked. "Why's he kissing you in the first place? Wait, is he gay? Does he know you're not gay?"

Stupid Riley and his questions, Gavin thought. "He's not gay. He's bi. He knows I'm not gay. He kissed me at my house about an hour ago, and I have no idea why. But we were talking about the next threesome, and he was telling me I need to try to get comfortable with another guy touching me," Gavin explained.

Riley didn't say anything, just looked thoughtful as he drank his beer. Gavin shifted around nervously, waiting for what he'd say. He wasn't expecting the question Riley asked.

"Do you want him to touch you?"

Well therein lies the rub—no pun intended, right? Did he tell Riley that for the last couple of weeks his dreams had been haunted by Lex's blue eyes? That his erotic dreams, which still mostly starred his ex-wife, had been invaded by hard muscles and a deep teasing voice? Gavin didn't know what he wanted, but the thought of Lex's arms around his shoulders made him shiver with anticipation. What would Riley think of him if he knew?

"If I say I'm not sure, but maybe, would that change anything between us?" Gavin couldn't look at his best friend while he waited for the answer. Thankfully, he didn't have to wait long.

Riley smacked him on his bare thigh. "Dude, you know you're my best friend. We've been through a lot of shit together, but if you start checking out my ass, we're so over. That's just fucking skeevy." Riley grinned at Gavin's look of horror. "I know I got it going on back there, but it is an exit-only type thing. You feel me?" Leave it to Riley to turn it into something about him.

"Don't worry, I'm not into hairy bubble butts, but if for some reason I go completely insane and get a hankering for one, I'll be sure to let you know so you can take preventative measures against any untoward advances I may make," Gavin assured him.

Riley's expression grew serious. "Really, Gav, I'm surprised you even had to ask. You know I don't give a shit about stuff like that. Besides, if I cut you off because you turned all fruity, you know that Sheila would totally kick my completely non-hairy ass." They both took a drink of their beers, and Riley watched the game for a second. "So you gonna be gay now?" he asked, still looking at the TV.

Gavin's phone picked that second to ring, saving him from having to answer Riley's question. He pulled it out of his pocket and stared at the screen. Shit, Lex. What the hell was he supposed to say to him? He stood up, gave Riley a look of warning, and went to the bathroom before he answered. He didn't need to give Riley anything else to bust his balls about.

"Hey," he answered.

"Doc, I'm so sorry—"

"It's not a problem, Lex, really. I overreacted. I just forgot you have poor impulse control, and you were probably just trying to help me get over the whole guy-touching-guy thing. I've had a little time to think about it, and I decided that it's fine. I'm fine. I still want to do the...that thing with you." He rushed it all out before he could get nervous, or Lex could call the whole thing off.

"Really, you still want to go through with it?" Lex asked. Gavin chuckled at being able to catch the unflappable Lex off guard.

"Yes, and I've decided I'm down for whatever. I will not freak out no matter what," Gavin assured him. Riley's exit-only comment flitted through Gavin's mind, and he amended his statement. "Um, except for any type of penetration of my...um...you know...back there."

Gavin let out the breath he was holding after stating his stipulation when Lex's bark of laughter came through the phone. "Doc, you are the weirdest man I've ever met."

"Yeah, I get that a lot. So Monday, eight o'clock, in front of the Starlight Motel. I'll be waiting," Gavin said.

"Okay, Doc, but I'm gonna email you some of the stuff I shoulda told you tonight, instead of shoving my tongue down your throat."

"And I promise to study up before then. Talk to you later then, yeah?"

"Yeah, Doc, later."

Riley almost fell on him when Gavin opened the door. "Asshole," Gavin said as he pushed him upright and went into the living room.

"So you're gonna do it then?" Riley asked.

Gavin grabbed his keys off the table and turned to face his friend. "Yeah, I am. Thanks for listening and for still being my friend. I'm going to go home now and freak out a little."

Riley surprised Gavin when he pulled him into a hug, a real hug, not just a man hug. "Don't freak too much, and if you need anything, you know I'm here," he said as he let Gavin go.

"Yeah, thanks. I'll give you a call this weekend, so maybe we can catch a game," Gavin said.

"Sure thing, dude."

GAVIN HAD READ the email, which he'd printed out, at least a hundred times. He'd had to look up a couple of the terms Lex had used, but if he told Lex that he'd looked stuff up, the man would probably laugh him off the planet. Although he had a vague idea of what some of the things were, he wanted to make sure he wasn't thrown for a loop. Apparently they were going to be doing what Lex referred to as "spit-roasting" the woman, Becca. Gavin thought there should be a more dignified word for the act, and when he apprehensively looked it up and read the description, he'd found it had nothing to do with pigs, thank god. After looking at some of the pictures on the Internet, he was pretty sure he could handle it.

Gavin was staring at the piece of paper when Lex knocked on the window of his car. It was time; no turning back now. He smiled at Lex and threw the paper on his passenger seat before getting out of his car. Standing behind Lex was a tall brunette, who was both pretty and shapely. Looking at the modest blouse and skirt she was wearing, Gavin would have never guessed she wanted to be on all fours with a dick in each end.

"Hey, Doc, this is Becca," Lex introduced him. "Becs, this is the doc."

"Hi, Becca. You can call me Gavin. Only the cops call me Doc." He was trying to be casual and not let his nerves show. It helped calm him when Becca smiled sweetly as she shook his hand.

"Nice to meet you, Gavin, Lex has told me all about you," she said. He hoped Lex hadn't told her about the last time, but what else did he know about Gavin that he could tell her?

Lex clapped him on the back. "Don't worry, Doc. I didn't tell her anything bad. Now let's go. I got the room already and put the supplies in there."

Becca put her arm through Gavin's and walked with him to the room. She didn't waste any time once they were inside, turning to Gavin and kissing him. Just as Gavin was getting into it, she stopped and started kissing Lex. For a moment, Gavin felt the same uneasiness he did the last time he was in this situation. He berated himself, but before he could start to freak, he decided to pull his shirt off and stepped in so he could kiss the back of Becca's neck. She moaned and reached back with one hand to pull him closer.

As he pressed against her, he found he liked the way her perfume and Lex's cologne mixed. He didn't startle at all when Lex's hands found his ass and pulled him even closer. The sweet sounds Becca was making and the way she writhed between them made Gavin's cock throb. Lex stopped groping his ass and pulled away to start shedding clothing. Gavin made use of Lex's absence to first palm Becca's tits and then unbutton her shirt.

She pulled out of his grasp. "Get naked, Gav, and let's get this party started," Becca said in a sultry voice. He didn't make her tell him twice. He took his pants off, and after a moment's hesitation, his boxers followed. Gavin stroked himself a couple of times as he watched Becca strip off her skirt. Lex ripped open the box of condoms and laid them on the bed.

Becca positioned herself, kneeling in the middle of the bed. She and Lex made eye contact, and as if there was some unspoken signal, Lex grabbed Gavin and planted one on him. Gavin's breath caught at the abruptness of it. It wasn't soft and gentle like the last time. It was a demanding, passionate kiss during which Gavin found himself fighting for dominance. Teeth were clashing, tongues were warring, and harsh breaths were coming from them both. Gavin's arms instinctively went around Lex's waist. The press of warm flesh against his own—only marginally weird because, though it was covering taunt muscles, it was still skin—had him grinding his hips, seeking friction for his straining cock.

Lex turned and pushed Gavin onto the bed, breaking the contact between their lips and bodies. Gavin stared as Lex climbed on the bed, and then Becca kissed Gavin, his lips, his neck, finally latching onto a nipple and sucking hard. He hissed and grabbed her head to press her closer, enjoying the flash of pain. The large, rough hands that could only belong to Lex were on Gavin's abdomen, and Gavin relaxed, letting Lex touch him until one of those large paws made its way down and cupped his balls.

Gavin tried to sit up, about to protest, but Becca's mouth covered his. He couldn't utter a word, when a warm, moist, what could only be...oh, god...tongue swept from the base of his cock to the crown. And then there was only the bliss of having his cock swallowed in one smooth movement. He moaned around Becca's tongue as it slid in and out of his mouth at the same time Lex started moving up and down on Gavin's length, with just the right amount of suction, complete with a swirling tongue across the slit every time he came up off Gavin's cock.

Becca released his mouth, but it was quickly filled again when she positioned her chest in front of his face, popping a nipple between his lips. This was something familiar—Gavin could deal with breasts. He worked one nipple with his mouth and the other with his right hand, as his left had found its way down to Lex's bobbing head, and he was surprised at how soft the short hair felt when he first ran his fingers through it before grabbing a handful to slow Lex down. He was going to come too quickly if Lex kept up that pace. Lex hummed, and Gavin bucked at the sensation as it flowed from his shaft to his balls. He pulled the hair clasped tightly in his hand so he could get Lex to pay attention to his command to stop.

"Oh, that's so hot," Becca said from above as she watched Lex give Gavin the best damn blow job he'd ever had. Becca pulled away from Gavin, leaving his mouth free to protest against Lex mauling his crotch—except the only thing that came out was a loud gasp when Lex grazed the crown of Gavin's cock with his teeth. Oh, god, he'd never thought that teeth and his cock together would ever be a good thing. Lex took him deep once more, and just when Gavin thought he was going to lose it, Lex tightened his grip on the base, effectively slowing his orgasm, before releasing him with an audible pop.

Gavin turned slightly to press his face into Becca's neck, reminding himself he and Lex weren't alone in the bed. He then found the soft mound between Becca's legs and slipped a finger into her slick tunnel, causing her to moan and push into his hand. Gavin concentrated on doing all the things he knew had made his ex go crazy while Lex positioned himself behind Becca, and whatever he did had Becca begging for what they'd all come to do.

As if they were all of one mind, they separated. Gavin and Lex rolled on condoms as Becca got into position. Gavin slid into the velvety smoothness of Becca's tight, slick tunnel as Lex fed his cock into her mouth. The sight of Becca there between them, wanting them to use her, turned Gavin on the way nothing else ever had. He had a slight twinge of conscience for thinking of Becca as just something to use to get off, but the way she moved, as if she couldn't get enough, quickly blew that thought out of his mind.

Gavin thrust a few times before they seemed to find a rhythm that worked for all of them. He then watched, mesmerized, as his cock pushed into the willing flesh and then reappeared again until his attention was snatched away by the sound of Lex's voice.

"Yeah, that's a good girl. Take it all, hmm. Oh yeah, just like that." Apparently Lex was a talker during sex, and Gavin found that instead of being distracting or off-putting, the deep tone of Lex's voice actually heightened his arousal.

Gavin looked up to meet Lex's intense gaze and took a second to ponder why Lex was looking at him when there was a naked female body to feast his eyes on. He answered his own question when his gaze took in the rippling muscles of the other man's abs as he thrust forward. Lex's skin was glistening with sweat, and Gavin felt the urge to take one tiny lick to see if it was as tasty as his brain was telling him it would be. How had he never noticed how sexy another guy could be?

Gavin leaned forward to get better leverage for his thrusts. Lex took it as an invitation, and Gavin found himself pulled into a kiss over Becca. He didn't fight it as Lex took his mouth in a sloppy open-mouthed kiss that was sexy beyond anything he'd ever experienced. It kicked the erotic factor up somewhere around ten notches, and before he knew it, his hips were jerking erratically, signaling the onslaught of his orgasm.

Lex let him go. "Come on, Doc, fuck her good; make her take that fat cock," he encouraged. Gavin was a little embarrassed to have Lex's sex talk directed at him, but he was too far gone to let it dampen the fire in the pit of his belly. His balls tightened, preparing to explode.

"Gonna come," Gavin groaned as he let loose his intense climax. Gavin lost control of all his senses during his release. When he was coherent enough to remember that he wasn't alone, his eyes settled on Lex, who was staring at him with a look Gavin couldn't quite put a name on but made his skin tingle. He looked away, pretending to be interested in making sure the condom stayed on as he pulled out.

Lex flipped Becca over as soon as Gavin moved out of the way, and Gavin watched as Becca once again took Lex's cock down her throat. Gavin got an eyeful of Lex's impressive equipment before he sunk back into her mouth. Lex buried his face between Becca's thighs, and all that was left was muffled moans and wet slurpy noises like a porn movie come to life. Gavin couldn't stop himself from wrapping his hand around his semi-hard cock and stroking it as he watched them.

Becca jerked and shuddered through her orgasm, and in true porn fashion, Lex got on his knees, stripped off the condom, and proceeded to come all over Becca's chest. When Lex saw what Gavin was up to, he pointed toward Becca. Gavin then got into position and added his own contribution to the little puddles on Becca's bouncy D-cups. Gavin wished he had a camera, sleazy as that sounded, because hot as it was to watch guys come on chick's tits in porn, it was way hotter to be the one doing it.

Unfortunately, then there was awkwardness as the three of them caught their breaths. Gavin wasn't sure what was supposed to come next, so he sat there waiting. Becca smiled up at Lex, and he smirked down at her.

Becca turned to look at Gavin. "Honey, you just earned your place in my bed if you ever want to do that again."

Gavin's chest puffed out. Yes, success! He'd proven to himself that he could do it, and even more importantly, Lex was there to witness his triumph. He'd forgotten for a second that Lex was still sitting on the bed with them, naked as the day he was born. Why did nudity have to be so weird when you weren't having sex?

Lex smiled and clapped him on the shoulder, but Gavin had a hard time meeting Lex's eyes. Every time Gavin looked at Lex, he remembered where his dick had been, and that gave him a fluttery feeling in his stomach. Getting the best blow job of his entire life from a guy who he was hoping he could be friends with was a little bizarre; no, he amended, it was really fucking insane. How was he supposed to not think of what that mouth could do? He wasn't sure if he'd be able to look at Lex the same ever again.

TEN

GRADY SHOT LEX a dirty look as the phone in his pocket vibrated against his keys, making an annoying jingling sound. It was the fourth time in the last hour it had rung, but Lex refused to answer it in front of his partner. They were forty-five minutes into their second hour of sitting off the county road just on the edge of town; so far their speed trap hadn't netted them a single speeder.

"Are you going to answer your damn phone? It's driving me nuts," Grady growled.

Lex ignored him and readjusted the AC vents for the millionth time. All of June had been hot and humid, and the first day of July wasn't proving to be any different. His phone finally stopped its dance in his pocket and beeped to let him know he had yet another voicemail from Gavin.

Grady snorted. "You musta caught yourself a clingy one this time."

"When do you find out if you get that spot in homicide?"

"Should be pretty soon. Why, you planning a party for me?"

"Yeah, sure, that's why I want to know." The sarcasm practically dripped from his words but Grady, ever the sharp one, missed it completely.

"Make sure it's chocolate cake. I don't like anything else," Grady said.

Lex nodded and sighed as his phone started in again—persistent little bugger. "I'm gonna step out and get this real quick."

Grady shrugged and played with the vents on his side of the car.

Lex popped his door open and stepped out into the molasses that was passing for air that day. It was so humid that it was hard to breathe, and sweat beaded on his forehead immediately. He pulled his phone out just as the call was sent to voice mail. Ignoring the messages, Lex hit the callback button.

"Hey, sorry, are you at work?" Gavin asked after he picked up on the first ring.

"Yeah, stuck sitting in a car with Grady, didn't want to talk in front of him. What's the emergency?" Lex was only half-kidding. Gavin's ex-wife's trial for vandalizing his house had been a one-day affair a week earlier. The former Mrs. Addison had gotten off with a suspended sentence and some mandatory counseling, so now Lex tensed every time the doc's number popped up on his caller ID.

"It's not an emergency per se, but I kind of need to ask soon otherwise plans may change," Gavin said.

"Ah...okay, so what's the question?"

Gavin laughed. "Yeah, guess I should ask you before I expect an answer. What are you doing on the fourth?"

"I have to work in the morning, but I get off at two when the parade's over. Otherwise, I don't have anything special planned." Nothing special enough to keep him from spending the day with his favorite doc, anyway.

"Sweet. Do you want to come to my place for a barbeque? You can bring your mom if you want. Riley and Sheila and a few people from work are going to be here. There's going to be food and beer, of course, and you can bring your own bottle if you want. The best part is we can see the fireworks from my deck, so we don't have to brave the crowds to get a good view of them," Gavin rambled.

Lex had noticed in the last month of getting to know Gavin that he tended to ramble when he was excited. He was like a cross between an adorable hyper puppy and an overexcitable five-year-old. Lex found it endearing and another reason he was starting to like Gavin more and more.

"So am I going to get to meet the infamous Riley at this little shindig?" Lex had heard a lot about Gavin's best friend. Riley knew about his and Gavin's playdates, six in all, if you counted the first with Rach, and Lex wondered what sort of reception he'd get when they met.

"Uh, yeah, I guess. Is that weird since he knows? I mean he's not going to say anything in front of your mom or anything," Gavin assured Lex.

"Nah, it's not weird, and I'd hope he'd have better sense than to talk about sex in front of my ma. So what time does the party start, and do you want us to bring anything other than our own bottle?" Lex leaned against the car but jerked away when the hot metal burnt his bare arm.

"You can come whenever. I told everyone else to come around four, but Ri and Sheila will probably be here before noon. I've got all the food covered, so just bring your mom, if she wants to come that is."

"I'll talk to her. I'm sure she'll be excited to meet you," Lex said. Grady knocked on the window and pointed at his watch. "Hey, Doc, I gotta go. I'll let you know for sure tonight after I talk to my mom."

"Okay, cool, talk to you later."

"Yeah, bye." Lex put his phone away and got back in the cruiser. Finally, time to go see if there was any crime happening somewhere else. Lex hated speed traps.

"MA, SERIOUSLY, GAVIN said he had the food covered. It's not a potluck; you don't have to take all of this." Lex tried once again to talk his mom out of the cooler full of food he was getting ready to lug to his truck.

His mom gave him the look. "If he's anything like you, with no woman there to help, the only thing that he'll have to eat is meat and bread. It doesn't hurt to take a few things with us. It's just a couple of salads and some fruit."

"Uh-huh, macaroni salad, potato salad, fruit salad, glorified rice, brownies, and a pan of whatever you call those bars. Ma, he's going to think that we don't think he can throw a barbeque by himself. What if he gets offended?"

"Is he the type of man who gets offended easily? If he's friends with you, I somehow doubt that," she said as she followed him to the truck. He hefted the heavy cooler into the back and got in the cab with her.

"No, I don't think he is, but still—"

"Don't worry I'll tell him it was all my idea. Now start the truck. I'm melting over here." Lex knew there'd be no more discussion on the subject.

There were already at least four cars parked in front of Gavin's house when they got there. Lex parked on the street, helped his mom down from the truck and grabbed the cooler from the back. Voices were coming from the fenced-in backyard, so Lex went to the gate instead of the front door.

"Knock, knock," he hollered.

A tall, lanky, dark-haired guy came to unlatch the hook for Lex. "Hey, look! This dude brought enough beer for everyone," the guy called over his shoulder to the crowd assembled on the deck. Lex tried not to look too embarrassed as he glanced around for the host.

"Hey, Lex." Gavin waved as he started toward them. "Riley, stop being a dick, and help him with the cooler."

Ah, so this was Riley; it figured. Riley grabbed one of the handles on the cooler while flipping Gavin off. Lex let him help carry it to the deck.

"So you must be Lex's mom." Lex heard Gavin say behind them. His mom would lay into him for not making proper introductions. "I'm Gavin. It's good to finally meet you, Mrs. Turner. Lex talks about you all the time. I'm glad you both could come today." *Ha, the doc is such a suck-up*, Lex thought as he dropped the cooler on the deck.

"It's nice to finally put a face to the name, Gavin. Thank you for inviting us. Please call me Jean." His mom and Gavin were walking arm in arm across the yard when Lex looked up.

"So what ya got in the cooler?" Riley asked from beside Lex.

"Ah, some salads and fruit," Lex said.

"Oh, you didn't have to bring anything. I told Lex that," Gavin said while he settled Lex's mom in a chair on the deck.

"Oh, salads! I hope there's potato salad in there. I told Gavin that he should have bought something other than burgers and hot dogs." A pretty woman with wild hair said as she joined them.

Gavin laughed and Jean looked smug from her spot next to the table. "Shush, Sheila. I was going to have Ri get some when he went for more ice. We'd already talked about it."

The woman held her hand out to Lex. "I'm Sheila. It's nice to finally meet you, Lex." They shook hands, and she pointed to Gavin's best friend. "And that is Riley, in case you didn't catch it. Come with me, and I'll introduce you to a couple of the others."

Sheila latched on to Lex's arm and dragged him across the deck. She stopped to hand him a beer from one of the coolers. Lex looked back at his mom, but he didn't have to worry about her. Riley had pulled up a chair, and they were already chatting and laughing. Gavin was fiddling with the grill, and Lex wondered if he should offer to help. He didn't get the chance because Sheila apparently intended to introduce him to everyone in attendance.

He ended up standing with three others in a group, discussing the current heat wave. There was Matt, an anesthesiologist, who seemed a bit shy, but Lex thought he was kind of cute in a nerdy way. Karen, a surgical nurse, who was almost old enough to be his mom but was kind of hot and flirty as hell. Then there was Tara, who as far as he could tell, did something at the hospital with medical records, but he wasn't exactly sure of her title. Tara was beautiful, and if the smoldering looks she kept aiming at Gavin were anything to go by, totally hot for his doc. Gavin, however, seemed oblivious to the attention.

Lex tried to keep his mind on the conversation he was supposed to be taking part in, but watching Gavin as he talked and laughed with his friends kept his attention fluttering back and forth. When he caught Riley staring at him, Lex noticed the long thoughtful look he got. He'd have to watch himself around Riley. Most people didn't quite catch on to the fact that he had more than feelings of friendship for Gavin, but it seemed that the doc's best friend was more perceptive than most, and that could be a problem for their budding friendship.

Lex excused himself from the group, claiming he needed another drink, so he could talk to Gavin, who was in the middle of a story about something that happened in surgery, when Lex stepped up beside him. He finished the tale and everyone laughed.

"Hey, Lex, did you meet everyone?" Gavin asked. Lex felt the desire in the pit of his stomach like always when Gavin aimed that dimpled smile at him.

"Yeah, Sheila introduced me. I was wondering if you needed help with the grilling."

Gavin looked at his watch, "Oh crap, we should probably start that, huh? You hungry?" he asked. The question had been directed at Lex, but the answers came from about five other people. Yes, everyone seemed to be hungry. Gavin chuckled nervously. "Sorry, I'm not a very good host. Good thing Lex and the rumbly in his tummy are here to remind me." Gavin reached out and rubbed Lex's stomach.

The gesture was overly familiar, done in public, and completely unexpected. Though they had gotten quite comfortable touching while they were in bed—actually to be totally honest, Lex was comfortable touching, and Gavin had gotten comfortable being touched—it never carried over into their friendship outside the bedroom. Once they stepped out of the privacy the closed door provided, they never touched or talked about what they'd done. They'd been hanging out, watching ball games, going out for drinks or dinner, even worked out a couple of times, but nothing happened that wouldn't happen with any other friend.

"Dude, did you just reference *Winnie the Pooh*?" Riley asked with quirked eyebrows.

"And what if I did?" Gavin shot back. Lex tuned the two of them out as they went back and forth about Gavin's literary preferences. He checked out the grill. It was newer but not one of those damn propane grills. Props to the doc. The coals were hot, just right for burgers and dogs.

"If you want to get the meat, I'll start grilling," Lex offered. Sheila popped up at his side holding a huge platter of brats and already-formed hamburger patties.

"Here, I figured I'd go get it. The conversation they're having could take a while," she said.

Lex had to laugh. "How long can a debate take over who wrote better books: Dr. Seuss or A. A. Milne?"

"Oh, you have no idea. Just pray that they don't start in on how the chick that wrote Harry Potter totally ripped off *The Lord of the Rings*. That discussion took at least four hours," she whispered.

"Sheila, dear, do you want to help me set out the other food?" Jean asked. She'd gotten up and was putting beer bottles into a trash can to clear room on the tables.

"You don't have to do that, Jean, I'll get it." Gavin stopped arguing when he saw what she was doing.

Tara flounced over and put her hand on the doc's arm. "Don't worry about it, Gav. I'll help," she said while smiling up at him and rubbing his arm.

"Thanks, Tara, you're a peach," Gavin said. Lex watched as Tara lowered her eyes and licked her lips while twirling a piece of hair. God, could she be more of a cliché? Lex unkindly thought of his competition for Gavin's attention.

Sheila had gone to help Jean set Tupperware containers out on the table. It didn't take long for Riley to take her spot at Lex's shoulder. "Make sure you don't burn those burgers," he said, drawing Lex's attention back to the grill. "So, I'm surprised this is the first time we've met."

Lex finished flipping the burgers before he answered. "Yeah, I can see that you guys are close. Probably just scheduling conflicts. I work some weird hours." He wasn't sure if Gavin had been deliberately keeping them apart, but if he had been, why get them together now?

Riley made a noncommittal sound. Tara's laugh drew their attention. She was doing more flirting than helping, it seemed. Lex tried to control his jealousy, telling himself Gavin had every right to flirt with whomever he wanted even if it was a shameless hussy.

"So does he know?" Riley asked.

It caught Lex off guard, and he almost said no, but instead he asked, "Does who know what?"

"Come on, man, you know what I'm talking about," Riley said. He looked around to make sure no one was eavesdropping before asking, "Does Gav know that it's more than just sex to you?"

"I don't know what you're talking about," Lex said. Gavin had told Riley about their playdates, but Lex didn't know how much he'd told Riley. Like, did Riley know Lex took every opportunity presented to him to suck Gavin's cock? He wasn't going to accidentally tell Riley anything that could cause a problem for the doc.

"Yeah, right, I'll believe that when pigs fly outta my ass, bro. I see how you look at him. He may not get it because he really just doesn't get shit like normal people do, but that's why he has me."

"Okay, so what if I am looking at him how you think? What business of it is yours?"

"Anything that concerns Gavin is my business. He's not just my best friend; he's family. Me and him have history together. He's different and sometimes he gets himself into situations that may not be in his best interests. I already screwed up once with Cassie, so I need to know what exactly your plans are when it comes to him," Riley said.

Lex thought about the question as he moved meat from the grill to a platter. What had he been planning? As enjoyable as it was to have Gavin in bed with him, it was just sex; that's all there was to it and probably all there would ever be. He'd been pinning some kind of hope on the doc— what exactly he didn't know—maybe switching teams for him? The thought would be laughable if it wasn't so painful. Lex looked over at Gavin, who noticed Lex looking at him and smiled. It would hurt, but maybe Lex needed to put an end to his fantasies. Gavin had been a good friend to him, and he deserved one in return, not someone who held unreasonable expectations of where their relationship could go.

"I don't have any plans. We're friends; that's all," Lex said.

Riley gave him a long look before taking the platter from him. "Just don't hurt him. He's gotten attached to you really fast, and if you drop him, he'll be heartbroken. If you have to let him down, do it gently, okay?" Lex nodded and followed Riley to the table.

"Thanks for grilling, Lex," Gavin said. "I kind of suck at it, so I was trying to talk Riley into it, but he said he was a guest and guests shouldn't have to cook their own supper."

"Yeah, so he just let you do it instead," Riley said.

"He volunteered," Gavin protested.

"Boys, it's fine. Lex likes to grill," Jean said. "He's good with manly things." She held out plates to Gavin and Riley as they snickered at Lex. Lex shrugged it off. She could have said much worse, and she did look proud of him.

Everyone filled their plates and found seats around the deck. Gavin and Riley bickered pretty much nonstop until Gavin pulled a chair up next to Lex and sat down. "Jean, your potato salad is so much better than the stuff you buy at the store. I can't thank you enough for bringing all of this. Sheila was right. It's not really a proper barbeque with just burgers, dogs, and chips," he said.

"Oh honey, it was no problem. I was just happy you invited me, especially since Lex said we can watch the show from here," she said.

"It's my—" Gavin started but was interrupted by Tara sitting down on the arm of his chair and almost knocking his plate off his lap.

"Whoopsie, sorry about that," she said with a giggle. She put her arm around Gavin's shoulders. "This is so good, Gav. I don't think I've ever had burgers done the way I like them on the grill." She let him go to take another bite to show how much she liked the burger.

"Oh yeah, well, Lex was grilling, so really it's him you should thank," Gavin said. Lex didn't think it was his imagination that the doc seemed to be uncomfortable around the too-flirtatious woman.

"Thanks, Lex," Tara said without taking her eyes off her prize.

"No problem," Lex said. He had the sudden urge to leave. If he'd been there alone, he would have acted on it, but watching his mom have a good time kept him in his seat. Instead, he busied himself with his food and ignored what was happening not even a foot from him. It wasn't easy when Gavin kept trying to draw him into the conversation. He got up and wandered over to where Karen was standing off the deck, smoking.

"Hey there, get enough of the bimbo show?" Karen asked and offered him a smoke.

Lex declined. "Um..." He wasn't sure if he should disparage Gavin's friends and coworkers to one another.

"Don't worry. Tara will get her pound of flesh and move on. She has a thing for the doctors, hasn't figured out that they're just people like everyone else. You won't have to worry about putting up with your friend's annoying girlfriend because she's not looking for anything permanent yet," Karen said.

"Oh, well, it's not up to me to tell anyone who they should date anyway. How about you? You got a thing for doctors too, or do you prefer something a little more blue collar, like say...a police officer?" Lex asked. He may as well have some fun and flirt a bit.

Karen laughed. "If you were just a little older, and I was just a little younger, I'd be all over you." She looked him up and down before adding, "I bet that you know how to use your nightstick."

"Yeah, that and my handcuffs. Sure you don't have any cop fantasies?" he asked. Karen threw her cigarette in a can and put her arm through his.

"I think you and me are gonna have to grab a couple of beers and get to know each other a little better," she said. She wasn't really interested in him, but hell, they could hang out and have a good time.

A little bit of flirting and Lex was back to feeling okay. He had to keep reminding himself that Gavin was just his friend. Lex should be happy for him; maybe the doc would get a chance to get a little on his own. Couldn't begrudge the guy a good time when it was throwing itself in his lap, right?

ELEVEN

GAVIN WASN'T HAVING the best time. Tara, who was drunk and still drinking, was clinging to his side. The attention she was lavishing on him was making him uncomfortable. He'd been having fun when he was talking to Riley and Sheila and, well, just about anyone but Tara. Every time he tried to make conversation with anyone but her, Tara interrupted and made it obvious as to what she was doing.

Gavin looked around for Lex and found him sitting in the corner with Karen, Jean, and Sheila. Lex looked like he was having more fun than Gavin was. Karen was sitting on the built-in bench next to Lex, who had his arm on the deck railing behind her. They were laughing at something Sheila was telling them. Gavin longed to go over and join their group, but Tara was insistent on monopolizing his time.

"Gav, you should show me around your house," Tara said. She was trying to tug him toward the patio door, but he was staying on the deck.

"No, not right now. I need to be out here with my guests," Gavin explained.

Riley had caught the last part of their exchange and obviously misread Gavin's excuse as a real reason for him not to take Tara into his house. "It's no prob, man. Go show the chickie around. I'll make sure everyone has a drink, and no one will even notice you're gone." Gavin gave Riley a dirty look as Tara bounced at his side. "Just make sure you're back in time for the fireworks." He winked at Gavin as he turned to grab more beer from the cooler.

Gavin threw a glance in Lex's direction as he let Tara pull him along. Their eyes met, and he thought Lex looked annoyed. It didn't stop him from throwing Lex a please-save-me look before Tara managed to get the door open. Tara pushed him through the door, and they were alone in the cool semidarkness of his house.

"I wanna see your bedroom, Gavvy," Tara said with a slight slur.

Gavin shuddered; did she really just call him Gavvy? He decided to get the tour over with, and then maybe he could pawn her off on someone else for the rest of the night. He led her through the kitchen and living room. "Here's the hallway and there's the bathroom and spare bedroom," he said as they walked. He pushed his bedroom door open. "Here's the other bedroom and that's it, unless you want to see the laundry room in the basement, but I wouldn't recommend it."

Tara crowded him up against the wall, pressing her body to his. He could smell the combination of food and beer on her breath, and it wasn't at all inviting. She reached up to put her arms around his neck and pulled him closer to bring their mouths together. Gavin let her kiss him, but he wasn't an active participant.

"God, Dr. Addison, you have no idea how long I've wanted to do that," she said when she stopped. She was grinding against him, and the thought that he should be at least a little turned on made him wonder why he wasn't. Tara was beautiful and had a great body, but he just wasn't into her—there was no spark. She felt his lack of arousal, and the look on her face could only be described as confusion, until a slow smile took over her face, and she dropped to her knees.

She pulled his shorts down with a yank, and before he could protest, she had his flaccid cock in her mouth. Gavin let out a slow breath, because apparently it didn't matter that he wasn't into her, his body had a mind of its own. She sucked on him sloppily, but still the warm and the wet did their job, and his mind went back to the last blow job he'd had. Lex was the best, going down on Gavin every time they'd played together, so he closed his eyes and went with it, imagining it was Lex kneeling before him instead of a drunken woman.

"Hey, do you have condoms?" Tara asked after several minutes of sucking.

Gavin had to shake his head to get the image he'd been using out of his mind so he could think. "Um...yeah...in the...over there," he said and pointed to the nightstand.

Tara got up and dug through the drawer, holding up a foil package like it was a trophy she'd found.

At the sight of the condom, Gavin finally grasped what he was about to let happen, but he realized he didn't want any part of it. Tara beckoned him to the bed with a motion of her finger, and when he didn't move, she approached him.

"Don't be shy now, Gav. I've seen how you look at me. I know you want it."

Once again, Gavin found himself pressed to the wall by Tara's much smaller body, only this time he was confused. How had he looked at her? He'd barely noticed Tara until she'd made a nuisance of herself. He'd only invited her because Matt had asked him if he would. He pushed her away. "No, I don't want this."

Tara's smirk as she looked down at his flagging erection made Gavin cringe inwardly. She crowded him again, her fingers lightly running the length of his cock. "You're a man, and what kind of man would turn down an offer for sex?"

Tara's words smacked of something Cassie used to say and suddenly Gavin felt sick to his stomach. He pushed her away once again, a little more forcefully. "Please go back outside. I need a moment alone; I'm not feeling well." Gavin bent down and pulled his shorts back up.

"Playing hard to get is supposed to be the woman's job, but I guess if you want to play it that way, I'm game." Tara flicked the condom at Gavin so that it bounced off his forehead before landing at his feet. "See you out there." Tara turned and walked away, leaving Gavin standing there feeling dazed.

Gavin was shaking when he went out to the kitchen to get a glass of water. He felt nauseous over the whole situation. He actually felt like crying, which was just stupid. As he stood at the sink trying to collect himself, he wished Lex would come in so he had someone to talk to about what had just happened and how it had made him feel. Better yet, he wished he could just go and crawl into his bed and forget it, but he had people in his backyard who would probably be offended if he just disappeared. He bent down, splashed some water on his face, and straightened his back, holding his head up as he walked back out into the approaching night.

Riley slung his arm around Gavin's shoulders the minute he stepped out on the deck. "Gav, you sly dog, did you hit that?" Riley asked inclining his head in Tara's direction.

Gavin shook his head as he looked for Lex. Their eyes met briefly before Lex turned his attention back to the group around him. A shudder ran through his body at what he took as Lex's obvious rejection. He wasn't even sure what he'd expected. He didn't know what made him seek out the other man for comfort, something Riley and, to some extent, Sheila had always done.

Riley finally picked up on Gavin's anxiety. He led Gavin to the unoccupied corner of the deck, Sheila following close on their heels. "Okay, buddy, tell me what's going on," Riley said. Gavin recognized the professional bedside voice Riley was using.

He looked from one worried face to the other. "I'm not sure." It was an honest answer. He wasn't sure what was going through his mind. He wanted Lex for some reason he couldn't explain. He wished he and Lex were in a booth at Carlson's Pub just relaxing and shooting the breeze because everything was so easy when it was just him and Lex.

"Gav, baby, you're scaring us. Tell us what happened to freak you out," Sheila said. Gavin had no idea he had his freaked-out face on. He made an effort to relax the muscles of his face and tried a small smile. Sheila recoiled at the new expression, so Gavin figured he must have gotten something wrong.

"Dude, stop it," Riley said, "You're just making it worse, and I'm not made of stone, so I'm gonna laugh if you keep up the facial contortions."

"Sorry, could you go get Lex for me?" he asked. Maybe if he could just talk to Lex alone for a minute, he could get his bearings back. His friends exchanged a glance before Sheila shrugged and left to get Lex.

"What's going on, Gav? Did that woman touch your no-no place without permission?" Riley asked, trying to joke Gavin out of his little freak-out. Gavin made a face again while trying to laugh it off for Riley. "Shit, Gav." Riley was looking kind of freaked-out himself. Gavin wondered what he was thinking.

"Eh, what's up, doc?" Lex asked over Riley's shoulder. Just the sight of Lex's face soothed Gavin more than either of his friends had managed.

Riley stepped back to let Lex take up his position in front of Gavin. Gavin had to hold back the urge to hug Lex. He decided it would be weird if he did. He looked at Riley instead. "Could I just talk to Lex alone for a minute?" Lex was studying Gavin as Riley nodded and left them to join Sheila. Their eyes remained on him, waiting to jump in if they felt he needed them.

"What do you need?" Lex asked.

He was staring at Lex, needing just to focus on his face for a minute before he could speak. When he did, he didn't like what came out of his mouth any more than it seemed that Lex did. "Tara just sucked my dick."

"Um...congrats?" Lex looked confused at Gavin's blurted confession.

"No," Gavin said. He didn't want Lex to think he'd enjoyed it. It was important for Lex to know it hadn't been his idea, and it had been awful, even if Gavin couldn't bring himself to say it.

"No what, doc? What's going on?" Lex asked.

"I don't know, but I just need..." Gavin didn't know what he needed and wasn't that just the shits? Lex put his hands on Gavin's shoulders and looked up into his eyes. Gavin's stomach fluttered. Was this where Lex kissed him, and then everyone would know what they did? What he had done?

"I don't know what's wrong or what you need, but if you need something from me you can ask me for it. You know that, right?" Lex asked.

No kiss then. Gavin could feel himself relaxing. He nodded. "Could you just kind of stick close until people leave, please?"

"Yeah sure, come sit with us. You can sit between me and my ma; we'll protect you," Lex said with a smirk. Gavin let Lex lead him over to where he'd been sitting earlier. Tara tagged along but Lex kept his body between them, shielding Gavin from her unwanted advances.

"Hey, there's the host," Matt said. "You look a little pale. You feeling all right?"

"He's fine, just ate too much. He needs to sit down and let his food settle," Lex explained so Gavin didn't have to. Lex sat back down next to Karen on the bench and pulled Gavin down next to him. He put his arm on the railing behind Gavin. It was a casual gesture, but Gavin was comforted by the fact that Lex seemed to be sheltering him. Like he knew what Gavin needed and was willing to provide it.

"Oh, you poor baby," Jean said. She reached forward and patted Gavin's knee. Gavin smiled at her. He looked around and realized that everyone was sitting in the same group, no longer split into smaller ones. Tara was eyeing him from the other side of the deck. She was still drinking.

"It's okay. I'm feeling better now," he said and looked at Lex. He did feel better. He stifled the urge to lean into Lex's solid body. Sitting this close, he could smell Lex. It was comforting because Lex's scent was as familiar as his own.

Everyone was chatting around him. Riley and Sheila were giving him looks, but Gavin couldn't be bothered to try to puzzle out their meaning. The drinks flowed freely as people snacked on the leftover food. Gavin watched Lex deflect any attention Tara tried to give to him, easily and effectively shutting her down on Gavin's behalf. He was relieved when darkness finally descended for real. They shut off the outside lights and settled in to watch the municipal fireworks show.

"Wow, holy crap, it's like they're lighting them off just for us," Lex said in awe as the first one went off almost directly overhead.

"It's one of the benefits of living next to the park. I used to spend every fourth here with my uncle when I was a kid, and this was the best part," Gavin said.

"Agent would have a conniption if we lived here; the noise would scare the crap out of him," Lex said.

"He'd probably have a heart attack at his age," Jean added.

"Oh, that would be so sad," Tara said, trying once again to butt into the conversation.

Gavin tensed next to Lex. "Yeah, it would be," Lex said, brushing Gavin's neck with the hand that had been resting behind him on the railing. When Gavin didn't show any sign of acknowledging the touch, it turned into more of a caressing massage, helping to drain away the tension. Gavin sent up a silent thank-you to the darkness for giving Lex the cover he needed to touch him unnoticed.

The fireworks lasted a little under an hour, and the finale was big and loud and bright just like it should be. The light was turned back on, so people started saying their good-byes. Gavin was relieved when Matt, who was the designated driver of one of the cars, led Tara away after saying a quick goodnight. When it was down to just Riley, Sheila, Lex, and Jean, Gavin let out a sigh. They all turned to look at him. His three friends exchanged knowing looks but kept their mouths shut.

"Well, I don't know about all of you, but when I was younger, girls didn't act like strumpets at nice get-togethers. If we'd been at my house, I'd have asked her to leave about four hours ago," Jean said to no one in particular. She turned to address Gavin, "And you, young man, are certainly a gentleman to put up with that in your own home."

Gavin blanched at hearing her say that because he'd definitely not been a gentleman when it had come to Tara. He opened his mouth to say so when Sheila jumped in and saved him from making an ass of himself.

"Yeah, she was one pushy drunk broad. Good thing Gav's got better taste than that," Sheila said. Gavin swore she winked at Lex as she did.

"I keep telling you, Ma, it's not like the old days anymore. Women can act anyway they want nowadays."

Jean stopped putting the cover on one of the Tupperware containers she'd brought and looked at Lex. "Well, if you ask me, it was better when ladies acted like ladies and left the carousing to the men," she said primly. "Just look at Sheila here—she acts like a proper young woman should."

Riley tried to suppress his laugh, which resulted in a half hiccup, half snort, making Gavin giggle. He knew how ladylike Sheila could be at times. In response, Sheila smacked Riley and then went for Gavin, but Lex put his body at risk to protect him. She stopped just short of hitting Lex on the arm and looked surprised to see him there instead of her intended target.

"Violence never solved anything," Lex said. "I could arrest you for assault and domestic violence."

Sheila burst out laughing and hugged Lex. Gavin felt a little flare of jealousy that she could do what he'd wanted to do all night. "Oh, you're gonna fit right in," she said as she pulled back and patted him on the cheek. "Just be careful. Better men than you have tried to get in between those two"—she pointed at Gavin and Riley—"and it usually ended in bloodshed."

"I'll take my chances," Lex said. Gavin watched as Lex and Riley held a stare down.

"Okay, well then, we should get these leftovers into the fridge and head home. Lex?" Jean had finished packing up the last of the food. Lex snapped to at the sound of his mother saying his name. Riley smirked at his win, but Gavin was willing to call it a tie since Lex couldn't really ignore his mom.

Sheila helped carry things into the house. When Gavin realized Jean planned on leaving her leftovers in his fridge, he had to say something. "Jean, you should really take all that with you. I appreciate that you brought it, but I wouldn't feel right if you left all of that."

"Oh pish posh, sweetie, there's not much left, and if I take it home, Lex will eat it all and get fat. You know, he was a chubby child. He would just eat and eat..."

"Ma!" Lex exclaimed, looking a bit mortified by his mother's oversharing.

"Oh, Lex, you look fine now. You shouldn't be ashamed of something that you overcame," she said. It was then Gavin realized Lex probably got his pragmatism from his mom. "Anyway, you need some fattening up. You can return the containers when they're empty. Think of it as a thank-you for inviting us. I had a really good time."

"Don't fight it, Doc, just smile and say thanks," Lex advised.

"Thank you, Jean, and it was a pleasure having you here," Gavin said. He gave her a hug. She was surprisingly strong for an older woman, and she hugged him nice and tight. It made him miss his own mom, so he reminded himself to give her a call soon.

"Can I dump this ice water out somewhere, Doc?" Lex asked. He was looking into his cooler that now only contained ice and water since they were leaving everything else in Gavin's fridge.

"Yeah, just dump it over that side of the deck," Gavin said. He went over to see if Lex needed any help. He didn't, but it gave Gavin a chance to stand in the shadows where the light didn't quite reach Lex. "Thanks for earlier," he said quietly.

Lex dumped the water and turned to look Gavin in the eye. "It wasn't a problem, Doc, but maybe you can tell me what exactly happened sometime when we don't have an audience."

"If you didn't have your mom here, I'd ask if you wanted to stay and have a couple of beers, just the two of us." As soon as Gavin said the words, he knew that was what he really wanted.

Lex bit his lip and seemed to decide something. "I could take her home and come back."

"Are you okay to drive? I guess I should have asked earlier," Gavin said.

"Yeah, I only had a couple, and that was over two hours ago," he said. Gavin hadn't even realized Lex had quit drinking beer at some point in the evening. "I knew I had to drive and I..." he trailed off as if deciding he shouldn't say what he'd been about to say.

"And you what?"

"I wanted to make sure I was sober if you needed me," Lex admitted.

Gavin's heart beat irregularly for a minute. It took him a few more seconds after that to be able to speak. "Thanks. You're really a good friend, Lex."

Lex smiled but there was that weird look in his eyes again. "You're welcome, Doc."

"So your mom won't wonder if you just drop her off and leave again?" Gavin hoped he didn't sound as needy as he felt.

"No, I'm a big boy. I can do what I want without asking permission."

"Okay." Gavin walked with everyone to the gate and watched as Lex and his mom drove away.

"I like him," Sheila said. She gave Gavin a hug. "Are you going to be okay?"

"I'll be fine, and I like him too," Gavin said. He looked to Riley for his opinion. He hoped even though he and Lex had a little pissing contest at the end of the night that his best friend liked Lex; it seemed important.

"He's okay," Riley said.

"Just okay?" Gavin asked.

"Fine, he's cool. I like him." Riley gave in to Gavin's hurt tone.

"You'll always be my best friend; you know that," Gavin said as he hugged Riley.

"Yeah, yeah, hearts and flowers and BFF's forever and all that crap. Now let me go so I can go home with my woman."

"Thanks for coming, guys," Gavin said as they got in the car and waved good-bye.

He really had good friends.

His thoughts then turned to Lex coming back to him, and he shivered in the muggy heat.

TWELVE

"HE SEEMS LIKE such a nice young man," Jean said as they drove away from the doc's house. It was closing in on midnight, and she sounded tired.

"Yeah, he really is," Lex agreed. "I'm actually going to head back over there after I drop you off." He could feel her eyes on him, but he kept looking at the road.

"Isn't it a bit late?"

"He asked if I'd come back and have a couple of beers with him," Lex said. Her silence seemed to hold weight as he waited for her to say something.

"Lex, you know I try not to interfere in your life, and I'm very grateful you put up with me in your home." When Lex tried to interrupt to tell her he didn't just put up with her, she barreled on. "I know that at your age living with your mother isn't what you really want; it's not cool; I understand that. But sometimes, honey, I really wonder what you're doing with your life. You're such a good man, Lex, and I hate to see you alone."

"I'm not alone, Ma. I have plenty of friends," Lex argued. When he risked a look at her, he could see the concern on her face.

"I'm not talking about friends. You need someone to share your life with," she said and then coughed before adding quietly, "If the way you look at him is any indication, I think I know who you'd like that to be."

"Mother!" Lex exclaimed.

"Oh, don't be so surprised. I wasn't born yesterday. I've never seen you look at anyone the way you looked at Gavin tonight. It reminds me of the way your Aunt Rita looks at her 'friend' Sue." She'd actually made air quotes around the word friend.

"What?" His spinster aunt, his mom's youngest sister, had been...oh okay, yeah, now he saw it. His mom must have seen the realization on his face because she laughed.

"I would think that you, if what I suspect is true, of all people would have connected the dots way before now," she said, still chuckling a little.

"It's not like I've spent a lot of time with them. You're okay with it?" His mom had just outed him. She didn't know that he was technically bisexual, but she knew he had feelings for the doc, who was definitely a man.

"With what, dear? The fact that my sister has been in a loving relationship for over thirty years or that you seem to be smitten with that nice young man?" she asked cheekily.

The heat rushed up Lex's neck because his mom was right. He was indeed smitten with the doc. Everything about Gavin got his blood pumping. His intelligence, his looks, his offbeat sense of humor, the little whimpering noises he made in bed, and even the way he seemed to need someone to take care of him—Lex liked it all.

"I guess I thought you'd be surprised and maybe a little upset," Lex admitted.

"Oh, Lex, I learned a long time ago that you can't change people. They are what they are, and if you love them, you have to accept them for who they are. I may seem old-fashioned to you, but I've always been very open-minded. My friend Nelson is a confirmed bachelor, and he and I get on like nobody's business. And you were always different. It was hard to pin down just how you weren't like other kids, but it was there. All I care about is seeing you happy. So you should go get your man." She said the last sentence firmly.

Lex had a big smile on his face because his mom was the best. But when his thoughts turned to making Gavin his man, the smile fell away. "It's not that easy, Mom."

"What? Why not?"

"He's not... He doesn't want me like that." It hurt to admit it, but if Lex could say it out loud to someone else maybe he could believe it and start to move on.

She hit him on the bicep as they pulled into the driveway. "You must have your head in a hole. If he doesn't want you, I'll eat my shirt." She shook her head as she opened the door. "That man was making moony eyes at you all night. Now stop being a blockhead, and go tell him how you feel."

Lex chuckled. "Okay, okay, I'm going. Make sure you lock up before you go to bed," he said as she got out. "Hey, Ma?" She stopped and looked at him. "I love you, you know."

"I know, honey, and I love you too. Have a good night, and make sure you don't drive if you drink too much." She slammed the door, and Lex waited until she was inside before backing out.

He tried to stay under the speed limit on his way back to Gavin's, but it wasn't easy. He thought of what his mom had said about the way Gavin had been looking at him. She was most likely mistaken. Something had happened to spook the doc when he was in the house with Tara, making him seek out the comfort of his friends, and that would explain anything his mom had noticed. Lex had a hard time explaining what it was about Gavin that brought out the protective side in people. Maybe it was because sometimes he seemed so innocent and vulnerable, it made him appear so much younger than his years.

When he remembered the lost and confused look on Gavin's face earlier, he felt bad for even thinking about telling the doc how he felt about him. Maybe it was best to keep their relationship friendly. Despite his mom's adamant insistence that Gavin looked at him in the same light, Lex couldn't make himself believe it. So he made a decision that he hated, but he knew it had to be done to make sure Gavin was protected, even from him. With the weight of the world on his shoulders, he walked up the porch steps to the doc's front door.

He didn't even get his hand up to knock before the door opened. "I was watching for you," Gavin said with a shy smile as he let Lex into his home.

Lex didn't know how to respond, so he didn't. He slipped off his shoes and followed the doc into the living room where beers sweating on coasters and a couple of bowls of snacks sat on the table. Lex rubbed his flat stomach. "You're not trying to see if you can fatten me up, are you?"

Gavin giggled. "I don't know. The picture I have in my head of you as a roly-poly little kid is kind of sweet."

You're kind of sweet, Lex thought. That giggle was freakin' cute as hell, but Lex quickly stopped that train of thought. He'd made up his mind, and no amount of cuteness was going to keep him from staying the course, so he sat on the chair instead of his usual spot on the couch. Lex didn't miss the look Gavin gave him when he reached for his beer.

"So my mom thinks you throw a great party. Thanks again for inviting her," Lex said, looking for a safe topic of conversation to start with.

"It was my pleasure. I really like your mom. I still feel bad about the food though. She must have been cooking all day. I didn't realize she was so..." Gavin trailed off before he could finish.

"So what? Mouthy?" Lex didn't think that's what the doc had been about to say, but it was fun to tease him and watch the expressions pass over his face.

"Oh no...no...that's not...no. I was going to say she was older than I'd pictured, is all."

"Oh, yeah, I get that a lot. People think she's my grandma sometimes. But tell me the truth; you think she's pretty mouthy, right?" Lex couldn't help prodding at things that made Gavin squirm.

"She's really nice. I think you must take after her more than your dad." Gavin looked down shyly at his beer. He took a big swallow and shifted on the couch so he was closer to the chair Lex was sitting in. Gavin turned his beautiful brown eyes to Lex, and Lex had to stop from falling into their depths that never failed to fascinate him. "I wanted to tell you something tonight—before—out on the deck," Gavin said. "About what happened with Tara."

Lex didn't think he could handle details. He shook his head. "You don't have to tell me anything, Doc. It's good that you scored on your own." Lex didn't know how Gavin was going to take the next bit, but he had to get it out there. "I was thinking it might be a good thing if maybe we didn't go on any more playdates together." He paused when Gavin's face started to fall but rushed on. "I think you need to just go out and find a nice woman to date. Not someone like Tara, obviously, but someone who's good for you. You don't want to be stuck in the scene— those women aren't looking to settle down. You need to be out where you can find the ones who are."

Gavin's expression changed until it settled on sad and hurt. "But I'm not ready to get into a serious relationship yet," he said. Gavin had just given Lex the perfect excuse not to tell him how he felt. The doc didn't want a serious relationship, and Lex couldn't keep his emotions out of the bedroom any longer.

"I just can't do it anymore," Lex said.

"You don't want to be friends with me?" Gavin asked. The voice he used just about killed Lex's soul. He sounded so hurt and confused. Lex was out of his chair and next to Gavin on the couch before he could put a lid on his need to comfort the man he'd been falling in love with since he'd first seen him. Lex didn't pull the doc into his arms, instead, putting a hand on Gavin's shoulder to reassure him.

Gavin looked at Lex with the saddest puppy-dog eyes ever seen on the planet. "Did I... What did I do wrong?"

Lex took a deep breath because all he wanted to do was pull Gavin into his arms and kiss him senseless so he'd make those little noises that drove Lex absolutely insane with desire. "God, Doc, you're killing me. You didn't do anything wrong, and I still want to be your friend. I just don't think it's a good idea for us to share women anymore. It's too much for me."

Lex held himself back from hugging Gavin even though the doc looked to be on the verge of tears. But Gavin had other ideas, wrapping his long arms around Lex's stomach and burying his face in Lex's chest. "Thank you," he whispered.

Lex heard the words even though they were muffled by the fabric of his T-shirt. "For what?"

"For staying by me tonight, for coming back, and for still wanting to be my friend."

"So what happened with Tara that freaked you out so much?" Lex asked. Gavin shuddered in his arms. As much as Lex didn't want to hear the details of what had happened with Tara, it had been wrong for him to cut Gavin off when he'd tried to talk about it. He got the feeling Gavin needed to tell him, so he let the doc cling to him since he didn't seem too keen on letting go. He waited, and when Gavin didn't answer, he asked, "Do you need me to call her and ask her for a mulligan?" He was trying to lighten the mood, but the way Gavin pulled away and shook his head vigorously told him his attempt at humor had fallen flat.

"I just really want to forget all about it. Can we do that?" The look on Gavin's face made Lex want to pursue the matter, something had to have happened for Gavin to react so strongly.

Lex's training kicked in. If Gavin had been a woman, sexist as it sounded, Lex would have seen it sooner. Now that he saw clearly, he would have sworn Gavin had been, and still was, exhibiting signs of an assault victim. Why he hadn't picked up on it after noticing Gavin was practically in shock when he'd asked for Lex after his time in the house with Tara? Obviously, the smaller woman wouldn't have been able to overpower a man as big as Gavin, but still, there was something off about the whole situation.

Gavin must have seen something click on Lex's face because he stood up. "Maybe you should go. I'm kind of tired."

"Doc—"

"No, Lex, I don't want to talk about it with you now." Gavin crossed his arms and goddamn if he wasn't pouting like a child.

"You said you were going to tell me," Lex reminded him gently. Lex didn't want Gavin to feel bullied on top of whatever else he may be feeling.

"No, not now. I don't want to tell you anything," he said petulantly.

Lex stood up in front of him. "Why not, Doc? We're still friends and nothing's changed. Come on, tell me what happened. You know I won't judge."

"No, I want..." Gavin trailed off, but then in a firmer voice said, "I want you to leave. I don't want to talk about anything anymore. I'm going to bed, and then I'm going to get up," his voice rose with each word, "and I'm going to forget tonight happened, and you can either decide to be my friend"—a soft sob escaped his mouth—"or not, but I'm not going to care because I can't even deal with this, and there's nothing that you can do—"

Lex grabbed Gavin and pulled him against his chest. "Shh, it's okay, just shh...shh. I'm not going to make you talk if you don't want to," Lex reassured him as he felt the wetness on the side of his neck and knew he'd do anything Gavin wanted if only he'd stop crying.

Lex turned so he could sit on the couch, and the doc followed him down. He let Gavin cry. He could sit there all night if he needed to, but Gavin calmed after a few minutes, and then he felt Gavin's lips moving against his shoulder before he heard the words.

"Will you stay with me?" Gavin asked in a tiny voice.

"Whatever you need, Doc. Let's get you in bed, okay?" Gavin nodded against him but made no move to let go and get up. "You gotta get up 'cause you're too big for me to carry." Gavin nodded again, and this time he let go, getting off the couch without looking at Lex and then starting for the bedroom.

Lex went around the house shutting off lights and making sure the doors and windows were locked. With no idea as to what the hell he was supposed to do in this situation, he decided to just be there for his friend. Whatever Gavin needed, Lex would give him or die trying.

When everything was secure and the lights were all out, he made his way to the bedroom where Gavin was already lying down. There was a small nightlight by the door, providing enough light for Lex to walk across the room without having to turn on the overhead. He sat on the edge of the bed, wanting to assure Gavin that he would be there, before going to sleep on the couch.

"Hey, Doc, I'm going to grab a pillow and sleep on the couch. If you need me, you come get me, okay?" He shifted to stand, but Gavin's hand shot out and gripped his wrist.

"Will you stay?"

"Yeah, I told you I would. I'm just—"

"No, will you stay in here?" Gavin asked.

Lex groaned. The doc was really trying to kill him. How could he say no to that plaintive voice? He nodded and Gavin slid over to make room for him. Heaving out a sigh, he lay down next to the doc.

"Are you going to sleep in all of those clothes?" Gavin asked as he rolled onto his side to face Lex.

Shit, shit, shit! Lex sat up, pulled his shirt over his head, and threw it on the floor before lying back down.

Gavin snorted at him. "If that's how you want to be, who am I to judge?" he asked. Lex couldn't believe the doc was being a pain in the ass after he'd sobbed on Lex's shoulder and practically begged him to stay the night, so he unbuttoned his shorts and lifted his ass to pull them down his legs. Flipping them off with one foot, he watched them fly across the room.

"Happy?"

"No, not really, but it's a start," Gavin murmured.

"If you don't want to talk to me about what happened, then you best go to sleep before I change my mind and go home," Lex threatened.

Gavin shifted a bit closer to Lex. Lex closed his eyes and tried to fall asleep. It couldn't have been five minutes before the doc said, "When I was in college, Riley and I were roommates. We'd met through a mutual friend, and after our freshman year, we got a house with a couple of other guys. They were complete slobs, so as soon as the year was up, we moved into a little one-bedroom apartment because that's all the two of us could afford. We figured it was better than having more space but sharing it with more people." Gavin stopped to yawn. "We fought over the bedroom because it wasn't really big enough for two twin beds, and we both refused to get bunk beds. We tried having one of us sleep on the futon in the living room, but it never worked because our schedules were so screwed up. So finally, after about three months of no sleep and constant arguing, we went to one of those thrift stores for charity places and bought a full-sized mattress and box spring with half of our grocery money. We ate like paupers, but slept like kings. Do you think it's odd that I slept in the same bed with my best friend on and off for at least four years and never thought it was weird?"

Lex had turned toward Gavin as he was telling his story. They were face-to-face and only about a foot separated them. "Nah, Doc, I don't think it's weird. I think it sounds exactly like something that you would do."

Gavin reached out and touched Lex's face with one finger and ran it down his jaw. Gavin yawned again and said, "Thanks for staying. I don't know anyone else who would do this for me but Riley, and he only does it because we've been friends for so long he feels like I'm his responsibility. I don't like that he feels like I can't take care of myself, because I can. I know I'm not always the most aware guy, but I'm not stupid either."

"I know that, Doc. You're one of the smartest guys I know," Lex said, grabbing Gavin's hand and putting it back on the bed. The doc was smart but maybe just a little naïve. Lex would be okay with taking some of the responsibility off Riley's shoulders if only Gavin would give him an opening.

"Thanks, Lex, you're so nice and a really good friend," Gavin said on another yawn.

"Back at cha, Doc. Go to sleep now."

"'Kay, night, Lex," Gavin said in a sleepy voice.

"Night, Doc." Lex watched Gavin make himself comfortable, snuggling down on his stomach as much as he could and with just the sheet wrapped around him.

Lex thought Gavin had fallen asleep until he said in a soft voice, "I should have told her 'No' sooner, you know?"

Before Lex could think of what to say, Gavin's breathing evened out. He was definitely asleep. Lex watched him, wishing things were different because he knew he could make a guy like Gavin happy. He also knew it wasn't going to happen because he wouldn't push and possibly cause the doc any more problems. He'd try to put some distance between them, and if he couldn't get his feelings under control soon, he'd do as Riley asked and let his doc down gently.

THIRTEEN

GAVIN WASN'T SURPRISED when he woke up alone. Sad yes, surprised no. He rolled over into the space Lex had occupied and buried his face in the pillow. He took in a long, deep breath through his nose. It was then that he knew. The realization kind of smacked him in the face, but if he really looked deep down inside, it wasn't all that shocking. He let out a low, frustrated groan. He was so stupid. Banging his head into the pillow did nothing to halt the thoughts running through his mind. He stopped and lay there breathing in the scent of the man he'd somehow—who knows how these things happened—started to like way more than was kosher for a straight man to like another.

After wallowing in Lex's unique aroma for far too long, Gavin got out of bed and took a shower while working out some of his issues. As he was toweling off, now much more relaxed and in a better mood, he decided he'd probably have to do something with his newfound knowledge. He then wondered how one might go about confessing such a thing to the object of their affection. Did it work differently between two people of the same sex, or was it pretty much the same?

Gavin took a moment to worry about his own mental health, considering how easily his mind was accepting the fact that he wanted Lex and not just as a friend. Maybe he'd freak out about it later, but right at that moment, it just felt right, so he wasn't going to dwell on the specifics of what his new awareness actually meant for his life in general. There would be plenty of time to freak out after he figured out how to get Lex.

Dropping his towel, Gavin wondered what he'd do if Lex didn't think of him in that way? Oh holy crap. Lex had never said he would be open to a relationship with a man. Bisexual or not, what if Lex only dated women? If Lex had wanted anything more than friendship, he'd had plenty of chances to tell him. Just because Gavin wanted a relationship didn't mean Lex would be so accepting. Gavin dressed in a pair of shorts and a ratty old T-shirt, after deciding his house could use a good cleaning, and the mind-numbingly boring routine of dusting, vacuuming, and washing laundry would give him time to think.

It was when he was eating leftovers out of Jean's Tupperware containers that he knew telling Lex how he felt would be a lot harder than he'd first thought. His mind circled around the previous night's conversation, and he focused first on the fact that Lex thought Tara had forced him to have sex. Did Lex see him as too weak to fend off a woman? He hoped not and wished he could explain to Lex that he'd just not been that into Tara.

At first, Gavin had thought he was doing what he was supposed to do when presented with a woman who wanted sex. He'd had sex whenever Cassie had wanted it whether he'd been in the mood or not. That was how it worked—women called the shots when it came to sex, and it was the man's job to give them what they wanted. His mom had always told him that no meant no, but Tara had been saying yes. Hell, she'd been saying more than yes, but Gavin couldn't go through with it. He'd thought he'd failed in his duty as a man, but now that his feelings for Lex were evident, he knew why he got a stomachache when he thought about Tara touching him.

Which brought him to Lex. Gavin puzzled over why Lex didn't want to be in the same bed as him anymore—even with a woman as a buffer between them. Maybe Gavin had been too selfish in bed—he'd never given any thought to reciprocating any of the many oral services Lex had performed on him. Of course, then his mind had to supply him with memories of Lex doing just that. He cursed himself for not having the courage to open his eyes and watch Lex as he'd had his cock in that hot mouth. Gavin shivered as he washed out the containers. He never got that queasy feeling in his stomach when he thought about the things he'd done with Lex.

Gavin needed a plan. He'd always been good at making them, and once he had one, he always followed through. Go to college, go to med school, become a doctor, get a girlfriend, marry said girlfriend... Okay, so maybe some of his plans hadn't worked out, but the last plan had gotten him back into bed with Lex. He just needed to figure out how to make Lex want him the way he wanted Lex. Easy peasy, right?

He called it an early night and curled up in bed with a book, sighing as he snuggled down in his freshly washed bedding. He pulled the extra pillow next to him, cuddling it against his chest and burying his nose in it. He was glad he hadn't washed the pillowcase that still smelled like Lex.

GAVIN HATED WORKPLACE gossip, especially when he was the hot topic. He'd been garnering stares for most of the morning while he did his rounds. Finally, he just had to ask.

"So, Jenny, what's the haps?" he asked the surgical nurse who was scrubbing in on the glaucoma surgery he was about to perform.

Jenny looked up at him shyly. "I'm not sure what you mean, Dr. Addison."

He took the direct route instead of dancing around the issue. Jenny was young and new to the hospital, so he thought he could coerce her into telling him. It took the green nurses a while before they figured out the doctors weren't gods, and they didn't have to obey them without question. He usually didn't abuse that fact, but this time he needed to know what people were saying about him.

"Jenny, would you please tell me what they're saying about me?" he asked with his best beseeching look.

Jenny giggled—they always giggled—and said in a confidential whisper, "Just that you're officially back on the market because one of the medical records staff is saying that you and her..." She trailed off, watching his face for confirmation.

Oh great, he should have known that Tara would be the gossipy kind. What the hell was he supposed to say? *We had such a bad sexual encounter that my friend thought she sexually assaulted me?* That wouldn't do anything to help him.

"Well, since I don't kiss and tell, I can neither confirm nor deny any rumors pertaining to who I may or may not have gone out with, or if I have indeed even gone out with said person, but I will tell you this: I'm not looking for anyone right now, and even if I was, I wouldn't look for them here at work." He wanted to make sure he made himself clear on the subject.

"Just telling you what was being said like you asked. I'm engaged, so it doesn't really matter to me one way or the other."

"Thanks for telling me, and you could help me out if you wanted to spread what I said around a little." He hoped to nip the rumors in the bud because he didn't need the nurses vying for his attention, thinking he was looking for a new wife. He should have a talk with Tara, but he got a nervous knot in the pit of his stomach just at the thought of seeing her again. He probably wouldn't follow up on that, and besides, the damage was already done.

Jenny shrugged at his suggestion. "You ready, Doctor?"

"Yep, let's do this," he said. He walked into the one place in the world where he was most comfortable.

"I DON'T KNOW, Ri. I'm meeting him at Carlson's Pub for a couple of beers, that's all," Gavin said as he got ready to go out. His stomach was jittery and talking to Riley on the phone about Lex was not helping the way it should have.

"But, dude, are you going to say anything?" Riley asked.

"I'm not sure I should. This is the first time in three weeks he hasn't been working or busy. I'm kind of scared he may have been avoiding me."

"Why would he be avoiding you? We've been over this. You didn't do anything wrong. I'm sure he's just got a lot of shit on his plate."

Gavin wasn't sure that was the case. Lex used to be quick to accept any offers to hang out, but since the disastrous party, Lex had made every excuse under the sun to not see Gavin. Gavin was worried that he'd been too needy so Lex didn't want to deal with him anymore.

"I know, but I'm still worried. What if he just agreed to meet me so he could tell me face-to-face to quit bothering him? Lex is just too nice to ditch me without doing it in person," Gavin confided his deepest fear.

"I'll kick his ass if he does," Riley said. "I'm sure if you just told him what you're feeling—"

"I don't think I'm going to blurt it out because if he isn't interested, he'll probably be all weird about being friends with someone who has a crush on him," Gavin interrupted. Riley had been trying to convince him to just tell Lex how he felt, but Gavin wasn't ready. He'd made a plan, but so far, Lex hadn't been available for him to execute it. Maybe he could get Lex to commit to something that evening so he could start to put the plan into action.

"Ah fuck, man, you're not going to get anywhere with another dude unless you put your dick on the table. Shit, Gav, you're a guy. Do you get subtle hints from chicks that they're into you, or do they gotta come up and stick their tits in your face and basically say 'Hey I want you to fuck me' for you to get it?"

Gavin groaned at his friend's crass, albeit astute, observation of most men's awareness level when it came to subtle flirting. "God, Ri, fine. I'll try to see if I can at least let him know I'd be interested in something more than just platonic friendship with him."

"That's all I can ask of you, my man," Riley said before signing off.

GAVIN WASN'T HAPPY to see Lex sharing what he'd come to think of as their booth with two other men when he got to Carlson's Pub. To make matters worse, Gavin had to sit next to a stranger because Lex was sitting on one side next to another guy. Gavin almost choked on the jealousy he felt for the stout man sitting close to Lex.

"Hey, Gavin, I'm glad you could come," Lex said when Gavin walked up to the table. "Sit down and let me introduce you to a couple of my friends."

So okay, this was different; he'd never met any of Lex's other friends. Of course he'd introduced Lex to Riley and Sheila, so maybe this was quid pro quo at work. Gavin took a seat next to the young guy opposite Lex. He did his best to smile naturally at them.

"Gavin, this is Stu." Lex indicated the man Gavin was sitting next to. Gavin shook the man's hand. "And this little shit is Mike." Lex nudged the guy next to him with obvious fondness. The little green-eyed monster reared its head as he shook Mike's hand.

"Good to meet you, Gavin. Lex says you're some kind of doctor, huh?" Mike asked.

"Yes, I'm an ophthalmologist."

"Whoa, Lex, you got you a smart friend," Stu said in an exaggerated hick accent.

"Yeah, I can't even spell ophtha-what-cha-ma-call-it. Very fancy," Mike agreed.

Gavin blushed in embarrassment, and he didn't know why. He was proud of what he'd accomplished, but sitting with Lex and his friends, Gavin felt out of place with them pointing out his profession.

Lex laughed, and Gavin felt like Lex was laughing at him. It made him want to shrink down on the bench. "Yeah, Gavin's really smart, but he's a good guy." They laughed again, and Gavin suddenly wanted to leave.

He'd only wanted to hang out with Lex like they had before, but he could almost feel Lex putting distance between them. First, with the seating arrangement, and now with their social status. Gavin was afraid to find out what would come next.

Stu poured him a beer from the pitcher they were sharing, and Gavin gulped down half of it while they chatted among themselves. He gleaned a few things from the conversation: Mike and Stu were state troopers; Mike was married; Stu was fighting with his baby's mom; and Lex wanted to be a state trooper, apparently.

"Gavin?"

Gavin looked up at his name being said and realized that was another thing different—Lex was calling him Gavin. He couldn't remember more than a handful of times he'd heard his name come out of Lex's mouth, and usually it was when he wasn't addressing Gavin directly. It felt like someone was squeezing Gavin's heart and panic was near.

"Um...what?" Gavin had missed whatever was being said while he'd been lost in his own thoughts.

"I asked if you wanted another beer," Lex said.

Gavin knew that if he stayed sitting there in that booth, with Lex so close but so closed off and out of reach physically, he might do something stupid, like cry. He shook his head in response to Lex's question and stood up, jarring the table.

"I'm sorry. I just remembered that I need to...bake a cake..." Gavin used the first thing that popped into his head and couldn't figure out why baking a cake was in his head. He took in the perplexed looks on all three men's faces. "My friend's birthday and... I'll talk to you soon, yeah?"

Gavin turned and left. Lex didn't follow.

AFTER THAT NIGHT, Gavin had fallen into a sort of—he didn't want to call it a depression—a fugue state was probably somewhat more appropriate. He walked through life doing what needed to be done but nothing more. Riley and Sheila joked that they were going to set up a suicide watch if he didn't snap out of it. But Gavin had never thought about killing himself—it just wasn't in him—but he did think of hiding himself away or leaving on an extended vacation.

He couldn't seem to put himself to rights though. He went to work, hung out with Riley, and even went on a few dates Sheila had set up for him. He'd failed to impress any of the women enough to garner a second date.

Gavin saw Lex exactly three times in two months. The first time Lex called him to set up a time to hang out, Gavin got butterflies in his stomach in anticipation. When he showed up and Mike was with Lex, his heart sank, and he went on autopilot to get through the evening. When the next two times turned out the same, Gavin decided it was better to make an excuse when Lex called.

Gavin came to realize a relationship with Lex was no longer a possibility. He needed to move on, but he wasn't sure what he wanted. Lex had opened his eyes to a world of possibilities, and if only he could get out of his funk, maybe he could try some of them out.

IT WAS JUST another long day at the clinic, and Gavin was walking through it in a daze as was his normal state of late. He'd just sat down at his desk with his lunch when his intercom buzzed. He pressed the button and said, "Dr. Addison."

"Doctor, there's someone here to see you."

Gavin sighed. Why did people think that it was okay to interrupt his lunch? "Who is it?" Gavin asked, expecting either a pharmaceutical rep or another doctor.

"He says he's Officer Turner. He's wearing a uniform," the receptionist said quietly into the receiver.

Gavin's heart skipped at least five beats, and his hand trembled as he pushed the button again. "Can you bring him back?" Gavin didn't want to make a scene in the lobby. He'd be more comfortable in his own space.

"Sure, Dr. Addison."

Gavin stared at his lunch until the tap on his door announced Lex's arrival. "Come in," he said, managing to project his voice enough for Lex to hear, even though it felt like his throat had closed up.

The door opened. Lex stepped in, and Gavin's breath caught. How had he never noticed how completely amazing Lex looked in uniform? He shifted in his chair because apparently his dick thought so too. He chastised himself and his dick; he needed to be clearheaded about this. Lex was probably just dropping by to make sure that Gavin knew he didn't want to be friends anymore. No contact, cease and desist, whatever. But Lex's smile seemed genuine as he stepped into Gavin's office and closed the door.

"Hey, Doc, long time no see," Lex said.

"Yeah, Lex, it's been..." Gavin couldn't go on. He looked down at his sandwich to hide his face. The emotion in his voice was going to give him away. He didn't want Lex to leave, when he'd just called him Doc, and it made Gavin feel like melting into a puddle.

"Um, I just stopped by—"

"Sit. Er, I mean do you want to sit?" Gavin interrupted. He tore his eyes away from his desk and risked a glance at Lex.

Lex grinned as he took the chair directly in front of Gavin's desk. He crossed his leg, ankle on his knee, and put his hat in his lap. The way his utility belt clanked and jingled as he moved reminded Gavin that Lex was probably on duty. Why would he be there while he was supposed to be working?

"I wanted to—"

"Did something happen? With Cassie?" If something did, Lex's visit would make some kind of sense to Gavin.

The smile dropped from Lex's face. "No, Doc, why would you think that?"

"Just... You're here. I haven't seen you..." Gavin stopped to heave out a defeated sigh.

"Doc, you're the one who stopped accepting my invites, and you stopped calling me," Lex said, sounding as confused as Gavin felt. "I figured if I called you, you'd just make one of your usual excuses to get off the phone, and I wouldn't be able to ask you what I wanted to. That's why I'm here."

Well, now that Lex had spelled it out for him, Gavin could see where Lex would think he was the one doing the avoiding when in his mind Lex had been the one pulling away. "So w-what do..." Gavin stopped to take a breath to calm himself and his hopes down. "What did you want to ask?"

Lex's easy smile returned. "I was wondering what you're doing the weekend after next?"

Gavin looked at his desk calendar to see if it was his on-call weekend. "Looks like nothing so far," he said. The rumbling in his stomach had nothing to do with hunger pains. Gavin told himself to brace for Lex to ask him to watch his dog so he could go on a weekend trip with other friends or something equally as heart-wrenching.

Lex shifted so he was sitting forward with his elbows on his knees. He looked Gavin in the eyes, and for a minute time stood still. Gavin remembered he needed to breathe, and his shaky exhale broke up whatever moment they seemed to be having. "I wanted to ask you if you wanted to go up to Long Lake with me. My buddy has a cabin there. Mike usually goes with me, but his wife is throwing a hissy fit about something or other, and he's leaving me high and dry. So what do you say, Doc? How does a couple of days of fishing with me on a mostly deserted lake sound?"

Gavin thought he heard a hopeful note in Lex's voice, and his heart pounded at the thought of the two of them alone for two days. His plan would be easy to put into motion; he couldn't have set it up better himself. An insanely huge smile split Gavin's face. He wondered how long he could sit there looking like the Joker after he'd tied Batman to a missile he was about to launch before Lex would decide he'd made a big mistake.

"It would just be the two of us?" Gavin asked. He needed clarification. He didn't want any nasty surprises and end up spending his weekend with Lex and the boys.

"Yeah, is that okay? I mean, if you don't want to, I can go alone."

"No! No that's fine. I think it would be a lot of fun. Just tell me when and where and what I need to bring." Gavin hoped he didn't sound overly eager, but fuck it; if Lex thought he was acting like a kid who just found out he was going to Disneyland, so what? Lex's chuckle sent a tingle down Gavin's spine. He hadn't realized just how much he'd missed that sound.

"First Friday in October, and we'll leave after you're done with work. I'll pick you up at your place. Pack clothes for a couple of days, and make sure you bring a sweatshirt and some pants. Even though it's still warm, it can get cold at night, and it always seems to be a bit colder by the lake," Lex said.

"No food or anything?"

"Nope, got it covered, Doc. So I gotta go. I'm on my last break, and Grady's waiting in the car. Call me if you need to know anything else," Lex said as he stood up. He turned toward the door, and Gavin got up to walk him out. Lex stopped with his hand on the knob, his shoulders slumped. "Please don't back out on me, okay?" Lex asked without looking at Gavin. Before he could ask Lex what was up, Lex opened the door and stepped into the hallway. "See you, Doc." He left without a backward glance.

Gavin was left watching Lex's broad back as he walked down the hall and out into the lobby. He went back into his office and sat down. He ate his lunch without thinking about it. He'd gone over and over his encounter with Lex, and after about the twentieth time, it finally sunk in. He stood up and did a little jig.

"Dr. Addison?"

Gavin turned around and took in the bemused look on the nurse's face as she stood in the doorway to his office. He stopped doing his happy dance. "Can I help you?" He couldn't keep the happiness out of his voice. The nurse's wide smile in reaction to his obvious joy made him want to hug someone. He didn't, of course. That wouldn't be appropriate in the workplace.

"You have a patient in exam room one."

"Oh, thanks. I almost forgot I was at work for a minute." Gavin walked out behind her and nearly passed the room he was needed in. She stopped and pointed. Gavin grabbed the chart and went in. He tried to hide his happiness because he was, after all, delivering some bad news. It then took most of his concentration to be serious as he told his patient he'd be blind within the year.

Gavin felt bad for feeling happy in the face of sadness, but god, he was just so...happy, finally. He was going to spend an entire weekend with Lex, alone, in a cabin on a lake where most people only went in the summer. He admitted October was a strange time to go to the lakes, but he wasn't going to question it. He had a plan, and he was going to make Lex his.

FOURTEEN

LEX WAS BREATHING a bit easier when he got out to his patrol car. Even if he had to put up with Grady for another three hours, his day was definitely looking up. He'd pinned Gavin down to a weekend alone with no interruptions. He had to figure this thing with the doc out. He'd not been able to maintain a normal friendship with Gavin no matter how he'd tried to include the man in his life. Gavin had been resistant to every effort Lex had made to integrate him into his circle of friends. In the past few weeks, Gavin had become distant to the point where Lex wondered if he should just let the friendship slide into oblivion, no matter how much it would hurt.

Lex's heart, his mother—big surprise—and Sheila wouldn't let him give Gavin the heave-ho. Sheila had texted Lex on and off, encouraging him to get in touch with Gavin, but the doc had stopped accepting his invitations. As a result, Lex had been somewhat of a bear to live with, and his mother was getting sick of his prickly demeanor. Her pointed comments about him manning up and telling Gavin how he felt had finally driven him to make a decision. Lex had asked Mike if he would be pissed if he took someone else on his annual trip to the lake. Mike, being the good guy he was, asked for few details and happily stepped aside.

Things were going to come to a head one way or the other, and the fallout could be considerable. He thought briefly about calling Riley to inform him of his plans in case he needed backup once the cards were on the table. He was nervous and waffled back and forth, but in the end, he left Gavin's best friend out of the loop. He still wasn't completely sure if he was going to profess his undying love to Gavin or tell him that they couldn't be friends anymore because it was breaking his heart. Lex would have to decide, and having a few days to gauge Gavin's reactions would, hopefully, be helpful.

WHEN LEX PULLED up in front of Gavin's house just after noon on Friday, Gavin was standing on the porch with his duffle bag at his feet. He waved enthusiastically at Lex before picking up his bag and running down the steps. The doc reminded Lex of a puppy, happy to see his human after a long day apart.

"Hey, Lex, sure you want to spend an entire weekend with me?" Gavin asked as he threw his bag into the backseat of the truck and climbed in.

"I think I can tough it out. I'm sure it won't be easy, though."

Gavin tried to look like he was acting hurt instead of actually being hurt. "Geez, nice to know your true feelings," he pouted. Lex made a note to watch what he said, even jokingly. Obviously, Gavin was as unsure about where they stood as he was.

Lex chuckled and punched Gavin's arm playfully trying to ease the tension coming off the doc. "You're lucky I like you enough that you came in first after Mike ducked out. You can't guess how many people were sucking up to try to get an invite to the lake." Lex hoped that hearing he was the first person on Lex's list would make the doc feel better. Gavin's shoulders relaxed a little, and there was a small smile on his face as Lex pulled out onto the street.

"So why exactly are we going to a summer house on a lake in the middle of October?" Gavin asked.

"It's a tradition. I've gone every year since I was about seven. Used to be something me and my old man did. When he passed away, I decided it would be a nice way to remember him. He loved to fish but hated how crowded the lakes were in the summer, so he'd book us a weekend at a lake somewhere, and we'd go at this time of year. It was nice, just the two of us and maybe a couple of people that either lived year-round on the lake or were diehards," Lex explained.

"That's cool. It's nice, the way you're honoring his memory," Gavin said. Lex saw the question in Gavin's eyes.

"Hey, don't get all weird. This trip is supposed to be fun. I don't spend the entire weekend moping around missing my dad, if that's what has that worried look on your face," Lex said to answer the unspoken question in the doc's eyes. Gavin nodded. Okay, that was settled then. Lex tried for a laid-back attitude to put Gavin at ease. He was going to act like the months that had passed hadn't happened. Kind of like one of Gavin's do overs. Lex was calling a mulligan on life.

The drive was quick, mostly interstate, before they pulled off onto a two-lane county road, followed by a narrow, paved semi-private lane. Gavin eyed the cabins on the road as they drove toward their destination. Some were huge McMansions, but in between those, there were quaint little cabins that had survived the property boom. Lex pulled up in front of a small, A-frame log cabin with wings. One of the wings was a two-car garage and the other was a later addition to the main structure.

"A friend of mine bought the place a few years ago, and a bunch of us helped him add the garage and a couple of bedrooms," Lex said while pulling into the empty side of the garage. The other side was stuffed with water toys it was too cold to use. "That's why he lets us use the place every once in a while."

The door from the attached garage led into the kitchen. The A part of the house was a wide-open space with only the kitchen and living room. A huge brick fireplace took up one wall, and the other was all glass patio doors. Gavin's low whistle of approval made Lex smile. He loved the cabin's design with the exposed beam ceiling and the pine wainscoting. If he ever moved from his condo in the city, this was the kind of house he'd want.

"I love this place. I've always thought that I'd like to have something like this near a lake. Only thing is it would have to be bigger; gotta have room for the kids, right?" he asked as he led Gavin down a short hallway to the bedrooms.

"You want kids?" Gavin asked.

"Sure, don't you?"

"Actually, it sounds stupid, but I've always wanted like four or five." Gavin put his bag in the room that Lex showed him. Lex pointed out the bathroom next and then threw his bag into the other room.

"That's a lot of kids. Let me guess—you were an only child?" Lex asked as they made their way back to the main area. They'd never really talked about Gavin's family.

"Yep, got it in one. I always wanted brothers and sisters and thought it was mean of my parents not to give me any. I was jealous of my friends because they always had someone to play with. Of course they were jealous of me because I had my own room and didn't have to share my toys with anyone." They went to the truck to unload the rest of the supplies.

Lex started putting things away in the kitchen. "You want to grab a couple of armloads of firewood from out back? We may want a fire tonight; this time of year it can get cold." Gavin looked around for a door that led out back. "Just go out the patio door and down the steps, and there should be wood stacked under the deck."

Lex watched as Gavin took in the deck when he stepped out the door. The deck was almost as big as the house. It had a hot tub in one corner and a built-in fire pit near the center. Gavin found the stairs, and Lex tore his gaze away. He reminded himself they had a whole weekend. Lex would get to look all he wanted. He could fill up the little place in his mind where he'd stored his moments with Gavin—the place that had slowly emptied during the long drought without him. Gavin came in with an armload of wood and dropped it in the tub next to the hearth. He turned to go get more.

"Hey, I thought we'd fire up the grill and have steaks. That work for you?" Lex asked before Gavin could go back out.

"Yeah, sure. Can we eat on the deck?"

"Don't see why not. We'll have to dig out a couple of chairs and the table. They're in the little shed off the deck. I'll come and help you in a sec."

"Can we have a fire on the deck later too?" Gavin seemed to be nearly bouncing at the thought.

Lex stopped and put his hands on his hips. "What are you, five?" he asked, but the corners of his lips were twitching as he tried not to smile. "Next, you'll be asking me if we can make s'mores."

Gavin's eyes lit up. "Oh, dude, that would be so cool. I haven't had s'mores in forever. I would've brought stuff if I'd known we'd have a fire."

"Oh my god, sometimes you're so much like a kid I forget that you're older than me," Lex said. "Let's go get the table and chairs, and then we can go out on the boat for a couple of hours."

Together, they carried the furniture out and set it up. They each carried in some wood for the fire to make sure they had more than enough if it got cold. Lex grabbed the fishing tackle and Gavin some beer, and they headed out on the boat.

They had a good time. Lex was surprised at how easy it was to be with Gavin again. He didn't feel the need to fill the silences with chitchat because they weren't awkward. Lex ribbed the doc about not wanting to touch the leeches he'd brought for bait and made a big deal out of having to bait Gavin's hook. In truth, he thought it was adorable that a man who could cut people's eyes apart would be squeamish about putting a hook through a leech. In the end, Gavin caught the biggest fish and taunted Lex with it to get back at him. It was so much fun that Lex could definitely see what a future with Gavin would be like, if only he could make it happen.

Neither of them brought up the threesomes they'd had or that they'd stopped. Lex made a concerted effort to not think of the times he'd been able to touch Gavin or the fact he couldn't anymore. It was like they were different people, and Lex wondered if Gavin missed it as much as he did. He'd never ask because Lex didn't want to risk their rekindled friendship so soon. And he couldn't put off talking about what he wanted forever, but just a bit longer couldn't hurt.

Lex fired up the grill, and Gavin carried the food out to the table. They'd brought out a two-seat glider rocker that was supposed to simulate sitting on a porch swing. Gavin sat mindlessly rocking while Lex made their dinner, the doc's eyes tracking him as he moved from the grill to the table and back. He wondered what was going through Gavin's head while he stared like that.

When the steaks were done and on the table, Lex called Gavin's name. He didn't answer the first couple of times even though it appeared he was looking right at Lex. "Doc!" Lex finally raised his voice to get Gavin's attention. Gavin startled, making Lex chuckle. "Where were you? I've been calling you for five minutes. Dinner's ready."

"Sorry, zoning out, enjoying the scenery," Gavin said as he got up. Lex didn't mention that he'd noticed the scenery the doc had been admiring. The thought brought a smile to his face. He wondered if the doc had really been so captivated by him that he hadn't heard his name being called and what it might mean if he had been.

They sat at the table and talked about football as they ate enough steak to feed a small army. Lex liked the warm feeling he got when Gavin sat back with a satisfied groan after eating a meal Lex had provided. It had been too long since he'd felt that warmth.

Lex made a fire in the pit just as the sun was setting and pulled the rocker up so they could sit side by side as they watched the flames, enjoying a beer and the silence that only came when civilization was left behind. Lex once again found it hard to bring up the reason he'd brought Gavin to the cabin in the first place, not wanting to shatter the peaceful feeling. He chided himself for putting off the inevitable but reminded himself there'd be time enough for serious discussions since they had the whole weekend. Tonight he just wanted to enjoy the doc's company.

After a couple of beers, Lex got up and went into the cabin. He had a surprise for Gavin, and he came back out the door carrying the fixings for s'mores. He couldn't keep from smiling at the excited look on the doc's face.

"Thought I'd put you out of your misery. I saw how you were staring longingly at the fire like you just wished you had some marshmallows." Lex dropped the chocolate bars and graham crackers in Gavin's lap.

"You, Lex Turner, are my new best friend," Gavin said as he started to unwrap the candy bars.

"You're so easy, and I'm telling Riley you said that." Lex put two marshmallows on each of the metal sticks. Gavin eyed the puffy candies suspiciously. "What? S'mores were your idea."

"I suck at roasting marshmallows. I can never make them the way I want them." Gavin turned his puppy-dog eyes to Lex.

Lex sighed. "How do you want them?"

Gavin bounced in happiness. "I like them just golden brown on the outside but completely melted in the middle. When I do them, they always burst into flames."

"Fine, I'll roast yours, and you can try to do a couple for me since I don't mind mine a bit charred," Lex said. Hell, he'd eat coal if it made the doc happy.

"Okay, but you asked for it." Gavin extended his stick over the fire. It took less than a minute for him to start his marshmallows flaming. He pulled them back and blew out the flame, and then Lex reached over, grabbed Gavin's hand, and ate the burnt marshmallows off the end of the stick. Without a word, Lex put two more on, and Gavin went back to trying to keep them from catching on fire.

After Lex had eaten six of the doc's mishaps, he pulled the two he was roasting back for Gavin's inspection. They passed with flying colors, and Gavin held out his cracker and chocolate so Lex could put the marshmallows on. Lex took the newest burnt ones from Gavin's stick and made one for himself.

When Gavin bit into his perfect s'mores, he hummed his approval. "I feel really bad that you're eating a piece of charcoal, and mine is like the perfect example of what s'mores should be," Gavin said through a mouth full of goo.

"Yeah, you look heartbroken over it."

"I can't help it. I might have a little bit of a sweet tooth. Even though I feel bad, I can't help but enjoy this. It's just so good." Gavin smiled, revealing chocolate-smeared teeth.

Lex chuckled. "You are such a goofball, Doc." Gavin nodded and took another bite of his tasty treat. The doc was too much sometimes, and Lex had to stop himself from pulling Gavin in for a chocolatey kiss.

Lex handed Gavin another beer after they finished their s'mores, and they sat back in companionable silence. Later, after a couple more beers, Gavin shivered. The temperature had dropped enough that it was chilly even in the sweatshirts they were wearing.

"Cold?"

"Yeah, it's getting a bit nippy out here," Gavin answered.

Lex got up but stopped Gavin when he started to follow his lead. "Stay there. I'll be back in a sec." Lex went inside and grabbed the quilt that was draped over the back of the couch. He came back out of the cabin with it wrapped around his shoulders. "Stand up, Doc."

Gavin got up. Lex wrapped his arm and the quilt around Gavin before they sat back down. Lex kept his arm around Gavin's shoulders. Gavin didn't seem to mind, and if anything, he snuggled a little closer. Lex didn't make a move to change their position. He was enjoying the doc's firm body pressed against his and his scent after a long day in the sun on the boat.

Lex rocked the glider slowly and laid his head back to look up at the stars. Gavin finished his beer, set the bottle on the deck, and leaned back to gaze at the sky too. It was so peaceful. When Gavin's body relaxed into Lex's, he tightened his arm around Gavin's shoulders. Lex had missed being so close to his doc.

Out of the corner of his eye, Lex saw Gavin turn his head toward him, so Lex turned to Gavin, who smiled softly at him. Raising a shaky hand to cup Gavin's face, Lex let the rough pad of his thumb brush Gavin's cheekbone. "Eh, what's up, Doc?" he whispered.

Gavin looked into Lex's eyes, and Lex wished he could see Gavin's more clearly because in the firelight they were only dark, colorless orbs. Gavin licked his lips, and Lex's gaze shifted to his mouth. Oh, how he wanted to taste those lips again. It was one of his more persistent dreams: kissing the doc until he whimpered for more.

Gavin took a shaky breath before he leaned in. Lex froze when Gavin pressed his lips to Lex's. Lex let the breath rush out of his nose at the unexpected contact and waited for Gavin's next move. When Gavin didn't make one, Lex moved his hand from the doc's cheek to cup his neck and pulled him closer. He wasn't going to let this opportunity go to waste. He moved his lips and shoved his tongue into Gavin's mouth. Lex was taking full advantage of the opening the doc gave him.

Gavin turned and worked his arms around Lex's body to get closer. The soft moan Lex couldn't suppress spurred Gavin on. He ran his hands down Lex's back to the waistband of his jeans and tucked just the tips of his fingers inside. Lex shuddered as he tried to pull Gavin in for more contact. He wanted this so much and hoped Gavin wouldn't suddenly come to his senses and pull away.

Lex tried to break the kiss, but Gavin didn't seem anywhere near done. When Lex wouldn't let Gavin get his lips back where he wanted them, the doc growled his frustration out, making Lex chuckle. "Slow down Doc, you're going to kill me," he said because wasn't that the truth? Gavin had never been aggressive before. He was usually the "lie back and take it" kind of guy.

"I really am going to kill you if you don't let me—" Lex dove back in, stifling Gavin's words, and shoving them back down his throat with his tongue. Lex tried to pull Gavin up from the glider. Gavin protested, like he was happy to keep doing what they were doing right there on the deck, but Lex was stronger, or maybe his need was greater because soon enough, he had them standing and stumbling toward the door.

Gavin managed to get his lips on Lex's neck once they were inside the cabin, and Lex moaned as Gavin sucked hard enough to leave a mark on him. He liked the idea of the doc marking him, letting everyone know who he belonged to. Lex dropped the quilt on the floor and kicked off his deck shoes, and Gavin did the same. When Lex backed away from him, Gavin started stalking Lex. Like a big sinuous cat, Gavin moved with such grace that it left Lex breathless.

Lex backed through the room and down the hallway as he stripped his sweatshirt off and threw it at Gavin's face, making Gavin charge like an enraged bull. Lex laughed when Gavin lifted him off his feet in a fireman's carry and then had to put him back down because he had either overestimated his strength or underestimated Lex's weight.

"Doc, are you okay?" Lex asked through his laughter.

Gavin didn't give into the humor of the situation; the look on his face was pure determination. He moved in on Lex once again, and this time he pulled his own shirt off and dropped it at his feet. Lex's mirth died on his lips as Gavin pressed their naked chests together and took Lex's lips in a desperate kiss, plunging his tongue into Lex's mouth. The aggressive side of the usually docile doc was driving Lex mad with desire, so he turned them and pushed Gavin through the door into his room. He didn't stop until the backs of Gavin's knees hit the bed. The doc whimpered into Lex's mouth, and his aggression seemed to fade away as he turned to putty in Lex's arms. Lex pulled his lips from the doc's so he could nuzzle his neck.

"God, I've missed you so much," Gavin breathed out. Lex's heart thumped in his chest at the confession as his hands went to the buttons on Gavin's jeans. He yanked, and they popped open giving Lex access to push the denim past the doc's hips.

"What do you need, Doc? What do you want me to do?" He needed Gavin to tell him everything was okay, that he wanted Lex's hand and, hopefully, his mouth on him.

No answer came. Instead, Gavin's hand brushed against Lex's denim-covered cock. Lex groaned. He was going to come in his fucking pants just from the unexpected touch. He pressed into the hand that was hesitantly rubbing him and kissed Gavin again. Lex then pushed his own hand under the waistband of the doc's underwear and found the leaking head of his cock. Running a thumb over the slit, he delighted in the little sounds Gavin made as he pushed for more.

"What do you want, Doc? Tell me." Lex stroked the cock in his hand, and Gavin trembled.

"Y-your mouth, please, just your mouth."

Lex kissed him. "Your wish is my command," he whispered and dropped to his knees.

"Fuck," Gavin growled as Lex pulled his boxer briefs and jeans down to his knees.

Then there it was—the object of Lex's obsession, staring him right in the face. He rubbed his stubbled cheek up the length, enjoying the hiss of breath it drew from the man above him. He took the head into his mouth and swirled his tongue around the crown, reacquainting himself with the taste.

Gavin's hands were in Lex's hair, tugging roughly until Lex looked up. Their eyes met for the first time while Lex was in a position to pleasure Gavin. The shiver running down Lex's spine at Gavin's heated look shook him to his soul. That look had to mean something, right?

He let Gavin guide his head up and down his shaft a couple of times before he wrested control from him. Grabbing his ass and pulling until the head of Gavin's cock bumped the back of his mouth, Lex swallowed it deep. Gavin gasped and held Lex's head in place until Lex had to pull back or pass out. He let Gavin pump into his mouth, loving the feel of smooth skin sliding across his lips. There was no finesse, none of the many techniques Lex usually employed while sucking cock. He let Gavin fuck his mouth with abandon, and all too soon the doc's hips started jerking erratically. Gavin pulled frantically at Lex's head in an attempt to get him to let go, but Lex wasn't going to relinquish his hard-won prize so easily. He tightened his grip on Gavin's ass cheeks and held him while the doc came down his throat for the first time.

"Oh, fucking god," Gavin groaned. Lex looked up to catch Gavin watching as he swallowed the entire load. He slid his hand into his own pants and gave his cock a couple of quick jerks. He finally let Gavin's cock slip from his lips as he moaned out his own pleasure.

Gavin plopped down on the bed like his legs had suddenly given out. He looked a bit shell-shocked while Lex wiped his hand on his jeans and stood up. Lex then put his hands on the sides of Gavin's face and tilted his head so he could look into his eyes.

"You okay, Doc?" Gavin nodded as best as he could while Lex held his head. "Are you sure?"

"Um...yeah, just a bit wrung out," Gavin said, lowering his eyes. "Maybe we should go to bed?"

Lex swallowed down the hurt that rose at Gavin's words. He'd pushed it too far. Even if Gavin had started it, Lex should have known there'd be consequences if he didn't stop it before it went too damn far.

"That's a good idea," Lex said, instead of all the things he wanted to say. If he gave Gavin some time to work through what had just happened, maybe it would be okay. "I'm a bit tired myself." He bent and kissed Gavin softly on the lips. "I'll see you in the morning." Lex left Gavin sitting there looking stunned.

FIFTEEN

GAVIN COULDN'T FIGURE out what had just happened. One minute Lex was there, swallowing his fucking jizz, for Pete's sake, and the next minute, he was up and gone. Gavin ran through everything that had happened and still didn't know why Lex had left. Gavin suggested bed, thinking they'd get in, but instead of sleeping, they'd maybe continue what they'd started in some fashion. Gavin wasn't all that well-versed in gay sex, but he surely knew the basic mechanics of it. He'd been willing to at least try some things, maybe not all, but...but then Lex had...he'd left, just up and left him there with his dick hanging out. Literally.

The shower started in the bathroom next door. Maybe Lex would come back after he showered? Gavin waited. When the shower shut off, he strained to hear what Lex was doing. His heart dropped when he heard the bathroom door open and then what was obviously Lex's door closing. Gavin got up to grab his sleep pants and T-shirt. He gave the other bedroom door a glance before going into the bathroom for his own shower.

The bathroom smelled like Lex, the scent of his shampoo and aftershave hanging on the moist air. Gavin stepped into the shower. Thinking of Lex naked in the little stall only moments before gave his libido a little kick-start, but he was not going to jerk off when what he really wanted was in the next room. He stood for a while under the warm water—it felt good after the cool air of the house—thinking about what had happened.

Gavin had spent the day trying to figure out if Lex was interested in more than friendship. He'd tried the subtle flirting thing, and it had yielded exactly nothing. Only a few times, like when making s'mores, did Gavin think he'd maybe seen something in Lex's eyes that looked like desire. In a fit of desperation, he'd thrown himself at Lex, even though he'd never been so bold. Never one to initiate a sexual encounter, he'd feared Lex would push him away, denying him what he wanted more than anything. Lex had responded better than Gavin had anticipated, but then he'd left. Now Gavin had a sinking feeling that maybe Lex was just interested in sex.

While toweling off, Gavin decided he'd have to ask Lex flat out if he had a chance. All his carefully laid plans were chucked out the window because Gavin couldn't wait any longer. He put on his pajamas and threw his dirty clothes on the floor of his room. He took two steps toward Lex's door and then stopped. Anxiety was building up at the thought of blurting out the question. He took one step back toward his room and then three steps to Lex's. It became a sort of fucked-up dance as he argued with himself—two steps forward and three steps back.

A door popped open, and Lex grabbed a startled Gavin by the arm. "Come on, Doc, get in here before your pacing drives me insane," Lex growled.

"W-what?" Gavin asked as he let Lex pull him into the room.

"You were out there pacing for five minutes. I figured I'd save the wear and tear on the rug and make your mind up for you," Lex said as he pushed Gavin down on the bed. Gavin watched wide-eyed as Lex walked around the bed and got in the other side. Lex pulled the covers over both of them. "If you were scared to sleep in a strange place, all you had to do was ask, and I'd have let you bunk with me in the first place."

"I'm not scared." Gavin rolled on his side so he could look at Lex.

"So you were just wondering if I wanted a cuddle then?"

Gavin choked and was glad it was dark enough so Lex couldn't see the blush he could feel crawling up his neck. "Um...Lex?"

"Yeah, Doc?" Gavin could hear Lex trying to suppress his laughter.

"Do you...um...I mean have you ever dated a guy? I mean like not just sex or..." Gavin trailed off because it was an awkward question to ask. Lex rolled to his side and propped his head up on his hand so he was looking down at Gavin. He was thinking too much for Gavin's taste before he answered.

"I had a boyfriend in college." Lex finally said.

"So you haven't dated seriously since college?"

"I haven't seriously dated a man since college. I had a few girlfriends, even one that I lived with for a couple of years," Lex clarified.

Gavin bit his lip. He felt his chances had just gotten slimmer because college was a long-time past. He had to know for certain. "So does that mean you don't date guys anymore?"

"No, it means that though I haven't recently, I have before, and I'd be open to it if the right guy came along," Lex said.

"So what would the right guy be like? Would he be like the guy you dated in college?" Gavin didn't want to get his hopes up because maybe he wasn't Lex's type.

"Hell no, I mean, I really thought I was in love with the guy, but we were incompatible. He wouldn't talk about anything, never told me things that bothered him, so they festered and... Crap, Doc, you don't want to hear about that, sorry. It still makes me mad when I think of how everything went down."

"I'm sorry I asked. I was just curious as to what type of guy you would consider going out with." Gavin rolled to his back so he could look straight up at Lex.

Lex grinned. "Well, Doc, I'll tell you then, so you don't have to wonder anymore," Lex said. "Let's see. I like a guy who's smart—the smarter the better—and funny—gotta have a sense of humor. Of course, I'd like him to be attractive. I'm partial to blonds, especially if they have brown eyes that shine with this light that seems to come from nowhere, but it's always there when I look into them. I also find it hard to resist guys who love s'mores, are afraid of leeches, have wacky friends, ask people they hardly know for sexual mulligans..."

"OH MY GOD!" Gavin exclaimed. He tried to sit up as Lex's words sunk in, but he knocked his head into Lex's and flopped back onto the pillow. They both rubbed at their injured foreheads, and Lex laughed as Gavin groaned.

Lex leaned down so his face was right in front of Gavin's. "I also like klutzy guys that head-butt me when I'm trying to tell them I would really, seriously, without a doubt, want to date them if they were so inclined." Lex brushed his lips lightly over Gavin's. "Are you, doc?"

Gavin was speechless, but Lex waited until he could compose himself enough to speak. "Are I what?"

"Not an English professor, that's for sure. Are you so inclined? Do you want to date me?"

Gavin licked his lips because they seemed really dry all of a sudden. He knew the answer to Lex's question, but he'd never planned past getting Lex to see him as a potential...boyfriend? He had no idea what dating another man entailed exactly. Like, was one of them supposed to take on the woman's role? That didn't seem right, but heck if he knew gay-dating protocol.

"I've never done this before." Gavin mentally smacked himself for stating the obvious when Lex's lips turned down in a slight frown. "I'm not sure how to go about dating a guy, but I've been thinking about it a lot lately, and I don't know, but I really like you, and I have these feelings I don't know what to do with because even though I think sometimes they're wrong, they really don't feel that way, and I'd just like to maybe—"

He could feel the smile on Lex's lips as they pressed against his. No, nope, this didn't feel wrong at all. Gavin kissed him back, but all too soon Lex pulled away. "It's not hard. Dating is dating, and it's pretty much the same as with a woman." Lex paused for a moment and then added, "Oh, but usually there's more sex." Gavin could see Lex was joking, but he was curious as to how dating another guy worked.

"I can deal with that, I guess, but what about going out on, like, dates and stuff?"

"We used to go out all the time. It's really no different, but if it will make you feel better, more comfortable to know what it's like, I'll take you out tomorrow night on an official date," Lex offered.

Gavin liked the thought of going on an actual date with Lex. But then he remembered they were on Lex's annual remember-the-good-times-with-his-dad trip. "Nah, I can't ask you to cut the trip short—that wouldn't be fair."

"It's not a problem. I'll take you to the Yacht Club. It's just across the lake," Lex said.

"I don't think I brought the right clothes for a fancy restaurant." All he had packed were jeans and long-sleeved T-shirts.

"It's just a name. The owners have slips so you can dock your boat, so everyone started calling it the Yacht Club. They changed the name because nobody actually knew what people were talking about when they called it by its real name. People eat there in swim trunks and flip-flops during the summer, so I think you'll be fine in whatever you have," Lex explained.

"Um, okay, I guess that would be okay." Gavin tried to hide how excited he was. He had a date, an official date, with Lex.

Gavin wondered what would happen next. They were in bed together. Lex was still propped on his elbow above Gavin, looking at him in the dim light from the hall. Gavin licked his lips and watched as Lex's eyes followed the movement. He took a chance and reached up to pull Lex down to him. Lex didn't put up any resistance when Gavin kissed him. He didn't know what having a boyfriend would mean for the rest of his life, but kissing Lex was rapidly becoming his new favorite pastime.

Gavin ran his hand along Lex's stubbly jaw down to his thick neck and let his thumb rub over his pronounced Adam's apple. Feeling all the distinct differences between the male and female bodies just from the neck up did nothing but speed up Gavin's heart rate. He was thinking about seeing what other differences pushed his buttons when Lex pulled back, ending their kiss.

Lex smiled sweetly down at Gavin. "We should get some sleep. I'm getting you up at the butt crack of dawn to go fishing." Gavin groaned in frustration because he was so hard, and Lex wanted to sleep? Lex laughed at Gavin's groan, probably misinterpreting it as a protest against the early wake-up call.

Lex got up to turn off the hall light and crawled back into bed, leaving a space between them. Was it okay for Gavin to move closer? Would Lex freak when he found out that he was a cuddler? Gavin lay there pondering his next move, until he finally rolled over, away from Lex, in irritation at his own indecisiveness. He jumped when Lex's arm snaked around his waist and pulled him back flush against the hard plane of Lex's chest. Then Lex settled in behind him and pressed a soft kiss on the back of Gavin's neck.

"Go to sleep, Doc. We got plenty of time to answer all your questions tomorrow."

Gavin shivered at the soft puffs of air on his neck, goose bumps rising on his arms. How was he supposed to sleep with a half-naked Lex pressed against him? He guessed he'd have to try because this *was* happening. "Night, Lex," he said on a yawn.

"Night, Doc."

It was honestly only seconds later when Lex's soft snores lulled Gavin into his own slumber.

THE DAY HAD gone by in a blur of fishing, grilling, eating, and more fishing. Hanging out on the boat and deck with Lex had been easier than Gavin had expected. They hadn't really talked about all the things Gavin wanted to know, but he didn't want to get into a deep discussion when Lex had been enjoying himself. Gavin had decided if being in a relationship with another guy was like this all the time, it was a wonder that more guys didn't switch teams. It was like hanging out with Riley, except Riley's touches didn't make his skin tingle, and there were never any stolen kisses that left him wanting more. Yeah, no, this thing with Lex was different.

Gavin, fresh from the shower, looked at himself in the mirror over the sink. He checked to make sure the shave he gave himself with the borrowed disposable razor didn't miss an unsightly patch of whiskers.

He was nervous about going out with Lex. After their perfect day, his sudden bout of nerves over going out to a restaurant was confusing to say the least. But, it was probably because it was a date, and he'd never been great at dating. Gavin had to admit there was also a niggling feeling in the back of his mind that going on a gay date could potentially cause a problem, especially out in the backwoods. The last thing he wanted was for his first date with Lex to go badly. What if Lex reconsidered wanting to be with him? Gavin really, really didn't want that.

"Doc, you look like a GQ model. Stop primping, and let's get a move on," Lex said from the doorway where he casually leaned on the doorjamb, watching Gavin.

Gavin stepped back from the mirror and wiped his sweaty palms on his jeans. "Just wanted to make sure that crappy razor you gave me didn't flay my skin off." Gavin joked to ease his nerves.

"Don't bitch, beggars can't be choosers; you should have brought your own," Lex said. Gavin had the strongest urge to kiss the smirk off Lex's face but held back like he'd been doing all day. He'd let Lex take the lead because he was still unsure what was acceptable when it came to showing affection toward the other man.

"I thought I'd be holed up in a cabin with only you seeing me turn into Grizzly Adams, not going out to a fancy yacht club," Gavin said before Lex pulled him in for a quick kiss.

Lex nuzzled his neck. "I don't mind when you're a little rough, Doc." He rubbed his own stubbled cheek over Gavin's smooth one. "Makes the sparks fly when I do this." Gavin's breath hitched, and Lex chuckled when he pulled back. "We better get going, or I'm going to throw you down and have my way with you."

Gavin bit back the "Yes, please" that was on the tip of his tongue and followed Lex out to the dock. They took the boat across the lake, and Lex maneuvered it into one of the slips with an easy grace Gavin couldn't help but admire. Lex held his hand out to help Gavin onto the dock and then put his hand on the small of Gavin's back as they walked to the front door. Gavin tensed at the public display. Lex removed his hand and maintained a proper amount of distance between them but not before giving Gavin a look that he couldn't interpret. Was he upset? Disappointed? Gavin wished he was more experienced and not so nervous about screwing up.

"Would you like a table or a booth?" the hostess asked when they walked in. "You can pretty much have your pick; it's slow in here tonight, even for the off-season."

"We'll take a table. Do you have something in a corner?" Lex asked with a devilish wink.

Gavin watched the hostess, who flushed and then put her hand on his man's arm in that way women do when they're flirting. "Sure, I have the perfect table for you. Just follow me." As she grabbed a couple of menus and walked ahead of them, the way her hips swayed was greatly exaggerated—probably for Lex's benefit.

Gavin trailed along behind, trying to stuff his jealousy away as he reminded himself that Lex was there with him and that Lex wanted him. He'd seen Lex flirt on many occasions, so he should be immune to the way Lex affected whomever he set his flirtatious sights on, but it didn't stop Gavin from putting his hand on Lex's back in a possessive manner, much the same as Lex had done to him outside the restaurant, staking his claim for the hostess to see.

Lex turned with a knowing grin, and Gavin realized Lex had been trying to make him jealous on purpose. Gavin sat and Lex took the seat to the right of him instead of across the table like he would normally have done. To start, Lex ordered a bottle of wine with a small appetizer, and after the wine had been delivered, Lex sat back to study Gavin, making him fidget.

"So you're too nervous to let me touch you in public but not too nervous to make sure the hostess knows we're here together as more than just two friends out for a meal," Lex said.

Gavin searched Lex's face to figure out if he was mad or just amused. His expression said Lex was leaning toward amused exasperation. "I guess I'm just not sure where we stand. And I'm really not sure that I want to be all... What do they call it nowadays? Out and proud? I mean, do you tell people that you...you know?" Gavin asked.

Lex huffed out a gruff laugh. "Doc, I don't tell anyone anything. What I do, or should I say, who I do in my own bedroom is nobody's business but my own. It wasn't that big of an issue for me in college since I was far enough away from home that nobody who knew me had to know what I did or who I did it with. Now, I guess as far as my friends and my mom go, I wouldn't hide it from them, but it's probably best not to broadcast it at work. I'm not sure that my fellow officers are all that accepting of alternative lifestyles, as our sensitivity training calls it." He waited a few seconds while Gavin absorbed what he'd just said. "I'm not going to push you to do anything you're uncomfortable with, but I'm not sure I can hide that we're more than friends from people who see us together. Shit, both my mom and Riley knew after watching me around you for less than an hour."

The look on Gavin's face must have been something to behold because Lex's laughter was so loud it drew the attention of the few other patrons dotted throughout the dining room. "What? Riley knew what?" Gavin asked. Seriously, what had Riley known, and why the hell wouldn't he tell Gavin if it would have saved him some heartache?

"He never told you." Apparently it was news to him that Gavin didn't know whatever it was he thought Riley knew. "I thought maybe he had, and that's why you were acting so weird every time we got together after your party."

The implications of Riley knowing that Lex liked him and wanted to be more than friends, as long ago as his party, made Gavin go cold. He'd spent months freaking out, and Riley could have just told him Lex wanted him too. What possible reason could Riley have had not to tell him?

"He didn't tell me anything...but how...what... I spent so much... God, I'm such an idiot, and I'm going to kill Riley when I see him." He was so... He didn't even know what he was.

Lex leaned forward and put his hand on Gavin's leg under the table. "Doc, I'm sure he had his reasons for not telling you. Probably because this was something you needed to work out on your own. I wouldn't be too hard on the guy. He did sorta threaten me and warned me not to hurt you."

When Gavin thought back to some of the things Riley had said, he could see Riley had been pushing him to tell Lex all along. God, everything would have been so much easier if he'd known. He shook his head to clear it, and then it dawned on him what else Lex had said. "You couldn't hide that there was more than friendship between us from Riley and your mom at my party. What does that mean exactly? Because Riley already knew we were going out and doing things." Gavin wiggled his eyebrows instead of coming out and saying fucking the same woman at the same time. "So what was it that Riley saw? Oh, and your mom?" His voice rose at the last because what did Lex's mom know?

Lex smiled and rubbed Gavin's thigh before taking his hand off so he could eat some of the stuffed mushrooms the waitress had stealthily dropped off before scurrying away. "Apparently, I was looking at you in a way that gave them the idea I might like you a little more than just as a friend," Lex said around the food in his mouth.

So Lex's mom knew too. Was he the only one who was totally oblivious? "Your mom's okay with this?" Gavin motioned between the two of them to indicate what he meant.

Of course the waitress showed up right then to take their order. As Gavin waited for Lex to finish, he thought about what it would be like to tell his parents he was dating a man. That would go over like a lead brick. The thought made his tongue stick to the roof of his mouth, so he gulped his wine. It was something he'd deal with later, much later.

"My mom is surprisingly open-minded on the subject as it turns out. She's one of the reasons we're here right now," Lex said after the waitress left. "She was so sick of me growling at her that she suggested I bring you instead of Mike and hoped that maybe I'd get up the nerve to tell you how I feel." Lex looked down at the table after his confession.

Gavin was having a hard time digesting all the new information. He had a lot of questions, but the middle of a restaurant, no matter how few people were there, was not the place for him to get his answers. Only one question nagged at him, and he couldn't help but ask, "How do you feel?"

Lex looked up, with a slow smile spreading across his face, making Gavin's chest tighten. "Well, Doc, I pretty much like you more than anyone else in my life right now except for maybe my mom."

Gavin's heart stuttered and skipped. A warm fuzzy feeling formed in his belly because that's exactly how he felt about Lex. "Me too," he admitted quietly.

Lex looked around at the other tables before he pressed a quick kiss to Gavin's lips. "Good to know, Doc, good to know."

SIXTEEN

GAVIN WAS A damn cute tipsy drunk, so Lex was extra careful in making sure Gavin got safely from the boat to the dock when they arrived back at the cabin. It wouldn't be good if the drunk doc took a dip in the chilly lake. Lex was having a hard time keeping his head in the game. Their first real date had gone smoothly after a couple of bumps. Based on the questions the doc had asked, Lex was sure Gavin hadn't begun to grasp what being in a nontraditional relationship would mean for the rest of his life. Lex just hoped he would be strong enough for the both of them when the shit hit the fan, and he just knew it would at some point.

Gavin almost took a header when he caught his toe on one of the flagstones leading to the cabin door, and Lex snapped back to attention in time to catch him before he hit the ground. The doc giggled, and Lex reveled in the fact that he didn't have to suppress the urge to kiss him. When Gavin responded enthusiastically, Lex smiled as he pulled away. For all his hesitation, the doc sure didn't object to Lex's overtures.

"I think I'm a little drunk," Gavin said through his giggles, so Lex made sure he was steady on his feet before he let him go to unlock the door.

"Yeah, I noticed that too. I'll have to remember to cut you off after three next time. I think it was the fourth glass of wine that tipped you over." Guiding him into the cabin, Lex settled him on the couch before he bent and pulled the doc's shoes off. Gavin sighed as he wiggled his toes and raised an eyebrow as he used his foot to rub the inside of Lex's thigh.

"Can we have a fire?" he asked. His toes grazed the bulge growing in Lex's jeans. Lex grabbed the questing foot and put it on the floor before the uncoordinated man could accidentally do him some damage.

"You can have whatever you want, Doc. All you gotta do is ask." Lex went to the fireplace and started the fire he'd readied the night before but hadn't gotten around to lighting. The flame took off quickly, and Lex turned to find Gavin staring at him. "What do you want to do now?"

Gavin made a show out of thinking, scratching his chin and furrowing his brow. "We could watch a movie and cuddle on the couch." He looked pretty pleased with himself over the decision, and once again, Lex felt the need to kiss him. He couldn't get over how everything about this man made him want him more.

Lex sat on the couch and pulled Gavin into his arms. He kept telling himself this was real, and he could do this anytime he wanted now that the doc was his. It hadn't sunk in yet, because it had been far too easy, and in Lex's experience, nothing good came this easy. He'd been prepared to cajole and fight and give up if it seemed an insurmountable task to get Gavin to see that they could be more than just friends. To have Gavin come to him, to ask him if he'd be willing was something Lex hadn't been expecting.

As their lips met and moved together, Lex's heart pounded furiously in his chest, not out of excitement, but in fear. What if Gavin had second thoughts when they went out and had to face the world as a couple?

Gavin pulled away from the kiss. "I thought we were going to watch a movie," he said as he let his hand trail down Lex's face to rest on his chest.

Lex wondered if Gavin could feel how hard his heart was pounding.

"Fine, hold on a sec." Lex got up and asked, "What movie do you want? Bill doesn't have a very big selection. What are you in the mood for?" He skimmed the titles, noting not much had changed since he'd last been there.

"Something funny," Gavin said. Lex could hear Gavin moving around behind him as he put the movie in and grabbed the remotes. When he turned around, the doc was sitting on the couch in only his underwear and T-shirt. Raising an eyebrow, Lex got a shy smile in response as Gavin crooked a finger at him, and he went to the sweet man willingly, dropping the remotes on the coffee table as he passed.

Stopping in front of Gavin, Lex watched as the doc unbuckled his belt, mesmerized by Gavin's long, dexterous fingers as they popped the buttons on his jeans one after another until his fly was gaping open. He sucked in air when Gavin's breath ghosted over his abdomen as he placed a chaste kiss just above the waistband of Lex's briefs. Lex stood as still as a statue when Gavin buried his face in his stomach and inhaled. His cock twitched, looking for attention, but Gavin seemed satisfied to just breathe Lex in.

Lex chanced a move, lifting a hand to smooth Gavin's curly, blond locks back from his forehead. How many times had he dreamed of having the doc like this? He didn't want to force the issue so soon, but he really wanted Gavin to touch him, his hands, his mouth, anything. Those thoughts made his hips jerk, and Gavin looked up at him.

"Sorry, Doc," Lex said in a thick voice. "It's been awhile."

Gavin pushed at Lex's jeans until they dropped to the floor, and Lex stepped out of them. "Come down here," Gavin said, pulling on Lex's hand as Lex complied. "Turn the movie on." Lex obeyed. "Can you just..." Gavin pulled Lex's arm around him, and Lex knew what to do from there. He pulled the quilt over and covered them, settling the doc into his side. And then Gavin was all over him, making it like cuddling an octopus. Where'd he get all those limbs?

"Settle, Doc," Lex said, soothing his hand down Gavin's arm and holding his hand to still it.

"I'm sorry. It's different being held than doing the holding," Gavin said with one of those looks he'd been giving Lex all day. Lex had come to think of them as the doc's "I don't really know how to be with another guy, so sorry if I'm fucking this up for you" looks. It was cute and frustrating at the same time.

He tried to reassure Gavin every time he shot him one of those looks, but so far he'd been unable to convince the man that there was no right and wrong when it came to what they did. Whatever Gavin felt like doing was okay with Lex, but he was so timid Lex wondered if the issue wasn't just because he was a guy. It was the only time he allowed himself to think about Gavin's marriage and what Gavin had been like with his ex-wife.

"Babe, just relax. There aren't any rules here, so if you want to be the one to do the holding, then by all means do the holding," Lex said. Gavin's wide-eyed look had him confused. "What?"

"Did you just call me babe, or am I drunker than I thought?" Gavin asked, his nose adorably scrunched up. Lex kissed the tip of it.

"Yeah—baby, doc, sweetie, dear, honey—they're all the same unless you prefer one over the other," Lex said.

"Doc is not interchangeable with any of those others," Gavin said. Lex was impressed the man could use such large words; the alcohol must be wearing off.

"Is to me."

Gavin giggled. "But you've been calling me doc since the first time you talked to me." He buried his face in Lex's chest and giggled some more.

Lex rolled his eyes even though Gavin couldn't see it. "Yeah, well, Grady calls you doc too, so I'd love to see you tell him what it means to you now." The thought made Lex want to giggle too.

Gavin sat up. "Oh my god, Grady... He's not like...eww... I don't think he's my type." The serious look of disgust on the doc's face made Lex want to tease him, but Gavin's hand under the quilt came to rest on his cock. Gavin rubbed lightly over the rapidly expanding flesh.

"Ah, Doc, if you want to watch this movie, that's not a great idea," Lex said through clenched teeth. Gavin's light touch turned firm, and his face turned into Lex's neck. Gavin nuzzled in and rubbed his nose along Lex's stubble.

"I like this. I thought it would feel weird to kiss someone with hair on their face, but I kinda really like it," Gavin said, his voice muffled by Lex's neck. "For some reason, it actually turns me on even more: the constant reminder that it's you I'm kissing. Even if I close my eyes, I still know because of your stubble and your smell. You don't smell like anything I've ever smelled before. I know the cologne you use, and I know other guys who use it, but it smells different on you. Better. Makes me want to taste you."

Gavin proceeded to do just that. He ran his tongue along Lex's neck and up to his ear. He sucked on Lex's earlobe, until he got a moan, and then moved on to the ultra-sensitive skin just behind Lex's ear. He sucked until Lex knew there was going to be a bruise. The pain from Gavin's teeth grazing his skin sent a shot of white-hot pleasure straight to Lex's groin.

"I don't wanna watch the movie anymore," Gavin murmured. Lex tilted his head so Gavin's lips could find more skin.

Fuck, Lex really wanted this, but he'd wanted to have a conversation about what Gavin expected first. Gavin was terminally confused about the entire situation. Apparently, the only thing he seemed to be sure about was the fact that he wanted Lex. Christ, how could he stop when Gavin's hot mouth was working its way down his neck? Tomorrow...tomorrow they'd talk since they had a two-hour drive with nothing to do but talk.

"Doc, wanna go to the bedroom?"

Gavin was up and halfway down the hallway before Lex even knew what was going on. Well, that was sort of an answer. Lex chuckled and shut off the TV before following him, getting to the bedroom door just in time to see Gavin bend over to slip his boxers off his feet. That ass was a thing wet dreams were made of, and Lex let out a low whistle, getting an over-the-shoulder smile in return. He couldn't remember a time when he'd gotten out of his clothes faster.

Gavin turned and gave him an admiring onceover. "Wow."

Lex didn't stop to preen even though Gavin's appreciation made him feel ten feet tall. There were so many things Lex wanted to do with Gavin, but he was limited because he'd failed to bring the proper supplies. He didn't worry about it too much, though, since the doc probably wouldn't be ready for anything too invasive anyway. Lex smiled at his clever turn of phrase.

Gavin wrapped his arms around Lex, molding their bodies tightly together, and shuddering when their cocks made first contact. Oh boy, this was going to be a study in control for Lex since he didn't want to push Gavin too far and scare him off. Still, the thought of sinking into the tight heat of the doc's body made Lex struggle for breath.

"Lex," Gavin gasped when Lex canted his hips, and their erections slid together.

"On the bed, Doc," Lex said, pushing Gavin gently down and following as Gavin spread his legs, allowing Lex to settle between them. The way their bodies fit together so naturally had Lex's head swimming with the possibilities. Gavin thrust his hips up into Lex, grinding their groins together. Lex leaned down to kiss him, and if kissing was the only thing he was allowed to do, Lex knew he could get off just from Gavin's soft lips and sweet whimpers. But Gavin obviously didn't feel the same way because he was drilling his hard cock into Lex's belly.

Lex kissed down Gavin's jaw to suck up a mark on his neck while Gavin moaned as he forced his hand down between them. Lex bit down on the flesh he'd been nibbling when Gavin's hand gripped his cock and gave a firm stroke. Releasing the doc's neck, he rose up so Gavin had room to use his hand. Oh, Christ, Lex wasn't going to last. It was too much. Too much skin pressing against his own, too many needy sounds coming out of the man underneath him, and finally having Gavin's hand wrapped around his swollen member was just too much. It was causing Lex's brain to go haywire. He needed to get Gavin off before he lost it.

Lex used his hand to move Gavin's off his cock before he kissed the questioning look off Gavin's face to let him know he hadn't done anything wrong. Lex then lined their cocks up, gathering what precum he could from both leaking heads for lube, before he got them both in hand and gave a pump.

"Oh, holy hell, fuck," Gavin hissed.

"Yeah?"

"Oh, yeah," the doc moaned.

Lex thrust his hips so Gavin would get the idea, and soon they were pumping in and out of Lex's fist, causing more friction than either of them could handle. Gavin's hips lost their rhythm first, and Lex couldn't hold back when the warm fluid from Gavin's cock hit the head of his. Lex shuddered through his orgasm and then dropped down on Gavin's chest, causing a sharp *oof* to leave his beautiful mouth.

"Sorry, Doc."

"'S okay."

Lex lifted his head to look at his lover. He wanted to make sure Gavin was okay with what they'd done, but the blissed-out expression on his face put Lex's fears to rest. Lex rolled off, and Gavin instantly burrowed into his side.

"We should clean up, Doc. We'll be stuck together if we fall asleep like this."

Gavin didn't loosen his grip, but he did pull his face away from Lex's body long enough to ask, "And that would be a bad thing, how?"

Lex chuckled. He supposed the cleanup could wait for a bit.

"So you don't mind if I don't tell anyone about us?" Gavin asked. The doc was sitting with his leg up under his butt and turned on the seat to face Lex. Lex had lectured him on sitting properly in his seat because the way Gavin was sitting made the seat belt he was wearing more of a hazard than a safety measure, but his words had fallen on deaf ears.

"I can't force you to acknowledge our relationship, especially when I have no intention of outing myself at work for the time being," Lex said. He'd been answering some of Gavin's questions and also reassuring him that there was no handbook on gay dating, as the doc referred to it. It was like hetero dating—fly by the seat of your pants and hope for the best. Lex flicked his eyes to the right just long enough to take a quick look at Gavin. He wore a thoughtful, slightly confused expression as he absorbed what Lex had said.

"So, let's just say, hypothetically, of course, that we're still together in a year, and we want to, like, maybe move in together, would you still want to be in the closet at work?"

Lex was startled by the question. "Um...the odds..." He cut himself off. He'd wanted this so badly, and here he was about to tell Gavin the odds they'd still be together in a year were pretty low. "The odds that you'll ever want to live with me are pretty low, Doc. I'm not easy to live with," he said with what he hoped looked like a playful grin.

Gavin sucked on his bottom lip, and Lex started to get nervous at his silence. "I'm gonna tell Riley and Sheila. It should come as no big a surprise since...you know. I'm not sure about my parents. I think they may not be too happy about it. I'll probably wait..." He trailed off, leaving the "until I know if this is going to work out" from the end of his sentence.

"Doc, you know I wasn't saying I thought the odds of us staying together weren't good, right? I mean, we're just starting out, so anything could happen, and with you... You're not exactly...crap. What I'm trying to say is you're more likely to dump my ass and go back to a safe relationship with a woman—" Gavin's loud snort cut him off.

"You do remember the circumstances in which we became acquainted in the first place, right?" Gavin asked. Lex smiled. "Huh, glad you think it was so humorous."

"I was smiling because I think it's hot when you talk all smart-like."

Gavin rolled his eyes. "Don't try to get me off the subject. You were telling me how I was going to ditch you for some safe and sane relationship with a woman because we all know how well that turned out for me last time."

"Fine, if we're still together in a year and want to move in together, I will tell everyone at work that I'm bi and in love with Dr. Gavin Addison and that we're going to move in together so we can have all the gay sex our little hearts desire," Lex said.

"I'm writing that down because that's exactly how you're going to have to say it in a year," Gavin said with a huge smile. Lex watched from the corner of his eye as the smile faded, and the doc bit his lip, blushing at his self-assured prediction.

Lex put his hand on Gavin's knee. "You got it, Doc. You better write it on the calendar so we know when my time's up."

Gavin released his lip and the smile reappeared. "I don't think I'll need to write it down. I'm pretty sure I won't ever forget this weekend." He covered Lex's hand with his own and squeezed.

"Me either."

"Good to know, Lex, good to know."

LEX KISSED GAVIN at his front door. He hated to leave the doc, but he needed to get ready for his shift. He also needed a couple of hours alone so he could just wallow in his happiness. The fact that Gavin was actually contemplating a future with him made him feel wonderful. Lex had wanted to blurt out that he loved him already so the ball would be in Gavin's court, but he didn't because it was too soon, and he wasn't completely stupid.

His mom didn't say a word as Lex unloaded his truck. She watched him with a small smile on her face until he'd brought everything in. Finally, as he was cleaning out the cooler in the kitchen, she decided she'd waited long enough.

"So, I expect you to invite him over for dinner soon. You did tell him I have no problem with anyone who loves my son, right?"

"It's a little too soon for such a strong word, Ma." Lex gave her a stern look. "I won't let him get near you unless you promise to dial the love talk back a notch."

"Why? Don't tell me you didn't tell him how you feel?"

Lex fidgeted, still feeling like a little boy under his mom's disapproving glare. "I told him I like him a lot. It's too soon for I love yous, Ma. We're guys, so if I told him that, he'd run for the door so fast he'd break the land-speed record."

"You'd better not wait too long. I have a feeling Gavin is one of those people who needs to know where he stands. Get over your macho bullshit, and do it soon because that boy is just what you need."

"Ma, you can't know—"

"Yes I can, and I do. I'm your mother. I've been watching you all your life, and these past couple of months I've seen two things that I never have before." She touched Lex's forearm and held his gaze. "I watched you fall in love and then into despair when you thought it wasn't possible to get what you wanted. Those are two of the most powerful emotions I've ever seen on you, and he was what caused them both. Now that you have him, you'd better find a way to keep him."

"Ma, it's just—"

"No, I don't want to hear it. I know it's not going to be easy, but you know what your dad used to say." Lex knew she was serious when she invoked his father's name.

"Nothing worth having ever comes without a lot of hard work," Lex said as his mother nodded.

Lex would find out just how prophetic those words were.

SEVENTEEN

GAVIN SAT AT the kitchen table staring down at the letter in his hands. He should have known. His paperboy never laid his paper nicely on his doormat. It was always out in the dew-covered grass. Shit, he'd once found it in the lower limbs of the tree in his front yard. So yeah, it should have struck him as suspicious that it was placed neatly in the middle of his welcome mat when Lex had picked it up while dropping Gavin off that afternoon.

Opening the paper to check out the entertainment section, so he could to see if there was a movie he could take Lex to for a second date, an envelope addressed with very familiar handwriting fell out.

He'd seen too many lists and balanced too many checkbooks over the years not to recognize Cassie's handwriting. Dropping it like it was on fire, he squelched the urge to stomp on it before he, instead, picked it up again. Now he was just staring at it, fearing what he'd read once he got up the nerve to open it.

They were just words, he told himself one more time as he pulled the flap open and took out the single sheet of paper. Gavin had gotten what he wanted when Lex agreed to a relationship with him, but the letter in his hands felt like the past trying to pull him back and away from the man he wanted for his future. A faint whiff of Cassie's perfume made Gavin's stomach lurch like he was on a roller coaster instead of sitting on one of his kitchen chairs. Closing his eyes, he took a couple of breaths, and that scent brought back memories—ones that he cherished, not the most recent ones that made him sick.

Dear Gavin,

I'm so sorry for everything I've put you through. I know nothing I can say would ever be enough for you to forgive me, but I need you to know that I have never stopped loving you. I know it's no excuse, but I was going through a very rough time, and now that I've gotten the help I so desperately needed, I can see that what I did to you was wrong.

I know I shouldn't ask, but I'd like for us to get together. I would like to apologize in person. I would really like to see you again. I've missed you so much, Gavin. I know I said some things that hurt you, and I want you to know I never meant any of them. Now that I'm on medication, my moods are more stable. I wish you would consider giving me another chance, but if you can't, then please at least let me tell you how very sorry I am face-to-face.

I'm staying with my parents for the time being. Please call me? I know you are a good, kind man so I will wait for your call.

Love you,
Cassie

Gavin was trembling by the time he finished reading Cassie's words. That was his Cassie, not the cold bitch who had been putting him through hell. He wondered what medications she was on; what had her diagnosis been? The doctor in him was curious, but the husband he used to be was elated that the Cassie of old was back and maybe they... Oh, oh no, what was he thinking? He had Lex now, and Cassie, well, she'd been bad, very, very bad. Could he really forgive her after everything she'd put him through?

He got up and grabbed his phone. The first person he wanted to call was Lex, but he couldn't. He didn't want to drag Lex into his mess. Besides Gavin knew he wouldn't be able to make a good decision if Lex was there distracting him. Which left Riley, who would be just getting ready to watch the late football game. In a flash of inspiration, he called to order pizza before dialing Riley's number.

"Got pizza on the way, if you leave now you should get here about the same time as the pizza guy," Gavin said after Riley grunted hello.

"Dude, you're home early. So gonna spill your guts or what?"

"Come over, and I'll tell you everything," Gavin said with a grin, anticipating Riley's next words.

"Gross, no way man. I'm never talking to you again if you give me any details about you and that copper having butt sex."

Gavin choked on his response. Not that he hadn't expected something so crass to come from his friend, but the way he'd said it and the fact that anal sex was something Gavin hadn't yet given much thought to left him speechless.

"Heelllooo," Riley singsonged when Gavin's silence stretched.

Gavin coughed and banished the images from his mind. "There was no anal intercourse, merely fellatio and frottage," Gavin said in the most scholarly tone he could invoke.

Riley sniggered and then called—probably to Sheila—God, Gavin hoped it was only Sheila there. "There was dick-sucking and something else, but he says no butt sex yet." Gavin heard Sheila's voice but couldn't make out what she said. There was a muted thump. "Ow, why you gotta hurt me like that?" Sheila had probably hit him.

Gavin's ears burned. "Just get your ass over here and bring Sheila. You can watch the game here." Why couldn't he just have normal friends?

"Man, the game's already starting. If we leave now, we'll miss half of the first quarter. Can't you wait until it's over?" Riley whined.

"Let me talk to Sheila."

"Fine, we're on our way," Riley grumbled knowing Sheila would make him do whatever Gavin wanted.

"I knew you couldn't resist," Gavin said, smug about getting his way.

"Fuck you." Riley hung up.

Talking to Riley had already made Gavin feel better. Riley and Sheila would give him advice he could trust. He turned the game on and made sure there was beer in the fridge.

The pizza showed up just before his friends did. They settled in the living room in front of the TV with the food and beer.

"So you told Lex how you feel, and now you two are together?" Sheila asked.

"Yes, we are."

"I'm really happy for you, Gav; he seems like a really nice guy," Sheila said.

"Are you goin' steady? Did he give you his letterman's jacket?" Riley asked. Sheila smacked Riley while Gavin ignored him. Riley went back to watching the game.

"How do you feel about all this?" Sheila asked. "I mean it's kind of a big change."

"I'm not sure, but I know he's what I want. Um...but could I tell you something without you judging?" Sheila nodded. "He's in the closet at work, and I'm not sure that I'm going to tell anyone except you guys for right now until I'm more certain of where we stand." He watched as Sheila's look turned guarded, and even Riley started paying more attention to Gavin than to the game.

"He's forcing you to keep quiet about this?" Riley asked. "That's fucked up."

Gavin shook his head. "No, it's not like that at all. He just doesn't know how well it would go over at work. I don't blame him, you know. We've all heard stories about how it can be tough for guys with jobs like his." There was conviction behind Gavin's words. He truly believed it was because Lex was a cop that he didn't want to come out. He didn't think it had anything to do with Lex being ashamed of him or their relationship.

"But, Gav, honey, that can be a really hard burden to carry; the secrecy has been known to kill relationships," Shelia said.

Gavin appreciated their concern, but it wouldn't be a problem; he could handle it.

"I've already decided I'm okay with his decision. I just wanted to let you know so you didn't accidentally say anything that could get back to someone he works with. I'd hate to cause him problems with his job." It was time to tell them the real reason he'd wanted them to come over. It would also have the added benefit of changing the subject. "I need some advice on something."

"Use Astroglide, and be the giver not the getter. That's the best advice I can give you," Riley said as Gavin got up to retrieve Cassie's letter. Gavin ignored the comment because, hell, what could he say; it sounded like good advice to him.

"Ugh, Ri, shut up. You never complain," Sheila said. Riley's surprised look at Sheila's comment made Gavin laugh. He didn't want to hear about anything they did in the bedroom besides sleep. Although it did explain why Riley was so ready with an explanation of what pegging was when Gavin had asked while refuting his exit-only claim. Gavin filed the information away for later use.

Gavin handed Cassie's note to Sheila. Riley leaned in to read it at the same time, and neither one of them looked thrilled at what they were reading.

"Oh, fuck no! You are not even thinking about seeing that bitch again," Riley said when he looked up.

"Oh, Gav, honey, please tell me that you aren't considering this," Sheila said the same thing but with more tact.

Gavin stared at his hands because looking at his friends was too much for him while he told him he was thinking about going to see Cassie. "I'd really like to at least talk to her. I mean, I think it might help both of us to get some closure." They were quiet. What must they be thinking? "I loved her for so long, and I think I never really stopped. Do you think you can ever really stop loving someone who you loved so much?"

Sheila got up and squeezed in beside Gavin on the chair. She put her arm around his shoulders and said, "Oh sweetie, I know that you love her. It's okay if you still do, but after all she did, you have to admit she's not good for you. I don't care what excuse she had, you don't treat people you love like she treated you. You deserve so much better."

"Yeah, like your cop. Even if he is closeted, he still looks at you like he cares, which is more than I can say for the Ice Queen," Riley added.

"He's not all the way in the closet, just at work. His mom already knows, and it's family that's important." Gavin didn't know why he felt he had to defend Lex, but in doing so he opened a whole new can of worms.

"So, how long are you planning to wait before you tell your parents?" Riley asked.

"Riley, can we please focus on one crisis at a time," Sheila admonished. "Now, I think you need to tell Lex about the letter. First, because she's violating her probation by contacting you, and if she was the one who brought it here, she's also violating the restraining order you have. And second, this is something that you should be open about with him, because whatever you decide, if he finds out and it doesn't come from you, it could cause problems. You really don't want to have secrets this big this early in a relationship."

"Are you done now?" Riley asked, shooting a pointed look at his girlfriend whose frown answered his question.

"No. One more thing, Gav. If you do decide to see her, please make sure you don't go alone. I'll go with you if I have to, but you do not go alone; you got me?" she asked.

"Yeah, I got you. Thanks, Sheila. You know that if Riley wouldn't take it too hard I'd upgrade you to best friend status instead of him." Gavin was trying to lighten the mood a little. He hated that he was the source of so much drama recently. He'd thought after how well the weekend had gone things could finally get back on an even keel.

"Okay, okay, you girls break it up now, and you"—Riley said pointing at Gavin— "answer my question."

"I don't know," Gavin said.

"You know your momma is going to flip a shit," Riley said.

Didn't Gavin know it? His mom still treated him like a small child. He'd been homeschooled by his mother, and they had been very close. He'd chosen to go away for college because, frankly, she was smothering him. He'd have had a much harder time convincing his parents to let him go if it hadn't been for his uncle's intervention and promise to keep an eye on Gavin. His mother's over-involvement in his life was the reason he'd decided to stay, instead of going back home, when he finished med school. Then, he'd used Cassie and her family as his excuse to stay after they'd gotten married, and his house after his uncle died.

His parents weren't too religious, but they had attended church regularly. It was one of the only places Gavin had social interactions with his peers growing up. He had never heard his parents say anything bigoted, and they'd always been for equal rights and so on, but he wondered if it was one of those situations where everything was all well and fine until it touched them personally. The thought of telling them about Lex gave Gavin nervous heart palpitations.

"I'm just going to keep it quiet for a while," Gavin said.

"Uh-huh, and what happens when they come for Thanksgiving this year? You going to hide Lex while they're here for a week?" Riley asked.

"Lex will understand. Now shut up and watch the game," Gavin said. He was done talking.

GAVIN SMACKED HIS alarm clock, but the damn noise wouldn't stop. It took him a few seconds to realize it was his phone, not his alarm clock, that had woken him. He looked at the clock. Who the hell was calling him at a quarter past six in the morning? "Yeah," he said groggily when he got ahold of his phone to answer it.

"Hey, Doc, did I wake you?" Lex asked, sounding wide awake and chipper to boot.

"Yeah, I don't have to be in until nine this morning, so I was sleeping," Gavin said, more alert upon hearing Lex's voice.

"I'm sorry, Doc. I thought you'd be up. I'll let you get back to bed then."

"No, I mean, I'm up now anyway. I thought you had a shift last night. Shouldn't you be sleeping?" Gavin asked as he sat up.

"I just got off, and I thought I'd call you to say good morning before I went to bed."

A warm feeling crept through Gavin's chest. It was nice that Lex called just to say good morning. Gavin felt a little giddy. Lex obviously liked him as much as he liked Lex. If they lived together, Lex would have come home and crawled in the bed with him, and they could have...

"Doc? You still there?"

Gavin cleared his throat. "Why don't you come here? I'll make you some breakfast or supper or whatever. Do you eat before you go to bed?" The sexy thoughts about Lex were making Gavin sound stupid.

Gavin shivered when Lex's chuckle came through the phone. He was certain Lex made that deep, throaty sound just to get to him. "Doc, I know you can't cook. If you want me to come over to see you before you go to work, just say it. That way I can stop to get some doughnuts for you."

"Lex, do you want to come over so I can see you before I go to work?" Gavin asked. Cripes, he blushed because he'd never been that forward in his life. May as well have asked the man if he wanted to come over and get naked.

"I'd like that. I'll be there in about fifteen, depending on how long the line is at the bakery," Lex said. Gavin could hear the smile in his voice.

After hanging up, Gavin started the coffeepot and got into the shower. He washed quickly, not wanting Lex to wait if he showed up early. He was pulling on his undershirt when Lex knocked. Gavin looked down at his boxer briefs. Since Lex had seen him naked, it probably wouldn't shock him to see Gavin in his underwear.

Gavin opened the door with a big smile for the man standing on his porch with a bag in one hand and the other poised to knock again. Lex's eyes traveled Gavin's barely covered body, and he quirked his lip.

"Well, I hope that's not how you greet everyone who comes knocking on your door." Lex stepped into the entryway next to Gavin. He leaned in and pecked Gavin on the cheek. "I brought you breakfast. I hope you made coffee."

"The pot's on. I was just getting dressed." He followed Lex into the kitchen.

Lex turned and leered. "Yeah, I can see that, and I don't mind if you don't finish. I could get used to eating breakfast with this view."

Gavin blushed. He'd probably never get used to hearing Lex say stuff like that. "I'll just go put on some pants." Gavin went to his room and slipped on his slacks, forgoing his shirt—he didn't need to get crumbs on himself before work

Lex was sitting at the table with a cup of coffee and a doughnut in front of him, and Gavin had a moment to look at Lex while he had his guard down. Lex looked tired and Gavin felt bad for keeping Lex from his bed after he'd worked all night. And he hated that he had to tell Lex about the letter from Cassie before he'd gotten to sleep, but he couldn't put it off because if he did he may never get up the courage to broach the subject again.

"Hey, come sit down and have a doughnut. I didn't know what you liked, so I got a mixed dozen," Lex said with a weary smile when he noticed Gavin lurking.

Gavin bent to kiss Lex as he passed on his way to the coffeepot. "I'm going to get fat if I keep letting you feed me. You know that I'm going to eat like four of those, don't you?" He poured himself a cup of coffee and sat next to Lex.

"I don't mind a little meat on my men," Lex said. "So what did you do last night?"

Gavin ate half a doughnut in one bite and pointed to his mouth as Lex waited for his answer. He swallowed and took a sip of coffee, gearing up to tell Lex about the letter. "Well, Riley and Sheila came over, and we had pizza and watched the game. I told them about us and..." He trailed off wondering how best to put it.

"And what?" Lex asked, probably expecting to hear some funny story about what Riley had said.

"Well, I asked them for some advice because, well—" Gavin got up and grabbed the letter from the counter. "—this was in my paper when I got home yesterday." He handed Lex the letter and waited patiently while he read it. His face was expressionless. Gavin had hoped he would have some kind of reaction, so he'd know what Lex was thinking. The transformation from Lex, his friend, to Lex, the cop, was noticeable; his shoulders squared; his jaw clenched, and it was like a curtain dropped over his eyes.

"You know that this is a violation—"

"I know. Sheila was kind enough to point that out last night," Gavin cut him off. "I'm not showing it to you because of that."

Lex sat back in his chair, his eyes still hiding his thoughts from Gavin. "Okay then, why are you showing it to me, Doc?" he asked. "I mean if not for my help, then what?"

"I was thinking that I'd like to see her." Gavin looked at the doughnuts, which no longer held any appeal, as he waited for Lex's reaction.

"Okay, why?"

Gavin looked up to meet Lex's eyes as he answered. "I still love her," Gavin admitted. Lex flinched at his words. "I don't want her back, but I'm sure that in her own way she probably still loves me too, like she said in the letter. I just feel like she deserves for me to at least meet with her to hear what she has to say. I think it would do us both some good."

Lex didn't say anything at first. He held Gavin's gaze, and Gavin tried not to fidget under the weight of Lex's stare. When Gavin was sure he was going to be the first to cave and look away, Lex blinked. His eyes went back to normal. "I can't tell you what to do, and I'm not going to point out all the reasons why I disagree with you on the fact that she deserves anything from you. I can only ask you to be careful because I really don't want anything to happen to you now that..." Lex stopped there.

Gavin smiled because he thought he knew what Lex was going to say, and for the second time that morning, the happiness bubbled up inside him. "Sheila already offered to go with me, but I was thinking I'd just set something up at her parent's house with them there. I hope you're not upset. I just wanted you to know what I was going to do. No secrets between us because I don't want that." Gavin covered Lex's hand with his own.

Lex turned his hand to lace his fingers with Gavin's, giving them a squeeze. "Okay, Doc, no secrets; that's good. I want to know when you're going, if that's okay," he said, and Gavin nodded. "Okay, well I should get home to bed, and you should get ready for work." Lex got up, and Gavin had no choice but to follow him to the front door since their hands were still entwined.

Gavin took the initiative and used Lex's hand to pull him in so he could press their bodies together. "I'm really glad you came over this morning, and I wish you could just stay and sleep in my bed and be here when I get home," he said, voicing his thoughts before he could censor himself.

Lex kissed him quickly. "I'd be gone before you got home. My shifts are from six to six this rotation, but I guess it's the thought that counts." He kissed Gavin more thoroughly before releasing him. "I'll call you soon. See ya later, Doc." He opened the door and stepped out onto the porch.

"Hey, Lex." Gavin called before Lex could take the steps down, and Lex turned his head to look at Gavin. "Sleep tight." Lex nodded and Gavin watched until he got into his truck and drove away with a wave.

That had gone better than Gavin had expected. He really did wish Lex could have slept in his bed even if he'd been gone when Gavin got back. Knowing he'd slept there would have made Gavin feel good. Crawling between the sheets with Lex's scent on them... Crap, he'd have to jerk-off before work or risk being a walking hard-on for the rest of the day. He made a note to himself on his way to the bedroom not to invite Lex over in the morning unless they could do more than talk before they had to go their separate ways.

EIGHTEEN

LEX MOVED AROUND Gavin's kitchen like he owned the place. He'd cooked more meals in there the past two weeks than he had in his own home since his mother had moved in with him. It felt good to be back in the kitchen. He'd always enjoyed cooking and feeding the man he loved—yes, he loved Gavin—made it even better. When the door opened, and the man in question stepped in with an appreciative smile on his face, Lex's knees turned to jelly.

"Something smells awesome," Gavin said as he put down his messenger bag. He didn't even take off his coat before he stepped into Lex's arms.

"I'm making baked enchiladas." Lex kissed Gavin deeply enough that he could verify the doc still had his tonsils. "Go take off your coat and grab a beer. I'll just be a second. Just gotta get this in the oven." He gave Gavin a push to get him moving.

Lex couldn't keep his eyes off the doc as he removed his coat and bent down to take his shoes off. That ass still had him pitching a two-man tent every time he saw it. Gavin grinned when he stood back up and then walked slowly to the fridge. Lex was sure Gavin knew what he was doing, but he always acted so damn innocent Lex found himself fighting the urge to throw Gavin down and sully him.

"How long do we have until it's done?" Gavin asked. He popped the top off his beer and took a drink while his eyes traveled the length of Lex's body. Lex turned and put the pan in the oven as goose bumps popped out from Gavin's perusal of his body.

"Only half an hour." Lex knew that look. The doc was thinking naughty thoughts behind that innocent façade. Lex turned to lean on the counter, and Gavin's lower lip poked out as he chewed on his upper one. It was his thoughtful look, and Lex wondered what was on his mind. Then, as if he'd made a decision, Gavin put down his beer and took the few steps that put him right in front of Lex. Leaning in to kiss him,

Gavin's hands went straight for the button on Lex's jeans, and Gavin had Lex's pants open and halfway down his ass before Lex could react.

Lex broke the kiss only to have Gavin nuzzle into his neck. "This is kind of sudden. What's up, Doc?" He was surprised at Gavin's assertiveness—the doc had been hesitant to instigate anything beyond a kiss until now. Their relationship still had that fresh-out-of-the-box feel to it, so Lex hadn't questioned Gavin's tentativeness. But Gavin instigating some sort of sexual encounter in the kitchen seemed out of character, and Lex wondered if something was wrong.

"Nothing's up; just want to try something," Gavin said. His hand found Lex's erection, and Gavin moaned into Lex's neck before abruptly dropping to his knees. Lex could only stare with wide eyes at the sight of the doc on his knees before him. Gavin pulled Lex's underwear and jeans to his knees and licked his lips, which were hovering just inches from the head of Lex's cock.

"Um, Doc, what are you doing?" Lex had a pretty good idea of what was about to happen, and he was totally on board but had to wonder why now, all of a sudden, Gavin thought it was time for him to attempt his first blow job.

Gavin looked up at him and rolled his eyes. "Isn't it obvious?" He wrapped one hand around the base of Lex's cock and grabbed his hip with the other.

"Doc, do you really think this is the right time and place—" Oh boy, that was so not what Lex expected. There were no tentative kisses or experimental licks; Gavin had just fucking swallowed his cock in one fell swoop. What the fuck? Did the man not have a gag reflex or what? Gavin pulled off slowly and looked at Lex. He took the time to give Lex a grin and a cheeky wink before he did it again. Lex's knees just about gave out. If Gavin kept that up, this was probably going to be the shortest blow job ever recorded.

Lex clutched at the countertop behind him to keep from grabbing the doc's bobbing head. What Gavin lacked in technique he more than made up for in enthusiasm and, fucking-A, he could deep throat like a pro. The warm, wet suction was almost more than Lex could bear, making his eyes roll back in his head when Gavin moaned around the cock buried in his throat.

"Fuck, Doc, I'm gonna come," Lex panted. He wasn't kidding; he was like right there, and he whimpered when Gavin pulled off.

"Grab my hair," Gavin said. When Lex just stood there with a stupid look on his face, Gavin grabbed one of Lex's hands and put it on his head. "Grab my fucking hair."

Lex was stunned out of his stupor by the command in Gavin's voice. He put the other hand on the doc's head and gathered a fistful of silky curls. Gavin licked his puffy lips, and his eyes glazed over as Lex guided his head back into position.

"Babe?" Lex didn't know what Gavin wanted, and he didn't want to hurt him.

"Just do it. Hard," Gavin whispered. He licked the weeping head of Lex's cock before taking him back in.

Lex didn't think it was a good idea. He'd never really had that type of blow job before, one where he was in control. He'd always let the giver, well, give. He pulled Gavin's head into him slowly, but the doc had other ideas because he pulled Lex's hips forward, resulting in an almost brutal thrust. Lex tried to pull back, but Gavin pushed against him, fighting for the control he'd tried to give up.

"Doc, I can't—"

Gavin pulled and pushed at Lex's hips. Lex had no choice but to give in to that demanding mouth. He let out a groan of frustration as he held Gavin's head still, fisting his hair as tightly as he could. He pumped his hips and felt his cock hit the back of Gavin's throat on each thrust when he dared to go deep. He watched Gavin's face for signs of distress, but if anything, the look on the doc's face was one of bliss as Lex used him. Watching his cock slip between the doc's lips as he just took it again and again was the hottest fucking thing Lex had ever seen.

It didn't last long. How could it? Lex pulled away as he felt the pressure that had been building in his groin getting ready to unspool, and Gavin let him go, but fisted Lex's cock, and right as he came, Gavin closed his eyes and took it in the face.

"Oh fuck, Doc," Lex groaned. He spread his legs as best as he could with his jeans still around his thighs and slid down the front of the cupboard. His bare ass hit the cold tile, and he pulled Gavin into his lap where he lifted his shirt and cleaned Gavin's face, all but his lips, which he kissed to get a taste of himself from his man.

Gavin buried his face in Lex's neck as soon as Lex pulled back to look at him. Lex stroked Gavin's wild curls, while holding him to his chest as he waited, not knowing what had brought on the episode and not wanting to pressure Gavin into explaining.

"Was that too much?" Gavin asked. His voice was muffled, but Lex had a feeling the question would have been voiced quietly anyway.

"Which part?" Lex asked.

"Any of it? All of it?"

Lex stopped stroking Gavin to pull his head out of his hidey hole so he could look him in the eye. "Why would you ask that?"

Gavin looked down and wouldn't meet Lex's eyes again. "I just don't know if that was weird or not."

"Was it what you wanted?" Lex asked. Gavin hung his head, but Lex caught the slight nod before he did. Lex grabbed Gavin's chin, forcing him to meet his eyes. "Then it wasn't weird." The question still burned in Gavin's eyes, so Lex kissed him. "It was fucking hot, if you want to know the truth."

Gavin jerked away. "Really?"

"Oh, you have no idea what you just did to me," Lex said. "I will let you do that anytime, anyplace, and you won't hear one word of protest from me." A shy smile gave Lex hope that he'd put Gavin's fears to rest. He patted Gavin on the thigh. "Now get up so I can get our supper out of the oven before it burns."

"I'll just go wash up quickly," Gavin said as he stood. He held out a hand for Lex and pulled him up too. "Maybe you should come with me."

"No way. We eat first, and then I'll show you something new too," Lex said as he pulled his pants back into place. He had plans for the rest of the night, but they needed food first.

"I'M ON MY way right now. Don't you dare leave without me," Lex growled into his phone.

"I told Sheila not to call you," Gavin said. His voice was an octave higher than normal, which meant Gavin was well on his way to a total panic attack.

"Well, she did, and I'm going with you, so just sit tight. I'll be there in five minutes," Lex said and hung up before the doc could protest again.

Sheila had called Lex while he'd been hanging out with Mike, trying not to think about Gavin's meeting with his ex-wife. After having supper with Sheila and Riley a few nights earlier, the four of them had decided that Sheila was the best choice to accompany Gavin to his ex-in-law's house to face Cassie. Sheila had gotten hung up at work and couldn't make it, so she'd tapped Lex to go in her stead. They'd already gone over why Riley was the worst choice. He wouldn't be able to hold his tongue when it came to "the beast," as he lovingly referred to Cassie.

As Lex pulled into Gavin's driveway, the doc rushed out the door and into his truck before he could even shut the engine off. Gavin looked nervous—not that Lex blamed him. Reaching over, he grabbed the doc's hand.

"You okay, babe?"

Gavin sighed. "I'm just not sure this is the best idea, Lex."

"I've been telling you that since you showed me the letter," Lex agreed.

Gavin rolled his eyes. "I didn't mean that, I meant you coming with me. It's sort of like taking your new girlfriend to meet your old girlfriend," he explained.

Lex fluttered his eyelashes and made a kissy face at the doc. "Wow, nobody's ever called me their girlfriend before. It makes me feel so special."

"Stop it; that's not funny. You know what I meant. If she finds out about us, the first call she'll make is to my mom, and then there will be hell to pay because she had to hear it secondhand. I really don't need that on top of what she and my dad are bound to say about the fact that you're...you know, a guy and all," Gavin said.

Lex backed out of the driveway and tried to think of something reassuring to say, but there really wasn't anything that would ease Gavin's fears about how his parents were going to take the news that their son was in a relationship with another man.

"I'm not going to throw you down and fuck you in front of her, you know. I'm perfectly capable of keeping my distance when I need to," Lex said.

Gavin squeezed Lex's hand. "I know you are. I'm sorry. I guess I'm just a little more stressed about seeing Cassie again than I thought I'd be."

"It's no problem. I understand. We'll get through this, and then I'll take you out to buy you that Halloween costume I've been promising you," Lex said with a wink.

"I'm not going to Riley's party dressed as a naughty nurse; you know that right?"

"Oh, don't worry your pretty little head about it now. I have a great idea for our costumes," Lex said. Gavin chuckled and rolled his eyes again. Mission accomplished, the situation was out of DEFCON 1 status.

They made the rest of the drive in silence, each lost in his own thoughts. Lex pulled up in front of the Stevens's residence, turned off the engine, and asked Gavin, "You ready for this, Doc?"

"Yeah, I want to get this over with. I thought this was a good idea up until about now."

"You'll be fine. Let's go."

Once out of the truck, Lex walked next to Gavin, who was taking his sweet time going up the walk to the front door. It was the first test of Lex's resolve not to do anything to let on that they were more than friends. He shoved his hands in his pockets to keep from touching the doc.

Gavin rang the doorbell, fidgeting with his hair as he stood on the stoop. An older woman opened the large oak door, her face lighting up in obvious pleasure when she saw him.

"Oh, Gavin, honey, it's so good to see you," she said as she hugged him.

"It's good to see you too, Mom," Gavin said but then pulled away. "I mean Cora or Mrs. Stevens... I'm not sure what to call you anymore."

Her smile seemed genuine when she said, "You can call me whatever you feel comfortable calling me, honey. I want you to know that Tom and I have nothing against you."

Gavin relaxed visibly at the woman's warm words, and then Cora noticed Gavin wasn't alone on her porch. "Um, this is Lex. He's a friend of mine. Lex, this is Cora, my mother...ex-mother-in-law," Gavin said in introduction.

She looked Lex up and down and then smiled. "It's nice to meet you, Lex," she said as she shook his hand and then added, "I don't blame you for bringing backup, Gavin. I'm just glad you didn't bring Riley."

Lex chuckled. Cora came across as a really nice lady—too bad her daughter didn't get some of that charm. "It's nice to meet you too, ma'am."

"Yeah, I figured I wouldn't get a word in edgewise if I brought Ri, and we might need an ambulance by the end of it," Gavin said.

"They never did get along," Cora explained to Lex.

Lex was surprised by the way the two of them joked with each other after all the woman's daughter had done to Gavin. It was a testament to what a forgiving man Gavin was, but Lex hoped it wouldn't bite them in the ass in the end.

Cora led them to the back of the house into a large kitchen. Cassie was sitting on a corner bench at the table in the breakfast nook. She looked up and smiled at Gavin, but a frown replaced it when she caught sight of Lex. Lex watched Cassie as she then schooled her emotions and smiled once again.

She didn't stand; instead she held one hand out toward Gavin. "Gav, oh my god, it's so good to see you again." Gavin took her hand and sat next to her on the bench. Cassie didn't release his hand once he was seated.

"It's good to see you too, Cassie. You're looking well," Gavin said. He looked up at Lex and motioned for him to sit too. "Cassie, this is my friend Lex. Lex, this is my Cassie."

Lex's spine stiffened, and his hand faltered halfway across the table. He took a deep breath and shook Cassie's hand even as his heart started beating a little faster. He tried to convince himself it had just been a slip of the tongue. Gavin was used to calling her that, and it was easy to fall back into old habits.

Cassie eyed Lex suspiciously. "Lex, you look familiar. Have we met?"

He'd been there the day she'd been arrested and also in the courtroom during her short trial, but he didn't figure she'd have noticed him on either occasion. "I don't think so. I just have one of those faces that make people feel like they know me," Lex said.

She nodded and turned her attention to Gavin. "I thought we'd have some privacy," she said as she placed her hand under the table. Lex tried to stuff his jealousy down. Gavin was his. He was vindicated when Gavin reached down and pulled Cassie's hand back up to the tabletop.

"There's nothing that we need to discuss that Lex can't hear. He's a good friend of mine," Gavin said.

Cassie spared Lex a quick glance before going back to making serious eye contact with Gavin. "Did you finally get rid of that jackass Riley and his slutty girlfriend?" she asked. Her tone was haughty as if she thought they were beneath her.

Gavin pulled back a little. Cassie had already crossed a line with Gavin. "He's my best friend, and Sheila is not slutty; she's very nice." Gavin defended his friends.

Lex covered his grin. Cassie had quickly gained a strike against her, and he was happy she couldn't help but show her true colors. He had a feeling Cassie was going to try to woo Gavin back with sweet words and promises. Her whole excuse of wanting to apologize had struck Lex as wrong from the get-go. Lex was sure she'd had ulterior motives, and her hand on Gavin's thigh right off the bat proved his instincts were right on.

Cassie waved a hand in the air in a dismissive gesture. "Oh, Gav, you never were a good judge of character. If it weren't for me, you'd have had a whole cadre of undesirables hanging around," she said as she reached out and put her hand on Gavin's cheek. "You're just too nice to pick your own friends. Everyone always takes advantage of you because you're not too bright when it comes to what people are really like." She shot a pointed look in Lex's direction.

Lex bit his tongue, holding in the nasty retort that was just nagging to get out. He was going to strangle that woman if she kept it up.

"Cassie, you know I hate it when you say things like that. Be nice; if you don't have anything nice to say about someone, don't say anything at all," Gavin said like he was scolding a child.

Cassie laughed and patted his cheek. "You sound just like Mona. Did I tell you I talked to her the other day? We discussed getting together when they come up for Thanksgiving. She even mentioned that maybe we could do the holiday together," Cassie said. Her eyes narrowed as she watched Gavin for his reaction.

"Why are you talking to my mom?" Shock was written all over Gavin's face, and his hand reached instinctively for Lex's, but he stopped just before they made contact.

Cassie was watching every move Gavin made, and her jaw clenched when she saw the gesture. "Because she still considers me a part of her family. Do you really think she'll just give up a wonderful daughter-in-law for whatever you bring home next?" The question was a jab aimed at Lex.

"We're divorced, Cassie. You're no longer a part of her family, and you shouldn't be talking to her behind my back. I've never told her about what you've done because I didn't think she needed to know, but if you keep this up, then—"

"Then what, Gavin? Huh, what are you going to do? You going to tell your mommy why we separated in the first place? I'm sure she'd like to hear all the gory details about what her son wanted and—"

Gavin stood up so abruptly that he almost knocked the table over. "Stop it, Cassie. Just stop. I'm done with this. I have no idea why I even agreed to see you. I thought you'd changed. I thought that you'd gotten help and were back to the person you used to be, but you're still a mean woman." His voice shook like he was on the verge of tears.

Lex watched Cassie as Gavin was talking. Her expression never changed from the vindictive amusement she'd had when she was trying to spill Gavin's secrets in front of Lex. Lex had no idea what she was talking about, but whatever it was, it probably wasn't as bad as Gavin thought. Gavin was naïve enough to think certain sexual acts were shameful, but unless he'd wanted to harm someone in some way, whatever Gavin had wanted from Cassie would probably seem tame to most people.

"I'm not mean, Gavin. I just tell it like it is. I'm going to tell your mother everything if you don't reconsider this divorce. I want another chance," Cassie demanded. She looked at Lex. "I'm sure your friend here would only want what's best for you."

Lex stood up and grabbed Gavin's arm. "I think it's time we go." Lex started pulling Gavin along with him. Cassie was bat-shit crazy. Why would she want another chance if whatever Gavin had asked her for had set her off so badly that she'd tormented him for months? Nope, no way was she getting even a little close to Lex's man ever again.

"Gavin, you heard me. I mean it. I'll do whatever I have to, and you know I will," she screamed. Cassie got up, but before she took two steps in Gavin's direction, Lex pulled his badge out and shoved it in her face. She stopped short.

"Yeah, I thought so," Lex said. "Now you listen to me, ma'am, I heard that threat, and I will remember it. If anything happens to Gavin or his property, I'll know where to look. The restraining order is still in effect, and any violation of your probation will be reported next time. I'll personally make sure of that."

Cora came into the room just as Lex finished his little speech. She put her hand over her mouth, her eyes tearing as she looked at Cassie. "Oh,

Cassie, you said you just wanted to say you were sorry." Cassie's mom had had no idea her daughter had planned more than an apology.

"He brought a fucking cop!" Cassie yowled like it was an excuse for her behavior.

"Ma'am, Gavin and I are leaving now; thank you for your hospitality. I'd keep an eye on her if I were you." Lex ignored Cassie's outburst as he pulled Gavin to the front door.

"Cora, I'm so sorry," Gavin said.

"Oh, honey, you have nothing to be sorry for. I wish I would have known. You take care now, okay?" she said as they stepped out of the door.

"Thank you," Gavin said over his shoulder because Lex was dragging him to the truck. Lex could hear Cassie, who'd stayed in the kitchen, screaming out threats he didn't care to hear.

Lex opened the door and stuffed the doc into his seat. He walked around and tried not to slam his door too hard. "That is a seriously messed-up chick, Doc. You need to be careful. I don't trust her." Lex turned the key in the ignition.

"Lex, about what she said..." Gavin said worriedly. His cheeks were flushed, and his eyes had that wild look in them.

"Don't worry about it, Doc. I don't give a shit about one word that came out of her mouth." Lex drove faster than he should to get them back to Gavin's house. The doc was all fidgety, and they needed to talk. He just hoped he could convince Gavin whatever it was he needed to say wouldn't change how Lex felt about him.

NINETEEN

GAVIN WAS RELIEVED once they got into his house. Being home always made him feel better. Lex followed him quietly into the kitchen and waited patiently as Gavin started the coffeepot. He avoided meeting Lex's eyes because he was afraid of the judgment he'd see there. Lex, along with Riley and Sheila, had warned him meeting with Cassie was a bad idea, but he'd gone and done it anyway. So now it was only fitting he should have to pay the piper by being forced to tell Lex everything. He watched the coffee drip slowly into the carafe while trying to think of a way to start. Lex cleared his throat behind Gavin.

"Doc, I'm going to be in the living room if you want to talk." He put his hand on Gavin's shoulder. "You don't have to explain anything to me. What went on in your marriage is nobody's business but your own, but I have a feeling it's not as bad as you're making it out to be. Maybe if you just get it out into the open, you'll feel better." Gavin nodded, and Lex's hand left his shoulder before he turned to walk out.

Gavin waited until the coffee was done brewing and poured two cups. He was going to tell Lex what Cassie was holding over his head. He was ashamed to admit what had driven the final nail into the coffin of his marriage, but Lex was right; he needed to get it off his chest. He handed Lex his coffee, and Lex murmured his thanks. Gavin sat on the couch and turned to pull his legs up. He cradled his coffee cup in his hands while thinking about how to start.

Gavin took a deep breath. He knew he was about to change what Lex thought about him, but he didn't see a way to avoid the conversation. Focusing on his coffee cup, he said, "Cassie was always the aggressor in our relationship. I mean she always initiated sex, and if I tried, she shut me down, so I stopped trying pretty early on. At first it was fine because she wanted to have sex a lot even after we got married. Everyone had told me that 'once you put a ring on their finger they stopped spreading their legs.'" Gavin stopped and blushed because those were Riley's words, not his, and they felt weird coming out of his mouth.

Lex chuckled. "Sounds like Riley."

Gavin smiled because Lex had hit the nail on the head. "Yeah, Riley. So anyway, the last couple of years she kind of stopped wanting sex, at least with me. I wondered if she was cheating on me and then..." Gavin stopped and took a deep breath because what he was going to say next would sound bad. "I started to fantasize about her with other guys, you know? About watching other men have sex with her in front of me, and it turned me on."

He ventured a quick peek at Lex. Lex was sipping his coffee and didn't look disgusted by Gavin's confession at all, so Gavin gathered up his courage and went on. "I finally asked her if she was cheating on me. We had a big argument about it because she denied it, and I wasn't convinced. I guess I still don't know if she was cheating on me back then. Of course, we had this amazing makeup sex, and afterward I told her about what I'd been thinking. I thought I could tell her anything, so I brought up the idea of having another guy join us. Part of me figured that if she was cheating on me anyway, I may as well get to see my fantasy played out by watching her have sex with someone else. What could it hurt if we both agreed to it, you know? Besides, I was desperate to do whatever she wanted to get her to stay, and if it meant letting her have sex with other guys, then that was what I was prepared to do."

Lex's hand was warm from his coffee cup when he laid it on Gavin's bare ankle. He rubbed his thumb across the exposed flesh. "Okay so you wanted to watch your wife get fucked by another guy. Kind of explains why you liked the threesomes so much. But still, I don't get why all the shit from Cassie. It's not like you suggested that you fuck someone and she watch. If she didn't want to do it, why not just say so and move on?"

"She was so mad, said it was perverted that I wanted to watch her get gangbanged—her words not mine. It started this whole downward spiral, and the last couple of months she'd just poke at me with comments about how I wasn't a real man. She said it was pretty bad that I knew I was such a bad lay that I'd offered to let her fuck around so she'd stay. She said that I wanted to watch some guy fuck her so I could see how a real man would do it." Gavin was ashamed to admit the things Cassie had said to him because on some level he'd believed all of it. She had always told him he was lucky he had her, that she was too good for him, and he'd believed that too.

"Then she set it up so I'd walk in on her with the fucking UPS man." Gavin could feel the old anger bubbling up again but tamped it down. "The worst part was, as I was standing there watching this guy fuck my wife, she said, 'Don't worry, Darren, my husband likes to watch me get fucked, don't you, Gav? You want him to fuck you next, sweetheart?' in the most taunting voice she could because she knew how much I hated when she mocked me. It was so humiliating. I just turned around and ran out because I knew if I had to look at the smirk on that guy's face for another second, I'd snap and maybe do something I'd regret later." Gavin stopped because his hands were shaking so hard the coffee was sloshing over the rim of his cup and onto his thigh.

Lex took the cup from Gavin and set it on the table. Lex pulled Gavin into his lap and wrapped his strong arms around him. Gavin bent down so he could nuzzle his face into Lex's neck. He'd never felt as secure as he did in Lex's arms, breathing in the man's scent. It should bother him, make him feel emasculated that he needed Lex's strength, but for some reason, it didn't.

"So I still don't get why she's been harassing you," Lex said into Gavin's hair.

"Because I wanted the divorce. She thought that she could do whatever she wanted to me, and I'd stay with her, but when I asked her to leave, she got nasty. I think maybe she really believes that I'm sick in some way, that I wanted what I wanted because I'm perverted, and maybe I am," Gavin said because it sure felt like he was. Who jerked off thinking about their wife getting fucked by some faceless stranger?

"Babe, you are so far from perverted it's almost sad."

"What do you mean?" Gavin smooshed his nose farther into the crease of Lex's neck.

"I mean you are so straight-laced you'd give Mister Rogers a run for his money. Just so you know, the whole getting off thinking about your wife cheating isn't a new thing that you invented. There's tons of adultery porn out there," Lex assured him.

"You're kidding me." Obviously Lex was yanking his chain or maybe just trying to make him feel better about it.

"No, I'm not, I could totally see you in his cardigan singing about wanting to be my neighbor," Lex said. Gavin pulled his face out of Lex's neck so he could see his expression. The smirk told him Lex had intentionally misunderstood him. Lex shrugged. "It has something to do with men needing to know their partner is desirable to others. It gets us revved up to know other guys want what we have, and it makes our partners more desirable to us because they're wanted by others. Basic human psychology. Didn't you take that in college?"

"I must have missed that lecture," Gavin said. "So what now?"

"What now, what?"

"What now that you know my shameful secret?" Gavin bit his lip in worry.

Lex tightened his arms around Gavin's body. "Nothing, because I don't think you have anything to be ashamed of. What happens between two people in the privacy of their own home is nothing that needs to be talked about by anyone but the people involved. I was worried that you wanted to kill puppies and have sex in their blood. This, what you just told me is nothing. I thought maybe you were blowing it out of proportion, and I know that it doesn't feel that way to you because it's how you feel, but trust me when I say there's a lot worse things you could have wanted. I hope that makes you feel a little better."

"It does some, but what if Cassie tells my mom?" The thought of his mom hearing about his perversion was worse than telling Lex about it himself.

"Then that's on Cassie, but I do think maybe you need to tell your parents what's been going on with her so they may take what she says with a grain of salt and not just swallow it without question. I think you also need to be careful because Cassie's unhinged and probably unpredictable. I don't think she's got a mental health issue. I think she's a malicious bitch who's pissed because she didn't get her way."

"Lex, that's not very nice. She's seen a doctor—"

"I saw how she looked at you, Doc. She wants what she wants, and she said it herself—she'll do anything to get it. She wants you. I thought she was the one who started the divorce proceedings, not you. Now at least I can kind of get why she's going after you, but I don't get how she thinks fucking with you will get you to take her back." Gavin could see the concern on Lex's handsome face but also the calculated cop mind working behind it.

"She thinks I'll give in if she makes my life hard enough because she knows I'm not strong. She knows I need someone to lean on." Gavin hated that about himself too, but he knew his own weakness.

Lex's hands left his body and grabbed his face. "Well now, Doc, you have me to lean on, and believe me, I'm one protective son of a bitch, so she better stay the fuck away from what's mine," he growled before kissing Gavin possessively. Gavin couldn't help the way he melted into Lex's arms.

"WHAT THE HELL are you two supposed to be?" Riley asked as Gavin and Lex stood at the door to his and Sheila's condo.

"Guess," Gavin said as Riley led them through the party to get drinks. Sheila was standing near the makeshift bar. She hugged Lex and then Gavin.

"I don't know," Riley said as he handed them each a smoking glass. He pointed at Lex. "You look like you dressed as Gavin on a day at the clinic where the director is in." He looked over Gavin and was about to say what he thought when Sheila cut in.

"And Gav looks like Riley on a day when he showed up for his shift in the ER after drinking an entire bottle of rum." She laughed and high-fived Lex.

"Bitch." Riley straightened his boobs and flipped the hair of his long purple wig at Sheila. "So tell me, since I have no clue."

"Dr. Jekyll and Mr. Hyde, you doofus," Gavin said. "What the hell are you supposed to be besides a big purple-haired drag queen?"

"Um, that's exactly what I am," Riley said. He preened for his audience.

Lex looked him over. "I have a friend who could teach you how to tuck that in better." He pointed at Riley's crotch bulge.

"No hiding that thing. It's massive!" Riley smirked before he wobbled off to greet more guests, leaving Gavin and Lex to mingle.

The party was fun, but he and Lex had to bow out early so they could hit Mike's party too.

When they arrived at Mike's door, they were greeted by the man himself. "Hey, it's a good thing you two showed up. It's not a party until Jekyll and Hyde make an appearance."

"Lex told you, didn't he?" Gavin asked.

"No way, man. I'm just that good." Mike ushered them inside and introduced Gavin to some of his friends. He handed Gavin a beer, but Lex refused his because he had to work in a few hours.

Gavin was glad Mike had forgiven him for his standoffishness when they'd first met. He didn't know what Lex had told Mike, but he never made Gavin uncomfortable about it. Mike was a decent enough guy; he was kind of like Lex's very own Riley, just not as sassy.

Gavin was listening to the guys talk about work when he caught something that made him turn a questioning look at Lex. "You're changing jobs?" he asked, wondering why it was the first he'd heard of it.

Lex looked a little sheepish. "Well, I just heard about it myself a couple of days ago, but yeah, I'm gonna be a state trooper." He was smiling and Gavin smiled back, but something about the way Mike was watching them made Gavin nervous.

"Congratulations, I guess, but why didn't you tell me before?" Gavin asked.

Lex actually fidgeted; the man never looked nervous, never, so the back of Gavin's neck prickled. "I wanted to wait so we could discuss everything when I had all the details," Lex said.

"What details?" Lex wasn't telling him something, and it wasn't something good if he went by what Lex's body language was saying.

"Can we do this later when we're alone?" Lex asked.

Gavin didn't like the sound of that at all, but he let it go. After that, the party dragged for Gavin. The fun was sucked out of it by the concerned looks Lex kept throwing his way. He drank way more than he should have because he didn't want to think about what Lex needed to tell him about his new job. Then, Lex had to help Gavin to the truck when they decided to leave.

"Doc, please don't be upset. It's not really a big deal. We'll talk about it when I get off tomorrow," Lex said after he got in beside Gavin. He probably guessed why Gavin had gotten sloppy drunk. "I just didn't want to get into it until I knew exactly what was going to happen. I wasn't hiding it from you."

Gavin nodded drunkenly. "Sure okay, Lex, we can talk later. It's not like you're moving to Alaska or something right?"

Lex chuckled. "Yeah, I don't think there's much call for Minnesota state troopers in Alaska."

Gavin smiled as Lex leaned across the seat to kiss him. "Home, Jeeves, I'm a bit snookered and think I should take to my bed for the evening," Gavin said, trying for a passable English accent.

Lex laughed as he pulled out of his parking spot. "Just don't trip over Agent when we get there. He holds a grudge and will poop in your shoes if you piss him off."

Gavin hummed. He liked Lex's dog, but he could see the old mutt taking revenge if he felt slighted. "Can he sleep in my bed with me when you leave?"

"No way, Doc. He'll get spoiled, and then you'll never get him to sleep in his own bed again. Then when my mom comes home, and he gets in bed with her, I'll have to explain that it was your fault, and she'll give you this look every time she sees you," Lex said.

"Fine." Gavin pretended to pout the rest of the way home.

Lex practically had to carry Gavin into the house. Leaving Gavin in the bathroom, he went to check on Agent to make sure the dog was down for the night. When he found Gavin standing against the counter in the bathroom, instead of in the shower, Lex stripped them both and followed Gavin into the stall. Lex even held him up and scrubbed the makeup off his face because Gavin looked like his legs were turning to rubber the longer he tried to stay standing.

"You're a bad drunk, Doc," Lex said as he toweled Gavin off.

"Ahh, I think I'm a good drunk cuz I got you to wash me and dry me and..." He pulled Lex's still damp body into his. "I got you naked and wet too." He rubbed up against Lex's hip, letting him feel how hard his cock was.

"Okay, I take it back, you're a naughty drunk," Lex said, but he didn't push Gavin away. He grabbed Gavin's ass and pulled him closer. Gavin lifted one of his legs and wrapped it around Lex's hip. Lex groaned, and before Gavin knew what was happening, his other leg was lifted, and he was forced to wrap his arms around Lex's neck to keep from falling.

"You're just a he-man aren't you?" Gavin tightened his legs around Lex's body and let the man support his weight, trusting that Lex wouldn't drop him.

"You have no idea." Lex bit at Gavin's neck.

Fuck, it was such a turn-on to be manhandled by Lex. Gavin's mind turned to other ways he wanted him. He'd been too afraid to ask for the thing that he'd been thinking about for the last week or so, but the alcohol made him brave.

Gavin watched himself in the bathroom mirror over Lex's head as he said, "I want you to fuck me." Lex's questing lips stopped, and the hands that were massaging Gavin's ass squeezed almost painfully tight. "Please, Lex, I really want you to." Gavin lifted so Lex's cock went from being trapped between them to under his ass. He felt the head brush between his spread cheeks and shivered.

Lex whimpered at the contact but then shook his head. "No, Doc, not like this." He made Gavin release his legs so Lex could put him down. "You're drunk, and I won't do something like that when you don't know what you're asking for."

Gavin could see the desire in Lex's eyes; his pupils were completely lust blown. How the man could control himself Gavin didn't know, but he knew better than to beg because Lex wouldn't do something he thought was unethical, and what he was asking of Lex crossed that line.

"Okay, but soon," Gavin said, following Lex into his bedroom.

"I'll do anything you want, Doc, when you're sober enough to ask for it." Gavin stuck his tongue out because Lex was ribbing him about not being able to ask for it when he was sober.

They got into bed. "I'm gonna ask you." Gavin kissed Lex and rolled away from him.

"What, so because I'm not going to fuck you when you're drunk, it means that I gotta go to bed with a hard-on?"

Gavin snuggled back into him, his ass pressed into Lex's groin. He wiggled a little, letting Lex's hardness rub against his ass and tried not to giggle when Lex groaned. "What's wrong, babe? Can't sleep?" Gavin teased.

Lex rolled away and rummaged through the nightstand. Gavin's heart pounded in anticipation as he thought about the supplies they'd bought and stashed in there. He only hoped he hadn't pushed Lex too far, that he'd be gentle.

When Lex fitted his body back next to his, Gavin could feel the cold lube Lex had applied to himself. But instead of putting his cock in the crease of Gavin's ass, Lex pulled Gavin back and pushed between his thighs. Gavin held still as Lex's cock slid between his thighs, and his hot breath ghosted across Gavin's neck. The head of his cock nudged Gavin's balls and sent a tingle through him. Lex's hand wrapped around Gavin's cock, giving him a slick fist to push into.

"Yeah, that's it, Doc. Squeeze your legs together a little more...oh fuck..." Lex moaned as Gavin pressed his thighs together, giving him more friction as he fucked them. Lex's hand worked Gavin's cock in time to his thrusts.

"Lex, I'm gonna come," Gavin panted when he felt his orgasm mounting. He never lasted very long with Lex; it was a little embarrassing how quickly the man could make him come.

"Come for me, baby," Lex said as he pumped Gavin faster. Gavin let go and came over Lex's hand. Lex was still thrusting between his thighs, and Gavin tried to not let his muscles turn to jelly. When Lex's sticky hand grasped his chest, Gavin didn't know what came over him, but he grabbed it and took two fingers, covered in his own seed, into his mouth. The bitter, salty taste of his own come filled his senses as Lex shouted out Gavin's name, the wetness spreading between Gavin's thighs and over his balls.

Lex pulled his fingers from Gavin's lips and rolled him to his back so he could devour his mouth. "You're so fucking nasty, Doc," Lex growled when he let Gavin up for air. Gavin tried to turn his head to hide his face, but Lex grabbed his chin. "It's sexy as hell. Don't you ever be ashamed of what we do in bed or what you want, got it? I'll never shame you for what turns you on, so don't be afraid to tell me. I'm not Cassie."

Gavin still had a hard time looking Lex in the eyes, but he nodded, and Lex kissed him again. He waited patiently as Lex got a rag from the bathroom and came back to clean up their mess. He liked it when Lex took care of him; it made him feel like Lex loved him. Gavin certainly hoped Lex would eventually love him because he was pretty sure he loved Lex.

TWENTY

LEX HAD AN uneasy feeling as he got ready for his shift. He couldn't put his finger on it, but something seemed off in the doc's house. He walked around trying to figure out if something was out of place, but nothing caught his eye. He took a few deep breaths as he stood in the living room and gave it another quick pass. Nothing. He didn't like leaving Gavin alone when he felt there was something he was missing.

He went to the kitchen where Agent was snoring on his bed. Filling a glass with water, he shook a couple of aspirin into his palm. He whistled low, and the dog's ears pricked up. "Come, Agent." It took Agent a couple of seconds to get up and heel to Lex's side. Lex led the old mutt into the doc's bedroom. He put the glass and pills on the nightstand and helped Agent up on the end of the bed before he leaned over and kissed Gavin softly on the lips.

Gavin murmured in his sleep but didn't wake up enough to acknowledge Lex's good-bye kiss. Lex smiled, thinking the poor guy was going to be hungover when he got up. Checking to make sure he had everything he needed, he patted Agent on the head.

"Keep an eye on him," Lex commanded. Agent growled and lay his head down on his front paws. He was snoring before Lex left the room. Lex shook his head. He wasn't sure what he expected his nearly fifteen-year-old dog to do, but he felt better knowing Gavin wasn't alone. Plus, it would be a nice surprise for the doc; Lex rarely gave in when it came to long-established rules like no dogs in the bed.

He pulled on his coat and stepped out onto the porch. The first of November was dawning on a crisp note; Lex could feel the edge of winter in the air. When he backed out of the doc's driveway, he noted the white sedan parked across the street but only because it was facing the wrong way to be parked on that side of the road. He huffed out a breath; he still had forty minutes until he was on duty, and he hated writing parking tickets—he wasn't a meter maid—so he drove by the car without a second thought.

"I HATE THE day after Halloween," Grady groused as they took a drive through one of the nicer neighborhoods. Even here, Lex noted the pumpkins smashed on the road and the occasional egged car or mailbox.

"Just be glad we weren't on last night," Lex said. He'd worked previous Halloweens, and the only night to be on duty that sucked more was New Year's Eve.

"Yeah, I heard they arrested four vampires and a couple of werewolves last night," Grady said.

Lex chuckled because that was nothing new, but the guy who had been dressed as a hot dog was something else. "Can you imagine walking around naked with your dick in a bun all night?" he asked when he couldn't get the picture out of his head.

Grady guffawed. "He wasn't naked. He had pasties on his nipples and socks and shoes on. And technically, even his wiener was covered if you count the ketchup and mustard. "

They both had a good laugh over the look on Santiago's face when she'd relayed that story to the entire squad room. When the radio went off, Lex quieted to hear what was being said. He only caught the end, so he shushed Grady and listened when it was repeated.

His heart thudded, and he felt the blood drain from his face. He looked at Grady and asked, "Did she say 1222 Grover Avenue?"

Grady shrugged. "I think so... Why does that ring a bell?"

"Oh god, oh god." Lex chanted as he hit the lights and sirens and made an illegal U-turn. "Just radio it in that we're responding."

"What the fuck, Turner? That's halfway across town. Someone else has to be closer than us," Grady hollered as he held on for dear life.

"Just do it because we're going."

"They were just calling in because the fire department had been called. We'll just be standing around for nothing anyway," Grady said, annoyed.

"Switch over and see what's happening," Lex gritted out through clenched teeth. "It's the doc's house, Grady. We've been there. That's why the address rings a bell." Lex shouldn't be taking his fear for Gavin out on Grady, but Christ, why couldn't the man just do what he asked? Finally, he listened while Grady told dispatch that they were responding to the call.

Lex sped across town, flying through red lights and swerving around the light traffic. When he caught sight of the smoke rising over the trees, his heart jumped into his throat. He bit his tongue and swallowed the sob that threatened to escape. He ignored Grady's pleas for him to slow down; nothing was going to stop him from getting to Gavin.

They pulled onto Grover just behind the ambulance. Lex swung the car up against the curb and threw his door open. He was out and running as soon as his feet touched the ground. "Turner, where are you going?" Grady called after him. Lex was already past the fire truck, heedless of the warnings shouted at him as he tried to get to the house.

Someone grabbed his arm, and he was almost pulled off his feet by the sudden loss of forward momentum. Grady came up behind him and grabbed Lex around the waist when he tried to fight off the fireman who had stopped him.

"Let me go. He's in there. I have to get him," Lex growled. If the doc had gotten out, he would have seen him on the lawn, and Agent would have come to him the minute he saw Lex. No, they were still in that house, and he needed to get to them; they were his responsibility.

"Calm down, Turner. The firemen are in there right now, and they'll bring him out," Grady said, his mouth pressed to Lex's ear.

"I shouldn't have left him. I knew there was something... I just couldn't figure it out... Oh god, Doc." Lex couldn't stifle the sob that tore loose from his chest as his knees went weak, but Grady's hold kept him up. The flames were licking up the back of Gavin's house, and Lex could feel the heat from the fire against his face. How long had Gavin been in there with all that smoke and heat?

There was chaos around him as shouts rang out. They were bringing someone out. Lex looked up just as one of the firemen in full gear came out with what could only be Gavin, wrapped in a blanket, over his shoulder, and the one behind him was carrying a smaller bundle in his arms. The paramedics rushed in to do their jobs. Lex fought against Grady's hold once again, and this time Grady let him go.

Lex made his way across the lawn, but once again, he was stopped before he could reach his goal. "Officer, hey, officer." Someone was trying to flag him down. He turned and saw an older man trying to catch up to him. "I saw someone parked on the street this morning. I think it may have been his wife," the man said.

"When was that?" he asked, but he couldn't stop looking over to where Gavin now lay on a stretcher. His hands itched to touch the doc and make sure he was okay, but the mention of Gavin's ex got his attention.

"Early this morning, I went out to grab my paper, and there was a white car parked in front of my house. I think I saw his wife. I can't be sure it was her, but it looked like her, anyway," he said. "Then probably half an hour later, the dog started barking like crazy, and he kept at it for ten minutes, maybe longer. I was going to come over to ask Gavin if he could quiet it down. I stepped out and saw the smoke, so I called 9-1-1. I don't know when he got the dog." The old man looked thoughtful, like that was at all important at a time like this, Lex thought.

Lex looked around and realized he and Grady weren't the only ones who had responded to the call. He motioned to one of the other officers, who jogged across the yard to where they were standing. "Will you tell Officer Nelson here what you just told me? Make sure you tell them everything you told me and anything else you can remember about the car and person you saw in it," Lex said.

"Okay, sure," the man said.

"Thank you," Lex said before he turned and made his way to the ambulance, ignoring Nelson's questioning look. Lex's mind reeled as he tried to remember if there was anyone in the car he'd seen as he left for work. He was sure it had been empty at that time.

He stepped up as close to the stretcher as he could get without getting in the way. The oxygen mask covered half the doc's grimy face. Gavin appeared to be unconscious, and there was blood running down from his head, mixing with the soot. Lex wanted to go to him and hold him just to assure himself Gavin was still alive but hung back and let the medics do their jobs. He listened as the paramedics talked between themselves until he was sure that none of Gavin's injuries were life-threatening before he turned to look for Agent.

Grady was standing over the dog while one of the firemen on his knees shook his head. "He needs to go to the emergency vet clinic over on Harper," the fireman said.

"He's my dog." Lex knelt down and buried his face in Agent's smoky fur.

Lex was torn. He knew Gavin would survive, and he really wanted to be at the hospital, but he had to take Agent to the vet. His barking may have been what saved the man Lex loved. He was spared from making the choice when Grady said, "I'll take the dog, Turner. You go with the doc."

Lex looked up at Grady. He'd have a lot of questions to answer later, but Grady was offering to help without asking them now, and he was thankful for that. Lex picked Agent up. "You're a good dog, Agent, a very good dog. I love you, and I'll be there as soon as I know the doc's gonna be okay." He handed Agent to Grady. "Thanks Grady. Call me as soon as you know anything." Agent's breathing was labored, and his eyes rolled wildly as Grady took him into his arms. Lex hoped it wouldn't be the last time he'd see his dog alive.

"I'm sorry, Turner," Grady said before he turned and walked off toward their squad car.

Lex walked back to where they were loading Gavin into the ambulance. One of the paramedics stopped him when he tried to follow the stretcher inside.

"Is he under arrest?" the medic asked. At first Lex didn't understand the question, but when he puzzled it out he shook his head. "Then what's the reason you need to ride along, officer?"

"I'm with him," Lex said. The paramedic looked confused, so Lex clarified it for him. "I mean, we're together. He's my boyfriend." The man's eyebrows rose up to his hairline. If the guy had been bald, they might have shot straight off his head with nothing there to stop them.

"Okay, I guess—"

"I'm going with you. My partner just left with my dog, so I have no way to get to the hospital," Lex said.

"It was your dog that bit him?" the man asked. He let Lex climb in after him.

Lex looked at the paramedic's name tag. "Albright, are you saying my dog bit my boyfriend?" Lex asked incredulous at the accusation leveled at his beloved pet. Agent never bit anyone in his entire life.

The doors closed and the engine started before Albright nodded. He pointed to Gavin's bandaged forearm. "There's a pretty nasty bite on his arm. Looks like he sunk his teeth in and either pulled or your boyfriend tried to pull away from him."

Lex nodded, but he had no idea why Agent would have bitten Gavin. "Why's he unconscious?" Lex was concerned about the fact that Gavin had not yet woken up. He was trying to remain calm, but it was getting harder by the second.

"Best we can figure from what Callard said when he found him was that he fell and hit his head and knocked himself out. That's where all this blood on his face came from. His vitals are stable, but they'll want to give him a CAT scan to see if he has a concussion, and then they'll most likely keep him overnight to monitor his lungs. He was on the ground, and in a room with a closed door farthest from the fire, probably saved his life since he was out cold, but he was still breathing in smoke for some time," Albright said, fiddling with various things before attaching them to Gavin.

"Can I make a couple of calls?" Lex asked. When Albright nodded, Lex pulled out his cell phone and called Riley. Getting no answer, he called Sheila. He gave her a quick rundown on the situation, and she agreed to call Gavin's parents and then meet them at the emergency room where Riley was working. Lex also called his mom who was in the cities visiting his aunt and uncle. By the time she hung up, she was practically hysterical about both Gavin and Agent being hurt. She promised, at Lex's insistence, to have her brother drive her back instead of coming on her own.

The ambulance jerked to a stop just as Gavin let out a low moan. His eyes opened slightly when he tried to raise his hand but couldn't. "Hey there, try to lie still. We're at County General. We're going to unload now. You've sustained a few injuries, and you need to be checked out," Albright said in a soothing voice when Gavin's eyes widened in panic.

Lex put his hand on the doc's leg, drawing his attention. "Hey there, Doc, you're gonna be fine. Just relax, okay?" Lex assured him. Gavin settled at Lex's words. The doors were opened, and Lex stepped out to face an agitated Riley.

"What the fuck happened, Lex? I thought you were staying with him?" Riley asked.

"I had to work. There was a fire. I don't have any of the details yet, but Gavin's going to be fine, maybe a concussion and smoke inhalation, but he wasn't burned or anything," Lex said.

"Don't forget the dog bite," Albright said. "Did your dog have all his shots? They'll want to know."

"Your dog bit him?" Riley asked, the look on his face thunderous.

Gavin was trying to pull on the oxygen mask as he was being taken out of the ambulance. "Doc, stop that. Leave it on," Lex scolded Gavin and then turned back to Riley. "I guess he did, but I don't know why. He's never bitten anyone before, but he's had all his shots."

They followed the stretcher into the ER. Gavin kept trying to get Lex and Riley's attention, and they kept telling him to lie still. "They won't let me treat him. I'm his emergency contact, and they all know we're friends, but I'll be able to keep you updated better than you'd usually be," Riley said when Lex was stopped from going into the back with them.

"That's fine. I have some more calls to make. Sheila's on her way, and she's calling his parents," Lex said before the door closed behind the doctors and nurses.

Lex paced a little and then called his sergeant to let him know that he needed to take the rest of his shift off and probably a personal day for the next shift. The Sergeant had already heard from Grady, and Lex could hear the question in his voice, but he didn't answer it. He'd come clean about his relationship with Gavin when he went in for his next shift, even though he'd hoped he wouldn't have to reveal his personal life in the two months he had left before his job with the state troopers started. He sighed when he hung up. He was relieved when Sheila came barreling through the door and into his arms.

"Oh my god, Lex, what happened? Do they know how the fire started? Is Riley in there with Gav? Is he going to be okay?" she asked in rapid succession before stepping back to wait for answers.

"Gavin's fine; he was awake when they took him back. Riley's back there, but he's not his doctor. He said he'd come out and tell me when they know something." Lex tried to answer all of her questions.

"I can't believe this. He's going to be heartbroken over his house. He loved that damn house more than anything. Did they say how it started?" she asked.

"No, and I'm sure they won't know for a while yet. They were still trying to put it out when we left," he said. "I need to make a call. Agent was in the bedroom with him, and I'm not sure..." Lex trailed off because now that he was sure Gavin was going to survive, his thoughts turned to his dog and the fact that the old mutt might not.

Sheila wrapped him once again in a tight hug. "I'm so sorry, Lex. Go and make your call, and if you need to leave, go. Riley and I will make sure that Gav knows everything. I'm sure he'd want you to be there with

Agent." Lex wanted to believe her, but he had really wanted to talk to Gavin before he left.

"I'm going to call Grady to see if he has any news. I don't want to leave unless I have to," Lex said. Sheila let him go and patted his arm in sympathy. He tried to smile at her to let her know that he was okay, but it probably came across as false as it felt. He stepped out into the bright morning light. It was still chilly, but that just helped to clear Lex's head as he dialed Grady.

"Hey, Turner, I was just going to call you. How's the doc doing?" Grady asked.

"I think he's going to be fine; haven't heard anything yet. How's Agent?"

Grady cleared his throat, which Lex took to mean not too good. "Well I think if you can get over here that might be good. He's got something with his lungs because of the smoke, and the vet says that at the dog's age it's going to be a pain in the ass for him to heal. I can't make a decision for you, but the vet says it's probably plenty painful for him just to breathe right now," Grady said.

Lex clutched the phone in his hand and took a couple of deep breaths. He understood what Grady wasn't saying. The vet who ran the emergency clinic was also the guy Lex usually took Agent to. Lex trusted him, but he needed to see Agent and make the decision himself. "Okay, I'll get a cab and be there in a few," Lex said. Then because he knew it would be harder to do in person he added, "Thanks for doing this for me, for letting me go with the doc and not having to worry that Agent wasn't getting the help he needed. I really appreciate it, Grady."

"Yeah, yeah, Turner, you're welcome; just get your ass over here," Grady said gruffly before he hung up.

Lex told Sheila he was going, so she promised to call him as soon as she had any news on Gavin. Lex then called a cab and made his decision. He thanked Grady once again, before he left as quickly as he could after Lex got there. As Lex listened to the vet explain what was wrong with Agent, it was clear he thought it would be cruel for Lex to prolong the dog's misery.

Lex ran the vet through his paces until the vet sighed and rubbed his face. "I'm sorry, but there's nothing more I can do for him. You could take him home and watch him suffer for a few days until he finally succumbs to the lack of oxygen, but you don't seem like the type to put an animal through that kind of torture. He's fifteen years old. He's had a good life, so let him have a good death."

Lex kept his composure as he nodded and signed the papers. The vet gave him a minute alone with his dog.

Lex lost it when he realized it would be the last time he'd hold Agent in his arms. He let himself cry into the dog's still smoky, dirty fur. He'd gotten Agent for his birthday when his father had pronounced him dependable enough to take care of Agent's needs on his own, and that's what he'd done—he'd cared for and loved his dog even after he'd realized that he really wasn't a dog person. Agent Mulder had been his constant companion as he fought to lose what his mom had called his baby fat, running beside Lex as he ran or rode his bike for hours to get in shape.

"I love you, you know. Don't think for one minute that I ever meant it when I told you I wished you were a cat. Ma loves you too, and I know you can't understand this, but if it weren't for you, she'd still be in bed crying over my dad and sister. I know you didn't mean to hurt the doc, and he was starting to love you too. Our lives won't be the same without you," Lex said through his tears. "Just know that I'm doing what's best for you. I couldn't stand it if I had to watch you in pain for the rest of your life. I hope it's true what they say, and you'll be chasing your ball in a grassy field in the hereafter because you deserve it, buddy."

Lex held Agent as the vet administered the lethal dose. He was assured that they'd keep Agent's body until he could get his own vehicle to pick it up for burial. He took another cab back to the hospital, wondering why he hadn't heard anything from Sheila.

Sheila was still sitting in the waiting room when he walked through the doors, and she smiled up at him as he walked over to her. He plopped down in the chair next to hers, and then she slipped an arm around his shoulders. "Sorry, Lex, I know it's hard. I lost my cat a few months ago, and I thought I'd cry forever over her."

"Thanks. He had a good long life, and it helps to know that. I've been preparing for this for some time now. I'm just worried about how my mom's going to take it." She'd loved the dog like a child. She'd taken care of him while Lex had gone to college. His father's insistence that Agent was Lex's dog was the only reason she gave him back once he had a place for him.

"Yeah, that's going to be hard; just know that we're all here for you guys. Riley came out and told me they have Gavin back getting scanned.

He'll let us know when they're done. He'll be admitted, and we can visit him when he gets to his room," Sheila said. "By then, his parents will probably be here."

"Oh, yeah, how am I supposed to handle them?" Lex asked. Gavin hadn't yet told his parents about their relationship.

Sheila tightened the arm she had around his shoulders. "I'd just play it off as friends for now. Gavin's mom is really overbearing, so brace yourself. To her, he's still a little boy, and she treats him like he's ten years old. Try to ignore it because it makes Gavin uncomfortable when people notice it. Not even Riley pokes fun at him for it, and that's quite telling, dontcha think?"

Lex shuddered at the thought of having to watch Gavin reduced to a child in his parents' presence, but he was more worried about how he was going to have to curb his need to show Gavin the affection he felt for him when they were there. He sighed and leaned back so he could rest his head on the wall. He hadn't gotten much sleep, and before he knew it, Sheila was shaking him awake so they could head up to Gavin's room.

TWENTY-ONE

BEING THAT GAVIN was a doctor, people thought it was funny when he said he didn't like hospitals. What he really meant was he didn't like being a patient in a hospital, not the hospitals themselves. He'd had a bad experience as a child, and though the doctors and nurses were great, the testing and treatment definitely was not.

Gavin had been given a CAT scan, and his brain was fine from what they could see, but the news didn't stop his head from pounding. They'd treated his minor injuries. The cut on his head, though it bled profusely, was actually quite small and just needed a bandage. The dog bite had required a few stitches. He was on oxygen and had a pulse oximeter on his finger because he had suffered from some smoke inhalation. Gavin had felt like he was going to cough up an actual lung at first, but by the time he was deemed ready to be moved to his room, the coughing had subsided to just the occasional fit. His throat was scratchy as heck, though, and downright sore. All he wanted was to drink a few gallons of water, but they made him settle for ice chips and told him not to talk too much.

Riley hovered whenever he had a break in patients. He wanted to know what had happened. Gavin told him all he remembered was waking up when Agent started growling. He'd smelled smoke, got out of bed too fast, tripped over a bunched up towel... after that things got fuzzy. He only vaguely remembered looking blearily up at Agent as the dog tugged at his arm, but he hadn't been able to regain enough consciousness to get himself out of the situation. The next thing he knew, he was in the ambulance with Lex.

Riley walked alongside Gavin's bed as they loaded him into the patient transport elevator. "I told Lex and Sheila where to find you. They'll probably be there waiting by the door," he said. His eyes kept scanning Gavin as he lay there on the bed. Riley was assuring himself that the ER doctor hadn't missed anything since he hadn't been allowed to treat Gavin himself.

"Is Lex mad?" Gavin asked. His voice was raspy; it hurt to talk. Riley flinched at the sound.

"Why would he be mad?" Riley asked. "It's not like you started the fire... Did you?" He shot Gavin a cheeky grin.

Gavin shook his head, which he realized was a bad idea after the fact. No, he hadn't started the fire. He didn't know why, but he had a feeling Lex would be mad. He'd been worrying about it the entire time they'd been working on him; well, that and his house. A tear slipped down his cheek as he lowered his eyelids, the first he'd shed so far but probably not the last.

Riley's hand on his arm as the elevator door opened made him look up at his best friend. "Everything's going to be okay. Don't worry so much." He held Gavin's arm as they rolled him down the hallway. "Oh, and your parents are on their way."

Gavin groaned even though the vibration felt like it was ripping his throat apart. His parents? Why would anyone think it was a good idea to call them? He wasn't at all sure he could deal with the added pressure his parents would put on him.

As they turned the corner, Gavin saw Lex standing in the hall. He was still in his uniform and had a couple of sooty streaks on his cheeks. When they got closer he could see that Lex's eyes were red-rimmed, and though he didn't exactly look angry, he did seem agitated. Lex met Gavin's eyes as they rolled him past into his room. Gavin was about to sigh in relief at Lex's lack of anger, but the feeling passed when Sheila was the first to enter his room while Lex hung back. Lex had to be mad, Gavin was sure of it.

A nurse bustled around hooking up the various machines and checking his IV. "I'll be back to administer some pain meds into that in a few minutes, Dr. Addison," she said before she left the room. He nodded instead of using his voice.

"Hey, Gav, how are you feeling?" Sheila asked as she lowered the bed's railing to give him a quick hug.

"Good," Gavin rasped. He tried to smile, but she noticed his tears and flicked one away with her thumb.

"We were worried about you. I'm so glad you're okay. I talked to your dad, and they're on their way. Should be here anytime now."

Gavin nodded. He was going to try not to talk too much. It hurt and his friends would understand. Looking over Sheila's shoulder, he was surprised to find Lex standing right there. He hadn't even seen Lex come in the room. But Sheila saw why Gavin was distracted and stepped back.

"Riley and I are going to go grab a bite to eat. We'll be back," she said. Gavin nodded again and watched them leave arm in arm. They passed the nurse who quickly pushed the hypodermic of pain reliever into Gavin's IV and left after telling him to buzz if he needed anything.

Lex stood there staring down at Gavin, still not saying anything. Gavin wished he'd start and get it over with. Waiting for Lex to lay into him over the fire, over Agent getting hurt, even over him being dumb enough to trip and hit his head instead of getting out uninjured was driving Gavin insane. Just as he thought he would have to say something to get Lex to speak, Lex practically threw himself onto Gavin's bed and into his arms. Gavin was so startled, it took him a few seconds to return Lex's crushing hug.

"Goddamn it, Doc, I can't leave you alone even for a few hours, can I?" Lex asked into Gavin's neck. Even though the words were teasing, there was emotion behind them, and the wetness on his neck could only be Lex's tears.

Gavin ran his hand through Lex's hair to soothe him. He felt horrible at being the cause of such strong emotion in the man he cared for so much. "I'm sorry. How's Agent?" he whispered in his rough voice. Lex shook his head, and his chest hitched with a sob. Lex clutched Gavin harder, making it even more difficult for him to breathe, but Gavin didn't care; he'd suffocate if that was what it took to make Lex feel better. Obviously Agent hadn't fared as well as he had.

Gavin rocked Lex as he let loose the pent-up emotions he'd been holding in as he waited for this moment. He shed a few of his own tears, for Agent, for his house, and for Lex's grief over his beloved pet. After an indeterminable amount of time had passed, Lex finally pulled back to look at Gavin.

"You look like shit, baby," he said. He ran a hand through Gavin's sooty hair. "Gotta say, I prefer you as a blond, Doc." He leaned in and brushed his lips against Gavin's.

"You don't look that great either," Gavin whispered. He'd never seen Lex as anything other than the big, strong, confident man he was. This softer side of his lover plucked at his heart strings and made him want to be the strong one for once. "Tell me what I missed."

Lex took a shuddery breath. "I had to put Agent down. He was pretty bad off, and it was better for him. I haven't heard anything about the fire yet except it's finally out. The fire marshal will probably be in touch as soon as they know anything," he said. Gavin didn't miss how Lex's eyes darted away from him as he'd finished.

He grabbed Lex's chin to make him look up. "I'm so sorry about Agent. I think I remember him tugging on me, but I couldn't focus and then... I don't remember anything until the ambulance. I'm sorry I killed your dog, Lex. So sorry."

A little flicker in Lex's eyes caught his attention. "You didn't kill my dog, Doc, but..." Lex looked away as his words trailed off. There was something Lex wasn't telling him.

"Tell me what else," he said, pushing his voice past his sore throat to make it more forceful.

"Well—"

"Gavin, my baby, oh my goodness look at you. We came as fast as we could. The traffic on the interstate was god-awful. You'd think that people would be at home on a Sunday morning instead of out clogging up the roadways—" Gavin's mom burst onto the scene with a flurry of words but stopped short. "Who's this?"

She'd gotten to the side of Gavin's bed, and her eyes were locked on the two men who were frozen in their taboo tableau. Lex had his arms around Gavin, and Gavin had one arm around Lex and one hand cupping the other man's face. They broke apart with jerky motions that would have been comical under other circumstances.

"Mom." Gavin looked from his mother to his father and back. "This is my friend Lex."

"Well he shouldn't be on the bed. Scoot, mister," she said through pursed lips as she shooed Lex off the bed. She took Gavin's face in her hands and gave him a good once -over. "Well I guess I should have expected as much." She pulled her huge purse up and sat it on the bed so she could rummage through it. "Aha, I knew I had a pack in here." She pulled out a packet of wet ones and proceeded to mop at Gavin's face.

Gavin sat patiently and let her finish because resistance was futile. He loved his mother, but she could be a bit much at times, and this was going to be one of those times. He met his dad's sympathetic gaze and then dared a glance at Lex. Lex was in a much better mood, it seemed. He stood off to the side, taking in the scene with obvious amusement.

"They never clean people up decently. How do they expect a person to get any rest and heal if they're all grimy? Look at your hair; it's almost black. They should have at least given you a shower before they put you in bed for the rest of the day. I'll talk to the nurse and see if we can't get some supplies, and I can give you a sponge bath and wash all that out of your hair. Criminy, are they really that understaffed that they can't give a person his dignity by letting him get cleaned up?" She stopped wiping Gavin's face and put her hands on her hips. "Well?"

"Um..." Gavin wasn't sure which question he was supposed to answer.

"Mrs. Addison?" Lex asked. Gavin knew Lex was soon going to regret drawing her attention to him, but he was glad he had.

His mother turned to face his boyfriend, her hand still firmly planted on her hip. "Yes? Lex was it? What's that short for? Alexander? It's an unusual shortening for that name; that's for sure, but I guess I could see it if your parents wanted you to stand out. How exactly do you know Gavin? He's never mentioned you, and usually Riley would be here. I'm going to give that boy a piece of my mind when he finally gets here. Do you know why he's not here, and Sheila come to think of it, where is she?" She fired fast, which left Lex no way to answer without interrupting.

"Uh, they went to grab something to eat, so they'll be back soon, I'm sure," Lex said, a perplexed look settling on his face. Gavin felt bad for him, but at least having his mother's word-vomit directed at him had wiped the amusement right off Lex's smirky face. "I was just going to say that the doc's...um...Gavin's throat is sore, and he can't really talk much, or I guess he shouldn't maybe talk a lot right now."

Gavin smiled at Lex; he was sweet when he was flustered. It was nice that he stepped up to be Gavin's voice so he didn't have to endure answering his mother's multitude of questions. Of course, she just waited because Lex had not answered the appropriate question. He watched Lex flounder under her stern look and had to jump in.

"Mom, I'm fine. You guys shouldn't have rushed—"

"Oh, you be quiet now. You're supposed to rest your voice, I guess. Of course we had to come. When you get a call that your child is being rushed to the hospital, well, you rush there too," she said as she tucked the blanket around him. "I was so worried, but your father, of course, wouldn't dare drive even five miles over the speed limit to get us here that much faster. I was sure that you'd be in a coma, and then we'd have to decide if we wanted to keep you on life support or pull the plug. Imagine having to make that decision for your own child; it would have been heart-wrenching. Even worse than when you were in the hospital when you were little, and they didn't know what was wrong with you. Oh, lordy, all those tests and—"

"Momma Mona!" Riley boomed as he walked into the room. He was the only one of Gavin's friends who had ever gotten away with calling his mother by her first name, and it was only because he used momma to preface it. His mother loved Riley, or rather, she loved that she could count on Riley to look after Gavin in her absence.

"Riley, where have you been?" she asked. Thankfully, she went to talk to him away from the bed.

"Hey there, son," his dad said. He put his hand on Gavin's arm and gave it a firm pat. He looked down at Gavin with the same expression he always had. He loved his son and wife, but my god, what had he gotten himself into? Gavin always thought of his father as a man who was on the periphery of things—he never really seemed to be completely there.

"Dad, you guys didn't need to rush down here," Gavin said quietly.

More arm patting as his dad said, "You know your mother; ever since that bout with Lyme disease you had, she's a nervous wreck the minute she hears you have a sniffle."

Gavin nodded because it was true. Lex came up to the other side of the bed with a traumatized look on his face. Gavin was used to that look. He'd seen it plenty of times on people who'd just had a run-in with his mother. He put his hand over the one Lex had resting on the railing of the bed and got a small smile in response. Gavin wished they were still alone. Things just felt right when it was him and Lex with none of life's other distractions to get in the way.

"Mr. Addison, I'm Lex." Lex reached across Gavin to shake Gavin's father's hand.

"Good to meet you, Lex. So how do you know Gavin?"

Gavin shuddered. Explaining how they'd met would mean getting into the whole thing with Cassie, and that would open a whole new can of worms. Gavin couldn't deal with any of it right then.

"We ran into one another one day and just hit it off, I guess." Lex added a casual shrug, making it seem as if it was as likely that was how they met as any other.

"I'm glad to hear it wasn't because you had him in the back of your squad car," his dad said with a small chuckle. "His mother would have him in the woodshed with the strap if he'd gotten arrested."

Gavin shifted in the bed. Geez, he'd known his mom would embarrass him, but he'd had no idea his dad would too. "Dad..."

"No, the doc's a good guy. I'm sure he's never done anything I could arrest him for," Lex said, seamlessly glossing over what his dad had said. Lex's hand turned under Gavin's, and his fingers rubbed Gavin's wrist in a soothing motion. Gavin lay back against the raised bed. He was tired all of a sudden, his family always having that effect on him. Lex noticed and brushed the hair from Gavin's forehead. "You tired, Doc?"

Gavin nodded as he unconsciously leaned into the touch. Lex drew away abruptly. Gavin startled, coming back to himself and remembering they had an audience. "Yeah, sleepy," Gavin managed to get out over the lump in his sore throat. He was drifting as he heard Riley's voice in the background explaining that Gavin's pain meds must have finally kicked in.

"HE SHOULD COME home with us. I can take care of him there. He has nowhere to stay here anyway."

Gavin awoke to his mother's voice. Keeping his eyes closed, he hoped maybe they'd settle this argument without him, and then he could tell his mother he was staying. He had his job and Lex, and even if he had to live in his car, there was no way he was leaving either of them behind.

"He can stay with us. We have a room, and he's welcome to stay as long as he needs. He's only going to be off work for a few days. It doesn't make sense for him to go all the way back home with you and then have to make the trip back." That was Riley.

Yeah, Riley, thank god for your logic but...

"He needs his mother, and he'll come home where he belongs. Now that he doesn't have Cassie or that house to tie him to this place, he may as well start looking into getting a job in La Crosse. There's no reason for him to stay here any longer." His mother's words struck Gavin hard in the chest.

Gavin popped an eye open and looked for Lex. He wasn't in the room, and Gavin wondered if his mother had something to do with that. He coughed, accidentally drawing attention to himself. The heated discussion stopped cold, and the four people in his room turned their eyes to him. Riley was angry, Sheila upset, his dad still not all there, and his mother had her eyes on her goal. Gavin could see the determination in the set of her jaw.

"Oh dear, did we wake you? We were just discussing your travel plans. I think we should head out as soon as you're released. I hope it will be in the morning because I'd hate to hit rush hour traffic. I can get your old room all ready for you. It won't be hard since it's still like you left it after Easter. I just need to refresh the bedding, and you'll have a place to get better without having to worry about anything," his mother said as soon as she noticed Gavin was awake.

"How are you feeling? Need anything?" Riley asked.

Gavin asked for the only thing he wanted. "Lex?"

Shelia smiled. "Jean showed up and talked to your parents for a few minutes before she convinced him to go home with her to eat and change. They should be back soon." She patted his leg. "Riley, why don't we take Mr. and Mrs. Addison out for some supper when Lex and Jean get back? I'm sure they don't want to eat hospital cafeteria food again."

"That's a great idea. What do you say Momma Mona? You want to go get something that's actually edible for supper?" Riley caught on quickly to Sheila's plan.

"I'm not sure. I hate to leave Gavin alone with people I don't know. I mean, who is this Lex character, and why's he hanging around when I've never heard a word about him? It's not like you to not keep me informed about your life, Gavin. I don't think that he's such a good influence on you if you think you need to hide him from your parents—"

"He's a really great guy, and his mom loves Gav like a son. They'll be fine for a couple of hours while we eat. Did you guys check into a hotel, or are you staying with us?" Sheila asked, interrupting and effectively changing the subject. Riley winced at Sheila's roundabout offer to let Gavin's parents stay with them.

"Oh well, we weren't sure what we were going to do. I guess if you have room and don't mind it would be nice. You know I don't like sleeping on hotel sheets. You never know if they actually changed them after the last people. Who knows what could be on those sheets when you lay on them. I've taken my own sheets along with me on vacation before. Remember, Roger, that time when I had to ask for them back when the maid accidentally took them off the bed? You should have seen their faces when they found out why I brought my own sheets. They tried and tried to tell me that their sheets were clean, but I wasn't born yesterday," Mona said.

"I'm going to call Lex and see how long they'll be. Maybe we can head out now if they're on their way." Riley pulled out his phone.

After a quick call and much more fussing on Gavin's mother's part, the foursome left Gavin in peace to wait for Lex and Jean and some much needed sanity.

TWENTY-TWO

LEX RUSHED THROUGH his shower and scarfed down the sandwich his mom handed him. "You ready?" he asked as he grabbed his keys. He wasn't in a hurry to get back to Gavin's mother, Mona, but he could bear her incessant babble for the doc. Lex had formed a not altogether nice opinion of the short, plump, verbose woman who seemed to run right over anyone who got in her way. Seeing the way she treated Gavin, it was a wonder the guy was even remotely normal and able to function in society. He wasn't sure about the father yet. The guy looked like he could be Gavin's older brother, but he didn't say much. Of course, when did he get the chance to talk with a wife who wouldn't shut up?

"Honey, slow down. It's not like he's going anywhere." Jean was finishing her own meal while seated at the counter. So far she had taken Agent's death fairly well, but Lex knew after she had some time to think about it would be when she'd need him most. He hoped he'd have Gavin's situation under control before then.

"I just don't want him to wonder where I am if he wakes up while we're gone." Lex grabbed his jacket and gave her an impatient look.

"They'll explain where you are," she said. "Now why don't you tell me what that phone call was all about before you try to hide it from Gavin?"

He shouldn't have taken the call from Grady in front of his mom. "They think the fire was arson. They brought Cassie in for questioning because the car she just registered a month ago matched the neighbor's description. I really would like to get back to the hospital before someone decides they need to tell Gavin what's going on," he said, not bothering to keep the tinge of irritation out of his voice.

"Lex, he's going to find out eventually. You can't protect him from this, no matter how much you want to." Jean got up and set her plate in the sink before putting her jacket on. "I know you want to be the one to tell him, but sometimes I wonder if you should back off a little when it comes to this mess. Just be there for him instead of trying to control how things happen or trying to fix everything that goes wrong when you can't control it."

Lex chewed his lip in thought. He understood where his mom was coming from. It was one of his faults; he'd done the same thing with her. He didn't know when to quit when it came to protecting his loved ones. How was he supposed to stand by and watch them get hurt?

They were halfway back to the hospital when Lex's phone rang. He dug it out and handed it to his mom when he saw it was Riley calling. Jean told him they were on their way, and Lex let out a breath when it sounded as if they'd have a little time with Gavin alone when they got back.

She hung up after a short conversation. "Riley and Sheila, the dears, are going to take the Addisons out for supper to give Gavin a little rest. They were just wondering if we were on our way so his mother wouldn't worry about leaving him alone."

Lex snorted in amusement. "What does she think will happen? He's in the hospital for Christ's sake. She worried they may come in and literally remove his balls instead of just—?"

"Lex! That is not very..." Jean began, but her laughter made her stop. "Oh boy, don't you say anything bad about his mother to him. You know how boys are about their moms," she warned when she got herself under control.

"Yeah, Ma, I know." He did. A mother was a mother no matter how...chatty.

GAVIN WAS LYING back, with his eyes closed, when Lex and Jean walked into his room. Lex hated to wake him, if he was tired, but he didn't have to worry because the doc's eyes popped open as they approached the bed. A slow, lazy smile took over Gavin's face, and Lex's face mirrored it.

"Look at you, dear; you still need a bath. You're filthy." Jean leaned in and hugged Gavin tightly. "How are you feeling?"

"Good...better at least. Thanks for coming, Jean. I feel bad about everyone rushing around."

"Oh don't you even think that. I'm happy to be here for you. You just let me know if there's anything you need, and I'll make sure you get it,"

Jean said. Lex loved his mom, but the look that crossed Gavin's face had him worried.

"What's up, Doc? Why the worried look?"

Gavin looked nervously from Lex to Jean. "My mom wants me to move back to La Crosse." Though Lex was glad to hear the doc's voice didn't sound as rough as it had earlier, the words hit him hard.

"And what do you want?" Jean asked.

"I want to stay here with Lex," Gavin said. His hand found Lex's and squeezed, and the weight lifted off Lex's chest. "But I'm not sure if my house will be—"

"You know you can stay with me for as long as you need to." The words were out of Lex's mouth before he could even think about what he was proposing. Gavin turned his surprised face to Lex. "I mean, if there's not another option, then there's always my place. That is, if you wanted."

"Thanks, Lex. Riley and Sheila will let me stay in their spare room for as long as I need, but it's nice to know that I have options," Gavin said.

"You do, and going back to La Crosse isn't one I'd endorse." Lex felt like he needed to express his feelings before Gavin gave it too much more thought.

"I'm sure you'll be able to work something out if going back isn't what you want," Jean said. A small smile played around her lips. "So, your parents seem nice."

"My mom's a bit overprotective, but I think her heart's in the right place, and my dad's just...well, he's quiet," Gavin said.

"I take it they don't know about you and Lex?"

"Mom, this is not the time to be discussing this," Lex argued.

"I'm just saying that they didn't really know what to do with you hanging around, so I assumed Gavin hasn't told them you two are a couple yet," she said like it was no big deal. How she picked up on all that in the few minutes she'd spent with the doc's parents was beyond Lex.

"Okay, fine. No, he hasn't told them. It's his decision as to when he does, so can we drop it now?" Lex asked.

"No it's fine," Gavin said. "I haven't told them. I know I should, but I'm afraid of what they'll say. Does that make me a bad person?" Gavin's voice was getting raspy again.

"No, honey, it just makes you human. Don't worry, I won't say anything out of line," Jean assured him. "Oh look, they're bringing you your supper."

Gavin grimaced at the tray the nurse's aide sat in front of him. Lex patted his hand and took a seat next to his mom by the bed. "Eat up, Doc. You don't want me to have to feed you," Lex said with a wink.

They made small talk while Gavin ate and listened. Lex wondered when he should break the news about Cassie. He was enjoying the peace of not having Gavin's mother in the room, and watching the doc eat always made him inexplicably happy.

After an hour, Jean made an excuse to leave, so Lex could have some time alone with Gavin. Lex really loved that woman. He was nervous, though, because he needed to get on with it and tell Gavin the truth, so he sat on the edge of the bed and took the doc's hand.

"Okay, what happened? What's wrong?" Gavin asked, his eyes searching Lex's face.

"I got a call from Grady after I left here." Gavin clutched Lex's hand. "They brought Cassie in for questioning about the fire. They think it was arson because they detected an accelerant. You know they got this thing that tells them right away now? Anyway, I wanted you to hear it from me instead of whatever detective gets the case," Lex said.

"I don't understand. Why Cassie? Just because of all that other stuff she did?"

"No, not just that. Your neighbor saw a car parked in front of his house, and he thought it was her in it," Lex explained. "I saw the same car when I left for work this morning, but it was empty as far as I could see. I'm sorry, Doc. I should have—"

Gavin put his hand over Lex's mouth. "No, it's not your fault," he said adamantly.

Lex was taken aback at Gavin's reaction. He'd expected sadness or whatever, but he didn't expect the doc to be breathing hard and for his eyes to be shooting fire. The man was pissed like Lex had never seen him before.

Lex removed the hand from his mouth but kept a hold on it. "It's not for sure; they're just following leads."

"Oh no, don't you try to handle me with kid gloves, Lex. I'm not some little...little kid that you have to protect. If she burned down my house, I'm going to...urrrgggghhh. I'm so mad. I don't think I've ever been this angry at anyone in my life." Gavin shook with rage, and his raspy voice was barely a whisper.

Lex saw the struggle play out on Gavin's face. He wasn't sure what it was, but he hoped that the doc wouldn't break himself before it was over. "Baby, you need to calm down a little. I get that you're mad, and you have every right to be. Hell, I'm glad you're pissed at her, finally—it's about damn time—but don't go overboard here. Let's let the investigators do their work, and if she's really to blame, then we'll concentrate on getting the best lawyer so she pays this time," Lex said, trying to talk his man down some.

He pulled Gavin into his arms and let him just be for a few minutes. The smell of Gavin's smoky hair eventually made Lex pull away. "So what do you think about asking the nurse if I can help you take a shower? Get some of this soot out of your pretty blond hair." Lex fingered one of the curls that hung limply over the doc's ear.

"You're trying to distract me," Gavin pouted.

"Is it working?"

"Yes." Gavin lay his head back on Lex's shoulder.

"You got stuff connecting you to the bed, baby. What do we need to do to get you in the shower? Oh, or better yet, should I give you a sponge bath?" The inappropriate thoughts of running a soapy sponge along the doc's naked body made Lex grin.

"I'll just push this little button and wait for the nurse. I'm a doctor, remember? I don't deal with the dirty parts," Gavin said as he pushed the call button.

"As I recall, Doctor, you are very talented when it comes to the dirty parts," Lex teased, distracting Gavin from his worry over his ex-wife. It worked because Gavin snuggled in a little closer and buried his face in Lex's neck with a satisfied little sigh. Lex held the doc tightly to his chest while they waited for the nurse to answer the call.

When a male nurse's aide showed up, he lectured Lex on the importance of not leaving Gavin unattended while he was out of the bed as he put extra tape on Gavin's bandages to keep the water out. He left after telling them to call when they were done so he could change the wet dressings.

Lex helped Gavin get out of bed and into the small bathroom. There was no shower stall, just a curtain that you pulled around to keep the rest of the bathroom from getting soaked. Lex untied the hospital johnny at the shoulder so the arm with the IV wouldn't get stuck and then slipped it off the doc's long, lean body. He reminded himself it was not the time or the place for him to get aroused. It didn't help, but hey, he tried. He positioned the hard stool in the center of the curtained-off area. Then Gavin sat on it as Lex hung the IV bag on the little hook above him. The way he looked up at Lex... Jesus, it almost killed him. The trust and longing mixed together on Gavin's angelic face about tore Lex to pieces.

"Be good, Doc. We're just getting you clean here. Nothing else." Lex bent to kiss him because he couldn't resist. Lex at least had the luxury of clothes to hide his arousal, but the poor doc had to try to hold his down with one hand, while looking like he wasn't trying to hide it.

Lex grabbed the shower attachment, turned the water on, and made sure it was the right temperature before holding it over Gavin's head. The soot ran out of the tangled mess of hair, revealing the deep, golden color Lex had come to covet more than the precious metal it was named after. Gavin took the nozzle and hosed down his body while Lex massaged shampoo into his hair.

When Gavin put his head back, eyes closed and mouth slightly open so Lex could rinse his hair, it hit Lex—he'd thought it before, but it had always been undefined and ethereal, something he couldn't grasp—but watching that trusting gesture, knowing the man sitting on the stool before him could have...could have so easily died in that house, without knowing how much he meant to Lex made him want to cry. He didn't, though, because he'd cried enough that day in private. In fact, he was a bit ashamed of how many tears he'd shed. Instead, Lex bit the sides of his cheeks and finished rinsing Gavin off but with the resolve that he'd tell the doc how he felt.

He toweled Gavin off very thoroughly, helped him into his new johnny, and walked him back to his bed. Lex hung the IV bag on the bed pole and pressed the call button.

"Thank you. I feel much better now," Gavin said, settling back against the bed.

"It was my pleasure. You look much better too." Lex sat on the side of the bed and held Gavin's hand. The nurse did his thing quickly and efficiently and left them alone. "Everyone will be back soon. Are you going to tell them that you're staying here?"

Gavin looked at their joined hands before lifting them to his lips. "I'm going to stay. There was never any question about that, really. Will you stay with me when I tell them?"

"I will. Doc, can I tell you something without you freaking out on me if it comes as a shock to you?" Lex's stomach fluttered in anticipation of what he was about to do.

"Lex, I'm not sure I can handle any more excitement today. I'm about full up on my quota," Gavin said with an apprehensive look.

"Okay, I won't tell you then."

"No, you can't do that. Now you have to tell me, or I'll worry about it, and I won't get—"

"I love you, Doc," Lex blurted. The hand in his squeezed so hard that Lex wanted to pull away, but he was too stunned by his own confession to do anything but stare wide-eyed at the doc.

"You do?" Gavin asked in that low, raspy voice so unlike his normal one that it sent a shiver up Lex's spine. His deep-brown eyes were huge limpid pools as they searched Lex's face for the truth.

"Yeah, I really do. Does that freak you out, like, way too much, because I know it's kinda sudden, and we just started going out, but I wanted you way before you even looked at me, so it's not really all that much of a shock if you think about it." Lex was rambling, but he couldn't help himself. When Gavin didn't say anything, he asked, "So what do you say, Doc?"

Gavin cupped Lex's face in his hands, and his eyes seared into Lex's like never before. "You are the finest man I've ever met. You make me believe I can be myself, and that's okay because I'm okay. I know my friends love me and accept me for who I am, but I never thought I'd find someone who would actually love me again after Cassie. I've known I've loved you for a while now, but I couldn't say it because I figured a guy like you could never feel the same way. I was willing to just be with you for as long as you'd let me. I'm not going to freak out, not even a little bit."

Gavin leaned in and the kiss he gave Lex was probably the sincerest thing Lex had ever felt in his life. The giant purse that hit him in the back was most definitely not as great.

"You get off him right now!" Mona screamed from behind Lex before she started tugging at his shirt.

"Mona, calm down. Stop hitting him." Lex heard Riley's voice but didn't see anything because the big old purse was flying toward his head. He put his arm up to shield his face just before the blow landed.

"You pervert. You sick man. Get away from my boy!" Mona was apparently not done.

"Stop, Mrs. Addison, please." Sheila was the next to try with no result.

Lex tried to grab the damn bag. What the hell did that woman have in there, lead? She was like a purse ninja as she evaded Lex's grasping hands and landed another hit to his shoulder.

"STOP IT!" Gavin's voice was what finally got through to the wild woman wielding the huge purse. Everything stopped at once, and all eyes turned to the man standing next to the bed, clutching his neck. "Mom, don't hit him again, or I'll..." Gavin's voice, barely audible at the beginning of his sentence, gave out completely so he just mouthed the rest. His wide, angry eyes found Lex and turned into a beseeching look.

Lex made his way through the crowded little room to Gavin's side. "Babe, you need to get back into bed," he said. Gavin tried to protest, but no sound came out. "Don't try to talk. Your throat is going to be really sore because of that. I'm sorry. Now get in bed for me, baby." Gavin shook his head, but Lex could be pretty insistent. He got Gavin back into the bed and covered before the nurse arrived.

"I'm sorry, folks, but if you can't keep it down in here, I'm going to have to ask you all to leave," she said. "We have other patients who need their rest."

"We're sorry for the commotion. I promise you won't hear another peep out of this room," Riley said. Lex took a moment to be impressed by Riley's transformation into a professional as he addressed the nurse. It was the first he'd seen the man as anything other than his usually clowning self. The nurse nodded and left them all standing there wondering what was going to come next.

"I want you out of here now. Roger, get him out. I don't want his perversion around my boy anymore. It's no wonder we never heard of him if that's what's been going on. It's just sick, you,"—Mona pointed at Lex and made a face of pure disdain— "you disgusting, perverted, nasty—"

"THAT," Jean's first word echoed through the room, "is just about enough of that." She walked farther into the room, not taking her eyes off Lex and Gavin, but nobody had to guess who she was talking to. "I won't listen to anyone talk to my son that way." She put one arm around Lex's waist and held out the other hand for Gavin, who grasped it like a drowning man clutching a lifesaver.

Lex took in Gavin's huge terrified eyes and knew he had to do something before he lost Gavin to his panic. "Ma'am, I'm sorry you had to find out this way. I'm sure it came as quite a shock, but I'm in love with Gavin, and he loves me too," Lex said calmly. Saying they loved each other got Lex some strange looks from the other people in the room, but it felt good. No, it felt right to say it.

Mona was shaking her head in denial. "No, no, Gavin is just confused. He's been led astray—he was vulnerable and you took advantage of him. He was grieving over the loss of his marriage to Cassie, and you stepped in and perverted him. He's not like you. He could never be like that." She seemed to run out of wind then, to everyone's surprise.

Though what she was spouting was complete and utter bullshit, Lex could see she believed what she was saying. She thought Lex had forced or tricked Gavin into thinking he was in love with another man. Lex had a brief moment of doubt about what had actually happened between the two of them, but when Gavin's free hand clutched at the back of his shirt, those doubts flew out the window. He was a rational man and knew there was no way he'd done anything wrong or perverted to the man he loved.

"I'm sorry, but I don't think you know what you're talking about," Lex said.

"Mona, I think maybe we should go." Gavin's father stepped away from the wall and into the fight. "You need to calm down. You've said some pretty terrible things to this man, and maybe we need to just step back and think about this before we try to discuss it with our son alone." The way he emphasized the word alone meant there would come a time when Lex would have to let Gavin face his parents on his own. For good or bad, it wouldn't be up to him to defend Gavin's choice.

Mona looked around the room, but for once she didn't say anything. She nodded her head slowly and let her husband take her arm. When they got to the door, Gavin's father turned to face Gavin and Lex. "We'll stop back tomorrow morning, Gavin. I think it would be a good idea if we could talk in private about this," he said. Gavin's mouth worked, but he was only able to croak. He nodded his agreement instead.

"We'll meet you in the parking lot. Okay, Roger? We just want to say good-bye to Gav," Riley said. Gavin's dad nodded and led his silent wife out.

Lex felt the tension drain out of the room. He turned to Gavin and was surprised by the look on his face. Apparently today was the day that the doc was going to keep him on his toes. "Doc, are you okay?"

The strained look of determination on Gavin's face didn't soften even as he shook his head. He motioned for Riley to come to him. Riley leaned in close, and Lex couldn't make out the barely-there whisper Gavin used to tell his friend whatever it was he wanted him to know.

Riley nodded and stood up. "Whatever you say, Gav. I'm just going to say, it's about fucking time, and leave it at that." He hugged Gavin and then turned and startled Lex by wrapping him in a tight embrace while Sheila said her good-byes to Gavin and Lex's mom. "Don't worry, copper; he's not going anywhere," Riley whispered.

Gavin grabbed Lex's arm as soon as Riley released him and pulled him down so they were face-to-face. He mouthed, "I love you" before kissing him so hard that Lex felt it in his toes.

Well, well, well, say hello to the new indomitable doc.

TWENTY-THREE

"ARE YOU SURE you want me to stay?" Gavin asked Lex one more time as they drove to Lex's condo. His voice was still raspy, but a full night of letting it rest meant he had a voice again. "I told you I can stay with Riley and Sheila. My parents are heading back in the morning so they'll have room."

"Doc, I really want you to stay with me, but if you're more comfortable with staying there, then just tell me," Lex reassured him yet again. "I don't want you to stay at my place if you really don't want to. I won't be mad, honestly. I just want you to do what you want to do without worrying about what anyone else thinks."

Gavin shifted in his seat so he could look at Lex. He'd asked Lex to pick him up from the hospital because he'd told Riley to tell his parents that they'd go out to supper and discuss whatever they wanted to then. Gavin needed a little more time to adjust to the fact that his life had undergone a major upheaval on not just one front but two. Time to gather his thoughts before he faced his parents.

He'd used his night alone in the hospital to sort through his life, and he'd made some important decisions. Watching his mom's reaction to his being in love with Lex had opened Gavin's eyes to the fact that it was his life. He had the right to make his own decisions about who he loved, where he lived—shit, just everything was his choice. He was taking back control of his life, and his parents would have to take a backseat to Lex.

Right now, the matter of where Gavin would stay was the most pressing issue. Lex said Gavin could stay with him for as long as he liked. Riley and Sheila had extended the same invitation, and after he talked to his insurance company, he'd have another alternative because they'd pay for him to stay somewhere if that's what he wanted. He had options, but the thought of sleeping with Lex in his bed every night sent a thrill through him. It was what Gavin really wanted, but he didn't want to seem too eager. He didn't want Lex to think he had to let him stay.

Gavin stopped that train of thought cold. One of the decisions he'd made in the hospital was that he was going to be more decisive when it came to his relationship with Lex. "I want to stay with you, but I don't want you to feel like you have to let me. I also don't want to get there and have you feel like you can't ask me to leave if I outstay my welcome. That's why I'm not sure because I'm worried that maybe it would be better if I stayed somewhere else to avoid that situation altogether." Gavin took a deep breath and waited for Lex's response.

"You may have a point." Lex's eyes stayed on the road, and he looked relaxed, but Gavin thought he detected a little edge to Lex's voice. Gavin realized he may have just talked himself out of Lex's bed and wanted to recant everything he'd said, but he wouldn't because it was how he felt. "How about you just come and stay with me for a couple of nights, and then you can call your insurance company and make a decision when you know all of your options?"

Now that sounded like a perfectly reasonable suggestion, so Gavin grabbed it. "Yeah, that would work," he said with a satisfied smile. "Are you still going to be able to go with me to meet the fire marshal tomorrow?"

"Yeah, actually, I took the rest of the week off."

"You didn't have to do that. I'm sure it was hard on such short notice." Gavin felt bad for causing Lex more problems.

Lex pulled his truck into his garage, shut it off, and turned to Gavin. "I explained the situation to my sergeant this morning. It's nothing less than they'd do for anyone else if it happened to someone in their family. I have the time since I never use it, so this is what it's there for, and I want to be there for you. It's all good."

The warm feeling was back. Lex had pretty much just called him family. He'd also probably had to tell his boss what type of relationship he had with Gavin to explain why he needed the time off. Gavin pulled Lex into a kiss to express how much everything the man did for him was appreciated.

They broke apart at the tapping on the window. Jean was standing by the door with a big smile on her face. Gavin blushed and opened his door. It was still embarrassing to get caught making out in the car by a parent—some things never changed.

Jean hugged Gavin tightly when he stepped out. "I'm glad you're here," she said, and he believed her.

"Thanks, Jean. I'm glad to be here. I feel strange showing up without anything. I don't even have any clothes. Do you see what I'm wearing? Doesn't Lex have any long pants? I never realized how short his legs were," Gavin said. It made Jean laugh just as he'd intended. Lex had told Gavin his mom had finally broken down over Agent after they'd left the hospital. Gavin had a hunch that his being there was partially to help Lex keep Jean out of the depression she was prone to falling into.

"Oh dear, yes, he's got short legs just like his father had. He's all body, that one. Come on in; I'm sure you'll want to rest a bit before you have to go out again." Jean pulled him along after her, and Gavin looked back to find Lex smiling at the two of them.

"I have a few phone calls to make, actually," Gavin said. Jean had led him to the couch, where he sat.

"That's fine, dear. Now do you want anything? A drink or something to eat?"

"No thanks, I'm fine."

"Hey, Doc, here's the cordless." Lex handed Gavin the handset, a notepad, and a pen. Lex was on top of things; had to give him that. "We'll give you some time to get your calls made." He leaned down and kissed Gavin before leaving him alone to try to start getting his life back together.

GAVIN FIDGETED AS he waited for his parents to arrive. Lex had dropped him off fifteen minutes early so he'd be the one his parents came to instead of the other way around. He felt like it gave him a little bit of an upper hand since it was going to be two against one. He'd barely stopped himself from begging Lex to come with him to hold his hand. He needed to do this on his own because it was time for him to grow up, and if his mom didn't like it, too bad.

He heard his mother before he saw her, which was par for the course. His parents came to the table where Gavin was seated, with mixed looks on their faces. His dad held out the chair for his mother, and she fussed with the bag of death—as Lex had coined her handbag after her assault on him—before she set it on the empty chair next to her. His father sat next to Gavin and gave him a small, sad smile. Gavin knew which way the wind was blowing just from the expression on his father's face and braced for the worst.

His mother took a breath in preparation to start in, but Gavin cut her off, leaving her with a look of surprise on her face. "I love Lex. I'm not going to apologize for that, nor am I going to justify my relationship with him. I will apologize for not telling you sooner, not because I feel badly about not telling you, but because I feel like it was a disservice to Lex to hide what I feel for him. He's a great guy, and he's been there for me through everything." Gavin stopped to take a breath but knew if he didn't rush on he'd be interrupted before he got everything out.

"Cassie has been harassing me since I asked her to move out. She's vandalized my house and my car. I don't feel like I need to get into the details of why I asked for the divorce. I've been assured that it's nobody's business but mine and Cassie's, but I will tell you that I was justified in asking for it. It had nothing to do with my attraction to a member of the same sex; Lex was in no way involved. I only met him because he's a cop and he kept having to respond to my calls to the police when Cassie did the things she did. The worst thing is that I know she's been talking to you behind my back, and I'm sure that whatever lies she's told you, you believe, and it hurts to know that you'd take her words at face value and not ask me if anything she said was true. But now they think she started the fire that almost cost me my life, so I guess you could say the proof is in the pudding." Gavin finished his rehearsed speech and looked from his father to his mother as he waited for their rebuttal.

To his surprise, it was his father who spoke. "Well, that is certainly a lot to take in at one time." Gavin couldn't help but look at his mother. She had her lips squeezed shut, and he wondered what type of conversation the two of them had had after they'd left the hospital.

"I know it is, and it's my fault for not telling you more about what was going on, but I know how much Mom worries, and I didn't want that," Gavin said. His mother once again took that telling breath, but his father's hand on hers stopped her short. It was amazing. Gavin had never seen his father take control.

"I see your point, Son, but if you were in danger, and I think recent circumstances point to that conclusion, then you should have told us," he said.

"I know and I'm sorry, but that doesn't change the fact that what's done is done, and I think Mom's reaction to Lex is the more pressing issue right now," Gavin said, trying to draw the conversation to what really needed to be discussed. Cassie was his past, but Lex was his future.

His mother's face showed a small sign of the disgust she had shown Lex the previous night.

"You're not gay," she hissed at Gavin before his father could stop her again. "It's disgusting and unnatural. I'm not going to let you—"

"Mona, stop it. We talked about this, and you promised not to do this. You know that Gavin had leanings toward—"

"Do not bring that up! He was just a little boy who was confused and probably misled by that...that nasty little boy."

Gavin watched his parents argue and suddenly a memory surfaced of a similar argument held years ago. Gavin had been six, no, seven years old, and he'd been in the church basement with...what was that kid's name? The face was clear in his mind's eye—a boy, a year older than himself—a boy Gavin had idolized because everyone wanted to be his friend. Hunter! His name had been Hunter. Hunter had held Gavin's hand and smiled at him with a gap-toothed smile before he'd kissed Gavin's cheek and told him they were going to be best friends. Gavin had gone home from Sunday school and told his mother he was in love with Hunter, and he would marry him when they grew up.

Her reaction to his childish fantasy had scared Gavin so badly he'd had nightmares for weeks afterward. His mother had taken him to the shed and spanked him with his father's belt while she told him to never ever say anything like that again. Boys only married girls. Hunter was a dirty, nasty boy who Gavin should stay far, far away from, or he'd go to hell. He'd cried because he didn't want to go to hell, but he loved Hunter.

His young mind couldn't comprehend why his feelings were so wrong, but his mom had to be right because she knew everything. He never talked to Hunter again. From that day forward Gavin never allowed himself to look at another boy in that light, and at some point, he'd simply forgotten he'd ever wanted to, until Riley. He'd been able to explain away his attraction to his friend as merely displaced feelings of friendship. His attraction to Cassie only cemented the idea that he was right. He wasn't attracted to Riley; he was just confused.

But then Lex had stumbled into his life, and he simply couldn't deny how he felt any longer. Gavin suddenly realized that he wasn't straight, and he wasn't gay; he was bisexual, and he was okay with that.

"Gavin, are you listening?" His father's voice broke into his thoughts.

"No, I wasn't," Gavin admitted. His mind was still trying to wrap itself around how he'd been forced to bury a part of himself so deeply he'd forgotten it was there. He glared at his mom, but she wouldn't look at him.

His father cleared his throat. "I said we have to admit your being in a relationship with a man came as quite a shock to both of us. Your mother is sorry that she overreacted to the situation, but her first instinct is to protect that which she holds dear. I would like to know how this relationship came about. As far as we knew, you were perfectly happy in a heterosexual marriage, at least up until the divorce, of course, so why now are you all of a sudden attracted to the homosexual lifestyle?" he asked.

Gavin now knew what Lex was talking about when he poked fun at how Gavin sometimes talked like he was giving a college lecture; apparently it was genetic. Gavin was confused as to why his father would be shocked Gavin was with a man after what he'd just remembered. It seemed both his parents knew more about Gavin's sexuality than he did. He decided to be honest with them because, after all was said and done, they were his parents, and he loved them. He wanted a relationship with them.

"I guess I can't say the actual homosexual lifestyle attracts me, it's more that Lex is the point of attraction for me. It's about the individual in this case. I found someone attractive, both in personality and physically, and that attraction turned into love. The fact that that person just so happens to be male is irrelevant in my mind; love is love is love," Gavin explained with a flippant wave of his hand.

"So you're saying that regardless of the sex of a person, you can be attracted to them for reasons that transcend the physical, thereby making the sex of that person not a factor. I understand that, but then why not just form a friendship with that person? You have a close friendship with Riley, but you've never, to my knowledge, been induced to have a sexual relationship with him. What makes Lex different?" his father asked.

Having an almost clinical argument over his choice of lovers with his father while his mother stared at them in horror was the most surreal experience of Gavin's life. He was sure he'd wake up back in the hospital, having been the victim of a massive head trauma. Laughter threatened to just bubble up out of him, and he wished Lex was with him to witness this insanity.

"I really don't know, Dad. I love Lex, and all I want is to be with him. I want to wake up next to him every morning, and when I go to work, I can't wait until I can go home and see him. I want to fall asleep in his arms, and I want to be as close to him as two people can possibly be, and that is just not something you can achieve without sexual intimacy. Can anyone really explain why one person elicits those types of feelings while a multitude of others don't? If every person you felt some type of camaraderie with gave you those feelings, this world would be an even more confusing place, don't you think?" Gavin asked. He left Riley and his long-abandoned feelings for his best friend out of it. His father could continue to believe what he wanted on that front.

His father hummed and nodded as he thought it over. Gavin's father was a very rational man, not prone to giving in to irrational feelings. His father would think it over and come up with an academic approach to his son's apparent deviation from the societal norm. Maybe there was still hope that his parents would be more accepting of his relationship than he'd dared hope.

"No, I'm done. I can't sit here and listen to the two of you rationalize this farce." His mother's voice cut down Gavin's last thought. She stood up. "You are not gay, and until you grow out of this ridiculous notion that you are in love with that man, you are no longer welcome in our home. When you straighten yourself out, give us a call. Come on, Roger, we're leaving now," she said.

Gavin could only stare with his mouth agape as her words ricocheted around his brain. He supposed telling her that he was, technically, bisexual wouldn't make things any better, so he just sat there. His father put his hand on Gavin's shoulder as he got up. "I'm so sorry, Gavin, but I have to go with her. I'll talk to her and keep in touch with you. Love you, Son," he said as he got up to follow his wife out of the restaurant.

Gavin sat there at the empty table. His thoughts were a tangled mess, and he felt all of his newfound resolve to be a better, stronger man start to crumble in the face of his revelations and his mother's rejection. The waiter, concerned that Gavin was having some sort of health crisis, called the manager to his table. He couldn't fault the waiter, since he still wore the bandages from his brush with his dresser and Agent, so the young man's assumption was justified.

"Sir, is there something we could help you with?" the manager asked Gavin.

"Cab?" Gavin croaked out through dry lips. It was the only thing he could think of because he was there without a car, and his parents had left... They had left him all alone. He tried to hold the moisture that was pooling in his eyes back, not blinking, to keep the tears at bay. He was a grown man, and he wouldn't cry like a baby in front of a bunch of total strangers.

The manager led him to the front of the restaurant, and when the cab showed up, he put Gavin in the back seat. Gavin broke out of his stupor long enough to give the driver Lex's address. In the relative privacy of the backseat of the cab, he let a couple of tears slip down his cheeks. When he got to Lex's place, he managed to get the money out to pay the cab driver and stumbled blindly up the walk to Lex's front door.

The door wasn't locked, so Gavin let himself in. Then he went in search of the one person he wanted to see, the only one who could make things right again. He found Lex in his bedroom. He was lying with his back propped up on pillows against the headboard with the remote in one hand and the other lying casually on his bare stomach. Yes, bare as in Lex only wore a tight pair of purple boxer briefs.

Lex's gaze left the TV screen. When they landed on Gavin, they went from surprised to concerned in less than a second. No! Gavin shouted in his head. He didn't want Lex to look at him like that because in the five seconds he'd been in Lex's presence his mind had gone from "I think my parents just disowned me, help me" to "I think I really need to fuck you, help me."

Lex must have smelled the ozone in the air as Gavin's brain sizzled with impure thoughts because he sat up at attention. "Doc, what's going on?"

Gavin didn't answer. He kicked off his borrowed shoes as he pulled the sweater off over his head. Lex's eyes widened when he realized what was happening. Gavin's pants landed with a soft thump on the floor. His breath was coming in lusty little pants. Gavin had never felt the need to connect on such a basic level with any other human being in his life. The drive to be inside Lex, to possess him, to make him his was so overwhelming Gavin thought he may pass out from the intensity of it.

"Lex?" Gavin let the name slip past his lips, not knowing what he was asking. Lex would know what he needed; he always seemed to know.

Lex put the remote on the nightstand and pulled the drawer open. He produced a little foil packet and a rather large bottle of lube from its depths. "Come here, Doc." Lex's outward calm did nothing to soothe Gavin's rapidly overheating mind. He walked around to Lex's side of the bed, and Lex turned so he could sit on edge. He pulled Gavin between his knees and buried his face in Gavin's chest. "Don't worry about it, Doc. We'll do whatever you need." Lex's breath was moist against Gavin's skin.

Lex worked the waistband of Gavin's underwear down over his stiff shaft, his cheek rubbing along the length as he pushed the material down until it all fell to the floor. Gavin's hips jerked in response to the slight stimulation. He knew what he wanted—no—what he needed.

Gavin pushed Lex back on the bed and returned the favor, sliding the purple fabric down Lex's muscular legs. With the evidence of Lex's own arousal staring him in the face, Gavin couldn't stop himself from bending and taking it into his mouth. Lex gasped and grabbed Gavin's head to keep him from moving too fast. He remembered he needed to help Lex relax so his body would accept the upcoming invasion. He suckled the head of Lex's cock as his hand groped for the bottle of lube.

With slick fingers, Gavin made his way to the only place on Lex's body that he'd yet to explore. When his finger slipped past the ring of muscled resistance, and the tight heat surrounded it, Gavin couldn't remember all the reasons they hadn't done this before. It took all of his concentration as he worked both his fingers into Lex while keeping his mouth on Lex's cock.

Lex didn't seem to be in any distress as Gavin added another finger and spread them like a pair of scissors as he'd been taught by Lex months ago. Lex moaned. "More, Doc." He clutched at Gavin's head to push more of his dick into Gavin's mouth. Gavin added one more finger, and when Lex pushed back against his hand he knew it was time.

Gavin let the cock slip from between his lips and slowly removed his fingers from their tight prison before he stood up and grabbed the condom. A shaky hand brought it to his mouth so he could tear it open with his teeth. The whole time Gavin was preparing himself, he was watching Lex, who was slowly stroking his spit-slicked cock. Lex looked amazing—all flushed and spread out on the bed. Lube dripped on the floor when Gavin accidentally overapplied it, but better safe than sorry.

Lex positioned himself on the edge of the bed, knees drawn up to his chest, presenting Gavin with one of the most erotic sights of his life. Gavin stepped in and bent to kiss Lex's lips.

"Go slow, Doc. It's been a long time," Lex whispered when they parted.

Words failed Gavin; he could only nod as he lined the head of his cock up with Lex's entrance. His initial push yielded subpar results, meaning he failed to gain entry, but on the second push he was successful. As the head of his dick popped into the man he loved, Gavin shuddered. It was like the world shifted in that moment, and everything became clearer to him.

Lex groaned as Gavin pushed into him and settled deep inside. Gavin waited through the adjustment period, clenching his ass cheeks as he tried to hold still against the tight sucking heat wrapped around him. He leaned down once again to kiss Lex, and he couldn't stop the words that rushed out as he looked into Lex's bright-blue gaze. "It feels amazing. Like nothing I've ever felt... No, oh god, no, that sounds so cheesy; that's not what I meant. I mean it's different because it's you, that feeling of being with you this way. It's not like anything else I've ever felt."

"I know, Doc. I feel it too. Now, will you please just move?" Lex asked.

Again at a loss for words, Gavin nodded and canted his hips to make the man beneath him moan. It was a heady feeling, and one that he wouldn't soon forget or take for granted because this thing Lex was giving him was so much more than just sex, and he knew it.

TWENTY-FOUR

"OH LEX, FUCK." Gavin's pistoning hips stuttered in their rhythm. Lex knew Gavin had found his release when the doc's lithe body slumped on top of him. Lex wrapped his arms around his lover to hold him close as his emotions overtook him. Lex knew what was coming so he held Gavin tightly, keeping him safe so he could fall apart.

From the minute Gavin had walked into the room, it was clear his meeting with his parents had gone badly. Lex had been surprised by the quick change in Gavin's mood, but he'd seen the need in the doc's eyes. Gavin had needed something only Lex could give him, and though it wasn't exactly the way Lex had envisioned their first time, it had been a way for Lex to show Gavin he was there for him, would always be there.

After a few minutes, Lex felt the uncomfortable sensation of the doc's cock leaving his body when he was no longer hard enough to keep the connection. Lex rolled over so they were lying on their sides, facing each other. He pulled back to study Gavin's tear-stained face before kissing the wet cheeks. Lex had never known a man who let his feelings show as readily as the doc. It would have made him uncomfortable with any other guy, but with Gavin, it made Lex want to wrap him in his arms and keep him safe.

"Do you want to talk about it?" Lex asked when Gavin was at the hitching-breath stage of his crying jag. Gavin shook his head and buried his face in Lex's neck. It was a gesture Lex had come to associate with Gavin's dual needs: to hide and to seek reassurance. It was heartbreakingly childlike in its innocence, and it got to Lex every time.

"My mom hates me," Gavin mumbled. He sounded so pitiful Lex wanted to cry along with him.

"She doesn't hate you." Lex pulled Gavin out of his hiding place so he could look into the eyes he loved so much. "She just doesn't understand, and she's probably upset that you didn't tell her right away. You need to give her some time to absorb this. How was your dad? He didn't threaten to beat the gay out of you, did he?"

"No, he seemed to be okay until my mom got up and told me I wasn't welcome at home anymore unless I straightened myself out. What am I going to do, Lex?" Gavin asked as another tear ran down his cheek. His face contorted, and before Lex could offer any advice, he clutched Lex's face between his hands. "I'm bisexual!" Gavin blurted.

"Yeah, Doc, I sorta figured that," Lex said. Why Gavin thought he needed to tell Lex something so obvious was beyond him.

"No, I mean, I think I've always been, but something happened when I was a kid, and I think I stuffed it away. I remembered something when my parents were arguing earlier and stuff started coming back to me. It made me realize that me being with you isn't as abnormal as I thought," Gavin said.

"What do you mean? I never thought it was abnormal. Why would you?"

"Because I thought I was straight all these years. But I'm not a mixed-up straight guy, Lex. I'm a normal bisexual guy." A small smile threatened to break through Gavin's tears, but his lip trembled once again. "One whose mother thinks he's disgusting and perverted. I guess Cassie was right in the end after all."

It took Lex a few moments to digest everything Gavin had just told him. Of course, it made sense that Gavin would have some sort of proclivity toward bisexuality because straight guys didn't all of a sudden form an attraction to the same sex. Lex had known from a very young age that he was different, and though he wanted to dig further into Gavin's past to find out what exactly had happened, he decided trying to reassure Gavin that there was still a chance his parents could come around was more important.

"Well, like I said, you need to give them time. If your dad isn't totally against you, then maybe there's a chance, right?" Lex had no idea if Gavin's timid father held any sway in the household, but he could hope, right?

Gavin's lower lip stopped trembling, and he quirked a little half smile. "Maybe there is. I think he was trying to analyze me. He'll probably go home and look up everything he can find on bisexuality and then present his argument to my mom, which should be interesting."

"Is your dad a shrink? You never told me what he does." Lex was intrigued.

Gavin shook his head. "No, he's an engineer with the USACE. Very rational. I think you'd like him. You should have heard our dinner conversation. He actually asked me why I never had a sexual relationship with Riley. It was embarrassing." Gavin hid his face again.

Lex nodded and chuckled at the thought of Riley and Gavin together. Not that he hadn't wondered himself if the two hadn't maybe been a bit more than just friends, but Gavin's tentativeness in their early days told a different story. "So he's not against this? Just curious as to why now?" Lex asked. If Gavin's dad was willing to accept them, then there was still hope his mom could too. Lex hoped she would because Gavin would have a hard time with his mother's rejection, and a long term rift would be taxing on both him and their relatively new relationship.

"I guess; I'm not really sure, but you should have seen him. He made my mom shut up for once, so he could talk." Gavin stopped and seemed lost in thought for a minute. "I don't remember him ever doing that before. I hate to say it, but I think I may have gotten the worst out of my parent's genes," Gavin said as the smile slipped from his face. "I have my mom's tendency to ramble and get emotional over the small stuff and my dad's analytical side that makes me want an explanation for everything.

"I think you're wonderful," Lex said. "The perfect mix of emotional and rational."

"You're wrong, but that's okay because I love you. You make me feel safe enough to show you my crazy. I've never had anyone I could do that with before. I'm glad it's you I can let see the real me."

Lex couldn't keep the smile from his face. God, the things this guy said sometimes just made his stomach flutter. It was a feeling he'd never experienced before. He'd been right to tell Gavin he loved him because surely that was what the strange feelings he was having were.

"I'm glad you feel that way, Doc, and I love you too." Lex kissed Gavin softly. "Now, why don't we go get cleaned up and then raid the fridge? I'm guessing you didn't eat anything."

Gavin looked down at his spent manhood, still encased in the used condom, and grimaced. "Yeah, I need to take care of that."

Lex got up and pulled Gavin off the bed and into the attached bathroom. He fished out the extra bandages they got at the hospital and made sure everything was ready so he could take care of Gavin's wounds when they were done in the shower. Gavin got in, waiting for Lex to join him, and then Lex stepped into his open arms.

"Thank you for everything, Lex. I don't know what I'd do without you," Gavin said as he turned them so Lex was under the warm flow.

"You're welcome, Doc. I'd do anything for you, you know," Lex said honestly. He accepted the soft kiss Gavin gave him before they washed up.

THE ENTIRE DRIVE to Gavin's house was tense. Gavin was trying not to show too much emotion over the fact that his house was going to be a disaster. They'd pulled off a trifecta, getting the fire marshal, the insurance adjuster, and Detective McDaniels, who'd been assigned the case, to meet them at the house. Cassie was still in custody, and they only had a few more hours to charge or release her.

Gavin gasped when they pulled up to the curb in front of his house. Lex was glad he'd talked Gavin out of visiting the previous day, with the excuse that the fire marshal and his inspectors were busy and they wouldn't be allowed within ten feet of the structure anyway. He touched Gavin's thigh, and Gavin turned to meet Lex's eyes.

"I know it looks bad, but maybe it's not a total loss." Lex tried to make Gavin feel better, but the tears were already welling up in the doc's eyes. So far he'd held them in check.

Gavin took a deep breath. "It's not that important, Lex. It's just a house, and everything inside was replaceable. The only thing I lost that I can't replace wasn't really mine. I'm so sorry about Agent, and if there was any way I could replace him, I would."

Lex smiled; it was a sad smile, but he hoped it would reassure Gavin once again that Lex didn't hold him responsible for Agent's death. "Hey, Doc, I know you feel bad about him, but really, he didn't have much time left, and you are not the one I blame. And just so we're clear, the only thing I couldn't live without made it out safe. I thank my lucky stars every day for Agent barking his fool head off so your neighbor got pissed enough to see what was going on. After we're done here, we're going to Mike's to give him a proper burial. I was going to wait, but I think we all could use some closure."

"Okay, then, let's get this over with so we can do that." Gavin leaned in and kissed Lex before he popped his door open with a renewed sense of determination.

They walked up to the two men who were having a conversation while huddled over a clipboard. McDaniels looked up from whatever the fire marshal was showing him. He didn't seem happy about what he was seeing. He held out his hand to Gavin, who was completely distracted by the charred remains of his house. Lex took the offered hand.

"Detective."

"Officer Turner, I heard you might show up today," McDaniels said. There was a hint of suspicion in the detective's eyes when he finally got Gavin's attention and shook his hand. "Dr. Addison, can't say it's good to see you again, at least not under these circumstances."

"Yeah, I'm not that happy to see you either," Gavin agreed.

The fire marshal stepped in and offered his hand. "I'm James Emmers, the fire marshal," he said as he shook hands. "We're close to done, so I can take you into the structure. There are some areas that we've deemed unsafe, but the front of the home is still structurally sound as far as we can determine. Your insurance adjuster was here yesterday and said he'd come back sometime today since we were still gathering evidence."

"So it was arson then?" Gavin asked.

James looked to the detective, who nodded, before he answered. "Yes, it was arson. We've determined there was accelerant poured over an extensive area. Also the fuse for the fire alarms was pulled as well as the backup batteries being disabled. Unless you did that last one yourself, I'd say whoever started the fire meant for you not to get out."

Gavin's eyes narrowed. He was probably thinking what Lex himself was thinking. Cassie had tried to kill Gavin, not just burn down his house. Instead of voicing his thoughts, Lex said, "She had to have been in the house at some point to do that, so she must have been planning it."

Lex put his arm around Gavin's waist, but the doc's eyes were on fire again. He didn't push Lex away, but he didn't lean into the embrace either. His posture remained rigid as he waited to hear what McDaniels had to say.

"I just put in a call to the station to press the formal charges: arson and attempted murder. There'll be an arraignment where they'll set her bail, but I don't suppose she'll get it since there's plenty against her, if that eases your mind at all. Now I need you to answer a few questions," McDaniels said. He looked from Gavin to Lex. "Both of you."

LEX TOLD DETECTIVE McDaniels what he'd done and seen on the morning of the fire. The look on the Detective's face remained impassive as he took down notes. Lex had been uneasy about revealing all to someone on the force but knew the rumors had most likely already permeated the entire station.

Lex went in search of Gavin after McDaniels told him he'd be in touch and took his leave. Gavin was standing with the fire marshal and another man, his insurance adjuster Lex assumed, who had arrived while Lex answered questions. Gavin gave him a little quirk of the lips when he noticed Lex standing a couple of feet away watching him.

"Well shall we go in then?" James asked.

Gavin nodded and held out a hand for Lex. Grabbing it, they went in the front door hand in hand. The flames hadn't reached the front of the house where the living room was, but the evidence of how hot the fire had been was there all the same. The wet carpet squished under their feet as they made their way along a well-worn path through the room. The flat-screen TV was melted into a pile of plastic mush on its stand; there was a thick coat of black soot everywhere; and the drywall was hanging down in sodden pieces in various places. There was a black streak extending from the door to the kitchen to the ceiling where the flames had tried to escape into this room.

Gavin shuddered and tightened his grip on Lex's hand. The insurance adjuster took notes and poked things with his pen every so often. Everything inside the house was unsalvageable, covered in soot and waterlogged, meaning it would all need to be cleaned out and disposed of. They had a long hard job ahead of them.

After their tour, Lex left Gavin to talk with the insurance guy while he called Mike and made arrangements to go out to his place to put Agent to rest. Lex needed to make sure that Gavin was still up to it, and if he wasn't, he'd just have to drop him off when he picked up his mom and do it with her alone.

Once Gavin was finished, they got in the truck to leave, but before Lex could start the engine, Gavin was next to him with his arms around his neck and his cheek nestled against Lex's. He rubbed their stubble together. "Remember when you told me that you liked it when we made sparks together?" Gavin asked in a shaky whisper. Lex nodded. "We need to be careful because that was the last time I ever want to live through a fire, and I definitely don't want to die in one either."

Lex laughed because the doc joking after seeing his house in that state was just too much for him. He tried to capture his lips, but Gavin moved away with a sly glint in his eye. "Doc, we still have things to do before you can be this flirty," Lex said, wondering what had gotten into Gavin. Lex had been sure this visit would send Gavin into a tailspin not get him all...horny.

"I know and I promise to be appropriately somber during the proceedings, but seeing my house like that and knowing I'm still here makes me feel alive. Weird, right?"

"A little," Lex admitted as he started his truck and put it in gear. "So what did the claims guy say?"

Gavin sat back on his side of the bench seat and buckled his seat belt before answering. "He says they will hire a company to go in and catalog everything and clean the house out." Gavin paused and then another reaction Lex hadn't been expecting hit. It was like a switch flipped in the doc's brain, and all of a sudden... Gavin punched the dash three times in quick succession. "THAT FUCKING BITCH, THAT FUCKING MOTHERFUCKING BITCH, SHE... FUUUUCCCKKK!"

The outburst surprised Lex so much his foot slipped off the brake pedal, and the truck lurched. He stomped down on the pedal to stop the forward momentum and threw the truck in park. He turned to Gavin. "Doc?"

"She fucked me, Lex. She flipped me over and fucked me hard. My insurance won't cover the actual replacement cost of the house. It only covers the estimated value, and the guy told me that there's no way I can fix the house with what I'll get out of the insurance company. Plus, I have to pay off the loan I took to pay her off in the divorce settlement, so there's even less. He said it would be cheaper to tear it down and rebuild anyway, but it won't really be my house after that, so what's the point?"

Gavin was seething, and Lex could understand why, but he'd never have guessed that Gavin could express his outrage in such a violent show.

"Oh, and let's not forget that she tried to fucking KILL ME!" he shouted. "She's crazy; there's no other explanation. She's out of her fucking mind, and who knows? They'll probably let her out to finish the fucking job because our legal system is fucking shit. I'm going to spend the rest of my life looking over my shoulder never feeling safe ever again!"

"Hey, Doc, come on now," Lex said in his most soothing talk-down-the-jumper cop voice as he reached out to grab the back of Gavin's neck to pull him closer. "That's not true. I mean some of it is, but I'm sure she'll have to serve some kind of sentence—"

"Not if they don't find her guilty," Gavin interrupted through clenched teeth.

"I don't think she can beat this if what McDaniels said is true. With the eyewitness putting her at the scene, the stuff that was in her car, and just a preliminary check on her financials, they have a pretty good case already. You add that to her prior harassment, and it's practically an open-and-shut case." Lex leaned in to rest his forehead against Gavin's. "Besides, I fucked up once not keeping you safe, it won't happen again; trust me."

Gavin sighed, closed his eyes, and let Lex rub the back of his neck for a few minutes. "I don't want you to feel responsible for me. I'm a grown man, Lex, and it's time I started acting like one. I want us to be equal—you take care of me, and you have to let me take care of you too because I think you need someone to do that for you, and I want to be the one to do it, okay?"

Lex kissed Gavin because it was one of those moments where the doc made him feel shattered with his honesty. "You got a deal, Doc. You want to stay home? Me and Ma can take care of Agent if you're not up to it."

Gavin pulled back and shook his head. "No, I need to be there. Let's go get Jean and do this so we can go home."

"Okay, Doc, whatever you say." Lex put the truck into gear.

A WEEK AND a half later, they'd settled into a routine, and things seemed to be going pretty well. Detective McDaniels had been right, and Cassie was sitting in jail waiting for her trial. Gavin had relaxed after the news had been delivered. He was happy and adjusting to the huge changes that had come his way. The doc was adaptable—that was for sure.

Gavin's house had been stripped by the company his insurance had provided. He had a huge list of the inventory of the contents and one estimate for the cost of renovating or rebuilding. He was mulling over whether to scrap the mess that was left and start from scratch or to cut his losses and sell the dilapidated structure. Someone was bound to buy it since his little plot of land was the kind of thing people were always looking for, considering it was right next to the park.

Lex was hoping Gavin would decide to sell for his own selfish reasons. He liked having the doc at his place and was in no hurry to have him leave. But Lex's new job threatened everything. Lex was back to work and about as happy as he'd ever been, but having a beer with Mike after his shift was quickly putting him in a black mood. Mike kept reminding him he'd soon need to make a decision.

"Man, you gotta tell him soon. It's not something you can spring on him at the last minute," Mike said.

"I know, but I was thinking I could commute or maybe take that room you said your cousin had and stay up there when I need to. Maybe I wouldn't have to move right away, and I could put in for a transfer after six months," Lex said. It sounded like he was trying to justify the fact that he still hadn't told Gavin his new job meant he had to move to a city up north that was a three-hour drive away. Lex lied to himself, making the excuse of not wanting to add to Gavin's stress as the reason for not talking to him about something so important to their future together.

Mike shook his head. "You know that transfers can take years if you don't have a really good reason. They're short on guys up there, which is why they're hiring. You need to figure out if what you have with him is the real deal and make your decision. You gotta ask yourself if he's worth giving up your dream for or does he think you're worth picking up and moving for? I'd ask him before you decide to chuck it at least, and maybe he'll surprise you."

"I don't know. I've got fifteen weeks of training up at Camp Ripley, and I'll have to see how he handles that news first. It's kind of early to ask him to give up his job, but I guess his ex took care of his house, which I think I'd have had a hard time getting him away from. I just don't know, Mike. What if he says no?" Gavin wasn't going to be happy about him being gone and basically in boot camp for almost four months, but that was the least of his worries. Asking the doc to pick up and move away from his friends and job was insane so early in a relationship.

"Well the only way you're going to find out is if you tell him. You need to tell him." Mike patted Lex on the shoulder. They finished their beers in a sort of somber silence as Lex contemplated his conundrum.

Lex continued to weigh the pros and cons of taking a job with the state troopers on the way home. When he made up his mind, he realized Mike was right—he needed to tell Gavin and let the chips fall where they may. Lex was going to ask Gavin if he'd go with him. He couldn't imagine his life without the doc in it now, and if Gavin wouldn't go, Lex would seriously consider refusing the job he'd wanted since high school.

Lex arrived home to find Gavin and his mom sitting together on the couch. Gavin had his arm around her shoulders, and she had her head thrown back against his chest laughing so loud they'd probably get neighbors pounding on the wall. Lex moved to stand in front of them and raised an eyebrow. Gavin looked up and burst into his own gale of laughter at the expression on Lex's face.

"Do I even want to know?" Lex was glad to see both of them in such a good mood but wondered if he was the cause, as was so often the case, of their mirth. He waited until the laughter died down for the answer.

"Jean was just telling me about the time Agent stole your girlfriend's bra, and your dad and him played tug of war with it because Agent wouldn't let go," Gavin said. Lex couldn't figure out why that was quite so funny until Gavin added, "Then you got grounded because they figured out that you'd snuck a girl into your room and tried to hide her behind the curtains. Oh my god, that's so freaking original, Lex!"

Lex shook his head. He knew it had to be something like that. The two of them were going to keep his life interesting if they kept ganging up on him. "Of all the Agent stories, Ma, you had to tell him that one?" he asked, but his lip quirked.

"Oh, Lex, come on; that was one of the funniest. Anyway, Gavin and I were thinking that we might like to get a cat. What do you think?"

The hopeful expression on Gavin's face made Lex wonder if this meant he was planning on selling his house. Hope swelled in Lex's chest at the thought. Maybe the odds of Gavin moving away with Lex had just improved. Lex knew he should tell the doc the news about his new job, but maybe it could wait. He wanted to enjoy the laughter of the two people he loved most just a little longer. His mom scooted over so Lex could wedge himself in between them on the couch. He put an arm around each of them and pulled them against him.

"I think a cat sounds like a great idea." Yeah, just a little longer, and then he'd fess up.

TWENTY-FIVE

GAVIN WAS IN his office when his cell phone rang. He couldn't help the smile that lifted his lips and made him sound like a love-struck teenager when he answered. "Hey, Lex, what's up?"

"Hey, Doc, when's your lunch?" Lex wasted no time getting to the point, and Gavin could hear the smile in his voice too. They were a couple of doofuses.

"Hold on, let me check my schedule," Gavin said as he checked his patient list. "I can take it around noon, and I have until maybe one thirty, why?"

"Wanna come pick me up, and we'll go out and grab a bite?"

"Of course I do. What time?" Gavin asked. Yeah, he was still excited about seeing Lex even though he'd been staying with him for two weeks.

"Noon is fine. See you soon, Doc. Gotta go." Lex hung up.

Gavin floated through his morning patients, and at a quarter to twelve he told the receptionist he was heading out for lunch. Driving to the police station, with a silly grin on his face, he felt life was pretty good right about then. He parked, but when he didn't see Lex in the lot waiting for him, he decided to go in to see if there was some sort of holdup.

He stopped and smiled at the female officer behind the desk. "Could you tell me where I could find Officer Turner?"

"He's in the back. I can call back and tell him you're here. What's your name?" she asked.

"Gavin." When her eyebrows raised, he added, "Addison." Lex would know who he was from his first name only, but the officer he was looking at probably wouldn't realize that.

She picked up the phone on her desk and punched in a couple of numbers. "Yeah, Grady, is Turner back there?" She waited presumably for Grady's answer. "I have a Gavin Addison out here looking for him." She paused to listen again and then smiled. "Ah that's what I thought. Okay, I'll send him back. Thanks." She hung up the phone and gave

Gavin a huge smile. "You can go on back. Grady said you've been back there before."

"Okay, thanks." Gavin walked to the door that led back to where he knew Lex and Grady had desks. The first thing Gavin noticed was the fact that a sort of hush fell over the room, and the second thing he noticed was all eyes turned to follow him as he made his way to where Grady was sitting. Lex was nowhere in sight.

"Hey there, Doc, long time, no see." Grady stood up to greet Gavin.

Gavin shuddered when he remembered Lex telling him when he called him Doc it was a term of endearment. It sounded wrong coming out of the short, balding older man standing in front of him.

"Good to see you too, Officer Grady. Do you know where Lex is? We have a lunch date," Gavin said. The grin on Grady's face alerted Gavin to his faux pas. "I mean we were just going to go grab some lunch. You could join us if you want. I'm sure Lex would be glad to have you along, and well, it shouldn't be a big deal if you wanted to, that is, if you don't have other plans." Gavin tried to fix his mistake by babbling.

Grady's grin widened into a smile, and he clapped Gavin on the back. "Don't worry about it, Doc. I wouldn't want to be the third wheel. Besides, the wife packed me a lunch today, leftover meatloaf sandwiches—my favorite," Grady said. "Turner should be out in a second. He's in with the Sarge working out something about his resignation. You know, he didn't even tell anyone he was applying to the troopers, not even me."

Grady looked a bit upset about his partner's lack of sharing, and Gavin knew the feeling. He still didn't know all the specifics of Lex's new job. It seemed to him, now that he gave it a little thought, Lex had been suspiciously tight-lipped about something he apparently had gone to a lot of trouble to obtain.

"Well you're not the only one he didn't tell," Gavin said, commiserating with Grady.

"Yeah, Turner's never been the talkative type. So you guys are together now? How's that going?" Grady asked.

Gavin was stunned by Grady asking about their relationship so casually, like it was no big deal, and he blushed and stammered when he answered. "Um...I g-guess it's g-good. Um, you know about it?"

Grady shook his head. "Man, how could I not? You should have seen him the day of your house fire; he was crazy. Then he takes a week off, and the rumors start flying about him and you, you know? But the best was when he came back for his first shift after that."

"What? What happened on his first day back?" Lex hadn't mentioned anything out of the ordinary happening, and he hadn't come home from his shift in a bad mood or upset.

"Well you know how it is, gossip, and then he strolls in and some of the guys were staring, and there were whispers, and then Lex stops in the middle of the room." Grady stopped to point out a spot, presumably where Lex had stood. "And he's got everyone's attention, you know, even a couple of detainees are watching him, and he cleared his throat really loud and said—"

"I'm in love with Dr. Gavin Addison, and we're living together. Anyone got a problem with that?" Lex interrupted to finish the story as he walked up to where Gavin and Grady were standing. He put his arm around Gavin's waist. "Hey, Doc, sorry about the wait. You ready to head out?"

Gavin was staring at Lex, with his mouth hanging open, while Grady practically howled with laughter next to him. Lex leaned in close to Gavin "I left out the part about the gay sex thing—too much information for some of these Neanderthals."

Gavin couldn't find the words to respond as Lex waved Grady off and turned them toward the door. He did, however, take in the looks of Lex's colleagues as they walked through the room. Some were smiling, but they weren't the ones who caught Gavin's attention. It was the few who were scowling in their direction that he noticed. It appeared there were a few who did indeed have a problem with that, but knowing Lex, he probably didn't give a shit what those guys thought. He could only hope Lex knew what he was doing and would be careful around those who may not be so accepting of his "lifestyle choices."

Lex led Gavin to his car and opened the passenger door for him. He slid into the seat, still too numb to argue that he should be the one to drive since it was his car. Lex got in the driver's seat and adjusted both the seat and mirrors before putting on his seat belt.

"Doc, seat belt." Gavin moved mechanically to pull the belt across his chest and buckle it. "You all right, Doc?" Lex's amusement over Gavin's shock had worn off, and he sounded worried.

"Do you really think that was the smartest thing to do? And why didn't you tell me you came out to everyone at work?" Gavin's voice trembled, but he couldn't help it. Lex's declaration was at once the most romantic thing he'd ever heard, and the ballsiest, maybe stupidest thing he could think of for Lex to have done.

"I told you that it would be all over the station by the time I got back. The sergeant probably didn't say much, but both Grady and McDaniels knew, so I figured why let them spread all kinds of rumors and have it get out of hand. Better to just come out with it, and let it either blow up in my face, or have it turn out like it did with everyone just kind of ignoring it. It's not like I'm fucking you in the squad room or something." Lex looked over his shoulder as he backed out of the parking spot before looking at Gavin. "Plus, I only got to put up with it until Christmas, and then I'm off until I start with the state in January."

Gavin nodded, guessing that made sense, because Lex didn't have too much time left on the force, but it also made him remember what he'd been thinking earlier. "Yeah, about that, Lex, we were supposed to have a talk about your new job, and then, well, you know with the fire and all, everything just kind of got pushed to the side. I'm sorry about ignoring your stuff, but maybe we could talk about it now," he said. Once again, he babbled because Lex's jaw twitched, and Gavin knew it meant Lex was nervous about something, which always unsettled Gavin.

Lex sighed, another sign Gavin wasn't going to like whatever it was Lex needed to tell him about his new position. He tried to puzzle out what could be so bad. Maybe he'd have to work horrible hours, or maybe... Oh... Gavin's stomach gave a lurch at the thought that maybe Lex would have to relocate, but hell, he was still going to be in the state. It wouldn't be that big of a deal. He would be at most what, five hours away, and though it would suck, it wasn't like they couldn't still be together—or was it?

"You have to move, don't you?" Gavin blurted. He couldn't wait for Lex to figure out a way to sugarcoat it for him. When Lex clenched his jaw and wouldn't look at him, Gavin knew. "Where do you have to go, and why didn't you tell me?"

"We've been kinda busy, Doc; not like there's been a good time to bring it up lately," Lex said. He was driving and Gavin could tell Lex was using that as an excuse not to look at him.

"So what, Lex? Were you just going to wait until you had to start packing to tell me I needed to find somewhere to live? You're just going to pack up and leave me here and never look back, aren't you?" Gavin asked, a note of hysteria making his voice crack. Then his stomach gave an even bigger lurch, and he knew what remained of his breakfast was going to make like Jesus and rise again at the thought of losing yet another thing in his life. "Pull over!"

"Doc, come on, can—" Gavin's loud, retching noise cut Lex off. He pulled the car to the side of the street just in time for Gavin to throw his door open and stick his head out far enough so his vomit landed on the ground instead of in the car.

Gavin heaved a couple of times until nothing came up. Lex rubbed his back as he sat there with the top half of his body hanging out the door. Gavin was shaking, not just from the throwing up, but because he knew for sure Lex was going to leave him behind. All that talk about being together, Lex's big declarations at the station and at the hospital in front of everyone had been a sham because Lex knew all along that their time together was limited.

"Baby, come on. Close the door, and let's go home so you can brush your teeth, and we'll get lunch and talk."

Gavin shook his head. No, he couldn't do this, not now, not just after he'd lost everything important to him. Fuck, he'd even lost his parents because he'd needed to be with Lex so much, loved him so much. He got out of the car and started walking down the sidewalk, not knowing or caring where he was going.

"Doc, stop!" Lex called from the car.

The car door slammed, and Gavin knew Lex would chase him. He could hear the rattling of Lex's duty belt behind him before arms wrapped around his waist, and Lex pulled him back into his chest. Gavin looked around the residential neighborhood they'd stopped in and wondered what the people in the houses thought was happening on their quiet little street. Surely they had no idea his world had just been shattered, and the burly cop restraining him had been the one to wield the sledgehammer.

"Doc, please listen to me," Lex said. His breath was warm on Gavin's ear and neck, making him shiver. He wanted to lean back into that strong embrace and let Lex put him back together once again, but he didn't.

"I can't do this, Lex. I can't lose you now. It's not fair," Gavin whined.

"You're not going to lose me. I was trying to figure out a way to make it work before I talked to you about it. First of all, you don't have to move.

You can stay in the condo as long as you want to, forever if you want, I promise, but please just listen to me before you sign the death certificate on this thing we got. Please, for once, just listen to me first," Lex pleaded. The tone of Lex's voice would have broken Gavin's heart if it hadn't already been done.

"So you are leaving?"

Lex sighed against Gavin's neck. "I have to go to Camp Ripley for fifteen weeks of training, and then my post will be up north, but I've been thinking about it, and I decided if you don't want to come with me, maybe I won't take the job."

Gavin stiffened; that was not what he'd expected to hear Lex say. He knew how much Lex had wanted that job. Jean told him ever since Lex's sister had been killed by a drunk driver on the highway, Lex's dream had been to be a state trooper so he could patrol the roadways that took his sister from him. To help keep them safe so other people wouldn't have to go through what they had.

"No, you have to take the job. You've worked for that position, and you can't just give it up for no reason." It was the truth, even if it hurt Gavin to say it.

"Doc, baby, please can we talk about this later? There's so much we have to discuss, and there's no reason to jump to any rash conclusions. You just need to know that"—Lex turned Gavin so they were facing each other—"I love you, and I meant it every time I said it. I may not say it often, but when I do, I really, really do mean it. I'm not ready to give up on this unless you tell me you don't want me anymore. Then I'll go. It will probably break me, but—"

Gavin stopped Lex with his lips but then pulled back when he remembered he'd just upchucked, and his breath was probably bad enough to kill the man he loved. Lex pulled him back and kissed him hard. He let Gavin go with a smirk.

"That was really gross, Lex."

"No, Doc, that was love," Lex said with a wink. "Let's go home and get Ma to make us some lunch."

THE INTENTION HAD been for Lex and Gavin to sit down and talk about their future. They'd been kept apart by differing schedules and Gavin's meetings with the Detective and District Attorney. Lex was supposed to tell Gavin about his new position and what it meant for their future. Lex wanted Gavin to move up north with him after his training was done. God, Lex's training—fifteen weeks with only a couple of weekend visits would be hell. Gavin had been thinking about everything for the last two days. It would mean looking for a new position, but he could easily do that even if it meant working for a hospital while he looked into a private clinic spot.

He was more worried about leaving Riley and Sheila behind. He'd been waffling back and forth and hadn't come to a decision yet, but Lex assured Gavin he had time. Shit, fifteen weeks without Lex in his bed—he couldn't wrap his mind around it. Lex wasn't pressuring Gavin, but he felt like the future of their relationship rested on his shoulders.

Jean helped him cook supper and then went to visit her friend for the evening so Gavin was alone waiting for Lex to get home when his cell phone rang.

"Hello?" He didn't recognize the number.

"Dr. Addison, this is Shelly from District Attorney Kotter's office. I have Mr. Kotter on the line for you. Please hold," the woman said.

That was odd. Usually she told Gavin what it was he needed to know or where he needed to be to meet the DA. There were a couple of clicks, and then the DA was on the line. He issued no greeting before he said, "Good news, Dr. Addison. We've got the plea agreement signed."

Gavin slumped into a chair and listened as the District Attorney laid it out for him. The talk he'd planned to have with Lex would have to be put off once again because they were going out to celebrate.

"Doc, I know this is going to be hard for you," Lex said. His worried expression was one Gavin had gotten used to seeing in the week leading up to the holiday.

It would be Gavin's first without his mom and dad present, and everyone was being so careful around him. He didn't want to feel the emptiness his parent's absence left in the pit of his stomach, but it was there, and it was affecting him whether he wanted it to or not. He didn't want to get into it with Lex yet again.

Gavin had made plans. He'd even prepared while he'd taken his shower. He wanted to clear his mind of everything and enjoy being with Lex for the first time since his life had been turned into the mess it was.

Gavin was going to give Lex something for always being there for him. It felt weird that at thirty-six, he was about to lose his virginity once again. The nervous butterflies in his stomach felt familiar, just like the first time when he was a teenager; some things apparently never changed. At least this time, Gavin would be giving it to someone he loved.

"I'm fine. I'll be fine," Gavin said as he snuggled into Lex's side, almost crowding him off the bed.

Lex reached over to turn off the lamp, plunging them into darkness so completely Gavin couldn't even make out Lex's outline. Lex's chest lifted under his cheek as Lex sighed. "I'm so sorry about everything, Doc. I don't know if I'd have been strong enough to get through everything you've gone through in the past few weeks, and I'm sorry my crap is adding to your stress."

Gavin waited quietly because he knew what was coming. It would be the same thing Lex had been saying since Gavin had figured out about his relocation. He'd try to butt in, but Lex would shush him so he could say his piece once again. Gavin would let him get it out so he could put his plan for the night into action.

"You can take all the time you need to make up your mind. I'll come home whenever I can, and nothing will really change," Lex said.

"I feel bad, Lex. You should be thinking about your training and then looking for a home up there for you and Jean, not thinking about staying in someone's spare room while you wait for me to make up my mind." Gavin voiced his feelings once again. Damn it, he didn't want to talk about it again, but he couldn't stop himself from saying what he thought even if it meant delaying what he really wanted.

"I will be looking for something more permanent eventually, but I'd like for you to have some input too... Sorry, Doc, but I just can't give up hope that you'll want to—"

Gavin put his hand over Lex's mouth to stop him. They'd gone around and around on the subject without getting anywhere. Gavin needed time to think. He'd been preoccupied with the Cassie bullshit and his house. What little time he had free had been spent thinking about his future.

Lex had already obtained his dream, or he would as he rose through the ranks. Gavin had dreams too, and for once he was actually thinking about putting his plan into action on the career front. He needed to see if it was feasible to do it up north, so he could still be with the man he loved, and that would take some time. Once he decided, he'd still have to give two months' notice under his contract with the hospital that owned the clinic he worked for. He needed to decide soon because any delay on his part would make their separation that much longer, and that was if he chose to go with Lex in the end.

Gavin rolled on top of Lex, who grunted under his weight. Lex's breath ghosted across his lips before Gavin leaned down and kissed him. The rough stubble Lex refused to shave off scratched his own freshly shaved face.

Gavin shifted to straddle Lex's muscular thighs just below his groin. He broke the kiss as he sat up, running his hands down Lex's torso to feel all the lumps and crevices of the man's anatomy, something he'd become very familiar with over the past couple of months. Lex's breath caught when Gavin lightly ran his fingers back up to find his nipples and gave them a sharp pinch and pull. The hips trapped beneath Gavin bucked.

"Doc." Lex's voice was breathy with his blooming arousal.

"I've been thinking, Lex." Gavin released his hold on the sensitive buds he'd been torturing and let his hands wander downwards. "I think it's time for me to ask you." Lex's breathing sped up, and the flesh under Gavin's fingers quivered. He leaned forward to kiss Lex once again, but he had another motive. Gavin slid his hand under his pillow and retrieved the lube and foil-packeted condom he'd stashed there earlier.

"Baby? What are you doing?" Lex asked. Gavin knew full well Lex knew exactly what he was up to.

"I don't want to talk about this, Lex. I'm going to ask you one question, and you only get to give me a one word answer... It better be the right one," Gavin said as he resumed his seated position over Lex. The darkness gave him the courage he needed to bluntly ask his question. "Now, Lex, my love, will you please fuck me?" He waited. It seemed to take forever, as he counted the breaths coming faster from beneath him.

"Yes..." Lex said yes, but Gavin heard the reservation along with the desire in his voice.

Gavin ripped the condom packet open and groped in the darkness for Lex's hard cock. He smiled to himself as he deftly rolled the latex sheath down over the engorged flesh. He found the lube as he stroked Lex, making him moan and wriggle. He dribbled the lube down so his pumping fist spread it over the entire length.

When he had his lover sufficiently prepared, Gavin released him and got to his knees to climb into position. He'd thought about this for a long time, and it was long overdue. One of Lex's hands reached between them, and Gavin gasped when one of Lex's thick fingers breached his bottom.

The chuckle from below was unexpected, but the words that followed explained the source of Lex's amusement. "Someone's a boy scout, a naughty, naughty boy scout," Lex growled. He was fingering Gavin's already prepared ass. His finger twisted and probed until he pressed against Gavin's prostate, making him jolt at the intense sensation. That soft chuckle again. "Found it," Lex said as he pressed the spot again, making Gavin shudder with pleasure.

Gavin got ahold of himself and grabbed Lex's wrist to pull his questing digit from his ass. "I'm ready; no need for that." Gavin resumed his movements to get into position, but Lex pulled him down and claimed his lips in a demanding kiss. Gavin groaned into Lex's mouth as the invading tongue took over his senses. Lex fucked Gavin's mouth with his tongue, leaving him feeling almost violated by the time he was done.

Lex released him and whispered, "That's what I'd have done to your ass if you hadn't already slathered it in silicone-based lube." Gavin shivered at the erotic image in his mind of Lex's tongue buried inside him but there was no time for that; he was on a mission, and he wouldn't let Lex distract him from his goal.

Gavin's cock brushed against the slickness of Lex's as he crawled up and over Lex's straining erection. He got on his knees and reached back with one hand to hold the object he was about to impale himself on at the right angle for entry. He lined up, but just as he was about to push down, he was blinded by the small light on the nightstand when Lex reached over and clicked it on. After the total darkness, the light was too much, and Gavin had to close his eyes against it as he relaxed and let the head of Lex's member breach him for the first time.

Gavin had done a good job preparing himself, but the stretch was still just this side of painful. He took a couple of deep breaths as Lex swore from somewhere beyond his closed eyelids. He felt his muscles give in to his relaxation techniques, and when they did, he wasted no time finishing what he'd started. The feeling was indescribable. Besides the light, burning sensation, the feeling of fullness was strange. Gavin wasn't sure he'd find any pleasure in the act itself, but he was willing to try for Lex.

"Oh god, fuck yes, shit, Doc. Fuck, that's fucking amazing." Gavin's ass landed on Lex's balls. "Look at me, baby. Please, open your eyes," Lex pleaded.

Gavin swallowed and opened his eyes just a crack to assure he wouldn't be blinded again and then met Lex's bright-blue gaze. What he saw there in that look was pure, unadulterated love. There was no denying it—not that he ever had—but the raw show of emotion spurred Gavin to move his hips. He wanted to give Lex all the pleasure he could, wanted nothing more than to please him. Strange feelings be damned; this was something Gavin could do for Lex to show him how much he appreciated everything he'd done.

Lex didn't move an inch. He let Gavin do what he would, gave him control over this intimate act. Gavin rocked on the cock that speared him as he rolled his hips. When Gavin managed to get the right angle so his prostate was brushed at every movement, he started to move faster. He knew now why guys liked it on this end too. Gavin lifted up as he rocked, and the short deep thrusts made him bite his bottom lip to stifle the moans he knew would be loud enough to wake the neighbors.

All his attempts at keeping the peace flew out the window when Lex grabbed Gavin's cock and started pumping it with firm, measured strokes. He was aware of the noises issuing forth from his own mouth, but he couldn't bother to be ashamed as he took as much pleasure from the act as he hoped his partner was deriving from it.

Gavin didn't know when he'd started, but by the time he was ready to come, he was slamming down on Lex's cock, impaling himself with reckless abandon. The all too familiar feeling at the base of his spine and in his balls signaled his imminent release.

"Gonna come…soon… Lex, please…" Lex's hand sped up on Gavin's cock, and as he came, he let out a howl that made him sound like a lunatic. He wanted to fall into a boneless heap on top of Lex, but he could still feel the stiff dick in his ass. Lex hadn't finished. Gavin gasped for air as he tried to keep moving. Lex's hands found his hips and gripped them in a bruising hold. Lex used his grasp on Gavin's hips to bounce him haplessly up and down on his shaft.

"Fuck, not gonna...fuck!" Lex was almost as loud as Gavin had been. He pulled Gavin down hard so his cock was buried to the hilt as he came. Lex let Gavin fall to his heaving chest and wrapped his arms tightly around him.

Gavin was content to just lay there and drift with his face pressed into the side of Lex's, but Lex's voice broke through the heavy breathing. "God, Gavin, I love you so much. Please come with me. I don't think I can live without you," Lex said in a tremulous voice.

And Gavin knew what he needed to do.

GAVIN FIDGETED ON the hard bench. He felt like his tie was strangling him, and even Lex's hand in his couldn't calm his unsettled nerves. Jean was sitting beside Lex, and Riley was on Gavin's left with Sheila next to him. His entire support system had turned out and some of their friends too. Gavin noted Mike, Stu, and Lex's partner, Grady, in the back. Becca was sitting with Karen and Matt from the hospital; the only ones missing were his parents.

The bailiff stood and started his speech. "Please rise, the Honorable Judge Masterson..."

Gavin stood but tuned the guy out as his eyes were drawn to the other side of the courtroom. Cassie was standing next to her lawyer, looking put together as always, but her parents, who stood behind her, were showing the wear that the stress of this spectacle had put on them. Gavin felt a pang of guilt at the sad look Mrs. Stevens gave him before she tried a small shaky smile. Lex caught where Gavin was looking and squeezed his hand.

Things had gone so quickly, Gavin was still a little off-balance. Once Cassie's lawyer had gotten all the evidence the state had against his client, they had been quick to accept the plea agreement offered by the district attorney. Lex had helped Gavin through the entire proceeding with his legal knowledge and that of the judicial system. In the end, Gavin knew this was for the best.

Cassie had pleaded guilty to one count of arson in the first degree, and the DA had dropped the attempted murder charge, thereby shortening the entire process by months. Everyone had gathered in the courtroom for the second time for Cassie's sentencing. The best case scenario for Gavin would be if Cassie got the maximum sentence under the law, which was twenty years in jail and a twenty thousand dollar fine. The DA thought the chances were pretty good that the judge would take into account Cassie's prior record when he decided her fate.

Everyone sat quietly as Judge Masterson read through all the legal mumbo jumbo and then the words Gavin had been waiting for: "The defendant is to be remanded to the custody of the state for a period of not more than twenty years but not less than seven years. The defendant is also ordered to pay the maximum restitution charges of twenty thousand dollars under statute six-zero-nine-dash-five-six-two..."

Gavin's heart was beating so hard he thought he might pass out. There was a little bit of clamoring in the courtroom, causing the judge to bang his gavel to restore order. Lex put his arm around Gavin's shoulders and squeezed. Lex was smiling broadly at Gavin, and the words finally sunk in. Cassie would be out of his life for the foreseeable future. A weight he hadn't even known was there lifted off his shoulders.

Everyone rose to the bailiff's call to rise. Gavin was ready to be out of the courtroom and to get on with his life when Cassie's voice stopped him in his tracks.

"Gavin!"

Gavin turned to see Cassie struggling against the guards as she shouted his name.

"You perverted faggot asshole! How could you do this to me? I was the only one who ever loved you, you fucking bastard. You think that he can give you something I couldn't? Well let me tell you, there's no fixing you. You're a broken piece of shit. You hear me? I hope you rot in hell!" Cassie was still screaming as she was dragged out of the courtroom.

Everyone's eyes were on him, and Gavin wished, for once, he could disappear on command. A strong arm went around his waist, and Gavin let himself be led from the courtroom. Lex, Jean, Riley, and Shelia gathered around him to provide some protection from prying eyes.

"Gavin, could I have a word with you, please?" Cora asked. She was hurrying after their group to catch them as they made their way to their car.

Gavin turned to face the woman he'd once called Mom. He still cared for her. She'd never said or done a bad thing to him, so he held no ill will toward, her. "Cora, I'm so sorry." It was the only thing Gavin could think to say even if he had nothing to apologize for.

A tear tracked down Cora's cheek, and she used a handkerchief to dab at it. "Oh dear, I'm sorry; I just can't seem to stop crying. I wanted to tell you that we're so sorry for all the trouble Cassie caused you. I should have seen what was happening when she was staying with us. I feel responsible for you getting hurt," she said, her voice hitching with emotion.

Gavin left the security of Lex's embrace to take Cora into his arms. "I don't blame you. I'm sorry you have to go through this. I don't think anyone could have seen this coming," Gavin said. He didn't blame anyone but Cassie and himself for everything that had happened. "I need to go now. Take care of yourselves, and have a Merry Christmas or, well, at least as merry as you can, considering."

"Thank you so much, Gavin. You don't know what it means to hear you say that. You have a Merry Christmas too, and I hope you're happy with your new...um... I just hope you have a happy life from here on out," Cora said. She gave Gavin a final squeeze, and Mr. Stevens shook Gavin's hand before they left.

Jean flung her arms around Gavin's waist in a big hug. "I'm so proud of you. You are such a good boy, Gavin." She looked up at him with shining eyes. "I'm so glad you're part of the family. Lex definitely got it right."

Gavin hugged Jean while he gave Lex a questioning look over her shoulder. Lex shrugged and smiled, which was a typical Lex response of late when it came to his mother.

"I love you too, Jean. Now can we go home and eat that leftover fried chicken Lex hid in the back of the fridge?" Gavin asked.

"Oh man, if there's Jean's fried chicken, we're so in," Riley said as he slapped Lex on the back. Lex glared at their friend as they got in the car, Gavin sandwiched between Lex and Jean in the back seat of Riley's Jeep. Everyone was meeting them back at the condo for a little "Cassie's in jail...finally" party.

"I'm so glad this is over, and I'm happy that she got the maximum sentence. She so fucking deserved it," Sheila said. She turned and looked at Jean. "Oh sorry, Jean, excuse my French, but I just can't help it when it comes to her."

"No problem, dear. I think it's fucking wonderful too," Jean agreed. She giggled at the shocked looks she got from the other people in the car.

TWENTY-SIX

LEX FIGURED SOMETHING was up when the call came over the radio for their unit to come back to the station an hour before they normally went back in. The cake was a nice touch—chocolate, Grady's favorite—but it was for Lex, not his partner. It was Lex's last shift with the SCPD, and they were giving him a going-away party.

Lex smiled through the sergeant's speech and accepted the good-natured ribbing from his soon-to-be-former colleagues about going over to the dark side. It was all fun and games until Merriweather suggested the officers who were off shift, or would be when Lex's shift finished, should go out for a drink.

"I'm not going out to a gay bar," Grady joked. Lex knew it was a joke; his partner had, surprisingly, accepted his relationship without so much as a bigoted peep.

"Yeah, I'm sure that little boy toy you got at home wouldn't want you at one either, Turner," Santiago said with a chuckle. She was still a little jealous Lex had landed the hot doctor she'd been drooling over, but Lex took her comment as the joke it was meant to be.

"That's just fucking gross. Can we not talk about Turner's personal life?" Officer Kranz growled. Now that one, Lex knew, was not said jokingly. Lex turned to look at the big bear of a beat cop who had an undisguised look of disgust on his face. "I for one am glad you're taking your alternative lifestyle over to the staties. Good riddance, I say."

Lex could almost hear the quickened heartbeats of the people around him as they waited in silence for his reply. He didn't give Kranz the satisfaction of listening to him try to justify his relationship or stand up for equal rights. "Yeah, I'm glad I'm going too, but I will miss watching you take a shower, Kranz," Lex said with a saucy wink.

In retrospect, it was probably not the smartest thing to bait a homophobe by reminding him you've seen him naked almost as much as his wife has. But Lex guessed the black eye he'd be sporting for the

Christmas pictures that year would be a good reminder not to do it again.

Lex didn't punch back, and Kranz was pulled away by his partner who kept telling him Lex's faggot ass wasn't worth a suspension. The tussle pretty much ended the party. Grady uncharacteristically offered to finish up their paperwork, and there was no more mention of hitting Stuckey's for a beer afterward. Lex hit the showers in a conspicuously empty locker room and then went to the sarge's office to hand in his gear.

"Turner, I'm sorry about that. Kranz will be dealt with," Sergeant Tollefson said as he eyed Lex's swelling cheek. "Just so you know, most of the force has no problem with your personal life. It has no bearing on the job you do, and you've always been an exemplary officer. It's a shame we're losing you to the state. I hope they offer you what you're looking for, and if they don't, you're always welcome back here." He shook Lex's hand.

"Thanks, I appreciate that. It's been a pleasure working under you, sir," Lex said. He always did like his sergeant.

Lex stopped to talk to Grady for a minute before he left. They made plans to meet for a drink on Grady's next night off, with their respective other halves. They weren't friends, but they'd been partners for a couple of years, and that ending deserved a beer as a send-off.

Lex accepted the good-bye handshakes and a few hugs, mostly from the female officers who, strangely enough, probably wouldn't have hugged him if they knew he was still attracted to women. Funny how people's perceptions of you changed based on who you slept with, Lex thought. He got into his truck and prepared to go home and explain his shiner to his mom and his boyfriend, but he had a stop to make first.

Lex pulled into the parking lot of a strip mall and parked in front of the little shop at the end. He was being sneaky with his purchase, but he had to admit he didn't care. He hoped it would help sway the doc's decision about the move. Lex wasn't above a little emotional blackmail to get what he wanted.

The girl in the shop was helpful. After he picked out the perfect one, she made sure he had everything he needed to take care of it. He paid for his early Christmas present for Gavin and his mom and walked out with a whistle on his lips. He couldn't wait to get home. He knew he was in for some serious loving when the doc got a load of his gift.

They were in the kitchen, which was nothing out of the ordinary for the two of them. Sometimes Lex wondered if Gavin loved Jean more than him. It made him feel like a petulant child thinking it, but it only got worse when he suspected his mom felt the same for the doc. Lex shook his head at his tinge of jealousy, telling himself Gavin needed someone to fill in for the mother who had recently abandoned him.

Lex was gone so much with his erratic shifts that having the doc there to keep his mom company had made it a win-win situation for all of them. His upcoming training had been something that in the past he would have dreaded. Leaving his mom alone for that long would have been hard, but now, although he hated leaving both of them, he at least knew they had each other.

Lex set the bags in his hand on the floor and then placed the plastic carrier next to them. He crouched down and pulled the thing, as he'd been referring to the little fur ball he'd picked up on his way home, out of the carrier and into his arms. It mewled and looked at him with wide, blue eyes.

"Shh, quiet now, you're supposed to be a surprise," he whispered to the little orange kitten as he used one finger to pet its cute, tiny head. There was laughter coming in fits and stops from the kitchen since, apparently, they hadn't heard him come in. Lex kicked off his shoes and settled onto the couch with the kitty and the remote to wait for them to notice he was home.

He almost dozed off, lost in the serenity of petting the purring kitten in his lap with the smell of what had to be Christmas cookies wafting from the kitchen. Gavin's laughter coming from the other room got louder as he walked into the living room.

"Oh, Jean, seriously, it's not a penis; it's supposed to be a cane. I don't think snowmen even—Lex!" Gavin's surprised exclamation, when he was startled by Lex sitting on the couch, made the kitten dig its claws into Lex's arm.

"Shit, ouch, damn it, Doc, you scared him half to death." Lex pulled the little kitty claws out of his skin. Gavin's face melted into a puddle of awe at the cuteness before him.

"Jean, get in here. Lex got a kitty!" he hollered excitedly. He was on the couch scooping the kitty out of Lex's arms before Lex could even say hello. Gavin lifted the little ball of fur up to his face and rubbed his nose against the cat's and then stood up as Jean came into the room to see the new addition to the family.

"Oh hey, Lex, how was your day? Oh, not too bad; got punched in the face, but that's all good. It's nice to see you too, Doc... Oh, Lex, you big dummy, why'd you go and do something stupid like that? No reason, and I missed you too, sweetheart..." Lex held a conversation with himself as Gavin and his mom cooed over the kitten and started debating names for it while Lex pouted on the couch, feeling ignored. Geez, if he'd known he'd be sitting there alone without so much as a hello kiss, he'd never have gotten the darn fleabag.

Lex oomphed when Gavin landed on his lap and started placing little kisses all over his face. He grinned and tried to catch Gavin's rapidly pecking lips with his own. Gavin finally landed one on his mouth and slid his tongue between Lex's lips. Lex kissed Gavin slowly and sweetly until his mom coughed and then chuckled behind them.

Gavin pulled back. "I love him. Thank you so much for getting us a kitten, Lex. I've never had a pet before." The doc's eyes danced with happiness, making the gold flecks in his warm, brown eyes catch the light, looking like little sparks.

"I'm glad you like him, Doc, but you have to share. I only got one," Lex joked.

"I'm serious, it's the best present I've ever gotten...even if I have to share him," Gavin said with a smile. The small smile dropped from his face, and his eyes widened. He grabbed Lex's chin and turned his face so he could examine the swelling, bruised skin under Lex's eye. "What happened? Did a perp resist? Did you shoot someone?"

Lex grabbed the hand holding him in place and kissed it. "No and no. It's nothing, just a little misunderstanding at my going-away party."

Gavin's eyes narrowed to slits. "It was one of those assholes who think fags shouldn't be cops, right?"

Lex sighed and looked over the doc's shoulder to his mom. She was standing there holding the cat with a worried look on her face. He knew they both questioned his decision to come out, but it was over, and he didn't work there anymore.

"It was nothing, just one guy, and it was my last day. I don't have to worry about it anymore. Quit with the worried looks; everything's fine. What's for supper? Are we eating sugar cookies?" Lex asked, trying to lighten the mood.

Gavin's eyes searched his face for a minute before he leaned in and placed a soft kiss on Lex's bruise. "I just worry about you. It's not like you don't have a dangerous enough job without having to watch your back around the guys you work with."

"I know, Doc, and I'm always careful. Now get your boney butt off me, and get me food," Lex said and then laughed at the look on Gavin's face.

The doc stood up and glanced over his shoulder, trying to see his own butt, and when his attempt failed, he looked at Jean. "Do I have a boney butt?" It made Lex chuckle as his mom looked thoughtfully at his boyfriend's round little butt.

She walked over, presumably to get a closer look, but instead, she patted the butt in question. "Nope, it's cute and most definitely not boney; kind of a bubble butt if you ask me."

"Oh, lord, save me," Lex groaned. He got up and grabbed the doc up in a bear-hug. "I like your butt. So why don't you walk into the kitchen so I can watch it while you get me my supper?"

"Pfft, you're a big boy, so you can dish up your own plate, or does your mommy not let you touch the hot pans?" Gavin teased.

"Oh, you boys, let's go, I'll dish up for both of you, but I will not cut your meat," Jean said in a faux-exasperated tone. They laughed as she set the cat down on the couch and headed into the kitchen.

"I love that old broad," Gavin said with a fond smile.

"Yeah, she's pretty great, but if she hears you call her that, she'll wash your mouth out with dish soap." Lex let the doc go but held his hand as they went to get their supper.

THEY WERE SITTING on the floor in the living room, wrapping gifts, drinking wine, and just enjoying the warm feelings of the season. Every once in a while Lex noticed a frown mar Gavin's face. He replaced it quickly with a smile every time Lex saw it, but it still appeared more often than he liked. Even George's stalking and attacking of the ribbons and wrapping paper didn't lighten the doc's mood for more than a few minutes.

"What's up, Doc?" Lex asked when the frown line appeared again.

Gavin looked up and shook his head. "Nothing, just wondering if I should mail the presents I got for my parents to them or..." He trailed off and Lex wondered what the "or" was.

He leaned in and kissed Gavin's lips. "Why don't you wait, and if you want, we can take a drive down there," he offered. He didn't think it was a great idea, but if Gavin wanted to try it, he'd go with him.

Gavin smiled. "You'd go with me even knowing that my mom is liable to knock you out with her purse again?"

"Doc, I'd brave much bigger purses if it made you happy." Gavin laughed and Lex felt better. He wanted to finish up their wrapping and go to the bedroom to unwrap the gift that kept on giving.

"HEY, UNCLE TED, Aunt Ida, come on in," Lex greeted his aunt and uncle at the door. "Damn, can you believe this snow? How were the roads?" He took their coats and hung them by the door as they stripped off their boots.

"Horrible. So many cars in the ditches I lost count. First real snow of the season and everyone turns into a mindless idiot," Ted said.

"Yep, the same old, same old then. Ma's in the kitchen as usual. Come meet the new additions to the festivities this year." Lex led them into the living room where the rest of the guests were sipping warm drinks. "Everyone, this is my Uncle Ted and Aunt Ida. They just drove in from the cities. Ted, Ida, this is Riley and Sheila, friends of ours." He waited as they shook hands and exchanged greetings. "And over here is who everyone's been dying to meet." He walked toward a smiling Gavin. He took the kitten out of his boyfriend's arms and turned away from the look of surprise on Gavin's face. "This is George. Isn't he cute?"

Riley and Sheila were laughing, and his cousin and Jean's two friends, who were yearly guests, were smiling at his joke. "Lex, quit teasing Gavin," Jean said from the kitchen doorway. "Come here, sweetie. I'll introduce you properly." She crossed the room and put her arm around Gavin's waist.

Lex shook his head at the two of them, thick as thieves as usual. His mom had been the happiest he'd seen her during a holiday since his sister passed, and he thanked Gavin, and even Riley and Sheila, for that little miracle. His aunt and uncle greeted his boyfriend with hugs and greetings of "Welcome to the family." Lex cuddled the kitten and decided this was the best Christmas Eve he'd had in his life, even better than the year he got his first bike.

Everyone sat around drinking and snacking. Riley kept everyone entertained with stories of med school experiments that went wrong while Jean flitted about making sure everyone had what they needed. Lex noticed his mom glanced at the clock quite often and also out the window at the ever increasingly falling snow.

When the doorbell rang, Jean popped up and rushed to the door. Lex looked at Gavin, who just shrugged. As far as Lex knew, everyone who'd been invited had already arrived. Gavin paled and Lex turned to see his mom leading a very hesitant-looking pair of Addisons into the gathering in the living room.

"I'm so glad you two decided to join us," Jean said to Mona as she took the bags of presents out of her hands and handed them to Sheila to put with the others. "I was starting to worry when the weather got worse."

"The last thirty miles or so were pretty slow going, but you know what they say: slow and steady wins the race," Roger said with a small, anxious smile.

Lex couldn't take his eyes off Gavin as Gavin stood there staring. Lex wasn't sure, but he thought the doc might start crying at any minute.

Roger walked across the room first and took his son into his arms. "Gavin, I've missed you. Thank you for giving us another chance, son." He pulled back to look into Gavin's face.

"Dad?" Gavin asked, obviously at a loss for what to say at this unexpected turn of events.

Lex knew Gavin was having a mental breakdown at that moment, and he wanted to step in, but Jean's abrupt departure caught his attention. As much as he wanted to stay and watch how this reunion played out, his need to make sure his mother was okay was much stronger. Gavin had Riley and Sheila there to make sure he'd come through this, but his mom only had him.

He pushed the kitchen door open to find his mom standing at the counter with tears running down her face. "Ma, what's wrong?"

She wiped at her face and sniffed. "Nothing. I'm just so happy that they came. Gavin needs them, and they have no idea."

"How did you do this, Ma?" Lex asked. He'd had no clue she had talked to Gavin's parents, let alone got them to agree to come for Christmas.

"I've been talking to Roger on the phone since just before Thanksgiving, and eventually, I talked to Mona too. I just told them the truth, honey."

Lex shook his head. "What truth, Ma? I don't understand how you managed to change their minds about this."

"Well Roger didn't need his mind changed. He was fine with Gavin being with you, but he loves his wife and wanted her to come around so she wouldn't feel like he was taking sides," she said.

"But he was; the doc could have used a phone call from him at least."

Jean nodded and pursed her lips. "It was his choice. I told him what Gavin was going through, but he made a decision, and in the end it got them here anyway so there's that," she said. The disapproval was clear on her face. She agreed with him on that count, it seemed.

"So why are they here? What finally convinced his mom?" Lex asked.

"Well, Lex, I guess it was what I told them that made her see the light."

"Ma, come on, you're killing me. Tell me what you told them," Lex begged.

"I told them that they were wasting precious time, time that they'd never get back. That if, god forbid, something happened to one of them tomorrow, would they regret the time they spent shutting out their only child? I told them what it's like to really lose your child. How you spend every day missing them and how you'd give almost anything for one more hug, one more word. How when you lose your child, you lose a part of your soul; your heart is broken forever, and there's never peace for your mind. That being estranged for such a stupid reason made them the most pigheaded people I'd ever met because Gavin is a great man, and disowning him because he loves you is wrong. How can love be wrong?" she finally asked through her tears.

Lex wiped his own tears on the sleeve of his sweater and took his mom into his arms. "It's not, Ma, and I'm so damn happy that I got the best mother in the world for my own. I'm sorry if I've been neglecting you lately. I know this time of year is hard for you, and I should have made more of an effort to spend time with you."

She sniffed. "I know how your work schedule is and that you spend as much time with me as you can, probably more than is healthy for a grown man to spend with his mom," she said with a little laugh. She pulled away and took a dish towel off the counter to wipe her face.

"Besides, I have Gavin and George now, so who needs a big lug like you hanging around?"

"That hurts, Ma."

She hugged him again. "You know I'm joking. You will always be my little boy, and I will always love you most. Now let's go see if anyone's managed to get beat-up in there."

The living room was much quieter than it had been before the last guests arrived. Lex's brow furrowed when he realized Gavin and his parents weren't in the room.

"They went to the bedroom to talk," Riley supplied.

"Oh, okay, well you know what we need?" Lex asked the tense people sitting in his living room.

"A condom dispenser in the bathroom?" Riley asked. "Ouch, god, woman, you can't even stop abusing me on Christmas," he muttered when Sheila smacked him.

"It's not Christmas yet, and if you're not careful, Santa will beat you with the coal-filled stocking he leaves you this year," Sheila said. "Now stop making inappropriate comments. There are old people present, and what's the rule?"

"No sex jokes when anyone's parents are in the room," Riley recited like a chastised school boy.

"Good boy," Sheila said. She patted Riley's head and turned to Lex. "So what is it we need then?"

Lex was laughing along with everyone else when Jean said, "I don't know about all the other old people in the room, but I myself enjoy a good sex joke now and then." She winked at a snickering Riley.

"See, Jean's my new favorite senior. She gets me." Riley stuck his tongue out at Sheila, who hit his chin, making him bite it and cry out. "You're stho mean!" Riley lisped around his sore tongue.

Lex shook his head at their shenanigans. "We need to break out the brandy slush. What do you say, Ma? I know it's earlier than usual, but I think we could all use something stronger than your virgin eggnog."

"I'll get the glasses. You go get the bucket," Jean said. "Riley, will you grab the Squirt out of the pantry?" Everyone mobilized, eager to get a little alcohol into their systems after the unexpected surprise guests had harshed their mellow.

An hour later, when the Addisons emerged from the bedroom, the party was back in full swing. Riley was on a roll, telling the raunchiest jokes he could remember, and Lex's Uncle Ted had started trying to one-up him. Everyone was nearly in tears from laughter. Gavin also looked like he'd been crying, but Lex doubted it was from laughing too hard. Lex fought the urge to go to Gavin and hold him. Gavin made sure his parents were comfortable before he went to the kitchen. He made eye contact with Jean, and she got up to follow him under the pretense of refilling snack bowls.

Lex stayed in his seat, even though he was dying to go in there to see what was going on. "So..." Lex said in the general direction of Gavin's parents. He had no idea what to say to them.

Roger looked at Lex and smiled. The gesture was probably meant to reassure Lex, but instead, it made his stomach twist. Lex had a bad feeling about Gavin's parents' sudden arrival, and the look on Gavin's face after they'd talked wasn't doing anything to quash that unease.

"Momma Mona, did you get me a good present this year?" Riley asked, breaking in to cut the tension in the room. "She always gets me the best stuff. Last year she got me one of those old-timey doctor's bags, and the year before that she found this old microscope that still works."

"Of course, Riley dear, I found your present at the flea market over in Chisholm, just like always," Mona said. A small smile tried to twitch its way onto her face when Sheila caught Mona's jab at Riley and giggled.

Gavin and Jean came back into the room. Whatever tension Riley had eased ratcheted back up at the grave look on their faces. Gavin sat next to Lex, but not like he normally did. There was no cuddling in or hand on Lex's thigh. The doc sat stiffly and maintained his personal space.

Lex waited until the conversation started back up. Jean had always been good at defusing tense social situations. She had the group chatting and laughing within minutes. It helped to have Riley there too. As much as he joked around, he knew what was at stake for his oldest and newest friends.

"What's going on, Doc?" Lex whispered. He leaned in closer to the man who would usually be clinging to him but now would barely look at him.

"Nothing. We'll talk about it later, okay?" Gavin's voice was unsteady like he was on the verge of tears. Lex took Gavin's hand in his, only wanting to comfort him, but Gavin jerked away like he'd just touched a hot stove, his eyes darting to his parents.

"So, I can't touch you now?" Lex hissed lowly so only Gavin could hear. His feelings were hurt, and though he knew it was childish, he couldn't help it.

Gavin's big brown eyes were huge when he turned back to Lex, the tears he was holding back making them shine. "Just...not right now, okay? Give me a little time?"

"Fine, take all the time you need." Lex got up and stood at the window. He watched the snow fall and tried to calm down. Why was it so important to him all of a sudden that Gavin show him some affection? He'd waited for Gavin every step of the way, and it always worked out in his favor. Why was he so impatient for the doc to shove their relationship in his parents' faces?

Lex sighed and the window in front of him fogged with his warm breath. He drew a little heart in the mist and then wiped it away quickly. He'd wait for Gavin once again because the doc had chosen him, and in the end that's what mattered most.

As day slipped into evening, Gavin remained distant but fidgeted and sent pleading looks Lex's way. Lex smiled every so often to let the doc know he understood and would give him his space and all the time he needed, even though it was killing Lex inside to keep his unspoken promise.

They ate dinner and then opened presents. Everyone exclaimed about the thoughtfulness of the gifts they'd received and thanked the givers. The only presents still under the tree when everything was said and done was a box from Lex to Gavin and an envelope from Gavin to Lex. Lex had wanted to get Gavin something special, but the cat had been his big gift idea. He'd settled on a gag gift that made him smile when he thought of Gavin opening it. Gavin would get a laugh out of it. Lex would have to wait because they decided to leave their gifts to each other for Christmas morning, when they'd be alone.

When the time came for their guests to start leaving, Lex noticed Gavin became more agitated. The twisting in Lex's stomach turned into a lead ball as he watched Gavin, who in turn, watched his parents with a wary look. Something was up, and it wasn't looking like Lex was going to like whatever it was.

"Well, I'm going to go start the car so it warms up," Roger said when he and Mona were the only remaining guests. "You'll be ready to go in about ten minutes?"

What the...? Lex looked to Gavin, who nodded slowly as his father went out the door. "Doc?"

"Lex, can we talk for a minute in the bedroom?" Gavin asked.

Lex looked at his mom, who had tears running down her face. He knew what Gavin was about to tell him and couldn't believe what was about to happen. Lex wanted nothing more than to turn around and leave, so he didn't have to hear it, but his head nodded, and his feet carried him to his fate without his mind making the conscious decision to do so.

Gavin pulled his duffle bag out of the closet and sat it on the bed. He looked up at Lex, sadness making his eyes a deeper shade of brown. "I'm going to go home with my parents for my vacation. My mom wants me to take a step back to make sure that this is what I really want, and maybe if I do this—"

"Yeah, that sounds like a good idea, Doc." Lex interrupted Gavin's excuse for leaving him. Mona hadn't come to make amends, but instead to break them up, and Lex wasn't going to fight it. Hell, he just didn't have it in him anymore. The weight of everything they'd been through, and now were going to go through, settled on Lex's shoulders again, and he realized he couldn't do it any longer. He couldn't be the strong one all the time. He was done. If Gavin thought they needed time apart, well, then he'd get it. "So, you're leaving now?" Lex asked calmly.

Gavin's expression went from surprise at Lex's easy acceptance to sadness before he answered. "Yeah, I think that would be best. They have a hotel room for tonight, and we'll drive back early tomorrow." Lex nodded. There was nothing else to say really. "I'll call you, and I'll be back before you have to leave for—"

"It's fine, Doc. You go do what you gotta do." Lex turned away from the man he loved and started for the door.

"Lex, please, can we talk for just a minute?"

Lex sighed and his shoulders slumped. He was broken, and he didn't want a long drawn-out argument. Gavin had already made his choice, and it hadn't been him. "I don't think that's a good idea, Doc. I don't want to say something I'll regret, and right now, pretty much anything that comes out of my mouth would fit the bill." Lex put his hand on the doorknob. "I can't stay here and watch you leave me," he said. Seeing Gavin pack and leave would surely drive him insane. He opened the door to go.

"Lex, please, I love you, but I just need some time. Please don't make me leave like this," Gavin pleaded.

Lex looked back over his shoulder at the man who had been the center of his life for such a short time but had made such a huge impact on him. "I'm not making you leave, baby. You're choosing to leave, and I'm just not stopping you. Take all the time you need. Tell your parents that I wish them a Merry Christmas." Lex didn't stop for anything, not even his coat, which he regretted when he stepped out into the frigid night air.

LEX DROVE AIMLESSLY around town for over two hours. The warm glow from the windows of so many houses only served to remind him he'd never have what all those people behind all those windows had. He was destined to love a man who would forever question their relationship, making it impossible for them to have their happily ever after.

His mom met him at the door, when he finally went back home, wrapping him in a hug as soon as he stepped into the house. "I'm so sorry, honey. It's all my fault. I shouldn't have meddled."

Lex returned her hug. She'd been crying, and he knew she would take responsibility for the mess. "Nah, you did a good thing, getting his parents here. It just comes down to the fact that he doesn't really love me enough," Lex said. He was full of self-pity, and he knew it. "I probably don't deserve for him to love me like that anyway."

His mom pushed him away. "Lex Luthor Turner, don't you dare say that again! You deserve all that man's love, and he knows it. You didn't let him explain. He told me—"

"Mom, stop. I don't want to hear how he justified leaving me, especially when he knows I'm going to be leaving soon. As far as I'm concerned, this is over. I can't beg him anymore, Ma. I just can't. I gotta have some pride; at least give me that much," Lex said, his anger taking over to wipe out the sadness.

"But, Lex, would you just listen?"

"No, I'm sick of being the one who has to listen and understand. I know that everyone expects me to just roll over and take this, but I can't. I can't do it anymore. There's only so much one person should be made to take before they're allowed to give up. I'm gonna head to bed. I'll see you in the morning, and I'm sorry you had to be sad on another holiday. I was really hoping that this year would be different."

Jean picked up and held George in her arms as she cried silently. "I'm sorry too, Lex. I love you."

"Goodnight, Ma. I love you too." Lex walked through the living room where he saw that under the tree only the envelope which contained the gift Gavin had gotten for him remained. He stooped down and picked it up, thinking about opening it but, instead, taking it with him into his room. He shoved it in his sock drawer, determined to forget about it and Gavin.

He stripped and got into bed, but it felt too big without Gavin, so it took him some time to get comfortable. He decided he'd get a smaller bed when he moved so he could get rid of the memories his current king-sized bed held. Lex needed to start seriously thinking about moving on and not just in the physical sense. He'd wasted too much time on someone he should have let slip quietly from his life when he'd still had a chance of salvaging his heart, and now he'd have to learn to live with it broken.

TWENTY-SEVEN

IT HAD BEEN the longest, most painful week of Gavin's life, and he finally came to the conclusion that he was being stupid. He had taken to living in the joke of a present Lex had gotten him for Christmas. He'd laughed for ten minutes over the rainbow-colored pajama pants and pink hooded sweat shirt that read, "I'm not gay and neither is my boyfriend," which was funny because it was true in their case. It was the only time he'd cracked a smile since Lex had walked out on him on Christmas Eve— before he'd walked out on Lex.

At first Gavin had been surprised by Lex's easy acceptance of his plans to go home, but now Gavin knew he'd finally reached Lex's limit. He didn't even want to think about why Lex hadn't fought for him to stay. There were so many reasons for Lex to let him go. He was too needy, and he was too weak, and Lex was probably tired of fighting for him and getting nothing in return for his efforts. Lex had written Gavin off as a lost cause, and he couldn't blame Lex for having done it.

It had taken Gavin two days to realize he'd hurt Lex badly by leaving him. Lex was always so strong. Gavin hadn't known his leaving would break Lex the way it did. He deserved the silent treatment from Lex, but it still hurt. If only Lex would have let him explain himself, maybe they could have avoided their current situation, but unfortunately, Lex had decided to show his stubborn streak at the most inopportune time.

So there Gavin sat on his childhood bed, wrapped in the quilt Jean had made and given him for Christmas. He was crying again. He was being a big baby, but Lex wasn't answering his phone calls, and Jean was even being tight-lipped about what was happening at home. She'd only tell Gavin that Lex was fine. It hurt. Jean had left him to dangle in the wind, but he understood her first loyalties would always lie with Lex. She had warned him it was a bad idea to leave. She thought Gavin should at least sleep on it and talk to Lex before making his decision to go instead of telling Lex he had already decided. It was advice he now knew he should have taken. Gavin had hoped Jean would pass on to Lex that he'd only agreed to this separation to appease his mother.

His mother had promised him if he took some time away from Lex to reevaluate their relationship and still wanted to be with him, she'd accept it. She'd welcome Lex into the family without another word. How could Gavin pass up the chance to have his family back? He was sure if Lex would only let him explain, he would have understood Gavin's need to go.

Gavin had wanted to explain it to Lex before he'd left. He wanted Lex to know he already knew the outcome. He'd spend a few days with his parents, and then he'd be back because he wanted...no, he needed to be with Lex. Gavin wiped the tears from his face and threw the quilt off his shoulders. He'd hurt the man he loved. He needed to get back to Lex and try to repair the damage he'd done when he left.

Gavin crawled off his bed and took off the sweatshirt that was, if he was honest with himself, starting to smell a bit ripe. He dug through his suitcase and pulled out clean clothes. He went to the bathroom and showered and shaved. He got dressed and went to find his parents to tell them he was leaving. If they had a problem with that, then, well, he'd know there was nothing he could do to make things right with them. Why torture himself any longer?

They were sitting at the table having lunch when Gavin found them. His mom eyed him suspiciously. She knew something was up. It was the first time Gavin had been dressed since they'd arrived home on Christmas Day.

"Are you hungry?" his mother asked.

Gavin shook his head. His mother had changed. She no longer went on and on with the aimless babble. He wondered what had happened in the past couple of months to affect such a change, or maybe it was just toward him that she'd changed.

Gavin sat down. "I'm going home today. I miss Lex and Jean and George. They're my life now, and I don't think being separated from them is doing me any good."

His mom and dad exchanged one of those weird new looks that made Gavin nervous. "Okay, if that's what you want. I guess I'm surprised you lasted this long," his father said.

Gavin's brow furrowed at his father's response. "What do you mean?"

He shrugged. "I figured you'd turn around and go back about two hours after you got here. You lasted a lot longer than I'd have given you credit for."

"If you knew how much I hated being here, why didn't you tell me I could leave?" Gavin asked.

"You're a grown man," he said like it explained everything.

"But Mom said—" Gavin stopped when he realized the folly of what he was about to say. "Were you testing me?"

His father put his coffee mug down on the table with a sad shake of his head. "Son, I know this has been hard on you, but your mother needed to see how much you love him. Watching you mope around this house for the past few days was painful for me, but for her to really grasp how much you needed him, she needed to see it for herself." He explained in his calm, rational tone.

Gavin had never had an ill-thought toward his father in his entire life, but at that moment, he hated him. The way he could talk about Gavin's love for Lex with absolutely no emotion evident in his tone irked Gavin to no end. He wondered why he'd even bothered to try to win back their affection when he wasn't even sure they loved him in the first place. Gavin yearned for the kind of love Lex got from Jean, the unconditional, no-holds-barred love that, had it been visible, would have been able to be seen from space. His attention snapped back to his parents when his mother started talking.

"I'm sorry, Gavin. I know love when I see it. I'm not blind, and if you're this miserable without him, then who am I to get in the way? I still don't think it's the best option for you, but like your father said, you're a grown man, and you should be able to make your own decisions. You won't hear another word from me on the subject, and as long as you're willing to include us in your life, I will be civil to that...to Lex." His mother pursed her lips, and Gavin had a feeling she was stifling the urge to say more or maybe something other than what had sounded like a prepared speech.

"It may not even matter anymore," Gavin snapped as he stood up. They didn't realize this little farce may have cost Gavin the man he loved. He wasn't going to waste another minute. He was going home to beg for forgiveness for being so stupid, so needy, so blind to the fact that Lex had given him a type of love he'd only dreamed of. If Lex would once again be the better man because, god, he was. Lex was always the better man—the best man—then they could ring in the new year properly.

LEX'S CONDO WAS dark when Gavin pulled into the driveway. He used the key Lex had given him to let himself in, but there was no sign of life in the dark, chilly space. He walked into the kitchen. George's food bowls were gone, which meant they weren't just out getting groceries or something as mundane as that.

Gavin took the phone off the wall and dialed Lex's cell phone with it, hoping he'd answer if he saw Gavin was calling from home. Lex's voice on the line made his heart skip, but it was just the voicemail, the now all-too-familiar message breaking his heart a little bit each time it told him to leave a name and number.

"Lex, please call me. I'm home. I don't know where you are, but I really need to talk to you. Please, please give me a chance to explain. Please come home if you can, or call me, and I'll come to you, please, Lex..." He choked on a small sob because it felt like it was finished somehow, that his coming home to an empty house was the end of the line for them.

Gavin carried his suitcase into the bedroom and emptied it. He took his Christmas present and threw it in the washer, so he could put it on without smelling like a hobo. He turned the heat up and started a fire in the fireplace. He'd hunker down and wait for Lex to come back because after checking the fridge and seeing there was a jug of milk and other perishables in it, he was pretty confident he wouldn't have to wait too long.

He hoped Lex would hurry up. They only had three days before Lex had to leave for training. Gavin had missed Lex's touch so much he wanted to make the most of the time they had left. Gavin intended to plaster his body to Lex's and stay that way until Lex stepped out the door to leave for camp.

THE CLOSER THE hand on the clock crawled toward midnight with no call or sign of Lex, the more agitated Gavin got. Where were they, and why wouldn't Jean have told him if they were leaving for long enough they had to take the cat with them? His phone almost gave him a heart attack when it started ringing in the quiet house.

He frantically reached for it only to be disappointed by Riley's phone number displayed on the screen. "Hey."

"Why the hell didn't you tell me you were coming back for New Year's? What are you and Lex doing? Oh wait... I'm pretty sure I don't want to hear about you two fucking like rabbits instead of going out. I'm actually surprised you answered the phone," Riley said with a maniacal giggle.

"Are you drunk?" Gavin asked, ignoring Riley's questions. He didn't know how to tell Riley that Lex was still avoiding him, and he was sitting home on New Year's Eve waiting like a stood-up nerd.

"Of course I am, man; it's only an hour until midnight. So why did I have to find out from your dad that you came home today?" Riley asked.

"I didn't even think about calling anyone. I just wanted to get home." Gavin had briefly thought about calling Riley, but he'd wanted to be home alone when Lex got there. They needed to talk, and he had hoped they'd make up and then go to bed to do what Riley had thought they'd been doing.

"Yeah well, that big lug has been like a wet blanket since you left," Riley said offhandedly.

"You talked to him? Why didn't you tell me?" Gavin asked, sitting up straighter. It was the first he'd heard that Riley had been talking to Lex while he'd been in exile at his parent's house.

"Duh, man, he's my friend. I couldn't leave him drowning his sorrows alone. I tried to tell him you'd be back, but cripes, when that guy gets something in his head, he's the most fucking stubborn person I've ever met. I didn't think you'd want to hear what he was saying because, man, well you just don't want to know," Riley said, his tone ominous, making Gavin shiver.

"So he didn't tell you if he had plans to go somewhere with Jean today, did he?" Gavin asked, hoping Riley had information about his missing family.

"Nah, Jean's at her sister's house up in Duluth, I think. She took the cat because she says he reminds her of you. So wait, he's not there with you?"

"No, there wasn't anyone here when I got home. I'm waiting for Lex."

"Why didn't you call him?" Riley asked.

"I did, but he won't answer my calls."

"Dude, why didn't you call me and Sheila then?"

"I didn't think about it. I'm sorry, I was preoccupied, and I just want to see Lex, but I guess he doesn't want to see me."

"We'll come over so we can count down to midnight with you. I'll even let you kiss Sheila if Lex doesn't show up," Riley offered.

"No, don't. You guys stay and have fun wherever you are. I'm really not in the mood for company."

"Fuck that, dude, we're on our way. You'll have to give us a ride home in the morning 'cause we're taking a taxi, and we're gonna get smashed so hard. Be there in ten." Riley hung up before Gavin could protest.

Gavin looked down at his outfit and decided Riley and Sheila would just have to deal because he wasn't changing, and at least he smelled like laundry softener and not body odor. He got off the couch and went into the kitchen to see if there was something he could put out to snack on. He'd at least make an effort to be a decent host. He heard the front door. Riley and Sheila must have been closer than he thought they were.

"I'm in the kitchen," Gavin called. He had filled a bowl with chips and turned to set it on the counter behind him when the kitchen door banged open. Gavin startled, missed the counter, and the bowl landed on the floor sending chips scattering in every direction. Lex stood in the doorway glaring at him. "Lex!" Gavin couldn't keep the surprise out of his voice or off his face, his heart pounding in his chest at the sight of his lover.

"You were expecting someone else? Got a hot date, do ya?" Lex asked. Gavin knew by the tone and timber of his voice that Lex was drunk.

"Um, Riley and Sheila were coming to sit with me while I waited for you," Gavin said. "I didn't know when, or even if, you were coming." Gavin got down on his knees so he could scoop the chips into the trash bin. "I tried to call you."

Lex walked across the floor, paying no heed to the chips as they crunched beneath his boots. "Get off the floor, Gavin," Lex said. His tone was one Gavin had never heard before, and it sent chills through him. It was probably the voice Lex used on criminals because it was scary as fuck.

"Lex—" Gavin said as he stood up.

"What the fuck are you wearing?" Lex sneered when Gavin stood before him. Lex's lip curled into a parody of his usual smirk as he took in Gavin's outfit.

"It's... You got it for me...Christmas present..." he said, suddenly very unsure of his choice in clothing.

Lex stepped to Gavin so their faces were a mere inch from each other. "You look fucking ridiculous. It was a joke. Only you would actually fucking wear a joke gift around like it was..." Lex shook his head in disgust. "Fuck, sometimes I really wonder what the hell you're thinking."

The stench of alcohol hit Gavin hard but not as hard as Lex's words. "I'm... I'm s-sorry. I just wanted to feel close to you. I m-missed you," Gavin stammered.

Lex laughed in his face. "Yeah, I know you missed me, but that doesn't change the fact that you left, does it?" Lex asked, not backing off at all.

"I tried to explain, Lex please—" Gavin's words were cut off when Lex grabbed his upper arms and held him in a tight, not quite painful grip.

"I don't want to hear your excuses, Gavin," Lex snarled. "I've fucking done nothing but wait for you. I waited for you to figure out that you wanted me; then I waited for you to decide that you could be with me; then I waited to tell you I loved you so you wouldn't freak out. I waited for you to tell your parents about us; I waited for you to decide if you could live with me; and I'm still fucking waiting to find out if you'll go with me, so excuse the fuck out of me for being sick and fucking tired of waiting for you to make up your fucking mind." Lex tightened his grip on Gavin's biceps and shook him. "It's not that hard, Gavin. Either you love me, or you don't. You either want to be with me, or you don't."

Gavin was taken aback at all the emotion Lex had been holding in, the feelings he'd been hiding. The love Gavin always saw so clearly in Lex's blue eyes was nowhere to be found at that moment, and Gavin ached at the loss. He opened his mouth to tell Lex he loved him and wanted to move up north with him, but Lex cut him off.

"I don't need an answer, Gavin. I already figured it out," Lex growled, giving Gavin another shake. "Yeah, don't look so surprised. I may not be as smart as you, *Doctor* Addison, but I'm not a moron. It took me a little longer, but I got it."

"Got what?" Gavin asked, but he was afraid to hear what Lex would say next, dreaded hearing the words that would break his heart.

"That you don't love me; you don't want me because if you did, Gavin; if you loved me, you wouldn't need to think about it so hard. I don't have to think about loving you; I just do. I just know that I want to be with you, and I love you so much it hurts sometimes," Lex said. His voice had a painful, pleading edge to it that tore through Gavin's soul.

Lex punctuated his words with a painful little squeeze of his hands. He released Gavin so forcefully that Gavin stumbled and fell to his butt before he could protest Lex's words. He sat there looking up at the man he'd been pining for, but who was no longer willing to give him a chance to explain how much he loved him and how wrong he'd been to leave. Lex turned and left him there in his own mess. Their bedroom door slammed, and Gavin let out the sob that had been stuck in his chest, along with the tears that had been pooling in his eyes.

As if by some miracle of timing, the front door opened, and Gavin heard Sheila's laughter. "Hey, honey, we're home," Riley called out.

"He's not in the living room," Sheila said as she pushed the kitchen door open. She stopped short at the sight of Gavin sitting on the floor with crushed chips all around him.

Riley stepped up behind her. "Dude, no need to cry over spilled chips. Get up and give me a hug. I missed you," Riley said. He stepped on some of the chips as he made his way over to extend a hand to help Gavin up, and then he pulled Gavin into a one-armed hug. "I'm glad you're back, man, but what the hell are you wearing?"

Gavin's face fell; he was an idiot just like Lex had said. "Nothing, just a joke gift Lex got me for Christmas. I thought it would be funny when he got back," Gavin lied to save face.

"I think it's cute," Sheila said, dragging Gavin in for a hug of her own. "Good to have you back, sweetie. Maybe your man will stop being such a bear now."

Christ, how much time did they spend with Lex while he was gone?

"Can we go to your place? Lex came home, and I don't think he's really in the mood for company," Gavin asked in a quiet voice. He hoped to get his friends out before they realized he and Lex had pretty much just broken up.

Riley looked at him and then at the mess on the floor, misinterpreting the entire scene he'd walked in on. Riley pushed past Gavin and headed toward the bedroom.

"Ri, stop, don't. He's drunk and he's mad and hurt and just... Let's go okay?" Gavin tried to stop Riley's charge but had little to no effect on his progress. "Nothing happened," Gavin pressed.

Riley threw the bedroom door open. Lex had just gotten out of the shower and was standing in the middle of the room in a towel. He glared at Riley and then Gavin as he followed Riley into the room.

Riley pushed Lex with both hands. Lex wobbled but other than that didn't seem to be affected by the shove. "You fucking son of a bitch, if you ever lay another hand on him, I'll fucking kill you!"

"Riley, stop! He didn't hurt me, he just—" Gavin tried to get between them, but Lex pushed him so he landed on the bed out of the way.

"I said don't fucking touch him," Riley growled and pushed Lex hard enough to make him stumble back into the dresser. Gavin watched as something flashed in Lex's eyes, and his face twisted it into a mask of hatred as he stepped up to Riley again.

"What's it to you, huh? Maybe I should just punch him so you got an excuse to step in and play hero. That what you want, Ri? Now that I've done all the hard work getting him to fucking realize that he's into guys, now you want to swoop in and get what you've been after all this time but didn't have the balls to go for?" Lex asked sardonically.

Gavin looked from his boyfriend to his best friend, trying to comprehend what Lex had just said.

"Fuck you, asshole. You don't know shit, and I won't let you fucking push him around. He deserves better than that," Riley said. He stood in front of Lex with his shoulders thrown back, his chest out, and fists clenching. Gavin recognized Riley's fighting stance and got ready to step in to stop them before it came to blows. Gavin froze as Lex's next words shocked him and made the meaning of his earlier statement clear.

"Yeah, like you, right? I've been quite the patsy here haven't I, Riley? Does Sheila know?" Lex snorted. "Oh fuck, are both of you in on this? You gonna share him because, hell, I know how much he likes that, so I'm sure it wouldn't take much to convince him. Shit, a two-for-one special, who could resist?"

Gavin looked at Sheila when Lex mentioned her name. She stood, as if frozen, in the doorway, looking just as confused as he felt. She didn't make a move to get between the two warring men, which was probably a good thing, considering what happened next.

Riley threw the first punch. It landed on Lex's jaw and snapped his head back. Gavin scrambled off the bed and pushed Riley back away from Lex. Gavin was trying to read Riley's face to see if what Lex was saying had any truth to it. Gavin knew he was a bit slow to catch on to things, but his best friend wanting more than just friendship had never crossed his mind, even when he'd wanted it himself. Also, he couldn't see Sheila sharing anything, let alone her lover. There couldn't be any truth to what Lex was saying, could there? Only anger showed itself on Riley's face as he glared at Lex. Gavin turned to Lex, who was standing there looking dazed as he rubbed his jaw.

"You're drunk and you have no clue what you're saying. We're leaving," Riley spat at Lex over Gavin's shoulder. "Let's go, Gav; you can't stay here with him. I don't trust him."

Gavin didn't take his eyes off Lex. After Lex had gotten all the vitriol out of his system, he was just a broken man—one Gavin had broken. If Gavin chose to go with what Lex saw as a rival for his affections, it would be over between them, and there would be no fixing it. Gavin saw it clearly—his choice in that moment would make or break them for good.

"Gav, let's go," Riley urged. He grabbed Gavin's arm and tried to pull him toward the door.

Gavin held his ground against Riley's tugging. He had a sudden thought. He shrugged Riley's hand off and took a step toward Lex. "Lex, did you open the Christmas present I left for you?"

Lex turned his glare from Riley to Gavin. "What the fuck does it matter now?"

Gavin swallowed down the hurt at Lex's words. "Where is it?" Lex shook his head. "Lex, do you still have it?" Lex needed to read what Gavin had written. Why the hell hadn't Lex opened it on Christmas? Gavin shook his head at his own stupidity. He should have known Lex wouldn't have wanted to open a reminder of how they'd been before Gavin had made his critical misstep. "Where is the damn letter, Lex?" Gavin raised his voice, hoping to get through to Lex.

Lex rolled his eyes and turned to open the top drawer of his dresser. He pulled out the red envelope that still had a crushed bow on it. He held it up so Gavin could see it. "Here, you want it back? Maybe you can give it to Riley instead."

Gavin didn't take the offered envelope. "You open it right now, Lex. You should have opened it right away." Gavin's voice shook with emotion. He had to admit he was a little relieved that Lex hadn't read it yet because it meant there was still a chance Lex would forgive him. Maybe all of this could have been avoided if Lex had just opened the damn letter when he should have. Gavin hoped the words he'd written with so much love would fix things now, hoped it wasn't too late.

Lex sighed and tore the flap open. He pulled out the card and looked at Gavin, with eyebrows raised.

"I didn't know what to get you because nothing was good enough to show you how I felt about you. So I just wrote you a letter. It's not a poem or anything sappy and romantic like that; it's just stuff I wanted to tell you but was too afraid to say. Will you read it, please?" Gavin let all of his hope ring through in his voice.

"We'll wait in the living room in case you need us," Sheila said. She'd been quiet through the whole scene, and Gavin had almost forgotten they were still standing there. Gavin nodded and watched her lead a reluctant Riley out of the room.

"Sit by me?" Gavin asked Lex as he sat on the foot of the bed.

Lex sat down but left a lot of space between them. He opened the card, and Gavin closed his eyes and remembered what he wrote in there over two weeks before. It was all still true, and he hoped it would win back Lex's heart.

TWENTY-EIGHT

LEX HAD LEFT for the bar at an hour most people—well, at least those who weren't alcoholics—would deem unseemly, but he needed to get away. Away from the loneliness, away from the memories, and away from that damn envelope that kept calling to him from his dresser drawer. His plan was to get drunk, find a person or two to go home with, and fuck himself into a stupor so he could finally get some sleep that wasn't haunted by sparkling, brown eyes. It had been an excellent plan and one he could see coming to fruition with the arrival of Becca.

Lex was already well on his way to drunk enough to not care that the only person he wanted to be spending his night with was currently at his house. He hadn't listened to the voice mail, but he'd seen the number and since he'd talked to his mom before heading out, he knew the only other person who would be calling from that number was Gavin. Knowing Gavin was there, probably waiting for him, only spurred him to drink more to drown out the pull the other man had on him.

Becca had seemed somewhat amiable to Lex's plan, but then she'd asked after Gavin. Lex tried to remind himself there was nothing worse than a morose, self-pitying, heartbroken drunk, but Becca had been a friend for a long time, and her concern had broken him down. She'd listened to him pour his heart out and let him cry on her shoulder before putting him in a cab and sending him home.

The cab ride home had been just long enough for Lex to get his tears under control. Once he'd accomplished that, the fire in the pit of his stomach, fueled by his anger at Gavin's leaving, was back. By the time they hit the curb outside his condo and he saw the soft glow of lights he hadn't left on in his windows, he was practically spoiling for a fight.

Confronting him while Gavin was on his knees in his kitchen was not how Lex had planned to start off the discussion. Seeing the surprise and hope turn to sadness, and then pain, on Gavin's face had been almost unbearable. Lex struggled against the urge to hold Gavin and comfort him. He'd been in such a hurry to get away from those feelings that he'd released Gavin more forcefully than he'd meant to. He hadn't meant to hurt him, but Riley's accusations rang true in Lex's ears—he couldn't be trusted not to hurt the man he loved so much it made his chest ache.

Which brought him to the here and now where he stood, with an aching jaw and a sour stomach, clutching the letter Gavin had written. He felt he had to read the letter because he owed it to Gavin after he'd hurt him, so he'd read what Gavin had written to make it up to him, even though the last thing he wanted to do at that moment was read a sappy love letter. But he sat on the bed, careful not to sit too close to Gavin, as he opened the card and realized Gavin's elegant script had replaced the once blank inside of the card.

My Dearest Lex,

I'm sorry this is the only thing I could think of to get you for Christmas. (Though I do hope later tonight I can give you something you'll enjoy a lot more.) I looked through every store for the perfect gift, but nothing said what I wanted. There was no gift out there that said, "Lex Turner, you are the most important person in my life, and I can't live without you either." So I just stopped trying and bought this card.

I'm so glad I met you. I keep thinking about everything that led us to this point, and though everything that happened in the past six months wasn't pleasant, I wouldn't change a thing. (That's a lie—I'd bring back Agent for you, and I would have never wasted so much time deciding I wanted to be with you.) But I wouldn't change any of the things that lead us to this point, because with every one of those trials set before us, I learned something new and fantastic about you that made me love you even more.

I wake up thankful every day because you are the kindest, most patient person I've ever met. When I look back, I know I wouldn't have put up with me and the things I did, but you were always there with a kind word or a hug when I needed it. (Don't think I forgot about the one time you gave me the only thing that could have made my world right again, because I remember it and cherish that memory above all.)

I love you, Lex, with everything I have. I've never felt this way about another person in my life, and the thought of you going away for your training makes my stomach hurt because seeing you every day is what has kept me sane during the mess my life has been recently. Not being able to look into your eyes, hear you call me Doc, or hold you while you sleep next to me for fifteen weeks will be one of the hardest things I'll have to do, but I will because I know what this new job means to you. I want you to have everything you ever wanted.

You asked me to go with you, to live with you for what I hope will be the rest of our lives. (Please tell me that's what you meant when you asked me because this feels like a forever kind of thing to me.) So my Christmas present to you is me. I want to go with you, Lex. I want to love you the way you deserve to be loved for the rest of your life. I want to have a family with you, and I want to make you happy, but if I never do another thing in my life but make you smile, it will be like I achieved the greatest thing on earth.

My answer is yes. Merry Christmas, Lex.

All my love,
Gavin

Lex read it three times—each time the words cut him a little deeper and made him realize what an ass he'd been. He was still hurt by Gavin leaving him without a thought to how he'd feel, especially when they only had such a short time left before he had to leave. He needed to put his hurt aside, unless he wanted to lose the only person who'd ever inspired so many strong emotions in him—both good and bad.

"Lex? Tell me what you're thinking, please?" Gavin asked tentatively. The bed dipped as he moved closer.

"I'm thinking that I'm still pissed...but I've been sort of an ass too. Why didn't you tell me this before you left?"

"I tried. I wanted to talk to you before I left, but you didn't want to hear me out. I hoped that you'd at least open the card on Christmas, and you'd know how I felt and forgive me for going. I'm sorry I left, and I know now that I should have stayed. If my mom never talked to me again, it would have been her own fault, but if I lost you by going, it was all mine. I'm sorry I stayed with them as long as I did. I should have realized then what my choice looked like to you, and I don't ever want you to think that you come in second to anyone or anything in my life."

"So why did you go?" Lex finally turned to look at his lover but couldn't hide the hurt he still felt over being abandoned. "Why did you leave me without a second thought?"

Gavin paled and shook his head as if to deny what Lex had said. "I never meant for you to think that I could leave you easily, Lex. It broke my heart, and I was stupid because I just wanted my family back. I was blinded by the prospect of them accepting me the way I am. My mom asked me to go—to just step back and give myself some space from you. I suppose she thought that if I wasn't so close to you physically maybe I'd be able to think with my brain, instead of my...you know," Gavin said as he blushed. "She promised that if I took a little time away and still wanted you, she'd be okay with it. I thought I could have it all—you and them."

Lex could see in Gavin the lost little boy who just wanted his parents' love, something Lex had never had to worry about. He felt like a complete and utter ass for not listening to Gavin sooner. He was sobering up quickly, and he knew he needed to beg for forgiveness and hope that his man was in a forgiving mood. Lex slid off the bed and onto his knees in front of Gavin before putting his head in his lap and wrapping his arms around his waist.

"Can you ever forgive me, baby? I really didn't mean to hurt you, and I promise I will never lay a hand on you in anger ever again. I'm so sorry. I can't even tell you how much I hate myself right now," Lex begged, hoping for Gavin's forgiveness. He wasn't a violent man, never had been. The thought that he'd hurt someone he loved turned his stomach.

Gavin ran his hands through Lex's hair, and Lex sighed at the touch. "Lex, you didn't do anything that I have to forgive you for. I know you'd never really hurt me; that's just not you. You don't have that in you. I could see how angry you were, and if you were ever going to hit me, it would have been then." Gavin stopped, taking a shuddery breath. "But I will forgive you if you do the same for me because I know I'm not innocent in this. I'll take responsibility for my part, and I'll forgive you yours if you'll do the same for me," Gavin said.

Lex nodded his agreement into Gavin's lap. "I love you so much, Doc. Don't fuck with my heart like that anymore, okay?"

"Oh my god, we're a couple of idiots," Gavin said and then he giggled. The sound had a slightly hysterical tinge to it, but Lex figured the doc deserved to be a bit crazy after all they'd been through.

Lifting his head to look at Gavin's happy face, Lex realized he'd missed him more than he could put into words. Lex surged up and landed on top of Gavin on the bed, which made the doc giggle even harder. "What are you laughing about? I'm the one on top," Lex asked as he smiled down at the doc. The weight that had been sitting on Lex's chest, making it almost impossible to breathe was lifting at the feeling of his lover beneath him once again, even if he was giggling like a lunatic.

"You do realize you lost your towel like halfway through your argument with Riley?" Gavin asked as he wiggled his eyebrows.

Lex looked down between them and shook his head. "Wow, guess I'm drunker than I thought."

"Yeah, um, Lex?" Gavin asked.

"What Doc?"

"You know you're going to have to apologize to Riley, right?" He looked worried as he ran fingers lightly over Lex's sore jaw.

"Oh god, I can't believe I said those things to him. He's going to hate me, isn't he?"

"Do you really think all that about him?" Gavin asked. His tone was skeptical, but Lex could tell the doc was mulling over the possibility that what Lex had said had some truth to it.

"Nah, I guess sometimes you see what you want to see, and I just wanted someone to shift the blame to. I felt really bad when you fell on the floor. I could have kicked myself, so I deserved the punch," Lex said.

"It's okay, Lex. If I thought you were really going to hurt me, I'd have kneed you in the balls. It hurt more that you made fun of my pajamas." Gavin stuck his lip out in a pout.

Lex nuzzled his nose against Gavin's cheek. "I think they're cute on you. I only said that because I wanted to hurt you, and that was mean. I'm sorry." He kissed Gavin's cheek. "Will you forgive me for insulting your jammies?"

"I'll forgive you anything, but just remember that I will kick you in the nads the next time you try to manhandle me."

"I thought you liked it when I manhandled you," Lex said with a sly smirk. He nuzzled his nose into Gavin's neck and felt a shudder run through the man beneath him.

"Seriously, Lex, we can't do this anymore."

Lex pulled back to look into Gavin's eyes, trying hard not to misunderstand what he was saying, but he couldn't think of anything they couldn't do anymore. "What are you talking about, Doc?" he asked, after not coming up with any possibilities.

Gavin put his hands on Lex's cheeks. "We need to talk about everything from now on. Say what we mean and mean what we say. No more misunderstandings. If I do or say something, and you get a feeling in your stomach that tells you I don't love you or that I want to leave you, you need to clarify it with me. Because in the extreme unlikelihood that would happen, I will come out and say it to your face, and I want you to promise the same. No more hurt feelings because we're afraid to talk to each other."

Lex nodded in agreement, but Gavin waited, still holding his gaze and stroking his face. "I promise, Doc, no more misunderstandings. We'll talk so much you'll get sick of hearing my—" Gavin pulled him down and sealed his lips over Lex's, effectively shutting him up.

A cough from the doorway made Lex stop and turn. "I see that you guys made up, so Riley and I are going to leave, okay?" Sheila asked hesitantly.

"No, why don't you stay? You can sleep in Ma's room; no reason to go out in the cold. I think we need to have a talk anyway," Lex said, never looking away from Gavin's eyes. He'd have to beg for Riley's forgiveness too. Riley had just been trying to protect Gavin like he'd always done, and Lex had taken it to a whole other level with his accusations.

"Are you sure?" Sheila asked.

"Yeah, stay. We'll come out and have a drink with you guys. Just let Lex put some pants on first," Gavin said with another little giggle. God, Lex had missed that sound—the sound of a happy Doc did his heart a world of good.

"Okay, but I wouldn't mind if he skipped the putting pants on part. I kinda like his furry butt," Sheila said. "Hurry up, and we can get one poured just in time to toast the New Year."

"Okay, but make sure Riley's not going to do any more punching when we get out there," Gavin said.

"Not promising anything," Sheila singsonged from the hallway.

"Ugh, let's go face the music," Lex said as he crawled off Gavin.

"Na-uh, you are going to go face the music. I'll be there to comfort you after that when Riley makes you cry," Gavin said dutifully.

"Thanks, Doc. So nice to know you care." Lex dug out a pair of sweatpants and put them on.

"Don't worry I got your back...and your furry butt," Gavin said. "But, Lex, can I ask you a favor?"

Lex turned to see Gavin worrying his bottom lip between his teeth. That unsure look made Lex think he'd do anything Gavin asked him right then. "Sure, baby, what do you want?"

"Just...could you never call me Gavin again unless you're sure it's over for good? Because it scares the crap out of me when you say my name."

Lex bent down so he could look into Gavin's eyes, the eyes he fell in love with long before he even knew the man behind them. "You got it, Doc." Lex kissed him, and it turned out to be perfect timing because Sheila and Riley hollered "Happy New Year" out in the living room as their lips met. Lex had a feeling it was going to be a very good year for them.

LEX AWOKE TO the excruciating pleasure of Gavin's lips wrapped around his cock. He had no idea how long Gavin had been at it, but he was right on the verge of exploding. Lex let the doc continue without alerting him to the fact that he was awake. He couldn't keep up the ruse though when Gavin pulled off. Lex's hand went instinctively to the soft curls to try to get the warm, wet suction back around his cock.

Gavin giggled as he pushed Lex's hand away from his head and crawled up his body. "I knew you were awake. I could tell by the way your moans changed," Gavin murmured into Lex's neck as he lay on top of him. Gavin had gotten really good at lining their bodies up just right, and Lex sighed at the pleasurable sensations as they coursed through his body. "I wasn't sure if you'd be up for it again before Jean gets home, but I had to try my luck." Gavin whimpered when Lex wiggled his hips and then gasped when their cocks rubbed together. "I'm a lucky, lucky boy."

"Yes, you are, Doc." Lex flipped them so their positions were reversed. "And you're about to get a whole lot luckier." Lex let the most lascivious look he could muster settle on his face. He got up on his knees and twirled his finger, indicating he wanted the doc on his stomach. Gavin raised an eyebrow but did as Lex asked.

Lex then straddled Gavin's thighs and leaned down to kiss the back of his neck. "You're going to enjoy this, I bet." Lex said. His voice deepened with the lust he could barely contain.

"What are you going to do?" Gavin's question was a breathy whisper.

"Oh, you'll see," Lex answered. "But first tell me, are you sore, baby?" He didn't want to overdo it. They'd been in bed for two days, and other than quick trips to the kitchen and bathroom and a few little naps, they'd spent most of their time buried in each other in one form or another. The bedroom smelled like a French whorehouse and it was starting to look like one too, with condom wrappers strewn on the floor and sheets that were just this side of being declared a biohazard, but neither man cared enough to do anything about it.

Gavin wiggled his ass against Lex's stomach. "Mmmm, I think I'm fine. Just start slow and we'll see."

Lex chuckled before he started kissing his way down the doc's smooth back, eliciting small moans from the man he was loving on. He stopped to nuzzle into the dimples at the top of Gavin's sweet ass and then finished tracking his way down to his goal. Gavin tensed and tried to wriggle out of Lex's grasp when he finally realized what Lex's intentions were.

Lex squeezed Gavin's cheeks in his hands and spread him. "Hold still, baby. You'll like this. I promise."

"But Lex...oh...oh...oh...my...god..."

Lex used the tip of his tongue to tease his lover's pink little opening, and he could tell Gavin was not going to put up any more resistance. Lex used every technique he'd ever learned, and there were a lot. The great thing about the lifestyle Lex had lived before meeting Gavin was he had plenty of experience in pleasing both men and women, and he'd always been eager to learn something new. He smiled into Gavin's ass as he speared him with his stiff tongue.

"Oh fuck is that your oh...tongue...oh god...why...why...oh...haven't we...oh... oh...done this before?" A squeal punctuated Gavin's sentence as he pushed back to get more of what Lex was giving. Hmm, that was a good question, Lex thought as he tongue fucked Gavin into oblivion. "Now...now...please...now," the doc begged after Lex had reduced him to a quivering mess with his talented tongue.

Lex, never the one to make his man beg too much, removed his tongue from Gavin's ass and looked around for an unopened foil packet. He couldn't see one and started to curse as Gavin shoved one, already opened for his convenience, into his hand. The almost-empty bottle of lube landed by Lex's knee. He grunted his thanks and quickly geared up.

"On your back, Doc," Lex commanded. He wanted to watch Gavin when he fell apart so beautifully under him.

Gavin flipped and wiggled into position. He looked up at Lex, finding and holding his gaze as Lex lined them up and sank into his own personal heaven. Gavin gasped when Lex bottomed out and lay on top of him, burying his face in Gavin's neck. "Oh god, that never gets old," Gavin murmured into Lex's temple. Lex nodded because he couldn't have agreed more.

Lex started slowly with shallow strokes because he wanted it to last. Gavin grabbed his face and pulled Lex up so he could lock their lips together. Gavin's breath came in sharp little puffs against Lex's cheek as he kissed him with everything he had. Lex had recently become a believer in soulmates. He was sure when the doc kissed him like that their souls were mingling and merging and would never be the same once they parted.

They moved together, bodies and mouths in complete synchronization, for long slow minutes. Lex tried not to think about the tight heat wrapped around him, but his brain refused to cooperate. He couldn't keep up that slow torturous rhythm despite his best efforts. Pulling his mouth away and breaking the kiss made Gavin whimper, but he groaned when Lex changed the angle of entry and brushed his prostate.

"You ready, baby?" Lex asked, and Gavin nodded frantically.

Gavin raised his legs so Lex could put them over his arms and lean forward. The doc was very flexible, and Lex took advantage of that, basically folding him in half. It spread him wide and left him vulnerable to Lex's every advance, so Lex snapped his hips and drove in deep, making Gavin gasp and clutch at Lex's arms. "Too much?" Lex asked after seeing Gavin's reaction.

"No, it's good. More, Lex, come on, you know I can take it," Gavin urged him on.

Lex placed a soft kiss on Gavin's lips before smiling at him. "I know you can, but I don't want to hurt you this late in the game."

"No pain, just do it, but a tad more to...oh yeah, there," Gavin gasped out in pleasure. Lex knew what he wanted and had obliged him, loving the way Gavin shuddered when he hit his sweet spot. Gavin's short fingernails dug into Lex's skin as he held on to keep himself from scooting up the bed with each thrust.

"Fuck, baby, you're gonna kill me," Lex growled, thrusting harder and at the right angle to make Gavin howl. "I'm not gonna last, so could you..."

Gavin took himself in hand and started stroking his leaking cock in time with Lex's thrusts. He used his other hand to double down his effort to keep himself stationary, nails digging in painfully, adding to Lex's war wounds. Gavin stiffened, but Lex kept up his pace as the doc's cock erupted between them, the spasming of Gavin's muscles around his own cock signaling the beginning of the end for Lex. He bit his lip and let his hips jerk erratically, no longer trying to do anything other than chase his own release, and it came quick and hard, making Lex cry out and then collapse on top of Gavin.

He lay there gulping down harsh breaths as his head spun. Gavin's fingers trailed across his back and then down his biceps where he'd left little crescent-shaped marks in Lex's flesh. When Gavin sighed in contentment, Lex closed his eyes so he could just wallow in the rightness of the moment.

LEX WAS HAPPILY cuddling Gavin on the couch in front of the fire, waiting for his mom to get back from her sister's. He'd managed to pry the doc off the bed and get him into the shower. The man was turning into a sex fiend before Lex's eyes. They'd cleaned the bedroom and opened the window to air the place out, even though it was well below freezing outside, and now Lex just wanted to hold Gavin until he had to leave. He kept looking at the clock—they were down to just over twelve hours left. Lex's mind kept drifting back to their bed, and he couldn't help but smile.

"What are you smiling about?" Gavin asked. He'd turned his head so he could rest his chin on Lex's chest and look at him.

"Just thinking about the last couple of days." His smile widened when the doc blushed.

Gavin was tracing little figures on Lex's chest with one finger as he asked, "Any one thing in particular making you smile like that?"

Lex wondered which thing would make Gavin blush the hardest because he loved the innocent look the red tinge gave him. He hummed low in his chest while he thought about it. "Well I have to say that getting woken up the way I was this afternoon was one of the best ways I could think of to wake up; so much better than an alarm clock. Makes me wonder one thing though."

The tips of Gavin's ears were red, and he wouldn't meet Lex's eyes. "Yeah and what's that?"

"Well I just wonder how, knowing that you've never been with a man before me, you're so goddamn good at it," Lex said. It was something he'd wondered about but had been afraid to ask. Gavin snorted and then giggled. It wasn't the reaction Lex had expected when he'd asked the question. "What? What's the joke?"

"It's so absurd that you won't believe me if I tell you," Gavin said through his giggles.

"I would believe anything you told me, Doc, so spill." He was intrigued, and now he had to know.

"Oh, fine, but I'll kill you if you laugh," Gavin said. His expression was so serious Lex almost told him not to tell for fear the doc would indeed kill him if he laughed.

"I promise." Lex crossed his heart.

"Okay, so you know how I was homeschooled," Gavin said. Lex nodded. "Yeah, so I didn't have a lot of friends, like the neighborhood kids thought I was weird and nerdy. So one year—I was twelve, I think— I watched this documentary on sideshows and decided I was going to learn to do something that would make all the kids like me because it was so cool." Gavin paused as if he was going over that time in his mind and trying to figure out how to explain it.

"Okay, so you were a dork, and you wanted to have friends, so you learned to suck cock?" Lex asked, trying to nudge Gavin to continue his story after he'd been silent for a while.

Gavin's eyes widened, and he clucked his tongue at Lex. "No, you dirty pervert, I had no idea what I was learning would come in so handy later in life, just plain luck on that one, I guess," he said. "No, I decided that I was going to learn to do the sword-swallowing act that I'd watched on the documentary. I was sure it would get me loads of friends."

Lex eyed his lover carefully, trying to imagine the doc as a knobby-kneed twelve-year-old. His mom had probably dressed him in khaki shorts and button-downs. It was surprisingly easy to picture; maybe it was due to the fact that Gavin still exuded a childlike innocence, so it wasn't a huge stretch of the imagination. "You're kidding, right?" Lex asked even though he knew the doc was serious.

Gavin sat up and looked around the room until he saw what he wanted. Lex smirked when Gavin grabbed one of the oversized candy canes that were being used as decoration from the vase on the table. They were pretty good-sized—at least as big around as a roll of quarters and perhaps a foot or so long.

Gavin started peeling at the cellophane as he explained. "The first step is to learn to control the gag reflex. It took me over six months of brushing the back of my tongue until I almost puked to get mine under control. Did you know that one in three people don't have a gag reflex at all? I'm not one of them, though," he said. He sounded disappointed about it. "The second step is to learn not to panic while swallowing something that could choke you to death. The third step is to learn to breathe through it. Most people think that you can't breathe with something in your esophagus, but you can, because the epiglottis only closes if you are actively swallowing, but not when there's just something in there. You have to learn to do it though, and if you panic it's impossible, hence step number two."

Lex loved it when Gavin was in smart-talk mode, but he wished he'd shut up. He was anxious to see if the doc could actually swallow the candy cane he had finished unwrapping while explaining the fine art of sword swallowing.

Gavin stood up and moved in front of Lex and turned sideways. He slipped the end of the cane into his mouth and sucked it as far back as he could. He then removed it and licked the entire length. Lex's cock stirred as he watched. The doc had no idea how erotic the little show he was putting on was.

"Have to get it wet so it'll slide better," Gavin explained.

"Wow, you really did learn lots of handy things when you were just a boy."

Gavin cocked his hip and gave Lex an exasperated look before he asked, "Do you want to see this or not?" Lex nodded so hard he looked like a bobblehead, but he kept his mouth shut. "All right then, the next step is to tilt your head all the way back so you have a straight column for the shaft of whatever you're inserting so it can go down. Then, it's just a matter of letting it slide in." Gavin tipped his head back, and Lex watched as he slowly put the candy cane in his wide-open mouth. The doc's throat moved as he swallowed, and the candy slowly disappeared until the hook was hanging over Gavin's lower jaw.

"Holy shit, Doc! That's fucking amazing!" Lex exclaimed as Gavin turned so Lex could see it from a different angle and their eyes met.

Gavin waited a few seconds and then pulled the candy cane back out and smirked at Lex. "Well, I can see that if you'd have been around back then, I'd have made at least one friend." Gavin looked pointedly at Lex's crotch where his cock played tentpole with his sweatpants.

"Oh yeah, baby, we'd have been really good friends," Lex said lecherously. "That little demonstration gave me all kinds of ideas."

Gavin huffed out a laugh and then surprised Lex by going around the couch and sitting on the back of it. Lex raised an eyebrow in question. Gavin fell back so he was upside down on the couch with his head hanging down and his feet over the back. He winked at Lex and positioned his head so that he had a nice straight column again and opened his mouth.

Lex growled at the invitation. He got up to take the doc up on it when the front door opened.

"We're home." His mom sang out, completely killing the mood.

Lex looked down at himself and cursed. No way could he let his mom see his massive boner. Gavin laughed and flipped off the couch with an easy grace. "I'll go distract her until you can get yourself under control." Gavin kissed Lex's cheek and went to find Jean.

"There's my baby!" Lex heard Gavin say cheerfully. Lex stared at his erection, willing it to go away, but it was stubborn. It didn't help that his mind insisted on replaying the entire event right up to Gavin offering the use of his throat to Lex. It was a good thing Gavin and his mother could natter on about nothing forever because Lex ended up having to go into the bathroom to splash cold water on his face to help calm him down.

"You know, when I was your age, we didn't have the Chinese food and the Mexican food and the Indian food. We had American food and that was it," Jean said as she happily dug another wonton out from its box. "We were really missing out." She smiled and popped it in her mouth.

"Really? Like there was, what? Only burgers and pizza?" Gavin asked.

"Well, you know things took a while to get here. If it wasn't for the cities, we'd all have been backwater hicks I suppose," Jean said with a chuckle.

Lex watched his mom and boyfriend chat over their takeout–Chinese food. He couldn't think of a better way to spend his last night at home than with his two favorite people eating takeout and talking.

"Lex, Lex, hello? You in there?" Gavin asked.

"Huh?" Lex had missed whatever they'd asked or were talking about that needed his input.

Gavin giggled and shook his head. "I just told Jean we're going to look at houses the first weekend you get free, and she asked if we'd decided where we're going to look." Gavin brought Lex up-to-date on their conversation.

"Oh well, I guess it doesn't make a difference to me which town we live in as long as we find what we're looking for," Lex said. He'd live in a trailer home if it was what Gavin wanted; as long as he was happy, that was all that mattered. He looked at his mom and asked, "Do you have a preference?"

Jean cocked her head and looked at Lex with a puzzled expression. "Why would it matter to me?"

Gavin gasped. "Oh my god, Lex, you didn't ask her to go with you? You just assumed she'd follow you?" Gavin turned to Jean. "You have to come with us."

"I'll be fine here. I have my friends here, and you boys don't want me hanging around all the time. It's time for you two to have some time alone," she said. And though she smiled, it looked fake. She obviously thought she'd be in the way.

"I want you where I can see you everyday," Gavin said, his voice holding an edge of panic to it. He turned to Lex, the pleading look plain to see in his eyes. "Please, Lex, make her come with us."

Lex laughed because that was the funniest thing he'd heard all night. Gavin didn't know his mom as well as he thought he did if he thought Lex could make her do anything. It was a good thing he was almost positive she wanted to go but was waiting for an engraved invitation. He should have asked her sooner, but like everything else, he'd assumed instead of asking. He turned to his mom. "Ma, come on. You know we want you to come. Stop giving the doc a panic attack and tell him you'll start packing."

Jean looked between the two of them, apparently judging the level of sincerity in their words. And then she smiled and nodded. Lex pulled her into a hug when he saw how shiny her eyes were. "Thank you, Lex," she said. "And you too, Gavin. Thank you both for inviting me. I'd love to come along."

Gavin got off his chair and joined the hug. "I love you both, but now I know where Lex gets it from," he said.

"Gets what?" Lex asked.

"The hardheaded, 'I'm just going to assume the worst until someone tells me different' thing you do," Gavin explained.

"Um, really, Doc, you should talk." Lex smirked.

"Okay, boys, stop needling each other, and go to your room," Jean said. They both looked at her in surprise. "Oh, don't give me that. I know what you both want to do, and you're wasting time. Now get." She kissed them both on the cheek and pushed them away.

They stood and looked at each other over Jean's head. "Did we just get sent to our room by your mother?"

"I believe so, Doc."

"Oh, you two, get out of here before I decide to make you spend your last night together watching an old movie with me," Jean threatened.

Lex took Gavin's hand and pulled him to the bedroom. He closed them in and turned to the man he loved. "Thank you, Doc." Lex pulled Gavin into his arms.

Gavin let Lex kiss him before he moved back to ask, "For what?"

"For making my mom feel wanted and loved."

"Well, she's been doing that for me for months. I do love her and want her with us, plus we'll need someone to help with the kids," Gavin said.

"Kids?" Lex squeaked.

"Oh yeah, baby, kids...lots and lots of kids," Gavin said with a mischievous grin.

"Oh boy, it's a good thing I love you, Doc, or else..." Lex let the words die on his tongue at the look in Gavin's eyes.

"I love you too, Lex. Now let's go see if I can show you any more tricks." Gavin left Lex's arms and crawled onto the bed. He held his arms out for Lex, and watched as Lex crawled up the bed and wrapped him in his arms. He didn't care where they lived; anywhere Gavin was would always be where Lex wanted to be. He'd found his one true love, and he wasn't going to let him go again.

EPILOGUE

LEX WATCHED AS Gavin's eyes lit up, and he just knew this was going to be the one. He got out of the truck and waited for Gavin to come around so they could walk in together. The house was what they'd been looking for on the outside; that was for sure. It reminded Lex of his friend's cabin, only it was at least twice the size.

"I still think five bedrooms is a bit extreme, Doc," Lex said as the real estate agent raised his hand in greeting.

"But, Lex, if we have lots of kids, we'll be glad for all the space. Plus, Jean can basically have her own wing—her own bedroom, bathroom and even a sewing room without encroaching on our space," Gavin said. His eyes danced as they took in everything around him. "Oh, and I already told you the cost per square foot is so much cheaper here than it was back home. This is a steal."

"Yeah, yeah, but what about heating it, and cooling it, and who's going to—?"

"There's a heat pump, which works for the AC, also; it's the newest technology available, costing pennies on the dollar compared to traditional heating and cooling systems." The real estate agent interrupted with the pertinent information.

"Good to see you again, Jeff," Gavin said as he held out his hand.

"I'm glad you guys could make it. This property just came on the market yesterday, and it's not going to stay there long. I've already heard rumors that one of my colleagues has an interested buyer. This house has everything you two asked for and more," Jeff said, always the salesman.

Lex shook the guy's hand and sighed. He'd let Gavin basically run roughshod over the whole process, and watching him house shop was like watching a kid let loose in a candy store. Lex had had no idea what he was getting himself into when he'd agreed to buy a house instead of a condo.

So far, they'd seen every house on the market in the area, and none of them had lived up to the doc's expectations. Lex had spent every one of his weekends free of Camp Ripley wandering through houses and listening to Gavin ask a series of questions that would have sent a normal agent to a corner to start rocking while sucking their thumb. Thank god for Jeff; he had the patience of a saint and all the answers.

"There's a small pond on the back of the property, and the previous owners got approval to drag it and add some sand. They used it as a swimming hole, of sorts." Jeff started his spiel as he opened the front door. "There's a three-car attached garage, but there's also an oversized detached two-stall garage off to that side with a small apartment above it." He pointed to the structure in question.

They stepped into the house, and Lex heard Gavin's little gasp of pleasure. The main structure was an A-frame and the back wall of the open living space was two stories high and all glass. Gavin went straight for it.

"Oh my god, Lex, you have to see this view!" he exclaimed. "There's a huge deck and then the river. Holy crap, can you imagine what all that land looks like in the summer when it's lush and green?"

Lex joined him at the window and had to admit it was quite the panorama. He'd been a bit hesitant to buy something out of town, but looking at all that space and knowing they'd be there together, a little isolated from the rest of the world, made Lex grin at the possibilities.

"The master suite is in the loft, and there's two bedrooms down that hallway along with an office and bathroom. The other hallway also has two bedrooms and a bathroom. The kitchen appliances are all less than two years old, and the countertop is granite, which the owners had imported from India," Jeff said as Lex and Gavin looked around the home.

Lex tuned out as Gavin started his usual inquisition. He had to admit this house was the best they'd looked at so far, and for some reason it just felt right. He still didn't think they needed all that space, but he didn't want to dampen the doc's enthusiasm on the family front. Lex himself wasn't quite ready for kids, but they'd get around to it eventually.

"You have to see the finished basement; it's a walk-out, and it's completely tricked out. The owners are willing to sell the house with the basement furnishings for extra," Jeff said. He led them down the stairs, and Lex was sold. This was their house.

Gavin practically squealed in delight. "There's a popcorn maker, and oh, is that one of those theater-seating couches? Holy crap, Lex, look at that TV. It's almost as tall as you. It's like a movie theater," he said as he flitted from one thing to another. "There's even a foosball and a pool table!"

Lex had to try to calm Gavin down, or they'd end up paying extra; even Jeff could tell the doc was sold on this one. "Doc, slow down," Lex said. He smiled at the doc's childlike exuberance over the entire setup.

Gavin flung himself into Lex's arms. "I want this one, Lex. This is where we can have a family, and Jean and George will have plenty of space, and our friends can come and hang out with us, and we can have parties and—"

Lex kissed Gavin to shut him up. He giggled when Lex stopped and kissed the tip of his nose. "Let's go see what kind of deal we can get," Lex said, and this time Gavin did squeal.

THE LAST OF the boxes were finally unloaded, and everyone was sweaty and hungry. "Where the hell is Riley with the pizza and beer?" Sheila asked no one in particular.

"I told you, you should have gone with him. He probably got lost," Gavin said as he put another box in the kitchen. Nobody listened to him when he'd suggested putting the boxes in the designated rooms as soon as they were unloaded, so he was busy trying to get things sorted.

"Nah, Mike's with him, and he never gets lost. They probably got distracted by something shiny," Lex said.

"Oh, you be nice. Those are good boys," Jean said as she stroked George's head.

"I agree, you three are too hard on them," Mona said from the kitchen. She insisted on washing all the dishes before they were put in the cupboards. Something about cardboard dust being toxic.

"So you're sure the house isn't in the hundred-year flood plain, right?" Roger asked once again as he stood looking out at the river. He'd been dubious about the house's close proximity to the river.

"Yes, sir, they have to disclose that ever since the big one in ninety-seven," Lex answered. He snagged Gavin's arm and put his around the doc's waist to stop the man from lugging more boxes around the room. Gavin smiled at him and kissed his cheek.

They all sat at attention when they heard the gravel crunching in the driveway. "Finally! I'm starving," Sheila said. She got up and went to the door to harass her fiancé about how long it took them to get the food.

Becca handed out paper plates and drinks. Everyone else was dirty and sweaty, but somehow she seemed to look like she'd walked off a photo shoot for yoga casual wear. She smiled coyly at Lex and Gavin, who exchanged a look that went unnoticed as she sat in the chair opposite them.

It was a feeding frenzy as everyone dug in, and the only sound in the room was chewing and the occasional burp. Lex looked at his family and friends and knew his life couldn't get any better than it was right then. He pulled Gavin into his side. He knew it was wrong, but he sent up a silent thank you to Cassie because, without her, he'd never have found the doc.

"What are you smiling about?" Gavin asked.

"Nothing really, just thinking how much I owe your ex-wife. I think I may send her a carton of cigarettes to thank her," he said.

"She doesn't smoke," Gavin said with a strange look on his face.

"That's not what they're for. In jail, smokes are like cash," Mike said with a grin.

"Why would you want to send her anything? What do you have to thank her for? She almost killed my sweet boy," Jean said with a scowl. Lex shrugged because he didn't feel like sharing.

Mona put down her slice of pizza and smiled at Lex in understanding. "If you do send her a gift, let me know because I'll add another carton. I think I'd like to thank her too."

Gavin burst out in laughter and soon everyone joined in. He turned to Lex and kissed him on the lips, right there in front of his parents. "I love you, you doofus," Gavin said.

"I love you too, Doc," Lex said and meant it more than he could ever have believed possible.

ABOUT THE AUTHOR

CL Mustafic is a born and bred American Midwesterner who mysteriously ended up living in one of those countries nobody can ever find on the map of Europe. Left with too much time on her hands—let's be honest here—it was the lack of television channels in her native language and too many voices in her head trying to fill the silence that led her to decide to give her lifelong dream of writing a novel a shot. So now, between shuttling kids back and forth from various activities and risking her life on the insanely narrow, busy streets of her new hometown, she loses herself in her own made-up world where love always wins.

Facebook: http://www.facebook.com/100010673946675
Twitter: https://twitter.com/CL_Mustafic
Website: http://www.clmustafic.com
Email: clmustaficwrites@gmail.com

ALSO BY CL MUSTAFIC

Satin Secrets

A story in the Beneath the Layers Anthology

ALSO AVAILABLE FROM NINESTAR PRESS

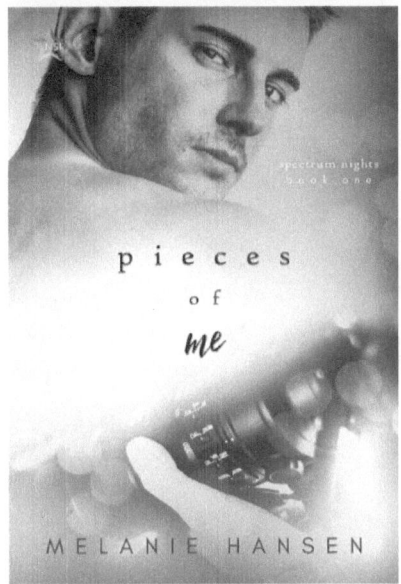

WWW.NINESTARPRESS.COM